RANDOM
HOUSE
LARGE
PRINT

How Beautiful We Were

How Beautiful We Were

A NOVEL

Imbolo Mbue

RANDOM HOUSE
LARGE PRINT

Copyright © 2021 by Imbolo Mbue

All rights reserved.
Published in the United States of America by Random House Large Print in association with Random House, an imprint and division of Penguin Random House LLC, New York.

Cover design: Jaya Miceli
Cover photograph: **Holding Hands_Selenite,** © 2015 by Daniel Arsham, courtesy of the artist and Perrotin

The Library of Congress has established a Cataloging-in-Publication record for this title.

ISBN: 978-0-593-21330-8

www.penguinrandomhouse.com/large-print-format-books

FIRST LARGE PRINT EDITION

Printed in the United States of America

10 9 8 7 6 5 4 3 2 1

This Large Print edition published in accord with the standards of the N.A.V.H.

For my beautiful, beautiful children

The people walking in darkness have seen a great light;
on those living in the land of the shadow of death,
a light has dawned.

—Isaiah 9:2

How Beautiful We Were

WE SHOULD HAVE KNOWN THE END WAS NEAR. HOW could we not have known? When the sky began to pour acid and rivers began to turn green, we should have known our land would soon be dead. Then again, how could we have known when they didn't want us to know? When we began to wobble and stagger, tumbling and snapping like feeble little branches, they told us it would soon be over, that we would all be well in no time. They asked us to come to village meetings, to talk about it. They told us we had to trust them.

We should have spat in their faces, heaped upon them names most befitting—liars, savages, unscrupulous, evil. We should have cursed their mothers and their grandmothers, flung pejoratives upon their fathers, prayed for unspeakable calamities to befall their children. We hated them and we hated their meetings, but we attended all of them. Every eight weeks we went to the village square to listen to them.

We were dying. We were helpless. We were afraid. Those meetings were our only chance at salvation.

We ran home from school on the appointed days, eager to complete our chores so we would miss not one word at the assembly. We fetched water from the well; chased goats and chickens around our compounds into bamboo barns; swept away leaves and twigs scattered across our front yards. We washed iron pots and piles of bowls after dinner; left our huts many minutes before the time the meeting was called for—we wanted to get there before they strode into the square in their fine suits and polished shoes. Our mothers hurried to the square too, as did our fathers. They left their work unfinished in the forest beyond the big river, their palms and bare feet dusted with poisoned earth. The work will be there waiting for us tomorrow, our fathers said to us, but we'll only have so many opportunities to hear what the men from Pexton have to say. Even when their bodies bore little strength, after hours of toiling beneath a sun both benevolent and cruel, they went to the meetings, because we all had to be at the meetings.

The only person who did not attend the meetings was Konga, our village madman. Konga, who had no awareness of our suffering and lived without fears of what was and what was to come. He slept in the school compound as we hurried along, snoring and slobbering if he wasn't tossing, itching, muttering, eyes closed. Trapped as he was, alone in a world in which spirits ruled and men were powerless under their dominion, he knew nothing about Pexton.

In the square we sat in near silence as the sun left us for the day, oblivious to how the beauty of its descent heightened our anguish. We watched as the Pexton men placed their briefcases on the table our village head, Woja Beki, had set for them. There were always three of them—we called them the Round One (his face was as round as a ball we would have had fun kicking), the Sick One (his suits were oversized, giving him the look of a man dying of a flesh-stealing disease), and the Leader (he did the talking, the other two did the nodding). We mumbled among ourselves as they opened their briefcases and passed sheets of paper among themselves, covering their mouths as they whispered into each other's ears to ensure they had their lies straight. We had nowhere more important to be so we waited, desperate for good news. We whispered at intervals, wondering what they were thinking whenever they paused to look at us: at our grandfathers and fathers on stools up front, those with dead or dying children in the first row; our grandmothers and mothers behind them, nursing babies into quietude and shooting us glares if we made a wrong sound from under the mango tree. Our young women repeatedly sighed and shook their heads. Our young men, clustered at the back, stood clench-jawed and seething.

We inhaled, waited, exhaled. We remembered

those who had died from diseases with neither names nor cures—our siblings and cousins and friends who had perished from the poison in the water and the poison in the air and the poisoned food growing from the land that lost its purity the day Pexton came drilling. We hoped the men would look into our eyes and feel something for us. We were children, like their children, and we wanted them to recognize that. If they did, it wasn't apparent in their countenance. They'd come for Pexton, to keep its conscience clean; they hadn't come for us.

Woja Beki walked up to the front and thanked everyone for coming.

"My dear people," he said, exposing the teeth no one wanted to see, "if we don't ask for what we want, we'll never get it. If we don't expunge what's in our bellies, are we not going to suffer from constipation and die?"

We did not respond; we cared nothing for what he had to say. We knew he was one of them. We'd known for years that though he was our leader, descended from the same ancestors as us, we no longer meant anything to him. Pexton had bought his cooperation and he had, in turn, sold our future to them. We'd seen with our own eyes, heard with our own ears, how Pexton was fattening his wives and giving his sons jobs in the capital and handing him envelopes of cash.

Our fathers and grandfathers had confronted him, after the evidence had become impossible to dismiss, but he had beseeched them to trust him, telling them he had a plan: everything he was doing was to help us reclaim our land. He had shed two cups of tears and swore by the Spirit that he hated Pexton as much as we did, wasn't it obvious? Our young men had conspired to kill him, but our old men found out about the plan and pleaded with them to spare him. We've already had too many deaths, our old men said; we've used up too many burial plots.

Woja Beki continued looking at us, dreadful gums still exposed. We wished we didn't have to look at them, but there could be no avoidance. They were the first thing we saw whenever we looked at his face: gums as black as the night's most evil hour, streaked with pink of various shades; tilting brown teeth, wide spaces between.

"My very dear people," he went on, "even a sheep knows how to tell its master what it wants. That's why we've gathered here again, to resume this discourse. We thank the kind representatives from Pexton for coming back to talk to us. Messengers are good, but why should we use them if we can talk to each other with our own mouths? There's been a lot of misunderstanding, but I hope this meeting will bring us closer to a resolution of our mutual suffering. I hope that after this evening we and Pexton can continue moving in the direction of becoming good friends. Friendship is a great thing, isn't it?"

We knew we would never call them friends, but some of us nodded.

In the glow of the fading sun our village looked almost beautiful, our faces almost free of anguish. Our grandfathers and grandmothers appeared serene, but we knew they weren't—they'd seen much, and yet they'd never seen anything like this.

"We'll now hear from Mr. Honorable Representative of Pexton, all the way from Bézam to speak to us again," Woja Beki said, before returning to his seat.

The Leader rose up, walked toward us, and stood in the center of the square.

For several seconds, he stared at us, his head angled, his smile so strenuously earnest we wondered if he was admiring a radiance we'd never been told we had. We waited for him to say something that would make us burst into song and dance. We wanted him to tell us that Pexton had decided to leave and take the diseases with them.

His smile broadened, narrowed, landed on our faces, scanning our stillness. Seemingly satisfied, he began speaking. He was happy to be back in Kosawa on this fine day, he said. What a lovely evening it was, with the half-moon in the distance, such a perfect breeze, was that the sound of sparrows singing in one accord? What a gorgeous village. He wanted to thank us for coming. It was great to see everyone again. Incredible how many precious children Kosawa has. We had to believe him that the people at headquarters were sad about what was happening to us. They were all working hard to resolve this issue so everyone could be healthy and happy again. He spoke slowly, his smile constant, as if he was about to deliver the good news we so yearned for.

We barely blinked as we watched him, listening to lies we'd heard before. Lies about how the people who controlled Pexton cared about us. Lies about how the big men in the government of His Excellency cared about us. Lies about how hundreds of people in the capital had asked him to relay their condolences to us. "They mourn with you at the news of every death," he said. "It'll be over soon. It's time your suffering ended, isn't it?"

The Round One and the Sick One nodded.

"Pexton and the government are your friends," the Leader said. "Even on your worst day, remember that we're thinking about you in Bézam and working hard for you."

Our mothers and fathers wanted him to offer specifics on exactly when our air and water and land would be clean again. "Do you know how many children we've buried?" a father shouted. His name was Lusaka—he had buried two sons. We had been to both of the boys' funerals and wept over their bodies, darker than they'd been in life and adorned with white shirts soon to merge with their flesh.

Lusaka's departed younger son, Wambi, was our age-mate and classmate.

Two years had passed since Wambi died, but we thought about him still—he was the smartest boy in arithmetic, and the quietest one too, except for when he coughed. We'd been alive for centuries combined, and yet we'd never heard anyone cough the way he did. When the cough hit, his eyes watered, his back hunched out, he had to hold on to something to steady himself. It was sad to watch, pitiful but funny in the way a heavyset man falling on his buttocks amused us. Doesn't your father know the path to the medicine man's hut? we would say to him, laughing the careless laugh of healthy children. We knew not that some of us would soon start coughing too. How could we have imagined such a thing would happen to us? That several of us would develop raspy coughs and rashes and fevers that would persist until our deaths? Please stay away from us with that ugly cough of yours, we'd said to Wambi. But it wasn't just an ugly cough, we would later find out. The dirty air had gotten stuck in his lungs. Slowly, the poison spread through his body and turned into something else. Before we knew it, Wambi was dead.

We could barely sing him a farewell song as we stood around his coffin, our tears drowning the words. Some of our fathers had to carry us home from the burial ground, faint as we were. Within five months of Wambi's death, two of us would be dead. Those of us who survived feared our death was close; we were certain we'd be the next, though sometimes we feared we'd be the last—all our age-mates would be dead and we'd have no friends our size with whom we could stick out our tongues and taste raindrops, no one to play with in the square, or fight with over the right to the juiciest mangoes.

We thought about our departed friends whenever we developed fevers or someone coughed around us. We feared someone in our homes would catch this sickness that had arrived like a thief in the dark and was now hovering outside every hut, waiting for its chance to enter. We worried for our entire families, though the disease preferred the bodies of children. We feared the first person to catch it in our huts would pass it on to another person, and the second person would pass it on to someone else, and before long our entire family would contract it and die, one after another, or maybe all at once, but most likely one after another, from the oldest to the youngest, in which case we might be the last to die, after we'd buried everyone. Our anxieties kept us awake at night.

We hated that we went to bed in fear and woke up in fear, all day long breathed fear in and out. Our mothers and fathers told us to have no worries for the Spirit would guide and protect us, but their words brought us no comfort—the Spirit had protected the other children and what had become of them? Still, we nodded whenever our parents made their assurances—our fathers as we bade them good night; our mothers in the morning if we woke up crying over a bad dream—for we knew they lied only to keep us calm, so we would have no nightmares, so we would wake up rested and run to school after breakfast, carefree and merry as we ought to be. We were reminded of our parents' lies whenever there was a new death, sometimes in our huts, sometimes in the hut next to ours, sometimes children younger than us, babies and toddlers, children who had barely tasted life, always children we knew. We were young, but we knew death to be impartial.

Please, you must do something, one of our aunts cried to the Leader, her baby limp in her arms. It was the poison—the baby was too pure for the filth in the village well's water, the toxins that had seeped into it from Pexton's field. One of our fathers asked if Pexton could in the meantime send us clean water, at least for the youngest children. The Leader shook his head; he'd heard this question before. He took a deep breath as he prepared to give his standard response: Pexton was not in the business of providing water, but out of concern for us he would talk to people at headquarters, they'd take our request to the government office in charge of water supply and hear what they had to say. Didn't the Leader give this same response last time? a grandfather asked. How long does it take for messages to move from office to office in Bézam? A very long time, the Leader replied.

Some of our mothers began crying. We wished we could dry their tears.

Our young men started shouting. We'll march to Bézam and burn down your headquarters, they said. We'll hurt you the same way you're hurting us.

The Pexton men simply smiled in response. They knew the young men wouldn't do it—we all knew that His Excellency would have our young men exterminated if they dared harm Pexton and our village would only be left further enfeebled.

We'd seen it happen already.

Early the previous year, we had watched as a group of six men set out for Bézam, water and dried food packed in their raffia bags. Led by the father of one of us—the one of us named Thula—the group promised the village that they would return with nothing less than a guarantee from the government and Pexton that our land would be restored to what it was before Pexton arrived. Day after day, we waited alongside our friend Thula for the return of her father and the other men, all of whom were our neighbors and relatives, three of whom had sick children. When they did not return after ten days, we began fearing that they'd been imprisoned. Or worse. A second group of men traveled to Bézam to search for and bring home the Six, but they came back empty-handed. Months later, the Pexton men arrived for their first meeting with the village. When our elders asked the Leader at that initial meeting where he thought our vanished men might be, he told them that he knew nothing, Pexton did not involve itself with the whereabouts of the citizens of our country, unless, of course, they were its workers.

On that evening in October of 1980, still smiling, the Leader reminded us once more that Pexton was our friend, and that, though we had to make sacrifices, someday we'd look back and be proud that Pexton had taken an interest in our land.

He asked if we had any more questions.

We did not. Whatever hope we'd had at the onset of that meeting had flown away and taken with it our last words. With a final smile, he thanked us for coming. The Round One and the Sick One began packing up their briefcases. Their driver was waiting by our school in a black Land Rover, ready to take them back to Bézam, to their homes and lives overflowing with clean necessities and superfluities we could never conjure.

Woja Beki stood up and thanked us too. He wished us a good night and reminded us to return for another meeting in eight weeks. He told us to be well until then.

^^^^^^^

ON MOST NIGHTS WE WOULD have left the village square and turned homeward.

We would have said little to each other as we walked in the darkness, our entire beings drenched with an unrelenting, smothering form of despair. We would have walked slowly, our heads hung low, ashamed we'd dared to hope, embarrassed by our smallness.

On any other night, the meeting would have been a reminder that we could do nothing to them but they could do anything to us, because they owned us. Their words would have served no purpose but to further instill within us that we couldn't undo the fact that three decades before, in Bézam, on a date we'll never know, at a meeting where none of us was present, our government had given us to Pexton. Handed, on a sheet of paper, our land and waters to them. We would have had no choice but to accept that we were now theirs. We would have admitted to ourselves that we'd long ago been defeated.

On that night, though, that night when the air was too still and the crickets strangely quiet, we did not turn homeward. Because, at the moment we were about to stand and start bidding each other good night, we heard a rustle in the back of the gathering. We heard a voice telling us to remain seated, the meeting was not yet over, it was just beginning. We turned around and saw a man, tall and lean, hair matted, wearing nothing but a pair of trousers with holes on every side. It was Konga, our village madman.

He was breathing heavily, as if he'd sprinted from the school compound to the square. He was exuberant and bouncy, not his usual lethargic self, the self that lumbered around the village laughing with invisible friends and shaking his fists at enemies no one else could perceive. We saw the glow in his eyes in the light darkness, his excitement apparent as he rushed to the front of the gathering, nearly floating in exhilaration. We looked at each other, too dumbfounded to ask: What is he doing?

Never had we seen the Leader so stunned as when he turned to Woja Beki and asked what Konga wanted—why was a madman disrupting the end of his meeting? Never had we seen Woja Beki as devoid of words as when he turned to face Konga.

Before us all stood a never-before-seen version of our village madman.

As if all authority on earth belonged to him, Konga barked at the Pexton men, told them to sit down, hadn't they heard him, were their ears so full of wax that sound couldn't penetrate it? The meeting wasn't over, it was just beginning.

The Leader, maddened by Konga's audacity, and running short on the decorum he'd brought from Bézam, reciprocated the bark, asking how dare a madman speak to him, Pexton's representative, in that manner. Konga chuckled, before responding that he had the right to speak to anyone any way he liked, an answer that prompted the Leader to turn to Woja Beki and demand to know why Woja Beki was standing there like an idiot, tolerating this insolent fool. Konga cleared his throat—everything in it—and spat out what we imagined was a glob of dark yellow phlegm between the Leader's feet.

We gasped. Did Konga know who the men were and what they could do to him?

The Leader glared at Konga. Then us. Then Konga again. He motioned for his underlings to pick up their briefcases. All three men lifted their briefcases and turned to leave. We took a deep breath, thankful the drama had reached its finale, but our relief morphed into greater perplexity when Konga asked the trio how they intended to return to Bézam. The representatives turned around, puzzled, if not alarmed.

What happened next, we could never have expected. Could never have imagined Konga would put a hand inside his trousers in front of the Pexton men and the village. Our mothers and grandmothers covered their eyes, afraid he was about to do a thing women should not witness, the thing they'd told us to never look at if Konga did it in front of us.

We kept our eyes open and watched as Konga caressed something in his trousers, his lips parted, stroking, stroking, no doubt an exaggeration. Gently, he pulled out something. He held it up and asked the men if it belonged to them. Our eyes widened, as did the men's—they'd recognized their car key, golden and glossy, in the madman's hand.

Before we could recover from the revelation, Konga asked the Pexton men where their driver was. The driver always waited in the car during the meetings, but with the key in Konga's hand, where could he be? Konga did not say. He merely, with a smile, informed the men that the key in his hand was indeed their car key and when they returned to the school compound they would not find their driver waiting.

We began talking all at once. What was happening? What was he doing?

Woja Beki started stuttering, bowing to the Leader, informing him that Konga was only playing a madman's game, the Leader should please understand that without brains Konga couldn't discern that the honorable representatives did not play games; of course the driver was fine, likely standing next to the car; of course Konga was going to hand over the key immediately; the Leader should please accept deepest apologies on behalf of the village; none of this was meant to disrespect our guests; travel blessings on their return to Bézam; all of Kosawa was grateful to them for coming once more to—

Konga commanded Woja Beki to shut up and step aside.

We wanted to hoot with delight. We yearned to jump up and clap, but we didn't—we were witnessing something extraordinary whose unfolding we dared not disturb.

Konga lifted his eyes to the sky, as if to commune with the stars. When he lowered them, he informed the Pexton men that they would not be returning to Bézam that night. The Leader and the Sick One and the Round One looked at each other and chuckled, amused at the idea that a madman was threatening to keep them captive. We thought it somewhat funny too, but we did not laugh, because Konga said it again, this time slowly, categorically: Gentlemen, you'll be spending the night with us in Kosawa.

He meant what he was saying, we could tell from his tone, and the Leader could now tell too, because he stopped chuckling. He looked at us in confusion, asking us what was going on, what was the madman talking about, his tone at first beseeching before turning demanding; determined as he was to get a response from us no matter the means.

We uttered not one word.

The Leader glared at Konga. Wrath was gushing out of the Pexton man's nostrils, but he had to contain himself. Raising his voice only slightly, he told Konga that whatever game he was playing was now over, it was time Konga handed over the key, he'd rather not use force, the night was certain to end badly if he did, he did not want that, considering how much Pexton cared for Kosawa, so it would be best if Konga quietly handed him the key so that this could all be forgiven and forgotten.

We did not expect Konga to obey, but neither did we imagine he would stare at the Leader for seconds, scoff, and burst into a prolonged laugh.

The Leader turned to Woja Beki, who quickly bowed his head.

"Get my key from him," the Leader shouted at our village head.

Woja Beki made no attempt to move. It was obvious to us why the Leader would ask this of Woja

Beki—the Leader could never debase his honorable personhood by getting himself, or his men, into a physical confrontation with an uncouth madman.

"Get my key from that idiot," the Leader shouted again.

Woja Beki remained frozen in his spot, perhaps ashamed, likely afraid, to look into the eyes of the big man from Bézam.

What came afterward, we'd long fantasized about doing ourselves—some of us had done it in dreams from which we woke up smiling—but it did not lessen our shock when it happened, when Konga, laughing no more, walked up to Woja Beki and spat in his face. We giggled, we gasped in horror, we half-shut our eyes. Woja Beki, without raising his head, wiped the saliva that had landed on his lips. Barely glancing at Woja Beki, the Leader, now a gesticulating bundle of fury and befuddlement, resumed his shouting, yelling at everyone, anyone, to get his key from the madman, someone get his key right now, otherwise there'd be severe consequences.

Not one of us did or said a thing.

None of us took it upon ourselves to tell the Leader that Konga was untouchable. We did not attempt to tell him that no matter what Konga did, however much he humiliated or hurt us or scared us, we could not touch him, because we do not touch men with his condition. We did not tell the Leader that for decades no one had touched Konga and no one ever would, because to touch a madman was to invite the worst curse.

If the Leader had sat down with us, we would have told him Konga's story, the story our parents repeated whenever we ridiculed Konga, every time they caught us skipping behind him around the village, laughing at his matted hair, his lone pair of trousers, his dirt-clogged fingernails. We would have told the Leader that Konga wasn't born a madman and that, hard as it might be to believe it now, he was once a proud, handsome man.

If the Leader had asked, we would have told him that long before we were born, when our parents were children our age, dozens of young women in our village dreamed of becoming Konga's wife and bearing sons as chiseled and long-limbed as him. His parents, long gone now, dreamed of the grandchildren their only child would give them. He was a fine farmer, a fine hunter, and a very fine fisherman. On any given day, our parents told us, Konga could be great at being anything—he was destined for a beautiful life. But then, one day, a hot day, he began complaining of voices that wouldn't stop talking to him. They were laughing at him, he told his parents, imploring him to kill himself, telling him he was going to live forever. They appeared in his dreams at night and emerged from dark spaces during the day in the form of men, women, and children who'd been in the grave for so long they'd lost most of their flesh. They seemed determined to never let him go, badgering him in a language he couldn't understand, surrounding him whenever he sat down to eat, chasing him around the village.

His parents took him to our village medium, who told them that nothing could be done—a vengeful spirit had taken Konga's sanity as punishment for an evil committed by one of his ancestors centuries before Konga was born. Konga was to spend the rest of his life as an atonement; the spirit could not be appeased. All his parents could do, the medium said, was to keep the front door of their hut open so Konga could come and go as he wished. They also needed to leave a mat outside their hut so Konga could find a suitable outdoor place and sleep comfortably on the nights the voices allowed him to.

By the time we were born, Konga had been sleeping under the sky for twenty years. With his parents gone and having left behind no siblings to feed him, our mothers took turns bringing him food and water under the mango tree. Some days he ate the food and drank the water; other days he ignored it until the flies came for it, and the ants marched into it, and the goats accidentally knocked over the bowls holding the rest of it, and our mothers sighed and took their bowls home, only to carry food to him the next time it was their turn. Many afternoons he sat half naked under the mango tree, scratching the skin that touched water only when it rained, pulling out thick chunks of crust from his nostrils. Occasionally, he sang a romantic ballad, his eyes closed as if he'd once been a character in a great love story. Sometimes he offered words of wisdom to his invisible friends, or chastised morons no one could see, his arms flailing, his face scrunching as he raised his voice to emphasize points that made no sense to us. He attended every wedding and funeral, watching from a distance, neither dancing nor crying, but he never attended the village meetings. On meeting days, he stayed in the school compound, uninterested in our plight. We thought him incapable of anger toward anyone but the voices in his head and the spirit that had ruined him. We thought him unaware of everyone and everything around him besides his immediate needs and the phantoms following him.

That evening, though, as he stood with the car key in his clenched and raised fist, we could see that he was capable of anger toward men, an anger that came out with no equivocation when he told the Leader that there was nothing the Leader could do to him.

The Leader, fatigued from railing to an unresponsive audience, paused and let out a deep sigh. He shook his head. He'd realized, it appeared, that he couldn't make us get the key from Konga and that there was nothing he could do to a madman in a dark village, a long way from Pexton's headquarters. We felt no sympathy for him—we had no capacity for that, occupied as we were in delighting in his despair. Beside him, Konga was now singing and twirling around. He waved the key in the Pexton men's faces, prancing as gaily as a groom on his wedding day, repeating over and over that the men would be spending the night with us, perhaps many nights—oh, what a wonderful privilege for them.

The Leader beckoned for his men to move closer to him. He whispered at length into their ears. The Round One and the Sick One nodded as he spoke, all of them intermittently looking sideways as they attempted to devise a strategy to retrieve their key, a plan they must have hoped would involve the least amount of debasement.

Seemingly satisfied with their plan and convinced of its strength, they took a step toward Konga, knowing nothing of the curse that would hold them and their descendants captive from that night till eternity. We leaned forward. The Pexton men took two more steps and stood closer to Konga. Konga moved the key to his lips.

"One more step," he said to them, "and I'll swallow this key."

We held our breaths. He would do it. We knew

he would. The Pexton men must have recognized this too, because the Sick One staggered, and the Round One's face grew more spherical, and they suddenly all seemed like children in a dark, deadly forest.

We turned our attention to Woja Beki, who had regained his speech and was now imploring Konga not to bring shame to our village. He begged for a full minute, calling Konga the son of the leopard, owner of a voice more melodic than music, bearer of a brilliance that rivals the sun's. He reminded Konga of how beloved he was, how blessed we were to have him, what joy there was in Kosawa on the day he was born, what—

The Leader cut him off and told him to stop speaking nonsense; his voice now had not a trace of politesse left. Its pitch rose as he shouted—looking at his underlings, who were still nodding at his every word—that all of this was nonsense, utter nonsense, to which Konga said the Leader needed to clarify exactly what the nonsense was, and the Leader responded that the idea of a madman preventing him, the Honorable Representative of Pexton, from returning home, was the exact definition of nonsense.

Konga doubled over, roaring with laughter. Deep in a trance into which we'd now fallen, we could scarcely move a muscle on our faces. Woja Beki pulled us out of our stupefaction by stepping closer to us and asking, in a quivering voice, if we were going to continue sitting there quietly while Konga insulted our guests—guests who had traveled for many hours to do nothing but assure us that our troubles would soon be over.

No one responded.

"If our honorable guests aren't back in their office tomorrow morning," Woja Beki went on, "soldiers will arrive by evening to look for them. I'm promising you, it won't be pretty when the soldiers arrive. They're not going to ask us why we did nothing to stop Konga. They won't be concerned about the fact that Konga is uncontrollable. They're simply going to mete out our punishment. They'll slaughter us, every one of us."

We looked at each other.

"Are you doubting me?" Woja Beki continued. "Wasn't it only last month that news reached us of how soldiers burned a village to ashes because one of its men split open a tax collector's head with a machete in anger? Where are the people of that village today? Are they not scattered around, sleeping on the bare floors of their relatives' huts? Would they say it was worth losing their homes for the sake of one man's heedlessness? If the soldiers can do it to those people, why won't they do it to us? This is a country of law and consequences, my dear people: we'll pay the price if we don't afford our friends here the respect we're required to give them. I'm begging you: please, please, don't let it happen to us. Let it not be that I did not say it. The soldiers won't care that this was the work of one madman. They'll put bullets inside all of us, down to the smallest child."

The men from Pexton nodded, a warning, it seemed, that it was all true.

Our collective sweat could have filled a dry well when our probable fate dawned on us. We knew what guns could do, but we'd never considered death by bullets.

One of our grandfathers stood up and turned to a grinning and swaying Konga. "Please," he said, "we don't want soldiers in our village. Please, Konga Wanjika, son of Bantu Wanjika, I'm begging you, give these men their key. Your father was my second cousin, and I'm now speaking to you on his behalf. Don't bring any more suffering on us. Drop the key on the ground, and I'll pick it up and give it to them. Go bring their driver from wherever you've hidden him. Let us all wish each other a good night and go home."

We thought Konga would heed the counsel of a man enlightened by age, a man who had lived long and mastered the difference between right and wrong. We thought the madman would remember that it was our duty to obey our elders and revere the words of the wise, a lesson we'd been taught and retaught since we were toddlers. In our cloud of bafflement, we forgot that, with the loss of his sanity, all that he'd been taught since birth had been washed away, diluted and pulled through his ears and out of his brain by that vengeful spirit. We forgot he was more newborn than adult now, possessing no sense of time, no awareness of the past or future, possessing only a faint consciousness of the spirit world from which we all came and to which we would return. We were reminded of how far from sane he was when he slid the key back inside his trousers and started laughing.

"Give him the key," one of our mothers cried out. The rest of our mothers joined in. Please, they said, we don't want soldiers coming here. We're begging you.

"Are you going to sit there and watch a madman invite abominations to your homes?" the Leader said to our fathers and grandfathers sitting at the front of the gathering, looking from one face to the next. "You're willing to die because of him?"

The soldiers might very well be on their way to Kosawa that moment, he said repeatedly. We ought to consider his words a final warning to get his key from that madman this very minute, or prepare ourselves for a bloody encounter.

The sound of our anguished murmurs rose. We could see clearly what lay ahead for us. We saw our village gone, poisoned and slaughtered. We saw in Konga our ruin.

We wanted no part of his madness.

The Leader pointed to our young men in the back and asked for volunteers to come up front, four strong young men to help him get the key from Konga.

No one stepped forward—we wanted to avoid a slaughter, but who among us dared touch a madman?

Woja Beki moved close to the Leader and whispered in his ear.

"Is this some sort of a joke?" the Leader said, his expression a convergence of shock, pity, and disgust. Woja Beki shook his head. The Leader gazed at us as if we'd just been revealed to be from another realm, a realm in which the laws bore no likeness to the ones ordinary humans lived by. "How could you believe such a thing?" he cried, arms raised and flapping in exasperation. "No one dies from touching a madman. No one has ever died from touching a madman. Does anyone here understand that?"

How could he appreciate laws that had not been imprinted on his heart?

"Get me my key right now," he said firmly, "or tomorrow you'll all regret it."

Woja Beki took a deep breath. Speaking as if he was using a borrowed voice he needed to treat with care lest he return it in a subpar condition, he looked at our young men in the back and told them that the future of Kosawa now rested with them.

"Your fathers cannot fight," he said. "Your mothers are old, your wives are women, your children are weak. If you don't do what is right, who will? I promise you, if you continue standing there and allow Konga to bring us harm, the wind will sing songs about a village that was laid to waste because its young men were cowards."

One of the young men stepped forward. Speaking in a voice no more steady than Woja Beki's, he said he would do it. His wife cried out, imploring him not to. His mother, her voice brittle, pleaded with him too. His father turned his face away.

Woja Beki nodded and half-smiled at him, a token of gratitude.

Three more young men came forward. We'll do it, they said.

Don't do it, voices cried from across the square. Do it, others shouted. Do you want to see them and their descendants cursed forever? the dissenters yelled, many rising to their feet. Do you want us all to be killed tomorrow morning? the encouragers responded, no less incensed. There has to be another way. There is no other way.

The quarrels began. Loud and fierce and clamorous.

We defy them tonight and we stand a chance of being free again, some said. We don't need freedom, we need to stay alive, others argued. Let us show them that we're people too. The soldiers are going to shoot us dead. The Spirit has sent Konga to tell us that we can and should fight. Fight with what? Fight with what we've got. What have we got but spears? We've got machetes and stones and pots of boiling water. How can you be so stupid as to think we have any chance? Konga has shown us we stand every chance. Konga is a madman. Perhaps madness is what we all need. How can you say such a thing? We were once a brave people, the blood of the leopard flows within us—when did we lose sight of that? We'll be dead tomorrow—is that what you want?

Everyone was standing, shouting; no one was listening. Konga and the Leader shook their fists at each other. The four young men stood between them, unsure of which side they were on. Most of us children began crying, our sad sounds lost in the chaos that had become our lives. Some of us cried for fear that death would arrive the next day, others for the illness that might lead to death the next month.

We all knew the truth: death was at hand.

When it had begun to appear the meeting would never end, Lusaka, the father of our departed age-mate and classmate Wambi, stood up and walked to the front of the gathering. He clapped to get everyone's attention. He continued clapping as the murmurs ebbed, until everyone was seated again and quiet.

He was one of the most peaceful men in Kosawa and rarely spoke, so whenever he stood before us everyone listened. The loss of his sons had diminished his frame, made him smaller than he used to be, but he seemed to have grown in wisdom.

"We won't come to an agreement tonight," he said, eliciting hums of agreement from all but a few of our mothers and fathers and grandmothers and grandfathers. "I'd like to propose a solution so we can at least put an end to this squabbling for now. Let me take these men home with me, and let Konga do what he wants to do with their driver and their key. I'll give them beds, and tomorrow morning my wife will give them breakfast. After they've eaten, I'll take them to see the graves of my sons who died from their poison. I'll show them the grave of every child we've buried, and they'll count the graves so that they'll know the number and never forget it. Then we'll keep them prisoner and I'll guard them until their employer stops killing us."

"Prisoner?" the Leader said. "Who do you think you are to—"

"What makes you think Pexton is going to leave us alone because we take its men prisoner?" one of our fathers shouted at Lusaka.

"And exactly how long do you suggest we keep them prisoner?" another added.

"You're crazier than Konga if you believe we can maneuver people in Bézam."

The commotion returned—everyone speaking, no one listening. The Pexton men and Woja Beki watched us, as if we'd lost all senses. Several of our grandfathers stood up to upbraid Lusaka: How could he be so naïve as to think Pexton would bow to our threats and demands? What made him think they cared? What would happen when the soldiers arrived the next day with enough bullets for every living thing in Kosawa?

"When the soldiers arrive," Lusaka said, "we'll tell them that if they kill one of us, we'll kill these men."

"And what if they don't care?" a mother cried.

"What if they let us kill the men and then kill us after? Does Pexton care if these men live or die?"

"It does," Konga replied, silencing everyone with the boom of his voice. "Pexton would never let anything bad happen to its men, because Pexton loves its men."

Most of our grandfathers nodded in approval, as if they'd seen evidence of this.

We believed it too, because it was now obvious that the Spirit had possessed Konga. Having gone mad and lost all knowledge of the near and far past, he had no way of knowing how Pexton felt about its men, so it had to be the Spirit speaking through him. Of this we had no doubt—the Spirit was in our midst and it was telling us to dare. Those of us who had been crying dried the remnants of the tears on our cheeks. Our mothers and fathers whispered to one another as they nodded and sighed deeply in relief.

Lusaka clapped again to quiet everyone. "It's simple," he said softly. "If Pexton doesn't stop killing our children, I'll kill these three of its children with my bare hands."

No one in the village square made a sound.

Lusaka wished everyone a good night and began walking to his hut.

Konga ordered the four young men to seize the Pexton men and Woja Beki and follow Lusaka. "Don't you dare touch me," the Leader said. The young men dared.

They grabbed one man apiece, each man resisting

in his own way—the Leader flailing his arms, his subordinates kicking and punching the air, Woja Beki wagging his finger and speaking with clenched teeth, ordering the young men to stop, reminding them that he was their leader, the blood of the leopard flowed thickest within him, he gave the orders here, they'd better not forget that. Konga asked for four more young men to come help. Eight rushed to the front, our friend Thula's uncle among them—a young man named Bongo, whose zeal to put an end to our woes awed everyone, being that he didn't yet have a child. Now reckoning with twelve men, the captives fought less, cursed more. Their voices receded. Woja Beki's wives' and children's whimpers became apparent. Two of his children were in our class. We did not attempt to console them; we'd long since stopped liking them.

Konga thanked us for coming and told us that the meeting was now officially over. He wished us a good night. "Tomorrow," he said, "everything is going to change."

Some of us walked home scared. Some of us floated, jubilant and light. Our friend Thula, thinking of her missing and likely dead father, walked head down, holding the hand of her little brother, Juba, a child who had died from Pexton's poison and come back to life through the mercy of the Spirit. Behind them, their mother and their father's mother walked slowly, hoping, we imagined, that they would soon have answers about the fate of their husband and son. Like every family in Kosawa, the Nangi family wanted liberation from their pain. We were all hopeful that night—we hoped even as we feared.

Tomorrow the soldiers will arrive, and we might be dead by sunset.

Tomorrow Pexton will surrender, and we might live to see our old age.

We tried not to think about our future. We wanted to hold on to that night for as long as we could, savor this optimism that had descended upon us, the faint promise of triumph. We wanted to be overcome with madness like Konga and relish the fleeting ecstasy wrought of fearlessness, anticipating our new lives as conquerors.

They'd proclaimed victory over us prematurely. That night, we declared war on them, and the next morning we awaited their arrival.

They should have known we're not easily defeated.

Thula

THE HUT IS WARM, BUT MY TEETH CHATTER. MY mind thrashes around, compelling me to imagine the spill of my blood after a bullet tears open my belly. I wonder how many bullets it would take to kill me—what would my corpse look like? I've spent my entire life around death, and yet I fear it. The mystery of it confounds me. How someone could be here and not here, in our world but also gone from it, with a nose closed off to air, eyes that won't open, a sealed mouth, a human but just a thing. I hate this world, but I don't yearn to leave it. I want to live long and see what life after a twisted childhood looks like, but I know death is eager to claim me—my journey to reunite with Papa might begin tomorrow. Once, after the funeral for one of my friends, I asked Papa about the crossing from this world to the next, how lonely and treacherous it would be, and he told me that it was different for everyone, it all depended on what kind of life a person had led, words that offered me no comfort. "You're not going to die for a long time, Thula," Papa said. A lie, we both knew it—what human can guarantee another long life?

Mama fastens the rope that keeps our front door closed. Her hands tremble as she makes knot after knot; she seems convinced a tightly locked bamboo door will prevent soldiers from getting to us. She hurries to do the same to the back door. Juba and I are in the parlor, sitting with our grandmother, Yaya—Juba is on Yaya's lap, I'm on a stool next to hers. Yaya strokes Juba's head with one hand, places the other around my shoulders. Besides the sound of Mama's efforts, our hut is quiet. Kosawa is quiet.

"My dear children," Yaya says, softly, "let's go to sleep. We need a good rest so we'll be ready to face whatever tomorrow brings." She is wrapped by a peace I haven't seen since the day Papa left. "If anyone comes to take something from us, we'll give it to them, even if it's our lives they want."

"Bongo and all the men are together right now, sharpening their machetes," Mama says as she reenters the parlor. Her voice is quivering. "If those soldiers think they can just come here and . . ."

"But, Mama, the soldiers have guns," I say, struggling not to cry. Papa told me, before he left, never to cry unless I must. "How will machetes help us?"

"Jakani and Sakani will take care of that," Mama replies.

I ask no more questions. The twins—our village medium and medicine man—are capable of incredible deeds. They're beyond human, but they're mortals; they too can die.

"We'll all sleep in my bedroom tonight," Yaya says, staring afar. "We'll dream the same dream, maybe a dream in which we see your papa and your big papa."

Everyone is silent again, listening to the quietness outside. Yaya rises first, leaning against her cane. Juba and I follow her to her bedroom. Without rinsing our mouths or changing into our sleeping clothes, we go to lie on either side of her. Mama sleeps on the floor, no one beside her for comfort now that Papa is gone and tradition forbids her from ever sharing a bed with another man. I hear Juba and Yaya falling asleep—their breaths turning into light snores—but I know that, like me and most of Kosawa, Mama will stay up all night; life gifts easy peace only to the very young and very old. Nothing can hinder my thoughts from rushing to the moment when Mama and Yaya and Juba are slaughtered in my presence. I wonder how long I'll spend dangling between this world and the next before finding myself among my ancestors, who I hope will welcome me and teach me how to be at home in their world. I pray they'll help me forget the few good things of this world. Perhaps it won't be hard for me to get used to this unimaginable land— Papa and Big Papa are already there, Mama and Yaya and Juba and Bongo will accompany me there. We'll be together again, but first we must die.

∧∧∧∧∧∧∨

MAMA AND PAPA CAUTIONING ME never to go near the big river is my first memory of life. Without their warning, how would I have known that rivers were not ordinarily covered with oil and toxic waste? Without our parents' stories about their childhoods in a clean Kosawa, their days spent swimming in rivers that ran clear, how would my friends and I have known that the sporadic smokiness that enveloped the village and left our eyes watery and noses runny wasn't an ordinary occurrence in the lives of other children our age?

The year my age-mates and I were born, while some of us were on our mothers' breasts and the rest of us were spending our final days in the land of the unborn, an oil well exploded in Gardens. Our parents and grandparents told us that the explosion sent crude and smoke higher than the trees. It filled the air with soot, a sight everyone thought was an omen, never having seen the likes of it before. By our sixth year of life, though, after our parents had come to know the fullness of the curse that came from living on land beneath which oil sat, they'd realized that what they saw that day was no omen—it was merely a broken oil-well head, long overdue for replacement, but why should Pexton replace it when the cost of its negligence would be borne largely by us?

One evening, when I am five, while sitting on the veranda with Papa, I ask him why the oil fields and surrounding dwellings for Pexton's laborers are called Gardens though there's not a single flower there. Papa thinks for a while, chuckles, and says, Well, Gardens is a different sort of garden, Pexton is a different sort of gardener; the oil is their flower. I ask Papa if the pipelines that begin in Gardens have an end—they seem to run on forever, wrapping around our village and passing over the big river, through our farms, and deep into the forest, the end nowhere in sight. Papa tells me that everything that has a beginning also has an end. In the case of the pipelines, they start at the oil wells and end in a faraway town many hours away by bus, a town near the ocean. There, Papa says, the oil is put into containers and sent overseas, to that place called America.

I ask Papa about America, if it has as many people as Kosawa, and he tells me that, from what he remembers in school, America has about seven thousand people, most of whom are tall men; the overseer at Gardens was from America. He and his friends came to Kosawa to get oil so that their other friends in America would have oil for their cars. Everyone in America has cars, Papa says, because the hours over there go by so fast that people need cars to get to places quickly and do everything before the sun goes down. I ask him if I can someday own a car and use some of our oil. Papa smiles at my question and says, Of course you can own a car, why not? Just make sure you buy a big one so you can use it to take me hunting; that way, I don't tire my legs trekking to the forest every time. Being that I hate Pexton, I say, I wouldn't want their oil in my car, so I'll need to buy a car that does not use oil. Papa tells me that cars must use oil, but I insist mine will be different. Papa chuckles at my fantasy. Then he starts laughing. He laughs so hard that I start laughing too, because the delight in his eyes tickles my heart.

Where is Papa? What did they do to him in Bézam? Could he still be alive?

In the early days after he did not return from his mission, I pictured myself sitting on the veranda, middle-aged and gray and weary, still waiting for my papa, waiting for an old man to show up and say, "Thula, it's me: your father, Malabo Nangi. I came back so we could continue chatting and laughing on the veranda." What will I say to that old man? What could ever make up for the loss of my dearest friend, my sweet papa, unlike all other papas in Kosawa, a papa who sat with his daughter at night and counted stars, who wondered with me if stalks of grass live in fear of the day they'd be trampled upon, who reminded me to never forget what it felt like to be a child when I grow up, never forget how it felt to be small and in need of protection, much of the suffering in the world was because of those who had forgotten that they too were once children.

Papa wanted many children, but all he got was Juba and me.

I never asked him or Mama why Juba and I are six years apart, but I remember the womb doctor coming to visit Mama several times when I was four, and also when I was five, and Mama sobbing after the womb doctor left. I remember Papa coming to sit with me on the veranda at such times, while Yaya stayed in our bedroom to console Mama.

Papa would look in the distance and ask me if I wanted to tell him a story. I would say yes and tell him the only story I knew, the one every child in Kosawa knows, about how three brothers once went to check on their traps in the forest and found a leopard caught in one of them.

Please, free me, the leopard cried to the brothers; I need to return home to my children, I've been in this trap for days and they have no one to protect them.

The brothers debated at length what to do— leopards were rare, and taking one back to their village would have brought them great fortune, but the leopard's pain was evident in her tears.

Ultimately, the brothers decided to let her go home to her children. In gratitude, the leopard made a cut on her paw and asked the brothers to use their spears and make cuts on their fingers too. On this day, the leopard said as she forged a blood pact with each brother, I give you my blood: it will flow in your veins and the veins of your descendants until the sun ceases to rise. All who seek to destroy you will fail, for my power in you will cause you to prevail. Go forth now, and live as indomitable men.

When the brothers returned to their village, they packed their belongings and left to create a new village, one in which every child would grow up to be as fearsome and dignified as a leopard. They founded Kosawa and anointed the eldest of the brothers to be their woja, for the blood of the leopard was most apparent in the strength that allowed him to tread upon snakes and scorpions. Through these brothers, we came to the world.

After finishing the story, I'd sit in silence, waiting for Papa's praise, which always came in the form of a semi-smile.

Sometimes he asked me to sing the song our ancestors sang as they laid the foundation for Kosawa, the song that would later become our village anthem. My singing voice is as pretty as a rooster's crow, and I took no pride in using it, but I knew Papa's heart needed a balm, so I would sing for him: **Sons of the leopard, daughters of the leopard, beware all who dare wrong us, never will our roar be silenced.**

Other times, at the end of the story, Papa would say nothing, and I would have nothing to add, because I knew I couldn't give him what he longed for. All I could do was wait alongside him and Mama for the day the womb doctor would come to our hut and leave with a smile on her face—which she did, the day Mama's belly finally got big enough for all of Kosawa to see that Papa's dream of a son was about to come true.

The evening Juba was born, Papa lifted me and spun me around as we both laughed, his eyes so full of gladness they glistened. The entire village sang and danced in our hut until there was no food or palm wine left, at which point everyone said their good nights. But I couldn't sleep. I woke up whenever Juba cried so I could help burp him when Mama was done nursing. When he urinated in my face while I was changing his napkins, I giggled; he was too perfect. Sometimes I worried Papa would stop being my best friend when Juba got older, they'd form a father-son duo and I'd be left out. But I also knew that Papa's love for me was boundless—the likely thing to happen was that Papa and Juba and I would become a best-friends trio. I'd learn how to wield a spear and go hunting with them and return home with the biggest kill Kosawa had ever seen.

I TOSS TO MY RIGHT. I toss to my left. My mind can find no rest. Beside me, Juba and Yaya sleep soundly. I think about calling out for Mama, asking her if I can come lie next to her, but I don't want to wake her up if she's sleeping too. I lie on my back and stare into the darkness. I think about how the air and water of Kosawa progressed from dirty to deadly.

Though Pexton has been here since Papa was a little boy, they didn't start becoming the cause of many deaths until three years ago, after they decided to add a new oil well at Gardens. It was then, with the increased wastes dumped into it, that whatever life was left in the big river disappeared. Within a year, fishermen broke down their canoes and found new uses for the wood. Children began to forget the taste of fish. The smell of Kosawa became the smell of crude. The noise from the oil field multiplied; day and night we heard it in our bedrooms, in our classroom, in the forest. Our air turned heavy.

At the end of that first dry season, a pipeline burst and oil flooded the farm of the mother of one of my friends—her family barely had any harvest that year; some days, I had to share my food with her during recess. Weeks later, a new spill turned into a fire that ravaged the farms of six families, forcing mothers to go searching for new land deep in the forest, a trek that left many with little strength for toiling. In the midst of all this, the gas flares got worse, the smoke blacker. For reasons we couldn't understand, the smoke always blew in our direction, never in the direction of Gardens and the hilltop mansion of the American overseer. With every new oil spill or day of gas flares so savage our skin shriveled and we needed to shout to hear each other over the screaming flames, Woja Beki sent someone to Gardens to talk to the supervisors, who, in turn, sent laborers to inspect the damage, patch up what they could of the old, rusty pipelines, and assure us that the spills were of no harm, the air was fine, Pexton was abiding by the law.

Not long before I turned eight, two children died in one month, both of them having suffered high fevers but otherwise different symptoms.

Papa and the other men of Kosawa made the coffins and dug the graves, and Mama and the women cooked for the bereaved families and wept alongside the brokenhearted mothers. We children did what we could to make the brothers and sisters of the departed feel less alone—we sat next to them in silence when they needed to cry, and let them decide what games we should play when they needed a break from their sadness. Nobody thought much about the fact that two children had died in one month—in a village of dozens of children, it was not uncommon for such a thing to happen. Only after my classmate Wambi began coughing while the rest of us laughed, and then began vomiting blood; only after we'd buried Wambi and coughs like his began echoing across the school compound and bouncing from hut to hut, some children urinating blood, others burning with fevers no amount of cold baths could bring down, several dying; only a few months before my brother, Juba, died and came back to life in Papa's arms, did parents start wondering if it was possible their children were dying from the same cause.

We did not initially suspect the oil field—it had been there for decades and, despite our hatred of it, we'd never before looked at one of our departed and linked their death to Pexton. We'd long ago convinced ourselves that our bodies had evolved to weather the poisons we daily breathed and that, by the mercy of the Spirit, the poisons by themselves were not enough to inflict us with diseases that herbs and potions couldn't cure.

Many parents thought it might be a curse, a jealous relative from another village targeting their children—a relative whose wrath was directed at a particular Kosawa family, but who was nonetheless going after all the children in the village to create the sense of a random act, render it untraceable. Or perhaps Kosawa had wronged the Spirit? Perhaps our parents needed to atone for one thing or another so their children might be spared? Our medium, Jakani, spoke to the ancestors and assured our parents that there was no need for atonement—the children's suffering was of this world, not from the spirit world; it was from something poisonous in our village which was entering their stomachs. But the dead children had eaten different meals, some of the ingredients bought from the big market in Lokunja now that few families could wholly depend on their farms for sustenance. The dead children had slept in different huts—what could they all have touched in common except for the ground upon which they walked, the fruits they ate from the same trees, or the water they drank from the village's well?

Papa's best friend, Bissau, was the first to suggest to Papa and our cousin Sonni that he believed it was the water. Before long, the theory began spreading through the village, parents wondering what was in the water their children were drinking—how could poison have found its way into a covered well? Woja Beki called for a meeting and invited the top supervisors at Gardens. Our parents begged the supervisors to take some water from the well, examine it, and tell them if it was the cause of the deaths. The supervisors, offering few words, took the water with them. When they returned, weeks later—the water had to be sent to Bézam for testing—they told our parents that the water was fine, but for the sake of caution it would be best if they boiled it for thirty minutes before giving it to their children. Mama boiled water for two hours every night so that Juba and I would be spared sickness and death. Her efforts were not enough.

Anyone could tell Juba's illness was no ordinary illness, this disease which started with him moaning from body aches before progressing to a fever so high his body gyrated like a fish on dry land. Sakani came over in the morning and gave him a potion to drink, but by nightfall his body had only grown hotter, no amount of wiping with a cold cloth sufficient to cool him down. When he began convulsing in Papa's arms, Mama and Yaya pinned his limbs to his body. I turned my face away, looking again only at the moment when his body turned motionless and Mama and Yaya began screeching, beseeching him: Wake up, Juba, please, open your eyes. Papa slapped Juba's cheeks and ordered him to open his eyes. Open your eyes right now, he cried. Open them. I'm commanding you.

Papa was still slapping Juba's cheeks when Bongo ran in with Jakani, both of them panting from the sprint they'd made from the twins' hut at the far end of the village. Without a word, Jakani took a package of grains from his raffia bag and threw them into his mouth, smacking his lips as he pulled out a knife and started making cuts on the soles of Juba's feet. He spat out the chewed grains all over Juba, roaring, barking, and hissing in one breath, and in the next, with his eyes closed, he began gesturing with force as he shouted at Juba, ordering him to start running back home immediately, return home before it was too late: Turn right, go over the bridge, take another right, watch out for the animal trap, jump over that puddle, don't worry about the wild pigs, keep running, take a left, keep going straight, run faster, Juba needed to run faster than that, good job, home was right around the corner, Juba shouldn't worry about his bleeding feet, once he got home Mama would take care of him, for now he had to hurry, the lion and the dog and the python were getting closer, they would get Juba if Juba did not run fast enough, stop looking behind, just keep running, ignore the mangoes, yes, the mangoes looked juicy, if he were Juba he'd want to taste them too, but as soon as Juba got home Mama would have better mangoes for him, the juiciest ever, so Juba needed to drop the mango in his hand and keep running, get out of the forest before the river rose too high, if that happened, Juba would no longer be able to cross it and return home, if the river got too high Juba would have to spend the rest of his life in that forest, alone, for eternity, he'd never see Mama and Papa again, was that what he wanted, good boy, now Juba was at the river, he didn't need to swim across, he only needed to take a big jump and he'd be home, yes, jump, of course he could do it, he had to do it now, the lion and the dog and the python were getting closer, they'd get him if he didn't jump, he had to jump now, jump . . . And Mama and Papa and Bongo and Yaya and I were all crying now, begging Juba to jump across the river, jump, please Juba, jump, please come back home, you can do it Juba, you have to jump right now, if you don't jump . . . Juba's eyes opened.

. . .

The next morning Papa is out of bed before the oldest rooster, having not slept all night. He throws a blanket over his shoulders, flies out of the hut, and storms into Woja Beki's house. Papa gives Woja Beki no chance to rinse out the night's taste from his mouth, or flick off any of sleep's crumbs from the sides of his eyes. There's only an abbreviated greeting between them—I hope you slept well, is all Papa says, according to Woja Beki's third wife, Jofi, who later gossips about the visit with half of the women of Kosawa.

Woja Beki is sitting in his parlor, still in his sleeping clothes, waiting for one of his wives to boil his bathing water, when Papa starts speaking, his voice louder than proper for a morning conversation, which is why, Jofi will later explain, she was able to hear the entire conversation even though she was far from the living room, in her kitchen, lighting her fire for the day, because that's just the kind of woman she is, minding her own business and staying far away from useless gossip.

Papa tells Woja Beki he wants to leave for Bézam as soon as possible to seek an audience with high-level government officials. He wants to have forthright conversations with as many of them as he can find. They need to look right at his mouth as he tells them how it feels for a man to watch his only son die because of this abomination they've brought upon our land. Maybe they know the number of children Kosawa has buried, but have they heard the stories of any of the parents of the departed children? Have they heard about how the days and months and years of these parents' labor and hope vanished in a single breath? Have any of these officials ever looked down helplessly upon their helpless child? He isn't going to sit back and keep waiting for Woja Beki—someone has to save his children, and whatever Woja Beki is doing is clearly not working.

Woja Beki listens in silence.

He knows—because the entire village knew less than an hour after it happened—about how Juba stopped breathing and Jakani brought him back to life. Woja Beki does not need to ask Papa where this heedless idea is coming from; he simply nods and shakes his head and nods some more as Papa swears by his ancestors that nothing will stop him from doing what he needs to do for his family. When Papa is done speaking, Woja Beki calmly responds that, indeed, everything Papa says is true: it is time for the village to start thinking of new ways to solve this problem.

His tone still tinged with the freshness of morning, Woja Beki agrees that none of the pleas he has sent to Bézam, asking the government to use its power to stop and punish Pexton, have worked, and nothing is getting better—he doesn't know what else to do. How can people not care about children? How can they not see that they're doing to our children what other people could one day do to their children? He ponders these questions often, he adds; he's found no answers. He was at the district office in Lokunja days ago and heard that Pexton was thinking about drilling another well. Another well? All those wells breathing poison on us every day, are they not enough?

After the last funeral, he says, he was unable to sleep. He went to Lokunja the next day to beg the district officer to speak to Pexton again on our behalf, ask them to find a way to, please, for our sake, replace their pipelines, because it wouldn't be long before the spills entered our homes and killed us in our sleep—but would they listen to him? The district officer told him that the pipelines were fine, that occasional leaks and spills meant nothing, pipelines the world over spilled. What was he supposed to say to such a statement? Should he have kept on arguing while they looked at him as if he were a madman? Say nothing and watch his people die on? He just didn't know what to do.

That night, from my mat, I listen as Papa gives Mama more details about his visit, whispering in the darkness. Mama is silent—she became tongue-tied the moment Papa returned from Woja Beki's house and told her of his plan to go to Bézam. I picture Papa lying on his back, his hands clasped on his chest, as he tells Mama about Woja Beki's theory that Pexton has been paying off people in the district office to shut their eyes, or turn them to the ground, or to the sky, to anywhere but the children dying in front of them. They all deserve the punishment that would inevitably be theirs someday, Woja Beki had said. How could people show such contempt for the laws of the Spirit? Was money so important that they would sell children to strangers seeking oil? "Look at me," he said to Papa. Look at how he always made sure to put some of his own money in the hands of bereaved families. Look at how he spoke to even the least in the village as if they were the most significant, because isn't that how it should be? Wasn't man's ability to recognize his fellow human what made him better than dogs? It was sad how the love of money was corrupting many; truly sad, he'd added with a sigh. But Papa was right, he went on, it was time for the village to take its complaints directly to Bézam.

Unfortunately, his back had been very stiff lately, so he couldn't manage the trip, and his counselors couldn't go either, old as they were—wasn't it a miracle they could still get out of their huts and walk around, one of them barely seeing, the other two half-deaf? But Papa could go on behalf of the village; Woja Beki's son Gono lived in the capital, and he would take care of Papa as if Papa were his own brother.

Mama must have fallen asleep somewhere in the middle of the retelling, because when he's done talking Papa says, "Sahel, Sahel, are you up?," and Mama says nothing, and I thank her in silence for not listening to the lies of that deceitful, dirty-teeth buffoon.

Two evenings later, Woja Beki calls a meeting of the village's able men and his three counselors. In his parlor, seated on the only sofa in Kosawa, his white-socked feet stroking the only rug in Kosawa, his head below a clock that sings whenever its long finger touches twelve, the rest of the men sitting on their wooden stools or on the bare cemented floor, Woja Beki asks his counselors if they think it a good idea for Papa to go to Bézam on behalf of Kosawa. The counselors either nod or shrug, and Woja Beki thanks them for their wisdom. Papa stands up and asks if he can get three men to go with him. No one puts up a hand. A man rises to say that leading a delegation to Bézam should be Woja Beki's duty, not Papa's. And besides, the man adds, Papa is not an elder, he's not even in the generation directly below the elders; he has no right to be the one to speak on behalf of the village. Many grunt in agreement, but Papa is not dissuaded—after giving the assembly the same speech he'd given Woja Beki, he prevents a protracted argument by announcing that he's not looking for anyone's understanding or blessings, even though he's doing this for their children too; he doesn't even want their gratitude, he only needs three men to accompany him. Bissau, Papa's best friend since childhood, is on his feet before Papa is done speaking. Four more men stand up. These are more men than Papa asked for, but he turns no one down—he knows that, like him, the men do not wish to travel to Bézam, but the salvation of their children compels them to.

My uncle Bongo is at the meeting, sitting next to Papa, but he doesn't offer to join. The moment he and Papa return home, Bongo begins imploring his older brother to reconsider his plan. Bongo is convinced Woja Beki will set a trap for Papa and his team. Some of the men in the team were part of the group that had once conspired to kill Woja Beki for his treachery. Woja Beki knows how much the men detest him for living in a brick house and drinking bottled water from Bézam and wearing new shirts and trousers from America, clothes he claims his sons gave him in appreciation for being a great father, matching outfits he loves to wear as he stands over the coffins of children, spilling water out of his fishlike eyes. But Papa cares little about that—in his desperation to never see his only son breathe his last again, he forges an alliance with a man he despises.

"Think about it, Malabo," Bongo says the morning of Papa's departure. We're all sitting on the veranda. Bongo is facing Papa, who's staring straight ahead. "Think about who you're trusting. Gono works for Pexton. His two brothers work for the government. They all work at jobs that supervisors at Pexton helped them get. Why would you trust them? You've never liked any of them since we were children. And their father—even the smallest child in Kosawa knows that a truthful word never escapes Woja Beki's mouth; if he says good morning to you, you go outside and see if the sun is indeed out before you respond. The man is a snake, and you're going to stay in his son's house and hope that he'll help you, even though we all know whose side they're on?"

"If you have a better idea, why don't you say it?" Papa says. "Do you know anyone who lives in Bézam? Someone who'll be willing to take us in and feed us and arrange meetings between us and the—"

"You think you'll go to Bézam and the government is going to shake your hand and say, 'Welcome, how can we help you?'" Bongo says.

"I'm not going there for a handshake."

"You're wasting your time. And causing your family great distress. For what?"

"Is the government a rock, a thing with neither brain nor heart?" Papa yells as he turns to face Bongo. "Is the government not humans like us—people who have children, mothers and fathers who know what it's like to have a sick child? I sat here and watched my son die and come back to life right in my arms. Did you not see it happen with your very own eyes? If the Spirit had not felt sorry for Sahel and me, Juba would not be sitting here with us today. And what did he die from? From something the government can put an end to. He's well now, but who can swear to me that he won't get sick again if he continues drinking this water? What's so crazy about me going to find someone in the government who I can talk to as father to father?"

"Do not go to Bézam."

"When you have a wife and children, you'll learn how to stand up and do what a man needs to do for his family instead of sitting here mouthing nonsense."

Bongo stands up and goes into the hut.

Yaya sniffles, though I see no tears—her eyes are downturned, she's too pained to look at her children. "My dear son," she says to Papa, "I may not be here when you return."

"There's nothing for you to worry about, Yaya," Papa says, his voice having rediscovered its gentleness. "I'll be gone for ten days at most."

"When I see your father on the other side, I'll give him greetings from you. I'll tell him that you grew up to be a good husband and father. He won't agree with your abandoning your family to march into a trap with your eyes wide open, but he'll be proud of you after I tell him how well you and Sahel took care of me."

"Yaya, please . . ."

Yaya leans on her cane, pulls herself off the stool, and enters the hut. Mama follows, carrying Juba on her hip, my unborn brother or sister in her belly.

I remain outside with Papa, neither of us speaking, both of us looking at the guava tree as the wind brings down the leaves. The dry season has just ended, heavy rains are on their way. Nights of thunderstorms will soon abound; on one or two mornings, we'll awaken to the sight of a rainbow. When the next dry season starts, later in the year, it will usher in the year 1980, a year I'm looking forward to because it's the year

I'll turn ten, my favorite number. On this morning, though, I must act as if I'm four times ten years old, for Papa's sake, so he feels less alone as he struggles to convince everyone that he needs to do this. I don't want him to go, but I know he has to do it, for Juba and me.

"Thula," he says to me after a long minute of us sitting in silence.

"Papa."

"Make sure, while I'm away . . ." He sighs. He does not turn to look at me as he tells me to watch over Juba and make sure to listen to Yaya and Mama and Bongo.

"Yes, Papa."

He tells me he's counting on me to be strong, especially for Mama—make sure she eats and sleeps well, for her sake and the sake of our unborn.

I nod.

"I don't want to come back and find that she and Yaya have not been eating because of their anxiety about my return. Bongo is a man—he doesn't know how to do certain things well, so I'm entrusting this to you. Take very good care of your brother."

"I'll do as you say, Papa."

"Get up and go get ready for school."

On the walk to school, between lessons, during recess, my friends ask me if it's true, if my father is really going to lead his group to Bézam, if they're going to march into the palace of His Excellency and demand that His Excellency remove Pexton from our land or else. I respond to no questions; I want everyone to leave me alone, or to go talk to the children or sisters of the five other men, some of whom also come to me for answers, seeking any assurance I can give that everyone will return home safely, that Bézam wasn't the vicious jungle of our imagination whence no one ever returned.

∧∧∧∧∧∧∧
ɯɯɯɯɯɯɯ

PAPA IS GONE BY THE time I return home from school.

I say nothing to Mama and Yaya besides greetings. I go into the bedroom and lie on my mat with my school uniform still on. I cover my head with my blanket and try to imagine life in a perfect world, but all I see is Papa's face. He and his group probably caught the bus at Gardens not long after I left for school, to begin the journey that would require them to change buses at least twice before arriving in Bézam a day and a half later. Mama calls for me to come eat, but I don't respond. I have no interest in food.

Bongo doesn't go out that evening to sit with his friends at the square. Mama goes to bed early. I rise and go to the veranda to sit with Juba and Yaya. We're all thinking of Papa, wondering what he's doing at the moment. We ask the Spirit to be with him. I think of his advice that I never forget how it feels to be a child when I grow up. I want to keep my promise to him, but I also want to forget I ever lived through such anguish.

We begin counting down the days, desperate for them to hurry to ten, which they refuse to. Day One takes a thousand years to get to Day Two, which takes three thousand to get to Day Three. Roosters won't announce a new dawn quickly enough, shadows won't lengthen at a generous speed. We spend every second with our ears searching for sounds of a return, scrutinizing noises from every direction, saying nothing beyond what is necessary, afraid we might utter a word that would put the others in even greater distress. The minutes and hours remain reluctant to leave us, though we beseech them to fly away. When the sun begins its descent, it appears to take a prolonged pause with every drop, to mock us, surely, for there is nothing here for it to take so long to admire, this ordinary view it has seen every evening since the day the Spirit created earth.

We visit the families of the other men. Mama goes to see her friend Cocody, the wife of Bissau, Papa's best friend—their two husbands are in Bézam, they're two anxious wives. Mama and Cocody talk in sad tones about their fruitless search for sleep every night. Another friend of Mama's, Lulu, comes to visit us; her brother, Lobi, went with Papa. Mama tells Lulu she's sorry for Papa's role in her family's pain, and Lulu asks Mama why is it that women feel they have to apologize for their men's failings—when was the last time a woman was the source of her village's suffering? Lulu's voice is not as loud as it often is, but she still pushes her tongue through the gap between her front teeth every time she speaks, the same gap her brother has, which makes me wonder what happens to the gap between people's teeth when they die. But no one has died. Has anyone died?

On the tenth day, I wake up early, sweep away the guava leaves in the front yard, and burn them at the back of the hut. I hurry home after school and dare not leave the veranda. I force myself to breathe. We all sit on the veranda, saying nothing to one another, our emotions warped and ineffable, our eyes dry from alertness. We wait till the darkness gets so thick we can scarcely see the torment on each other's faces.

Papa does not return.

On the eleventh evening, Mama and Bongo take turns sleeping and sitting outside until the sun rises and the dew dries. The next night, I cry in the darkness, begging Papa not to leave me, to please hurry back home to me. In the morning, Mama rises up with bloodshot eyes. She walks to Gardens and takes the bus to Lokunja, to the big market. She returns with fresh produce and kills two of our chickens. She makes a meal of grilled chicken and boiled green plantains with eggplant and tomato sauce on the side, Papa's favorite—she'd had a dream in which Papa returned and asked for something to eat. When

Papa does not return, Mama offers the food to those who come to tell us that Papa is surely on his way back, shaking their heads sadly as they rip off meat from bones with their teeth and lick their fingers before asking for a cup of water to wash down the meal.

By the fifteenth morning, Yaya can barely climb out of bed. Mama wipes her down because getting to the bathroom is too long a walk—first age attacked her legs, now heartache is finishing the job. More neighbors and relatives arrive to comfort us in the following days. Bongo visits the families of the other men to assure them that, though hope might be frail, everyone has to do whatever they can to stay strong. At school I avoid all eyes. I sit alone during recess, having no need for hollow words of comfort.

Twenty days come and go, twenty nights of nightmares.

Worse than the waiting is the punishing nature of time, its ruthless inflexibility. Our appetites disappear before us. What sort of news should we prepare ourselves for?

Woja Beki's son Gono arrives from Bézam on the thirtieth day.

I'm returning home from school when I see the car he hired in Lokunja dropping him off. I hurry home to alert everyone. We all run to Woja Beki's house, Mama holding her belly, Juba on my back. Even Yaya, who has barely eaten in days, picks up her cane and hauls what little is left of her body. Because, surely, it has to be good news. Or not the worst of news, at the very least. Gono hasn't returned with a carful of dead men, so it must be that Gono came to tell us why Papa's return has been delayed.

But Gono does not know where Papa is.

The Six arrived safely in Bézam two days after they left the village, Gono tells us. He was expecting them, because his father had sent him a message through the district office, so he went to the bus stop to meet them. He hugged them and took them to his house, where his wife fed them her special cocoyam porridge with smoked porcupine, and gave them mats to sleep on in the living room. His wife served them potatoes and fried eggs for breakfast, and then the men got on a bus with him to go to the government office, their bellies filled, their eyes bright as they gaped at quick-walking, fast-talking crowds, cars as far as they could see, houses sitting atop other houses, some structures so high they had to lift up their heads to see the roofs.

"I left them in the children-affairs office to meet with two directors of health I'd arranged for them to talk to—I'd been thinking that if the government could send some medicine to Kosawa, that might help," Gono says. "Then I went to my office, came back to get them two hours later, but they weren't there."

Our gazes upon him are cold as he speaks, standing in his father's parlor, encircled by us, the fathers and mothers and wives and children and brothers and sisters of six most likely dead men. The rest of the village is outside, wondering about the fate of their cousins and nephews and friends and neighbors.

"You went to get them after their meeting and you didn't find them because they had vanished like dust, is that what you're telling us?" Bissau's father asks.

Gono nods.

"Vanished how?" Bongo asks.

"I don't know."

"Do not lie to us," Bissau's wife, Cocody, shouts. She is pregnant, her belly bigger than Mama's.

"I swear it's the truth. The directors in the children-affairs office said they met with them, then sent them on their way. I thought they'd be waiting for me in front of the building, but I went all around the building, over and over, and I couldn't find them."

"You sold them to the government," a missing man's brother yells.

"I'd never—" Gono cries.

"You killed them," a voice behind me shouts.

"Kill my own friends? Why?"

"Grown men don't get lost."

"They don't. That's why . . . that's why this situation . . . I just don't understand. . . ."

"Tell us the truth, Gono," a mother cries. "Please, tell us the whole truth."

"I swear to you all on every last ancestor," Gono says, bending to swipe his index finger on the floor, lick the dust on the finger, and point it to the sky, "I swear upon all that I am that the government people promised me our brothers left their office alive."

Wives and daughters and mothers begin wailing, their voices flying through the double doors of Woja Beki's house, over the apple trees in his compound, along the path that leads to Gardens, through the supervisors' offices and the school Pexton built for the children there, past their clinic, into the meeting hall where the laborers gather on many evenings to reminisce about the distant homes they left behind to work for Pexton, onto the vast, grassless field on which stand structures of metal spewing fire and smoke, and down into the wells, where they become one with the oil.

I sit against the wall with my brother on my lap, watching my mother cry, her hand on her belly. I yearn to dry her tears, but I yearn even more never to see her tears again. Mama's crying has known no pause since the ten-day mark—so much does she cry that Yaya warns her that the baby will be born withered up if she doesn't do a better job of holding on to her liquids. But then, when Mama stops crying, Yaya begins, singing a woeful, discordant solo about the fate of a child born to a dead father, and then Mama is back to crying, and it's then I walk out of the room, because none of that is of any use to me; I'm better off spending my time thinking about the chances that Papa is alive, the odds that he'll stay alive until I'm old enough to go to Bézam and rescue him, bring him home, hear him laugh, watch him make Mama happy and teach Juba how to be a man.

"My dear sisters and children, are these tears necessary?" Woja Beki says, rising from his sofa. "Are there any corpses in front of us? What are we crying for? We don't know the full story yet, but Gono and I will get to the bottom of all this, I assure you."

Looking at Woja Beki's face, I wonder why he was ever born, considering there's an infinite host of unborn begging to be born, considering most of the unborn would be decent people if given a chance at life. Why does the Spirit keep on cursing the world with the existence of the likes of Woja Beki? I hate him for how he lied to Papa, and how he has no shame about lying to us, how he can look at us in our despair and fling untruths at us, rubbing pepper and scorching embers into the very wounds he inflicted.

I hate how, because of him, two days after the meeting in his house, Mama's grief pushes out our unborn before it is ready for this world. Mama screams when she sees the baby—its body is so small it fits in her palms—and her friends implore her to be strong, to let go, to bear her burdens like a woman. No one tells Mama that there'll soon be another baby—without Papa sleeping next to her, Mama will never have another baby.

Yaya barely has a voice left to cry with as we walk to the burial ground to bury the baby on top of my grandfather Big Papa. It doesn't seem that long ago when we walked this same path and crossed the small river to bury Big Papa. I still remember his casket at the front of the processional, balanced on the shoulders of Papa and Bongo and four other men, behind them Mama pregnant with Juba and holding my hand, three women holding Yaya, reminding her of how blessed she was to have shared decades with her husband, the rest of the village behind us, singing: **All lives must end, may your life never end.**

No one sings for the baby; our baby never had a life. There is no processional to the burial ground. Just a dozen of us. Our baby's body is not worth making a coffin for—one of our relatives holds it in her arms, wrapped in a blue sheet.

I promise myself that afternoon that someday I will make Woja Beki and his friends in Bézam pay for what they've done to my family. I know nothing about how a girl makes men pay for their crimes, but I have the rest of my life to figure it out.

Later that week, Bongo leaves with three men to search for Papa and the others in Bézam. Before he goes, Yaya falls to her knees. She begs him not to leave her childless, the worse curse that could befall any woman who's ever carried a child. Bongo promises her that not only will he return, he'll return with Papa's body, with or without life in it.

In Bézam, Bongo and the others sit on the steps of government buildings and promise parcels of land and goats to anyone who can offer them useful information. They sleep in an abandoned roadside shack, and from first light to dusk they walk up to anyone with a semblance of friendliness and ask questions, and give descriptions, but they only get headshakes. They roam a city so massive and frenzied it threatens to rip apart and swallow them at every turn. Eight days after their departure, they return empty-handed.

Still, night after night, Mama and Yaya sit on the veranda waiting for Papa, losing more flesh to despair. They take turns being the weaker woman—some nights Yaya feeds Mama with my help; other nights Mama and I feed Yaya. Many nights I feed them both, with Bongo's help if he's home. I force myself to eat a banana whenever I can—one of us needs to have a basic level of strength at all times. Only late at night do I consider my own pain, when I hope everyone is sleeping; it is then that I cry, imagining how different our lives would be if our ancestors had picked any other piece of the earth but this one. Images of my dead friends enter and exit my dreams. I think about what our unborn would have looked like if it had been allowed to be a fully formed child entering a kind world, a world where Papa wasn't gone and my surviving friends and I weren't spending precious minutes contemplating the day our turn would come to die.

· · ·

Three months after Papa's disappearance, the Pexton men arrive for their first meeting with the village. Before their arrival, Woja Beki tells us that we should be thankful to Papa and his group: something they did or said in Bézam must be why Pexton has decided to come speak to us. That makes no sense to me— why would people in Bézam cause Papa to vanish if they wanted to help him?—but I hope the meeting will be fruitful.

Yaya and Mama take a break from their seats on the veranda to attend the meeting, carrying along what shred of faith they have left that, despite Bongo's futile search, Papa might return alive, even if broken. Ours is the worst kind of mourning—not knowing if the men are dead, how they died, when they died; not knowing if there's still a chance we can save them. Yaya says this when she cries, that if she could only take her son's corpse and put it in the ground, then she could at least begin the journey to acceptance. But the men from Pexton offer us no information at the meeting. When one of the missing men's fathers stands up and implores the Leader to at least confirm to us that the Six are dead, so we can offer sacrifices to the Spirit on their behalf, help hasten their voyage to be with our ancestors, the Leader says that he cannot do that, he's not allowed to do that, Pexton cannot involve itself with superstitious matters.

For more than a year now, they've come to speak to us every eight weeks. On every occasion, Woja Beki dons a linen suit, and the Pexton men tell their old lies using new words. Mama and Yaya cry when it's over. Kosawa grows weaker. We were all on the verge of resignation until a few hours ago, when Konga took away the men's car key.

THE WEIGHT OF MY THOUGHTS puts me to sleep toward the end of the night. When I wake up, the first light of day has descended on Kosawa. I had prayed the sun would never rise, but risen it has, and now I too must rise, to face the guns.

Juba is still sleeping next to me, but Mama and Yaya are already up—I hear them whispering with my uncle Bongo in the parlor. When I enter, they stop talking to look at me, Mama feigning a smile. I want to know everything: Are the men of Kosawa ready for the soldiers? What did they spend the night doing? Are there enough machetes?

"I'm not going to school today," I say.

"Come," Mama says, stretching out her hand for me to walk to her. I don't move.

"There's no need for you to stay home," Bongo says. "School is going to go on as usual. Nothing's going to happen to you there."

"How do you know?"

"Because . . . everything will be fine, Thula. Just ignore all the things the Pexton men said last night, okay?"

"I can't ignore it. They meant it. They were serious. Mama, please?"

Mama does not counter Bongo. Her fake smile remains intact.

I glance outside through the door. All is calm. Why aren't the men running around preparing some sort of defense against the soldiers? Why doesn't Bongo appear like someone who stayed up all night getting ready for battle? It is evident from his oiled face and his kempt hair that he just took a bath. His machete is lying against a wall, sharpened and glistening at the edges. Am I supposed to trust that his relaxed demeanor is thanks to a conviction that the machete will cut down speeding bullets?

He looks at me half-smiling, his head tilted; he resembles Papa more than ever. Speaking in the deep voice they share, he tells me that there was a lot about last night that, as a child, I'd misunderstood. He says there isn't going to be any battle because soldiers are not coming to kill anyone. Yes, the Pexton men had uttered the words I heard, but the men did not mean that the soldiers would slaughter anyone. What the Leader meant was that the soldiers would slaughter the disagreement between Pexton and us and put an end to it all. The soldiers will be coming, that's certain, but only to have a conversation with the men of the village. Nothing more. Which is why all the children must go to school—the adults will stay home to await the soldiers.

Mama, with a genuine-sounding chuckle, adds that by the time I return home from school, the episode will be nothing more than a story I'll one day tell my grandchildren.

I don't believe Bongo and Mama, but I don't know what to say. I can't argue with them—I don't have the right to argue with my elders even if I believe they're not telling me the truth. I look at Yaya, hoping she'll say something wise to ease my perplexity, but words aren't my grandmother's favorite gift for her family at times like this—silence is.

I leave to fetch water at the well. I'm not going to school, I tell myself. I'll pretend to have a stomachache.

On my way to the well, I see some friends; it is clear from their faces that their parents just told them something similar to what Bongo said to me.

Like me, my friends are children born in 1970. We are boys and girls, age-mates and classmates. We crawled together and toddled together and now we walk together. Sometimes the girls play separately from the boys, and other times we play together, and

fight each other, and when we're done crying and tat-
tling on each other to mothers who sigh and ignore
us, we return to being friends, because we'll never
belong with another group of age-mates the way
we belong with ours. I have a few girl age-mates I'm
closer to than to the others; it's two of them I see as I
approach the well. They agree with me that there are
things the adults are not telling us. But they're going
to school. Apparently, everyone is going to school despite everything. "Think about it, Thula," one of my
friends says. "Would our parents send us to school if
they believed we'd be killed there?"

Fatigued from my restless night, I fall asleep in class
even before Teacher Penda is done with the first
arithmetic problem. Most of my classmates do too.
When Teacher Penda asks us what is going on, why
we all look so tired, we chirp in unison that nothing
is wrong, nothing whatsoever, we're just focused on
listening to him. We know our parents wouldn't want
us telling a government man that they've taken our
village head and three of Pexton's men captive. One of
my classmates almost says it, stammering something
about a long village meeting the previous night, but
the rest of us shoot him a glare so sharp we're surprised
he doesn't end up one-eyed, like Jakani and Sakani.
After this, we're all afraid that we might inadvertently
tell Teacher Penda what the village has done and in so

doing put our lives in greater danger. The fear keeps us alert for the rest of the day and forces us to answer every question, so that our teacher will suspect nothing.

I like Teacher Penda, even if he's a government man. Like the other six teachers at our school, he lives with Pexton's laborers at Gardens, in a brick house covered with an aluminum roof, one of many benefits to being a government man. Unlike every other government man we've ever met or heard our parents talk about, though, Teacher Penda is kind to us. He gives us only knowledge, which isn't a poisonous thing. But we know that doesn't mean he wouldn't betray Kosawa for the sake of money. He's not one of us—he's from a village on the other side of the country, a place where, he loves to tell us, a woman can marry three husbands if her beauty is too great for one man to bear. We've never asked him if he has a wife and children in his village—such questions are not for one to ask another—but we like him enough that we invite him to our family weddings and birth celebrations, which he attends only if we're good students.

I return home from school that afternoon to learn from Mama that the soldiers did not arrive as expected, but the adults are not concerned, they know the soldiers will come, they're prepared for them whenever they do arrive. The gleeful manner in which Mama says that makes me lose my skepticism; I become convinced that all will be well.

Mama tells me that she has prepared my favorite meal—fried ripe plantains and beans with smoked pig feet. Across Kosawa, mothers have prepared special meals for their families, as if the simple day deserved celebration. They've cooked rice and smoked-goat stew; leafy greens steamed with palm oil and mushrooms; boiled yams to go with okra sauce and bushmeat. The meals are made from ingredients both pure and adulterated, some from our dying farms and emptying barns, most bought at the big market, paid for with a portion of whatever the women earn from selling the animals their men kill in the forest. Some dishes are made possible by the benevolence of relatives with fertile lands who live in other villages, aunts and grandmothers and cousins many times re-moved who occasionally visit and offer us foods they still have in abundance. So delicious are the meals that we think little of sickness and death as we eat on our parlor floors. I give Juba some of my food when he starts eyeing my plate after licking his with his tongue. Some of my friends have bigger stomachs than I do, and their parents have many mouths to feed, so they and their siblings fight over the right to lick the sauce at the bottom of the cooking pot; oftentimes they quarrel so much their mothers intervene and draw a line in the pot with their fingers, giving each child a section to lick.

After we're done eating, my friends and I wash our

families' plates and pots—a quick chore for many, considering there's not much left to clean after all the licking. The rest of our chores that evening are more enjoyable than they've ever been: chickens and goats meekly take their sleeping spots in barns; the leaves and twigs we sweep in our front yards gather in perfect piles, which we transport to our backyards so they can crumble over time and merge with worms to serve as nourishment for our sickly soil.

With chores finished, and approaching twilight turning the air blue, we hurry out to play. Across compounds, friends and siblings start hiding and seeking, kicking balls of plantain leaves and rubber, everyone enjoying a hopefulness we'd feared we'd lost.

I'm happier than I've been since Papa vanished over a year ago. I don't know if a dialogue between the adults and the soldiers will bring Papa home, but I trust our men will take a stand that will force Pexton to do more than send us useless representatives.

Sitting with three friends on one of their verandas and watching a couple other friends jumping rope, I laugh as one of them keeps tripping on herself. When my friends stop playing and start arguing about one thing or another, I smile and listen. I've never found the need to use words unless I must. Papa says it's because I was born with four eyes and four ears and a quarter of a mouth better suited for smiling than for talking. On this evening, I have even less need for words, and I can't stop grinning, overwhelmed as I am with love for my village and its people. I listen to the laughter of my friends, and watch young men heading to the square to laze and linger and smoke mushrooms— the breeze is perfect for such an activity—and I can think of no better place to have been born in than Kosawa.

The next morning, while eating breakfast, I ask Mama if there's a plan for what the village will do with the captives, and Mama tells me that Bongo and Lusaka and the rest of the men are going to have a meeting later in the day to map a strategy, what to do if the soldiers don't soon arrive. My friends and I wonder, on our walk to school, and during recess, what the strategy might be. Would our men kill the captives? I hope they kill Woja Beki first, give him the worst possible death for betraying his own.

After my afternoon chores, I go to the square to meet my friends, and we take turns doing each other's hair under the mango tree. Again, I let them do the talking. Sometimes they yell at each other, because one friend wants to be heard above another, what they have to say is just too important, which confuses me because listening is far more enjoyable than fighting to be heard. Papa is the only one I ever truly yearned to talk to, because our conversations were like the rustling of leaves, slow and gentle, followed by silence. Now that he's gone, I prefer to spend more time alone in my head, pondering why the world is the way it is, wondering if the Spirit will one day decide to redesign it.

^^^^^^/

ON THE THIRD DAY OF the Pexton men's captivity, Yaya is taking a nap, and I'm sitting with Mama and Juba in the parlor. We are eating when we hear it, the sound of an engine over the noise of our chewing, something chugging down the narrow road from Gardens.

It's a sound neither loud nor bothersome, but it needn't be to be noticeable, because ours is a small village, too little for noises of certain sorts to find hiding places. Even with the oil field nearby, cars seldom arrive in Kosawa, for there is nothing past us, nothing but trees and grass as far as one can travel, which is why the sound of an approaching vehicle is enough to make us pause and change the direction of conversations, speculating on who's in the car and what they've come for.

The food in my mouth turns to garbage.

I look at Mama. Don't just sit there, I want to scream at her. Stand up. Lock the doors. Lock the windows. Do the triple knot you did the night of the meeting.

Yaya ambles out of her bedroom. She looks at us and walks to the veranda. We all stand up and follow her outside, palm oil from my food dripping down my fingers.

The men of Kosawa are coming out of their huts. They have nothing in their hands as they move toward the car—no machetes, no spears. Bongo is probably at Lusaka's hut, likely discussing the minutiae of the anticipated conversation with the soldiers. But shouldn't a conversation with soldiers involve weapons? I'm tempted to ask one of our neighbors this as he rushes to the square. I want to tell him that he's forgetting something—he and the other men can't go out to meet soldiers empty-handed even if they're hoping for a polite conversation—but as more men come rushing past our hut toward the square without weapons, none of them with the countenance of men about to collide with their doom, some of them chatting and laughing with one another, slapping each other's backs and rubbing their own bellies to show how well their wives had just fed them, I decide a new form of madness has descended upon the men of Kosawa.

What did Jakani and Sakani do to them right after the village meeting? The twins were supposed to prepare them for the soldiers' arrival and everything that would ensue, but it seems that, somehow, whatever ritual they did had the reverse effect.

Mama and the other mothers step off their verandas after the men disappear from sight. They whisper,
holding toddlers by the hand, babies on their hips and
backs. In silence, they start walking toward the square.
Though confused, we children follow our mothers,
for, surely, they wouldn't ever lead us to doom. We
walk in twos and in threes. I inhale, I exhale, half
unable, half unwilling to envision the scene we'll find
at the square.

The soldiers are out of their car by the time we arrive. They survey us as we approach. They assess
the mango tree under which Konga isn't napping.
Where is Konga? I'd asked Mama, but she'd said that
no one knows; no one has seen him since the night
of the village meeting. He had sent around word for
all the men of the village to meet him in front of
Jakani and Sakani's hut, but he never showed up there,
leaving the twins to preside over the rest of whatever
happened that night, things we'll never know.
     The soldiers look around at the square—at the
dusty front yards and slanted thatch roofs of the huts
that surround it; at the paths diverging from it; at the
powdered earth rising as Yaya and other grandmothers and grandfathers approach with hands gripping
canes, walking at the pace of toddlers, none of them
in any rush for life or death.

. . .

I'd imagined there would be at least half a dozen
soldiers, but there are only two, both dressed in uniforms of green with patches of red and black. One of
the soldiers has hair sprouting out of his chin like a
he-goat; the other one has cheeks that jiggle like the
belly of a well-loved pig. They look neither angry nor
happy, simply like men who've stopped by to pick up
something of little significance on their way to somewhere important.

I see Bongo walking up to the soldiers as the village
settles around them.

Bongo offers a hand in greeting. He says something
to the soldiers, too faint for anyone else to hear. The
soldiers nod. Bongo points toward Woja Beki's house.
The soldiers nod again and smile. I can't conceive what
Bongo could be saying to make the soldiers smile, or
how he could will himself to say something smile-
worthy to them after what the government has done
to Papa. It also makes no sense to me why the rest
of the fathers and uncles and grandfathers and older
brothers are smiling. I look at my friends, and they all
appear as baffled as I am, though, gradually, the looks
on our faces change to smiles—nothing seems wiser
for us to do in the moment than to join in the smiling. A smile that does not originate from my heart
hurts my mouth, but I know I must join in and do
my part. We had been taught to do this in school, to
follow the leader, and being that Bongo is our leader

in that moment, the sides of our lips rise as if pulled up by strings from the sky. Everyone in the square is likely thinking along the same lines, because soon all of Kosawa is smiling alongside the inaudible conversation. Perhaps a few of the smiles are real, but I doubt it—all around me teeth are exposed but eyes are wide open.

Consumed by upholding our grins, we don't wonder what the next step in the game might be until we look to our right and see Woja Beki walking toward the square, two of the young men who had dragged him to Lusaka's hut on the night of the village meeting on either side of him. Woja Beki is smiling, the young men are smiling as their steps lock with his, Bongo's smile broadens, the soldiers smile on, everyone acting cheerful for reasons no one knows except those who started this lethal game.

"Our dear soldiers," Woja Beki calls out as he hurries toward the front. "I'm so sorry to keep you waiting."

The soldier with the piglike cheeks shrugs and keeps on smiling.

"How can I waste the time of important men whose jobs don't allow them even two minutes to spare?" Woja Beki continues. "I'm truly sorry, my dear soldiers. I was visiting a friend, and before I knew it I fell asleep in his house. Fortunately, these fine young men woke me up. They tell me that you've come looking for the Pexton men? Is it true what I'm hearing, that they haven't been seen since they left our village?"

Both of the soldiers nod.

"I'm shocked to hear this. How can it be possible, when they left three days ago? This is absolutely unbelievable. I can't . . . I'm just . . . I have no words. None of this makes any sense. Please, let's go to my house so we can talk about it," he says, as he gestures in the direction of his house. "I'm glad my people have been keeping you company, but it'll be better if we can speak in private, don't you think?"

The soldiers nod again and turn around to follow Woja Beki.

"If you don't mind, my dear soldiers, I'm going to bring along these three young men to serve as witnesses to everything I say," Woja Beki says, as he gestures at Bongo and the two men who just escorted him to the square. "You must understand, a man in my position needs witnesses before he opens his mouth, lest his words be distorted."

The soldiers look at each other and shrug again, which makes me wonder if they've been sent to do nothing but nod and shrug. Looking at them and their air of nonchalance, I realize the men of Kosawa were not unwise to leave their weapons at home—there'll be no need for spears and machetes in today's proceedings. The soldiers have guns, holstered on their right hips, but they look nothing like men who possess any knowledge of, or interest in, pulling out the guns, never mind using them on us.

We remain standing in the square as Woja Beki and the five men walk away. Woja Beki's voice is vibrant as he unleashes words he hasn't had a chance to use in days, speaking so fast his sentences have no pause between them. "My shock is so great dear soldiers but we'll sit down and my wives will make us a good meal and we'll put our heads together and try to figure out where the men could be because there's no way men can vanish going from one place to another and I can tell you that in all my years I've heard no such story and believe me when I tell you that I've heard every sort of story there is to hear and my people standing over there will swear that the men got into their car with their driver and left after the meeting and the men said they were going home and I woke up the next morning and pictured them eating the breakfast their wives had prepared for them before going to their offices but you've come here to tell me that no one has seen them since that day and I can never understand how it's even possible. . . ."

After the group disappears behind a hut to take the path that leads to Woja Beki's house, my friends and I turn to each other, befuddled. What is Woja Beki doing here? Why is he speaking on our behalf? Is he no longer our enemy?

I look at our men. They wear no confusion, only satisfaction, because, clearly, what they wanted to happen is happening, and even if their children do not understand it, their plan is working, and as long as the Spirit remains benevolent, victory will be theirs.

. . .

We don't know how long we'll be waiting for Bongo and the others to return from Woja Beki's house, so my friends and I decide to make ourselves comfortable in case our wait stretches for hours. Waiting has become us—we've been waiting for one thing or another since the day we were born; what is one more wait of a few hours compared with a lifetime of waiting? Grandmothers and grandfathers, leaning on their canes, ask us to run back home and fetch their stools. Mothers ask daughters to bring back mats for them to place under the mango tree so they can sit and stretch their legs; also balls for toddlers to play with, to keep their boredom at bay. Older sisters and younger aunts who had hurried to the square with babies balanced on their hips, some of the babies naked except for the napkins tied around their buttocks, ask their little sisters and nieces to bring an outfit for the baby, and a banana, too, in case the baby gets hungry, and also the straw baby-carrier.

The children of Kosawa run off in every direction. I return with a stool for Yaya and a cup of water for Juba, but most of my friends return with baskets containing assorted items, for they share a hut with parents and multiple siblings and aunts and uncles and cousins and grandparents, huts to which their families add rooms with every new marriage so newlyweds can have space to share with their future children, and grandparents can keep their bedrooms, and unmarried aunts and older sisters and female cousins can have a room of their own while waiting to be plucked by a man, and unmarried uncles and older brothers and any other male relatives can be in the back rooms with separate entrances, no one ever needing to leave home unless they choose to.

Mama and the other mothers, having made themselves comfortable on the mats beneath the mango tree, whisper among themselves. Our oldest grandparents lean close to speak into each other's ears. Some of my friends' older sisters, girls who recently exited childhood and now walk around with the glow of new womanhood, exchange coy glances with boys who've decided they're no longer boys and are thus ready to prove they can do to a woman everything a man can. Eyeing the giggling girls, the soon-to-be men lick and pucker the lips on which stand countable strands of hair until a parent notices them looking at each other in a way people aren't allowed to look at each other unless they're ready to have babies, at which point the shameless adolescents turn their eyes away from each other and pretend that the only thing on their minds is the fate of Kosawa.

Fathers and uncles and grandfathers move farther away from the women and children to confer, nodding to whatever Lusaka is saying. My friends talk about Konga. They imagine he's in the forest, strolling without cares as animals roam nearby and birds tweet above him, listening to the voices of leaves when the wind forces them to speak.

At the far left corner of the square, Jakani and Sakani stand watching us. They're in the same spot from which they've observed every meeting, including the last one, which they witnessed in entirety, though they did and said nothing even after Konga arrived.

Sitting on the ground not far from our mothers, my friends switch from discussing Konga to wondering when our stand against Pexton will end, how it'll end. One of our classmates is getting sicker; he wasn't in school today. Another friend's baby brother fell ill; she had to stay home to take care of him so her mother could go to the farm. Whatever hope we had only days ago is fading; Kosawa can't shake off its desolation.

Every few minutes, my friends get quiet—death can be talked about for only so long. One of them suggests that we wait in silence. Another says that while we're silent we should pray in our hearts. Everyone agrees; if we've ever needed to pray without ceasing, now is the moment. I bow my head and start praying for Kosawa. I pray for Papa's return. I pray for Yaya and Mama and for all mothers to cry no more.

My eyes are closed when a friend nudges me. Lusaka and the other men are walking to retake their places behind the grandparents. I quickly see why—Woja Beki and the soldiers and Bongo and the two other young men are turning around from the path that leads from Woja Beki's house to the square. Mothers pick up babies and toddlers and stand up for a better view. Everyone stares at Woja Beki as he strides to the front of the square, exposing his spacious teeth, his eyes sparkling. The soldiers are on either side of him, Bongo and the young men a step behind.

We do not need to wait long for Woja Beki to begin speaking. He is beyond eager to tell us that his meeting with the soldiers has been a wonderful meeting—Hasn't it been? he says, looking at the soldiers, who both nod without interest, their demeanors unchanged.

"My dear people," Woja Beki says, "I put my head together with our fine soldiers here and our sons, and we agreed that we absolutely must find a good explanation for what is going on. We considered many different scenarios that could have happened, and then we said to ourselves, Maybe our dear friends from Pexton decided to make a detour to visit a relative on their way back home—which is possible, isn't it, my dear people?"

"It is," our parents and grandparents respond in unison.

"This is what I think, my dear people: I think that the wonderful men from Pexton went to visit someone who is a relative of one of them, and this relative, being a kind man, told his wife to prepare a bountiful feast for his dear relative and his friends, who have all accomplished something great by becoming workers for American people, and so the wife of the relative killed and stewed the fattest pigs and chickens and sliced and boiled the thickest yams, and the Pexton men and their driver ate well, so well that they decided that, because they were enjoying themselves beyond measure in the relative's village, they would spend a few more days there; it wasn't every day a man got a chance to reconnect with a relative and relax like that, and why shouldn't they take a break for a few days? Their jobs would wait for them, their wives could surely use a break from cooking for them, and their children would have some space to be mischievous, so this delay would be good for everyone. It's possible the men thought so. Is it not possible?"

"Anything is possible," our parents and grandparents reply.

"Our good soldiers think that the Pexton men are responsible men," Woja Beki continues. "Our dear soldiers think that our Pexton friends wouldn't eat and laugh and soak up life so much that they'd forget their responsibilities, but when we asked our good soldiers to come up with another theory as to where the men might be, they couldn't come up with any. The men have to be somewhere, but where? Their car did not have an accident on the way back to Bézam; otherwise, our good soldiers would have seen the battered car. The men didn't vanish, because it's not possible for grown men to just vanish, is it?"

"It's not."

"Weren't we all here when their driver turned their car on and started moving it back toward Bézam?"

"We were."

"Didn't we all watch with our very own two eyes as the car left Kosawa?"

"We did."

"So we have nothing more to tell our dear soldiers except the fact that the three Pexton men are somewhere out there, they didn't vanish into nothing, they're having themselves a good time, and someday soon, we're certain, they'll return to Bézam."

The Children

HOW WE LAUGHED ON OUR WAY TO SCHOOL THE NEXT morning. All the cracking up we'd done after the soldiers left still wasn't enough. We needed to dissect every detail—the way they'd looked at Woja Beki after he was done talking; the manner in which they had shrugged and walked back to their car. Did you see the looks on their faces? Aren't soldiers supposed to be intelligent? Many years from now, we said to one another, the children of Kosawa will compose a song about this first victory that ultimately led to our vanquishing our foes. They'll skip around in circles, just as we do today when we sing of how our ancestors carved up men from other villages who arrived here lusting over our land.

Our parents had talked about it late into the night, about Woja Beki's switch to our side. They said he was wise to agree to the deal the men of the village had offered him: help us deceive the soldiers and you'll get back your freedom. Of course he agreed. After days of sleeping on a bare floor and dreaming of his mattress and pillow, who wouldn't? And he executed his end of the deal masterfully. But our fathers knew they still couldn't trust him. They needed to keep him and his family confined to their house. Allowing them to move around the village freely would be a mistake; they would surely escape to Gardens and alert the supervisors. If that happened, it would be a matter of hours before Kosawa was covered in blood.

That morning, we walked to school as we did on all school days, in twos and threes, some of us through relatives' compounds, others in front of the twins' hut, and yet others past Old Bata sitting in front of her hut, husbandless and childless, the nightmare of all the girls except our friend Thula, who, on the rare occasion when she had gotten involved in an argument, had made it clear that she found nothing pitiful about having no children.

Those of us who walked in front of the twins' hut hurried along, as our parents had always warned us to do—to never, absolutely never, look toward the hut, lest our eyes wander inside it and we see things our mouths wouldn't be able to say. Our parents' orders notwithstanding, we'd all been tempted to take a peek—the things our parents forbade us from doing were precisely the things we most wanted to do—but none of us had thus far looked inside it, no matter how much our curiosity egged us on, because our parents had told us stories of boys and girls who once looked inside the hut and ended up with round black stones where their eyes had been. Sometimes we dared each other to go near the hut and see if our parents' tales had any truth to them, but, despite wanting to awe our friends with our bravery, none of us wanted to lose the eyes we so loved.

Though we'd never seen anything inside the hut, some of us had heard noises coming from it—the growl of animals interwoven with the rumble of thunder; babies singing a folk song; pots and pans banging over the sound of people laughing; a woman in labor begging the fetus never to come out; a man passing musical gas. When we told these things to our friends and cousins in other villages, they refused to believe us—their villages had mediums and medicine men but no version of the twins—but we believed each other, for we knew that the twins were capable of deeds many deem impossible.

Even before our parents warned us never to look the twins in the eye, we knew they were to be revered, these men who were born on each side of the rooster's crow, Jakani before, Sakani after. We couldn't tell them apart from a distance—they wore the same long gray beard and the same black-and-brown snail shells around their necks—but we could differentiate them if we looked closely enough: Jakani was right-handed, and Sakani was left-handed; Jakani was born with his left eye shut, Sakani with his right eye shut. They were older than our parents, but younger than our grandparents, most of whom were there the day the twins were born. One of our grandfathers told us that the twins' mother had been in labor for a week, moaning in pain so loudly for seven nights that no one in Kosawa had been able to sleep, not even the insects and birds and animals, all of whom began chirping and tweeting and bleating and barking and oinking collectively every night, their sounds growing wilder until the laboring woman's screams crescendoed to a peak, at which point the twins came out, looking like average babies except for one closed eye apiece and large heads with a patch of gray hair on their foreheads, patches that would eventually migrate to their chins.

Another of our grandfathers told us that, back when he was a little boy, he used to play hiding and seeking with the twins until Jakani began seeing playmates no one else could see and finding things no one had hidden, and Sakani started healing his playmates' cuts and scrapes with leaves he dashed into the forest to find, chanting healing prayers. A grandmother who died a good death from old age the same day as Wambi once told a couple of our mothers on her veranda, while a few of us lingered around to eavesdrop, that the twins had never shown any interest in women, not even when they were young men with fullness in their trousers. In the best days of their youth, while their age-mates flirted and courted and traveled to other villages to bring back girls who they hoped would give them at least half a dozen children, Jakani and Sakani stayed in their parents' hut to perfect their crafts, which, after they'd been mastered, brought in the money they used to build their own hut at the edge of the village, where they now lived together.

Far more than was appropriate, we wondered about what went on inside the twins' hut. Our mothers wondered too, as must our fathers, though they would never debase themselves to ponder it openly. More than once we heard our mothers saying that it was possible the twins slept on the same bed, Jakani on the right, Sakani on the left, arms around each other. We imagined they were speaking in a parable of sorts, because we knew with certainty that, although men could hug and hold hands with each other, there were certain things men did only with women, things like sharing beds, and lying on top of each other late at night to breathe heavily and cause the bed to squeak, the kind of things that our parents did when they thought we were sleeping, and which we couldn't wait to do one day, because we could tell from how frequently they did it, and from our fathers' grunts and our mothers' muffled moans, that it would be a delightful thing to do.

When we were younger, one of us had woken up at an evil hour with a bladder spilling urine and gone outside to empty it, only to see something she wished she had never seen. Ordinarily, she wouldn't have gone outside alone. We left our huts at night only when accompanied by a sibling, but this one of us had no other sibling besides a little brother, who would have been of no use as a companion, so she'd gone over to her parents' bed, to wake her mother up, but her parents were not in their bed. This one of us had hurried through the parlor and out the back door, believing she would find her parents outside—perhaps they'd gone out to urinate together—but when she stepped outside, she saw nothing of them. She only heard their moans coming from inside the kitchen. Our friend immediately lost the urge to urinate. She thought about hurrying back to bed, but the part of her made of curiosity had tugged her to look through a hole in the bamboo kitchen wall. In the dim light of a kerosene lamp, she saw it clearly—her parents naked, her mother lying on her back with her legs spread wide and feet high, her father's head deep between her mother's thighs. Our friend ran back to her bed and hid under her blanket, her heart loath to slow its pounding, her eyes unable to shut, until her parents returned early in the morning with the blanket on which they'd been lying on the kitchen floor. They took a new blanket from under their bed, climbed into bed, and covered themselves as innocently as if they hadn't just been doing unspeakable things to each other on the kitchen floor. The next morning, fatigued from struggling to unsee what she'd seen, the one of us had been unable to get up in time for school. When we asked her during recess why her feet appeared to be as weak as grass, she told us about her night, and a few of us told her that we'd seen similar things, and that, whatever she did, she could never tell her parents that she'd seen them, for it would make them ashamed of themselves, and making one's parents ashamed of themselves was never a good thing.

We believed Jakani and Sakani did no such things; what they felt for each other was more akin to what our parents felt for us than what our parents felt for each other, but we couldn't know this with total certainty, for the twins were palm nuts that could never be cracked open. They did and said nothing besides what they needed to do or say to bring us healing and peace. On the occasions when they took someone into their hut because a ritual couldn't take place anywhere else, they wiped away all memory, so that the person exited the hut with no awareness of what he or she had seen or done. That, we were convinced, was what happened to our fathers right after the village meeting.

Much as the men of Kosawa recognized the danger the twins' hut posed, there was no better place for them to go to prepare for a potential confrontation with soldiers. It is likely that, in those hours after the village meeting, some of our fathers cowered when the twins told them to enter the hut, while the rest of them urged the frightened ones to stand tall and be men. Or maybe Jakani chanted a solo that made everyone file in like ants marching at their leader's command. Ultimately, all of the men must have entered the hut, which was why Kosawa was quiet after we returned to our huts. Inside the twins' hut, we believed, Sakani gave the men a pre-battle potion to drink, to erase their anxiety and fortify their minds. We imagined that Jakani asked them to kneel in the center of the hut before calling upon the Spirit to possess them with a fearlessness so all-consuming they would overcome our enemies as utterly as the light overcomes darkness at dawn.

The men walked out of the hut in the morning with no memory of what had been done to them; we know this because our fathers' memories of the previous day were still intact, but none of them could recall what they'd done from late that night to the dawn of the next day. It was thus evident to all of Kosawa that, with the power bestowed upon him by the Spirit, Jakani had reached into the men's brains and turned off their memories. He must have restarted them only when the men were at a safe distance from his hut, after they'd left the confines of where the spirit and human worlds intersect. Our fathers, if they'd been aware of what the twins were doing to them, wouldn't have complained, knowing that everything the twins did was for the good of Kosawa. They would have been thankful that, in briefly shutting down their consciousness, Jakani had protected them from coming face-to-face with the Spirit, an experience no mortal could survive.

We had as good a time in class that morning as we'd had in months. When Teacher Penda lectured on the government, we tried not to laugh as he stressed that it was made of the country's most intelligent men. At the end of the lecture, one of us asked him to tell us more about His Excellency—what made His Excellency such a great president? Teacher Penda told us to list some traits a person needs in order to be a good leader. We called out several—friendly, kind, funny, respectful. Teacher Penda told us that His Excellency had all of these traits and more. His Excellency was the smartest man in the world, he said; not many countries were blessed to have a president like ours. We did not argue; we'd lived long enough to know he was simply saying what he was paid to say.

When he wasn't saying what he needed to say, Teacher Penda told us many truths. By the time we were eight, we knew more about where our oil was heading than our grandparents and their parents ever did. We knew because Teacher Penda taught us about America—how people there lived in big brick houses, and how they loved to mash their potatoes before eating them with objects called "ferks." He taught us how to speak English, though we could never speak it as well as the American overseer at Gardens. Sometimes we used English words when we played, saying things like "who cares," and "absolutely not," and "holy shit," to impress one another.

Once, one of us, feeling confident in his ability to speak English, had shouted out a greeting to an overseer who was visiting our village. Like the overseers before and after him, this American man lived in the brick house atop the hill facing the oil wells and the laborers' camp, a house as big as all our huts combined. The loneliness thrust upon him might have been why he visited our village that day, to feel any kind of human touch. The man's car had barely entered Kosawa when we gathered at the entrance to Woja Beki's compound, singing: **Motor car, motor car, I love you, motor car, take me to the capital, I want to be a capital.** When the driver opened the door for the American to exit, we angled for the best position to watch him. As he was walking toward Woja Beki—who was grinning like the idiot he was—our friend shouted, "Hello, man," which is how Teacher Penda had told us Americans greeted each other. Our mouths dropped. What was he doing? He had no right to speak to the overseer as if he were a friend. We saw the fear in Woja Beki's eyes too. How would the overseer react? The overseer turned to face us, smiling. His eyes embraced the eyes of the one of us who had called out the greeting, and he said, "Well, hello to you too, my little friends." We burst out laughing, poking each other in delight.

Did we just make friends with an American? For days afterward, we couldn't stop asking our friend to tell us how it felt to attract the attention of a man from America.

A few months later, on a day when our class was only half full because most of our friends needed to stay home due to a high fever or bad cough or an inexplicable rash and a multitude of symptoms, we talked about that afternoon during recess. We wondered if America was populated with cheerful people like that overseer, which made it hard for us to understand them: How could they be happy when we were dying for their sake? Why wouldn't they ask their friends at Pexton to stop killing us? Was it possible they knew nothing of our plight? Was Pexton lying to them, just as they were lying to us?

Some of our parents weren't even born when Pexton first arrived, back when the valley contained only Kosawa and footpaths lined with trees around which animals frolicked and birds sang. "Rest assured that we won't be here for long," the government men accompanying the oil explorers told our grandparents, when they came out of their huts with open mouths and hands on hips to see the strangers who'd appeared in their village. Even after a detailed explanation of the mission, our people still couldn't understand why the oil-seeking men couldn't plant palm trees and make palm oil if it was oil they wanted. When Woja Beki—who had just taken over leadership of the village after the death of his father, Woja Bewa—asked this question of the government representatives, the representatives told him that the oil beneath our valley was a special kind, it was the kind that allowed cars to move, a clarification that made our grandparents look at each other in mutual amazement—they had seen cars in Lokunja but they'd never wondered what got the cars to move. The representatives told them that drilling for oil would bring something called "civilization" to our village. One day, the government representatives said, Kosawa would have a wonderful thing called "prosperity." Could the men explain "civilization" and "prosperity" in our language? our grandparents had asked. The government men had said it was impossible for them to explain such terms fully, because it would be hard for our grandparents to understand what they'd never witnessed or considered a possibility. But as soon as "civilization" and "prosperity" arrived, they added, our grandparents would be in awe of what a beautiful life they offer; they would lose all comprehension of how they and their ancestors could have lived without the wonders heaped upon them by the rapidly changing world around them. They would pour libations over and over to thank their ancestors. They would sing songs of gratitude to the Spirit every morning for having put oil under their land.

Our grandparents had rejoiced upon hearing this.

They believed Pexton's lie, and for a long time our parents did too, convinced that if only they remained patient the thing called "prosperity" would arrive like a cherished guest for whom the fattest pig had been slaughtered, and all of Kosawa would live in brick houses like the one Woja Beki would eventually own.

Though our hatred of Pexton multiplied as we got older and our indignation deepened, we couldn't deny the fact that Pexton had offered our grandfathers jobs and a chance to partake in the wealth that would be created from the drilling. Pexton had told our grandfathers that if they came to work for them, for a certain number of hours a day, and did as they were told to do, they would earn a fixed amount of money a month. Our grandfathers, however, had no interest in losing ownership of their lives—every one of them had turned down Pexton's offer and returned to the thrill of killing for food as trees were felled all over the valley to make room for the oil field and pipelines and Gardens.

By the time our fathers came of age, around when Pexton began drilling its third well, it had become clear to everyone in Kosawa that the only way to partake in the oil wealth was to work for Pexton. But every time our fathers went to Gardens to apply for work, the supervisors told them that there were no jobs— all the jobs had been taken by men brought in from

villages around Bézam, men whose brothers and uncles and cousins and tribesmen worked in government
offices and had no doubt conducted secret meetings
and signed cryptic documents to ensure that whatever
prosperity the oil wells brought would be reserved for
their families and clans and tribes. Our fathers had
no one in Bézam to speak up and scheme for them to
get the coveted jobs, so they had continued hunting
and fishing before spills covered the big river, just like
their fathers before them. Meanwhile, men from far-
off places came to live in Gardens to do jobs that came
with the privilege of living in brick houses and getting
monthly envelopes of cash, money that allowed these
laborers to build fine houses in their ancestral villages
and send their children to schools in Bézam so the
children would one day get office jobs and drive cars
like American people, cars our parents' children could
only dream of touching.

We despised those laborers.

They'd been given what should have been ours, and
yet they shot us glares reserved for vermin whenever
we sat next to them in the bus that ran from Gardens
to Lokunja; a bus meant for them which Pexton allowed us to use out of solidarity, yes, but still, a bus
that took them from our land and brought them back
to our land.

We hated how, whenever a pipeline spilled in our
farms, it took them days to fix it, after which they
told our parents that all they needed to do to reclaim
their farmlands was to remove the topsoil and toss it

aside. When our parents tried to explain that doing so wouldn't work, since the poison went deep and the oil spread wide, and that perhaps the best solution would be for Pexton to get better pipelines, the laborers chuckled and asked if we expected Pexton to pack up and leave just because we didn't like them.

After these exchanges, the laborers returned to their houses to breathe the same air as we did, but not to drink the same water, or eat the same food—they had enough money to buy all of their food from the big market, and Pexton made sure that their water came in through pipes, not from a well, which was why their children weren't dying like us. When their children fell sick, there was a doctor from Bézam among them, someone Pexton paid to heal them so that their parents' minds would not be disturbed and their fathers could focus on doing the work that had to be done. When one of our fathers had asked at a village meeting if he could take his sick child to the doctor there, in case that medicine man had herbs Sakani didn't have, the Leader shook his head and said that it was best to keep the children separated—why confuse them about how the world works?

THE WEEKEND AFTER THE CAPTIVITY, while our fathers rested and our mothers did chore after chore, some of us loitered in front of Lusaka's hut, hoping to hear the Pexton men and their driver crying and begging for their freedom, likely having realized that we would never let any soldiers find them. Our mothers repeatedly yelled at us to leave the area, even as they frequented the hut, to take meals to Lusaka's wife so that she wouldn't have to shoulder all the burden of feeding the hostages. We knew our mothers went to Lusaka's hut not only to deliver the food—we usually ran such errands for them—but also to ask Lusaka's wife if she could let them into the makeshift cell so they could spit in the Pexton men's faces, tell them what despicable creatures they were, slap them, kick them, bang their heads against the ground for all the children Pexton had killed.

Lusaka's wife never allowed our mothers into the room to do it. She said no even to the mothers whose departed children still appeared in their dreams nightly, clothed in white, with tears in their eyes, speaking no words but showing every desperation to understand why they were dead, longing for their mothers but unable to touch them, the space between them never narrowing no matter how hard the mothers ran toward them for a hug and an up-close look to ensure they were well-fed in the world beyond.

"I don't think it right to mistreat the men on top of what they're enduring," Lusaka's wife told our mothers. Her duty, she said, was to keep them alive by feeding them. Still, she confessed, she couldn't stop herself from fantasizing about the best way to make them suffer a pain similar to the one she daily bore, the unbearable grief she would do anything to be free of for a moment. She'd thought about putting poison in the captives' food, she told our mothers, but she didn't want their deaths to be quick. She'd thought about letting them starve to death, but her husband and the village men would never allow it, and there really wasn't much she could slyly do to harm the captives, since her husband and the elders had frequent meetings in the parlor to devise their next steps.

It was at one such meeting that the elders decided to forbid all the members of Woja Beki's household from going past the village entrance or visiting another hut; keeping them at home was the only way to guarantee that they wouldn't run to Gardens or the district office to report the ongoings. We were in support of the measure when we heard about it—we'd always despised the two children in that house who were our age-mates; we had been excluding them from our games long before the dictate. It grated us how they loved to talk about sitting on "couches" in their "living rooms," and eating with "ferks."

As for the rest of the family, the village's abhorrence of them had so grown that even Woja Beki's third wife, Jofi—who used to bounce from hut to hut spreading news about whose husband had looked at whose wife in an unsuitable manner, and which young woman would likely never find a husband if she didn't change her snobbish attitude, and whose sick child would probably be spared, may the Spirit be thanked—even

she, who used to visit grieving mothers to swear by
her ancestors that her husband would not rest until he
found a way to avenge their children's deaths, speaking in that shrill voice of hers we so hated as she sat
in our mothers' kitchens with a plump body covered
with clothes from Bézam, even she had been banished
by the entire village, now that our hatred for her
family had been laid bare. The days when she used to
beam as she dragged her thick ankles around Kosawa,
pretending she didn't know our mothers rolled their
eyes after she left their company, those days ended the
night of the village meeting. Now she and her co-wives
hid from our wrath behind their brick walls unless it
was absolutely necessary to step out.

Day and night, our mothers monitored the movements of all three of Woja Beki's wives with a ferocity
we'd never seen before. Their viciousness surprised us,
considering they did not have the cold hearts of our
fathers and they would never have encouraged such a
behavior in us, turning our backs on our friends. But
we reminded ourselves that they had buried children,
and one of our aunts would bury a child four days
after the village meeting, the baby she'd held up to
show the Pexton men during the meeting. How many
children had Woja Beki's wives buried? None. How
many children in that house drank the well water in
its pure state? None. In addition to the clean water
Gono brought from Bézam, the family had a machine
that removed all impurities from the well water on
the occasions when they had to drink it. None of us

ever saw the purifying machine, and Woja Beki once brought some of our fathers to his house to prove to them that there was no such machine, the story was ridiculous, he was a victim too, but we believed it still, because we knew he and his family cared about protecting themselves only.

Perhaps our mothers were realizing, as we all were, that no one was coming to save us and we had to save ourselves by whatever means presented itself, including spying on and keeping under arrest people with whom we once shared meals and hugs. Visiting each other in kitchens and on verandas, our mothers spoke freely of the hatred they'd long concealed toward Woja Beki's wives, Jofi especially. "What makes me angry," one of our mothers said, "is how I wasted precious hours pretending to like her."

Having been warned by Lusaka that all our eyes were on them, and that if they were caught attempting to leave the village the punishment he would inflict on them would be unparalleled, the family curled into themselves, an island surrounded by crocodiles.

Sometimes, in the evenings, we loitered outside their house, hoping to hear the wives and children crying, but we heard nothing. Their windows and doors remained shut, each wife in her bedroom with her daughters, the sons all in one bedroom, every mother pondering how to save herself and her children when the chance arose. If some of us felt pity for them, we said nothing of it to our friends, for we all knew how essential the measure was to our ultimate victory.

Bongo

I SIT ON THE VERANDA NOW, FORCING MY THOUGHTS to stay far away from the burdens that will come with my new role. Thula is visiting a sick friend; she and a couple of her age-mates are probably doing their best to entertain him with ludicrous tales and theories, anything to distract him from the aches in his body. Knowing Thula, she's likely sitting in silence and nodding to one theory or another that her friends are defending, like the one I once overhead about the ocean, which none of them have ever seen, how it's bound to dry up someday because of American people like the ones at Pexton, because of all the toxic wastes they're dumping into rivers which will flow into the ocean and choke it dead.

Juba is next to me, on Yaya's lap. Sahel is in the kitchen, making dinner. We're not the family we used to be before Malabo vanished; we don't try to be. It's been over a year, and Yaya and Sahel cry still. But they're women—they must find a way to wipe their tears and keep on moving. We must all keep on moving. There are seven sick children in our midst now, three of them babies, all likely to recover, according to Sakani, may the Spirit be thanked. Perhaps our newfound hope is sustaining them, a sense that a winnable battle is being fought on their behalf. The air of Kosawa has grown lighter from the collective faith of its people: we know our time for doubt is gone.

I look at Yaya. Her cheeks seem to have sunk farther into her face now that she's lost most of her teeth. She appears calm, as if she hadn't started the day with a cry for her firstborn. When my father died, she began each day with a cry for one month; with my brother, it's conceivable she'll start her day with a cry for the rest of her life. May she never shed a tear for me. She's rocking Juba, who's four and too old to be rocked. Both Juba and Yaya show no signs of wanting their physical closeness to end. Malabo never liked it—he often asked Yaya to end it—but has such love ever been successfully curtailed? I know Yaya wants to rock a child of mine too, but she asks me no questions about when I'll get a wife. I know she wants me to forget Elali, choose another girl from the sibling villages, any of those jostling to be selected, but she doesn't say this to me. She says nothing, in the way mothers say everything while saying nothing.

. . .

A relative passes in front of our hut and wishes us a good evening. We wish him the same. I notice two of Lusaka's daughters walking toward us. The older one is tall, her body at the junction where slender meets fleshy. She's beautiful. I'm surprised by my sudden assessment of her. I hope it means I'm forgetting Elali. I should forget Elali. Another man goes between her thighs every night, and it's his name she moans, not mine. But it was my name she'd promised me she would say for the rest of her life—she promised me that a hundred times, from the first night in my bedroom till the day she sat next to a laborer on the bus from Gardens. She was never mine again after that day.

Lusaka's older daughter gets closer to us. I can't imagine her thighs are anywhere near as slender and firm as Elali's, but they're probably fine enough thighs she'll someday use well on a man. Something about the way she moves makes me want to start searching for a replacement for Elali, find a body I can lay claim to and grab and fondle as I wish, but I have no time for a courtship dance right now. There have been a few women since Elali got married—one of them allowed me to do to her something I'd never been bold enough to ask Elali to let me do—but the women did no more than keep me from ripping off my groin when hunger for a naked body turned my brain into sludge.

Lusaka's daughter sways onward, looking everywhere but my face. Her body is ripe for babies. Dead babies. I try not to think of dead babies. Do they realize it, the little girls of Kosawa, when they spend hours assembling babies of sticks and stalks with flowers for eyes, when they name and rock and sing to these things in an effort to preview their destiny as mothers—do they realize that their wish, if it were to come true, would be inevitable death? Shouldn't we remind them always that birth happens only so death may prevail? Was an awareness of this the reason why I never saw Thula partake in those games when she was younger, why she only looked on, brows twisted, while her friends doted on their creations, oblivious to death lurking close by?

I remember when a friend of Thula's brought her baby brother over. Thula sat with the friend and the baby and two other friends to the side of our hut. Not knowing I was watching, one of the girls lifted her dress and brought the baby to her empty chest, to experience the sensation of a baby breastfeeding on her. I could see the delight on the girl's face as the baby sucked whatever was there. The other girls giggled. On Thula's face was written: I'd rather die than be subjected to such an ordeal. That baby is still with us, having survived a long illness. But I really must think nothing of such things now. Better I think of the wife I'll someday have—heavy-breasted and smooth-skinned, never lacking for joy as she keeps the hut perfect, keeps me happy—how delicious her thighs will be. I know I'll have to aim for lesser thighs than Elali's, those limbs that held me tight and guided me as I explored the deepest hinterlands of the lush Republic of Elali.

"Good evening, Yaya. Good evening, Bongo," Lusaka's daughter says, suddenly standing in front of me. Her younger sister is beside her, a far lesser beauty in the making. I feel for the girl already—she'll soon find out that she is bound to someday be no more than a man's third or fourth choice.

Yaya nods at the sisters, smiling weakly. She continues rocking Juba.

"How's your father?" I ask them.

"Bongo, Papa wants you to come over immediately," the beauty says. Her teeth are small, as white as clouds that carry no threat.

"Bongo, did you hear what Wanja is saying?" Yaya says.

"Yes, yes," I say, realizing I'd been staring at her for too long. "Your father wants me to come?"

"Yes, please, he wants you to come right now. He says it's very important."

I nod and stand up but I find no need to hurry. I don't imagine that what Lusaka wants to talk about is of great consequence. We've secured the captives; they're going nowhere until we say so. We've deflected the soldiers. Woja Beki and his family are under surveillance. We have in place a plan for what we'll do at every stage till it's over.

I go to my bedroom and pull a shirt from the top of the pile of clothes on my bed—Sahel washed and ironed them today. My brother did well for us all by marrying a dutiful woman like Sahel, a woman who never complains but does as a good wife must do for her family. Maybe Lusaka's daughter will soon take over the washing and ironing of my clothes. I smile at myself, enjoying this new direction of my thoughts.

I walk behind Lusaka's daughter on our way to their hut. I marvel at her buttocks, gently sloped and dense, but my eyes must leave them more often than I'd like: I must acknowledge friends and relatives as I pass them sitting on their verandas. I tell everyone who calls me over that I can't stop to chat, nothing's the matter, all will be well.

I never wished to be a part of such an operation. I had hoped that the instigators of our misery would learn that it's possible to cater to their own happiness while leaving us the space for contentment, but in a world where many believe their happiness is tied to the unhappiness of others, what choice did we have?

When Konga showed up that night at the village meeting brandishing the Pexton men's key, I was at first aghast at his tactic and manners. I was thinking what my friends were thinking: Is this the right way to get what we want? Wouldn't it be best for us to wait for a better time to do this, perhaps a day in the future after we'd mapped out a step-by-step strategy rather than initiating a spontaneous rebellion based on a mysterious whim? I still can't say how I persuaded myself to obey the orders of someone who wields no power over the words coming out of his mouth, but the words were the ones we needed to hear that evening. I needed to hear them. My brother had said them to me, and I'd refused to listen to him. I'd let him travel to Bézam without my support on a journey where he could have benefited from my faith and counsel. I couldn't let him down again.

After my friends and I had dragged away and dumped the Pexton men and Woja Beki in a corner of Lusaka's parlor, Woja Beki cried out, upon hearing Konga tell us to bind their hands and feet and throw them in the back room, "Konga Wanjika, son of Bantu Wanjika, what did I ever do to you to deserve such treatment . . . ?"

I say similar words whenever I look at a mother collapsed in grief beside a dead child: Enemies of Kosawa, what did we ever do to you to deserve such treatment?

Many nights I lie in bed and imagine myself turning into a fan, blowing away the air over Kosawa, driving it past the hills behind Gardens, dumping it where strong winds will take it afar and bring back to us good air. I picture myself a wall that stretches from the sky to the inner core of the earth, allowing no pipelines to pass through, no poison to flow into our water. I want to give the children simple things.

Clean water. Clean air. Clean food. Let them soil it if they like it dirty—how dare anyone refuse them this right?

~~~~~~~~

I AM NEITHER KOSAWA'S BEST hunter nor farmer, and I won't be an elder for decades. Yet, after the soldiers left, the men of my village chose me to be their leader.

Lusaka stood in front of our gathering that evening and declared that we needed a new, fearless leader. An age-mate of my brother's named Tunis offered his services, but nobody was enthused about anointing him—passionate as he is, he enjoys a good laugh far too much, and he has newborn twin daughters at home, a life change certain to do nothing to make a man manlier. My cousin Sonni offered too; his father, my uncle Manga, agreed that his son, wise since birth, would make a great leader. But someone shouted that it wasn't right for a father to nominate his son. An argument was about to ensue over who had the right to nominate whom when Lusaka raised his hand to ask for silence. In the same spot where he'd asked us to take the Pexton men to his hut, he told everyone that he believed I should be the leader. He said no one present had done more for Kosawa in the past year. Several men nodded. No one stood up to counter him.

I wanted to stand and say the same about him, but he spoke without pause, giving me no space to slide my words between his. The reasons were many why he wanted me to lead, he said. I'd participated in digging a grave for every child who had died in the past two years. (About this he was wrong—after Elali told me she no longer loved me, I'd sat in my bedroom and stared at the wall a full day, disregarding Malabo's pleas that I eat, ignoring the wails coming from a hut where a nine-month-old boy had gone to sleep and never woken up. I hadn't gone to that baby's funeral or cared to know his name.)

Lusaka said I'd orchestrated the search for the vanished men in Bézam (I'd indeed assembled the search party and led the way around Bézam, but I'd done it not for Kosawa, but for my brother and my family). He added, incorrectly, that I'd been among the first to step forward when Konga called for volunteers to drag away the Pexton men (I was at the back of the pack of young men who went to the front). When, on that night of the village meeting, as per Konga's order, I arrived in front of the twins' hut and realized that some of the men of Kosawa weren't there, Lusaka continued—pointing at all of the cowards, their faces turned away—I'd gone to their huts and dragged them from beneath their wives' skirts, but not before telling their wives and children what the men were: cowering, wet chickens; phonies undeserving of the good in their lives (I'd said no such things. I'd only told the men that they had to come with me, though I now wish I'd insulted them inside their huts—no able man who sits at home while other men go to fight and die for his family is deserving of the honor of being called a man).

"Bongo was the one who negotiated with Woja Beki before the soldiers' visit," Lusaka said, which was true, though he was there too, along with two elders. But he was right—I was the one who told Woja Beki that Kosawa's future rested on his choosing a side and sticking with it: he could either choose his people or choose their enemies. He had chosen us, even if only for that afternoon. The soldiers had left, convinced that the Pexton men were not in our village. The battle was just beginning, but we were winning.

"Aren't we winning?" Lusaka asked the assembly of men.

"We are," they replied.

"Won't we keep winning?"

"We will."

"Yes, we will," he said. "And we can thank Bongo for that."

Every morning I ask the Spirit to grant me reasons to be grateful. I pray for protection upon my brother's children. Juba has nightmares from which he wakes up sweating, and Thula, ever since I returned from Bézam empty-handed, doesn't have much to say to me—I failed her father, I failed her. I long for the days when she was a little girl who would come into my bedroom at dawn, slip into my bed, and tuck her hands inside my shirt. Sometimes I'd tickle her just to hear her laugh. I loved watching her prominent, round eyes get wider. It was evident even then, by her heart-shaped lips, and her lengthy eyelashes, that she would grow up to be a beauty. She's now on the cusp of that, though with her thin frame it's unlikely hers will be the kind of body men in Kosawa will crave. The fact that she curls further into herself as she gets older, smiling at intervals but revealing nothing about her inner being, makes me worry she'll grow up to be too mysterious and her wondrous face will go to waste. Her father was inscrutable too; they did not share much of a physical resemblance, but her mind was a replica of his. Numerous were the evenings they spent chatting and laughing on the veranda. Now that he's gone, I worry she has closed herself off because she wants to share her thoughts with him and him only. She may not go around saying it, but she's angry with all those who colluded to rob her of her father. Alas, what can she do about her anger? There are moments when she's reading a schoolbook and she appears ordinary, but with every day added to the number of days Malabo has been gone, she speaks less and her anger reveals more of itself in the weakness of her smiles, which she's more likely to give while she's listening to her friends than when she's sitting in a hut in which her father no longer lives.

If she were any other girl, I would merely wish that

the Spirit mend her heart and free her of the agony she bears, but she's my brother's child. Without knowing the future—without knowing when I'll finish this work Malabo started and turn my energy toward finding a wife to bear me children—she might be the closest I'll have to a daughter for a while. That is why I want, desperately, as impossible as it seems, for her to grow up to be an unshackled woman, so that I may tell my brother, when we meet again, that though I'd failed at saving him from whoever felled him, I hadn't failed in keeping his children safe by doing everything I could so they could grow up in a clean Kosawa.

THERE ARE TWO OTHER MEN with Lusaka in his hut when I arrive—my uncle Manga, and Pondo, who is married to Woja Beki's only surviving sister. Lusaka has relied on the wisdom of the two elders since the captives came into his custody nine days ago, and I see no reason why I shouldn't do so as well, having known them all my life to choose right over wrong often. The men avoid my eyes as I pull a stool to join their circle.

"He's dying," Lusaka says the moment I'm seated.

"Who?" I ask.

"The Sick One," he tells me. "My wife just finished

cleaning his vomit. He's been vomiting all afternoon. You touch him, he's hotter than a pot of boiling water."

Manga and Pondo turn their eyes on me. Their look says: You're the leader—lead us out of this situation.

"We need to make a new plan," Manga says.

"I've tried everything, they won't talk," Lusaka says. "Last night I said to them: We don't need a long list of names anymore, just give us five or six names. The Leader looked at me as if I were a bowl of rotten food. The others barely opened their eyes."

"Maybe if we try beating them—" Pondo says.

"Beating them?" Manga says, sneering as if his age-mate has just uttered the unutterable. "One of them is dying and you want us to beat them—"

"If we don't get any information out of them, then what was the point of taking them prisoner? Wouldn't everything we've put ourselves through have been in vain?"

"Nothing's going to be in vain," I say.

"So we're going to keep them here till they die?" Pondo asks. "Is that the new plan? Sooner or later more soldiers will come looking for them. They'll ask more questions. Only the Spirit knows what they'll do to us when they find out."

"They'll never find out if we don't let them find out."

"You think Pexton is just going to accept that its men are missing?"

"Bongo, what should we do?" Lusaka says. He's whispering. We're all speaking in low voices, though we're keeping no secrets from the rest of the village.

My resolve weakens. I'd feared that one thing or another might not go as well as we'd planned, but I hadn't considered the possibility of any of the men dying on us.

Our plan, the plan the men of Kosawa have agreed on, is simple: keep the captives until they give us the names of men in Bézam who can help us. We want nothing else from them. Just names. After which we'll set them free. That was the plan we made after we stepped out of the twins' hut the morning following the village meeting. We'll never know why Konga didn't show up to join us that night as we assembled with our spears and machetes, ready to die for Kosawa, nor will we ever know what the twins did to us, but we have no doubt that whatever they did is what led us to the revelation that this battle would be fought not weapon against weapon, but weapon against wisdom.

Upon getting the names of our potential benefactors, a delegation will travel to Bézam with gifts of smoked bushmeat and dried spices and yams, bottles of palm oil, and eggs from our fattest hens. We'll offer these gifts to the men. We'll speak openly to them, since the captives have attested to us that they're men of power, yes, but also men of conviction and good hearts. Once we enter their offices, we'll go down on our knees and sing their praises before pleading with them to come with us to our village: Come see it for yourselves, the desolation of our children. We'll offer them Woja Beki's house while they're with us. We'll repaint the house; our women will clean it and fill it with roses and sunflowers—it will have a scent befitting our esteemed guests. The house may be far from Bézam, but it will look and smell like what we imagine the finest houses in Bézam look and smell like, a conjecture we'll come upon based on pictures of houses in America from the children's schoolbooks. Woja Beki will stay in the house with them—we'll spread his family across our huts, asking our women to swallow their bile. We'll tell the big men that our wives and mothers and sisters will cook for them only the things they desire to eat. We'll assure them that Woja Beki will treat them as the honored guests that they are, and that will be the truth—when we had presented this idea to Woja Beki as part of the condition of his release, told him that we would need to do with his house as we deemed necessary for the sake of accomplishing this mission, he had agreed; we'd suspected he would delight in the privilege of entertaining powerful men from Bézam.

We're not beggars, but we'll travel to Bézam and lie prostrate before these men, kiss their feet no matter how dusty their shoes, because we need their help if we're to grow old on our land. We'll make several trips to Bézam if need be; we'll continue traveling and pleading and gifting until we succeed in bringing at least one big man from the government and one powerful man from Pexton to Kosawa. When they

arrive, we'll make a feast to welcome them and present
them with parcels of land. After that we'll lay our sick
children at their feet, beg them to protect these helpless ones. We may be proud, but our pain has abased
us, and we will do this and more for the sake of our
descendants.

The responsibility for mining the crucial information
from the Pexton men fell upon Lusaka. We believed
that if the men could come to see him not as a foe
but as someone bent on ensuring their freedom, they
would be more willing to talk to him. If there was
indeed anybody the men could trust in Kosawa, it
had to be Lusaka—Lusaka was after all the one who,
once we brought the captives to his hut on the night
of the village meeting, had asked Konga if Konga
could kindly hand over the car key. Konga had tossed
the key to Lusaka as he walked out of the hut, not to
be seen again since then. Before joining us in front of
the twins' hut, Lusaka had led three men to the school
compound to search for the Pexton driver. They had
found the driver walking around in the darkness,
searching for the key. Lusaka had shown him the key
and told him to come along; the driver put up no
resistance as he was escorted to join the other captives.

"What will you do to us after we've given you the
names you want?" the Round One asked Lusaka when
he went to them with our request.

"We'll give you your car key and wish you a safe journey home," Lusaka replied.

The Leader scoffed.

"We will," Lusaka said.

"Liar," the Leader growled. "Where are the beds you said you'd have for us? Where are the graves of your dead sons? Do you even have dead sons?"

"I wish I had no dead sons."

"The moment we give you any names, you'll kill us," the Sick One said.

"We don't kill other humans," Lusaka replied. "That's what you do, not us."

"You won't get away with this, I promise you," the Leader said. "Your punishment will be severe."

"If you swear not to kill us, I'll tell you what you want to know," the Sick One mumbled.

"Shut up," his superior said.

"Don't be afraid of him," Lusaka said. "Tell me."

"The car," the driver said. "Please, don't let anything happen to it."

"We took your car to a safe place a couple of days ago, somewhere the children cannot touch it," Lusaka said. "I have the key, right here in my pocket. I swear by every one of my ancestors that when you give me the names we need I'll lead you to the car, hand you the key, and wish you a safe journey to Bézam."

The Leader burst out laughing. "So you think after you send us on our way all will be forgotten? 'Goodbye. Travel well. Wasn't it wonderful for us, keeping you prisoner in our village?'"

"All will be forgotten," Lusaka said, then turned and walked out of the room.

There was no point telling the men how all would be forgotten. No reason to inform them that, upon leaving Lusaka's hut after providing us with the information we need, and just before re-entering their car to return to the capital, they will spend an hour or so in Jakani and Sakani's hut. We will lead them to meet the twins blindfolded and they'll remain with the twins until their memory, from the time they arrived in Kosawa for the meeting to the time they enter their car to return home, is wiped away. So thoroughly washed off that when their families and friends ask them about their travels—what they'd said and done in Kosawa, why their trip had been longer than expected—they'll respond that they'd had car troubles which needed time to resolve; otherwise, it had been the usual trip—they'd said this, done that, nothing special, they were now just glad to be home.

Their families and friends might not know how to interpret the men's insouciance. They would confer with each other, asking how it could be possible that all four men were offering such scant details. Or maybe those who love them will ask each other no questions. Ultimately, no one will know what to think, and even if they contemplated it, nothing would be traceable to us—not one human will know what happened to them except the people of Kosawa. And if, for reasons now unbeknownst to us, Pexton and the government decided to send soldiers to ask us why the men had no recollection of the days when they were missing, we'd once again assemble in the square and express shock about how strange and inconceivable it was that the men had vanished after departing our village meeting; how unfathomable the times in which we were living.

But all that will come later, after we've made it to the next step of our plan.

For now, what matters is keeping the men alive and getting the names.

I tell Lusaka and Manga and Pondo I need to step out for air while I ponder what to do about the Sick One. I sit on a bench and consider what Malabo would do if he were here.

"Take me to the men," I say to Lusaka when I re-enter his hut.

At the back of the hut, outside the kitchen, Lusaka's wife and his sole surviving son sit in the twilight. The boy is drying his eyes as he listens to whatever his mother is saying in a soothing voice. Lusaka, ignoring them, unfastens the rope keeping shut the back room door. I enter the room with him and Manga and Pondo.

As my eyes grow accustomed to the darkness, I see

the Pexton men and their driver sitting in separate corners of the empty room.

I haven't seen them since the night of the village meeting. The Leader is sitting with his back against the wall, shirtless. His head is down; his hands and feet are bound in front of him. The plate of food beside him is uneaten. Across the room, I see their urine bucket. I'd been concerned about how they would be able to eat and urinate and scratch itchy spots with their hands bound, but Lusaka had assured me that they would do it just fine, that as prisoners they weren't entitled to maximum comfort. Every morning, Lusaka gets two male neighbors to help him walk the hostages, one after another, to the toilet. Once they're within the palm-frond walls, he unbinds them and gives them as many minutes as they need. The Round One and the Sick One make good use of their time in the toilet. The driver, however, never fails to complain that his feces is shy and won't come out unless he's left alone. To this, Lusaka responds that if the driver doesn't go during his turn he'll have to hold it, because Lusaka is going hunting, in which case the driver will have to clench his buttocks till evening. Every morning, upon hearing this, the man grunts and grinds his teeth and pushes until he can do so no more.

The Leader, for the entire time he has been in the back room, has refused to stand up and walk to the toilet. So resolute is he in displaying his superiority that he's been rejecting most of his food and surviving on the residues of whatever lofty lunch he ate before arriving in Kosawa. It becomes evident to me, as I look at him, that his bitterness and pitiful haughtiness must be the result of years of holding on to vast amounts of odious matter in every bit of his body.

"Good evening, Leader," I say to him. He does not respond.

Lusaka and the elders add their greetings to mine; they get no response either.

The Sick One moans. I move close to him and inspect him. He's lying on the ground. His shirt is soaked with sweat; he's shivering. The driver, with his bound hands, is struggling to wipe the sweat on the Sick One's forehead. The Round One is sitting away from the Sick One, still fully dressed in his suit. He looks into my eyes, expecting me to say something to him, but I say nothing. Everyone hates the Leader most, but ever since the first village meeting, something about the Round One utterly irks me.

I stoop next to the Sick One and ask him how he's feeling.

"Please, help me," he says. "I don't want to die here."

"What are you sick with? Does anything hurt?"

He turns his face away. Is he ashamed to say what is ailing him?

"What's your name?" I ask him.

"Kumbum."

"Honorable Mr. Kumbum, my name is Bongo. I want to—"

"I'm not an honorable anything," Kumbum replies. "I'm a sick man. . . . Please, I need to go home. . . .

My daughter is getting married in two weeks, there's a lot of preparation that still needs to get done, I need to go help my wife, please. . . ."

"What's your daughter's name?" I ask.

"Mimi," he says. "My first child." He sighs. "I've been waiting and hoping that the soldiers will come for us. But they won't. It's been nine days since you put us here. They're clearly searching for us in the wrong places; they're never going to think to start looking in people's back rooms. I need to go home. I'll tell you whatever—"

"You'll tell him nothing," the Leader says.

Lusaka joins me in stooping next to Kumbum. He feels the sick man's forehead and pulls his hand back. It is evident from Lusaka's eyes that Kumbum is warmer than he was earlier in the day. Lusaka moves to a sitting position and tucks his legs under himself. I switch from stooping to sitting like him. Manga and Pondo do the same, and we're all sitting on the ground now, facing Kumbum. We're looking at him panting and sweating, and, we hope, not dying in front of us. The Round One stares at us as if we're a spectacle. If only I could gouge out his eyes and bury them inside his fat body.

"Kumbum," Lusaka says, softly, "we'd love for you to go home and get ready for your daughter Mimi's wedding. We don't want you to die here."

"It's true," I add. "As soon as you give us the names of the big men in Bézam, anyone who you think we could persuade to—"

"Please, don't make me laugh," the driver says. I turn to him, surprised. I want to ask him who he thinks he is to interrupt our conversation and make us the object of his ridicule, but a man is dying in front of us, and his death might essentially be our death, so, rather than rebuke the driver, I ask, "Why would we make you laugh?"

"Because you're talking like people who were dropped from the sky and landed in this country only yesterday," he says. "No one in Bézam cares about villagers like you, okay? Absolutely no one in the government. No one at Pexton. No one whatsoever."

We know this may be the case, but we don't believe in such absolutes. What sense is there in having total certainty that something is one way and no other way? Who has lived through all the years the earth has existed and seen all possibilities? Though, from the way the driver is talking, one would think that many things in life are absolute and we simply do not possess the intellect to recognize that.

"Do you understand what might happen after these representatives give you the names and you go to Bézam and plead on behalf of your children?" the driver continues.

Yes, I understand what might happen, because my brother went to Bézam and never came back, I want to say to him. Yes, we might go to Bézam and never come back—does that mean we should never go?

"What might happen?" I ask him.

He shakes his head and breaks into a derisive laugh

reminiscent of the Leader's. He laughs long enough that he starts coughing. As if they'd rehearsed it, Kumbum starts coughing too. Their coughs—one dry, one with a trace of phlegm at the end—go on until Lusaka runs to his wife's kitchen and returns with two cups of water. The driver drinks all of his; Kumbum takes a sip when Lusaka brings the cup to his lips.

"What Tonka is trying to tell you," Kumbum says, panting at every word, "is that when you get to Bézam, no matter what you say there, people will just laugh at you."

"We're not stupid," Lusaka says. "We know Bézam is where evil has built its house and where it raises its children. But we also know that good men live there, it's impossible for it not to be so. We're simply asking you to direct us to a few of them."

"Do you not understand the words coming out of his mouth?" the driver shouts. "Are you deaf? Listen: there are no upright men in Bézam. No one there cares whether your children live or die. How else can we say it so you'll understand?"

"You're telling us that everyone in Bézam is a bad person?" Manga says.

"I'm telling you that you can go to Bézam and lie on your belly and crawl from one end of it to the other and cry all the tears you have in your eyes and nothing will change for you. The big men will take the gifts you bring, and they'll say thank you and they'll give the meat to their cooks to prepare.

While they're eating it, they won't even remember why you gifted them the food in the first place. Your children will continue dying until there are no more children left. These men right here in this room"—he gestures to the three Pexton men—"they're all you're going to get from Pexton."

I turn to Lusaka. He's looking at Kumbum, trying to decipher whether he agrees with what the driver has just said.

"How do you know all this?" Lusaka asks the driver. "Why are you so sure?"

The driver perks up as if he's been waiting for years to pontificate on this topic.

"You think you're the only ones suffering?" he says. "Villages and towns all over this country are suffering for one reason or another. You have no clean water. The village over there has soldiers raping its daughters. That other village has some other corporation cutting down its trees; the soil is eroding away. Or maybe precious stones were found under their land, and soldiers arrived with a government decree to secure the area and in the process killed people because . . . Do they need a reason? My wife—her ancestral village, it's not far from mine, in Bikonobang District—the government says they want the entire village for some project about protecting animals, everyone in the village needs to pack up their things and go find somewhere else to live. What do you think the people there can do about that? Nothing. Dozens of them travel to Bézam and cry and beg for help—you know what happens? They're told to go home and wait, help is on the way. So they go home and wait. And wait. Sometimes they return to Bézam, countless times. But nothing's going to change. Not for them. Not for you. You can go build a new country if you don't like this one; the people who own this country, they like it just the way it is."

I look at the driver but I can't figure out why he's saying the things he's saying. Is it spite? Is it anger? Is he inflamed that we dare dream of a new life when he has resigned himself to the belief that an idyllic future is not the birthright of the likes of him and us? He must be convinced he'll never be more than a driver, a small man who picks up scraps of food falling off the plates of big men. His father must have shown him how to pick up scraps; soon he'll teach his son how to do the same—smile, nod, take whatever they give you, thank them profusely, ask no questions, let them know they own the air you breathe.

"There is one thing you can do," Kumbum says.

"What can they do besides make more room for graves?" the driver asks.

"Help me sit up," Kumbum says, grabbing my arm. Given his condition, I wonder if it's time to unbind his hands, but I banish the thought—we have everything to lose if my attempt to show mercy leaves us outwitted.

When Kumbum winces in pain, Lusaka dashes out and returns with a pillow, which he puts against the wall for the sick man to lean on.

"I have a nephew," Kumbum says, looking at me. "He can help you."

"Is he with the government or with Pexton?" I ask.

"He's not with anyone. He's a newspaperman. He can write your story."

"How's that going to help us?" I ask. "Your driver just said that no one in Bézam cares about our story."

"The people who'll read the story are not in Bézam. They're in America."

"America?"

"Yes, America, the country of Pexton. My nephew works for a newspaper that is read by many people there. . . ." He pauses, as if, having used too much air, he needs to await a new delivery. "American people like to hear stories of what's happening in faraway places, so my nephew tells them stories about what's happening in our country."

"So your nephew is a Bézam man who works for American people?" Pondo asks.

Kumbum shakes his head. "No, he's an American man. . . . It's a long story. His father is an American man, his mother was my sister. . . . He moved here from America a few years ago. . . . His story's complicated. Please, just trust me, go see him."

"Why should we trust that he'll write the truth?" I say.

"Because that's the kind of person he is. When you meet him, you'll see for yourself. If there's a story that he thinks needs to be told, he'll tell it. He's not afraid.

He attends all sorts of meetings in Bézam to learn about people and write their stories. . . ."

"And if he writes about us and the American people read our story—"

"When the American people read about what a corporation from their country is doing to children in our country, they'll be angry. American people like to take action. Some of them might want to help you. I don't exactly know what they'll do, but—"

"But the Pexton people in America, they'll read this story too, won't they?" my uncle Manga asks. "What if they read it and tell their friends who also read it that our story is a lie and that your nephew is perpetuating falsehoods? The people in America have never seen our suffering with their very own eyes. No one from there has been to Kosawa, so Pexton can claim that they don't even know us."

Kumbum thinks for a few moments. "Yes," he says. "That could happen."

The Leader, who hasn't said anything for a while, chuckles. "You all amuse me. You really do—do you know that?" We pay him no attention.

"Leave for Bézam first thing tomorrow morning," Kumbum says. "Meeting with my nephew is the best chance you have. I'll write a letter to him, introducing you. I'll tell you how to find him. But first, please . . . you must let us go home. I'm begging you."

Lusaka gestures for me to step outside. Manga and Pondo follow us. The four of us confer for several minutes and agree on what we must do. I must leave for Bézam the next morning to find the newspaper-man. Lusaka and one other man will come with me; we'll decide who later. For now, we have to get Kumbum healthy. We must move him to somewhere more comfortable: Woja Beki's house. Pondo, as the husband of Woja Beki's sister, is best positioned to go to Woja Beki and ask him to take in Kumbum. Pondo will remind Woja Beki that if a Pexton man who's been declared missing were to die in Kosawa and his remains be found here, it wouldn't portend well for Woja Beki's relationship with the government and Pexton; he must do everything to keep the man alive.

The other two Pexton men and the driver will remain in Lusaka's back room. My uncle Manga suggests that my cousin Sonni be responsible for making sure that the captives are well taken care of in Lusaka's absence. I've never thought my cousin to possess much wisdom—he walks sluggishly and talks far too slowly—but this isn't the time to declare that. I nod and pray Sonni doesn't fail us. We carry on with the planning. A meeting of the men needs to be held im-mediately, so that everyone knows what's going on. But first the Pexton men have to be told that they'll soon be free. We must keep their hopes alive, lest the other three suddenly fall sick like chickens that have pecked on poisoned corn. We want them to walk with their own feet out of the back room. As soon as our delega-tion returns from Bézam, after having connected with Kumbum's nephew and received a guarantee from him that our story will be told to people in America, and that such a telling will indeed make a difference, the men will be captives no more.

We re-enter the back room and tell the men our decision. They're not happy about it, but they have no recourse.

In the hours that follow, everything we discussed outside the back room happens as we'd hoped. Woja Beki is shaken when he hears that Kumbum might die on us. He asks Pondo many questions about the sick man—are his symptoms contagious? is there a chance the stranger could get well and do something sinister to one of his wives or daughters? he needs to keep his family safe—and Pondo replies that he has no answers, he can give no assurances, we're all forging ahead with questions that cannot attach themselves to responses, at which point Woja Beki stops asking. He's learning, just as we're unlearning, that sometimes the best way forward is to do as commanded and offer no resistance.

Before I head to bed for a rest, I pack my raffia bag. Yaya does not cry when I kneel before her and ask for her blessings. She blesses me and wishes me a safe journey. She promises she'll take care of my brother's family in my absence. Sahel wraps up food for me and fills my water bottle. Juba gives me a long hug. Thula sits alone on the veranda and ignores my attempt to assure her that I'll return in a few days.

· · ·

We meet in the square before dawn—Lusaka, myself, and Tunis. The decision to make Tunis the third man was an easy one: Tunis's sense of direction is the best in Kosawa, and we'll need it to help us find the newspaperman's office, much as we had relied on it to help us navigate the city when we went to search for Malabo.

We are about to head for the bus stop in Gardens when we hear a rustling. I think it to be no more than the sound of an early-morning breeze bothering tree leaves, perhaps warning of a coming rain, but it is not stirring air. It is Konga. He's back in his spot, under the mango tree. Our thoughts solely on Bézam, we hadn't seen him sleeping under a brown sheet. I move a finger to my lips, and the other men nod, a signal that they too have seen him. Together, we lift our feet off the ground slowly and return them with delibera-tion—we do not want to awaken the madman and be forced to reckon with whatever is bound to come out of his mouth when he opens his eyes and sees us.

Too late.

"My guess is that you're heading somewhere im-portant," he says from behind us.

We stop. Should we turn around or keep walking? The voice is his, but which Konga is speaking? Our newfound sage, or longtime menace? Should we listen to what he has to say? Lusaka decides we should; he turns around to face Konga.

"Good morning, Konga," he says, moving toward the madman. Konga flips off his sheet from over his body and stands up.

"May I ask where you're all heading to?" he says. His politeness is uncalled for; from it I discern little about his current state.

"We're going to Bézam," I say.

"Bézam," he repeats. "And are you going to tell me why you're going to Bézam?"

I look at Lusaka. I decide it's better to let him do the rest of the talking, so I remain silent, looking toward Gardens; I hope we don't miss the bus. Lusaka says nothing for a while, clearly searching for the proper response to Konga's question.

"I'm waiting and waiting for a response and I've got nothing to do but more waiting so I'll wait until I have nothing else to do but wait," the madman says. He's speaking in a singsong manner, smiling. Patches of dried saliva are in the corners of his mouth. A large crust of snot is visible in his nostrils. I dare not avert my gaze from his face lest he think me afraid of him. I'm not afraid of him. If I'm to succeed as the leader of this operation, I cannot be afraid of anyone, sane or insane.

"We received some advice last night," Lusaka begins. "We were given the name of someone in Bézam who can help us, so we're going to meet him."

"And this person is . . ."

"This person is an important person. We were given very good advice."

"Would you like my advice on if the advice you got is indeed very good advice?"

Lusaka looks at me, and I nod, and he proceeds to tell Konga all what Kumbum had suggested we do. Konga does not blink as Lusaka speaks. He stares at Lusaka as if Lusaka has traveled a great distance to deliver stale news. I grow even more concerned we'll miss the bus—Lusaka is going into every detail of what Kumbum told us.

Konga continues staring at Lusaka after Lusaka is done talking. When he finally takes his eyes off Lusaka's face, they land on mine.

"You won't find what you're looking for in Bézam," he says to me.

"We might not," Lusaka agrees, "but that doesn't mean we shouldn't try."

"Why try when you know you're going to fail?"

"Isn't it better to try and fail than to do nothing?"

"What we need isn't one more failure, Lusaka Lamaliwa. The world is crumbling under the weight of failures. Look around you. What do you see besides failures? Do we need more of them?"

"No, but we need people bigger than us to join our fight."

Konga throws his head back and laughs. "Someone bigger, someone smaller, someone neither big nor small, which is better?" Lusaka looks at me—should we attempt a response to a madman's riddle? "You call yourself small," Konga goes on. "And you say it with no shame."

"There's no shame in admitting that we're in need of help from those with the power to free us," I say.

"Yes, yes, of course," Konga says, as if he's heard such rubbish too many times. "But let me tell you something, sweet child. Something you may never have heard before and might never hear again after today: we are the only ones who can free ourselves."

Right, I say to myself—the children die on, the gas flares rage on, the pipelines spill on, we're in danger of annihilation, and we're fully capable of freeing ourselves.

"That is all true, Konga Wanjika," Lusaka replies. "Our ancestors passed on to us great powers, and we can indeed do much for ourselves, but the thing is that we haven't been successful at it with Pexton. If we can tell our story to the people in America—"

"They came from America and destroyed us, and now you want to go to them and beg them to come save us?"

"It's not the same people," I say, though what I really want to say is that we have to leave now. "The people who own Pexton and the people who'll do whatever needs to be done to make Pexton stop hurting us are two different kinds of American people."

"But they're not different, beautiful young man," Konga says, walking closer to me and looking into my eyes—for the first time in my life, I feel as if he's seen me, not merely noticed me as one of dozens of young men in Kosawa. "You do understand that all people from overseas are the same, don't you? The Americans, the Europeans, every single overseas person who has ever set foot on our soil, you know they all want the same thing, don't you?"

How does he remember the Europeans when he has no memory?

"You're young," he says. "Someday, when you're old, you'll see that the ones who came to kill us and the ones who'll run to save us are the same. No matter their pretenses, they all arrive here believing they have the power to take from us or give to us whatever will satisfy their endless wants."

"Are you saying—?"

"I'm saying you should turn around and go back to your huts. Tomorrow we'll continue fighting for ourselves."

Tunis looks at me beseechingly. I can tell from his eyes that Konga has convinced him. He wants to return to his hut. He's ready to abandon our mission because a madman thinks we can defeat His Excellency and an American corporation all by ourselves. I'm tempted to tell him to hurry back to his wife and children and forget about ever joining our fight. I want to assure him that if his children were to die the stain of their blood would be on his palms forever. The words almost leave my tongue, but I hold them back and breathe it out—a man's anger is often no more than a safe haven for his cowardice.

I thank Konga for his advice and tell him that we did not pack our bags for this journey only to return to our beds, mission unaccomplished. Lusaka nods.

We've done everything we could possibly do and considered many options, I say. Going to Bézam today seems the best viable option we have left.

"There is a way that seems right to a man," the madman calls out as we turn our backs on him to continue our journey, "but in the end it leads to destruction."

We keep walking. Just as we settle on the path to Gardens, Tunis says what I'd seen in his eyes. "Perhaps we should heed Konga," he mutters, looking at the ground.

"Go home," Lusaka screams at him before I have a chance to respond. Lusaka is pointing toward Kosawa, his voice trembling with rage. "Go home, and after you've buried two sons you can come back and let me know whether it's better to listen to a madman or to listen to your heart. Turn around right now and never return."

Tunis does not turn around. We do the rest of our walk in silence.

⁓⁓⁓⁓⁓⁓⁓

WE TAKE THE FIRST BUS from Gardens just as the laborers are finishing their breakfast, and the second bus leaves Lokunja at noonday. From there, two more rides on crowded buses with little moving air. I take window seats every time and look at trees rushing past as I think about those childhood days, long gone, when Kosawa was far from untainted but abundant in carefreeness, when children had few worries, when I had Malabo.

He always had his age-mates, my brother, and I had mine—we kicked balls and climbed trees in separate corners of the village—but my favorite days were the days when our groups played together and I could watch him kick balls the farthest, climb trees the highest; even if it weren't so, it was so to me, because he was my older brother, so tall and strong, no one could ever be better than him. Whenever we went into the forest with the other boys to search for bush plums, he made sure I walked in front of him. Not just me, but also the little boys who had no big brothers—someone had to mind them, and if no one did, it was up to Malabo. Yaya said it was because he was a firstborn child, that firstborn children are innately responsible, though she could offer no explanation for all the firstborns in the village who continued playing with their friends while their siblings cried in a corner.

Malabo wanted everyone to feel safe. He was eager to protect me and desperate to make Yaya happy. Whenever our father, in his moments of fury, kicked away his dinner, Malabo would always be the one to pick it up so Yaya wouldn't have to.

You know that's how he is, Yaya always said with a shrug whenever I went to her to complain about my father's uncontrollable anger; you know he's not good at being happy. But why? I would ask. Because he was born that way, Bongo—that's why. But how come everyone else in the village smiles and he's the only person who never smiles? Because he's the way he is; why should he pretend he's like everyone else? Doesn't he get tired of being miserable year after year? I wanted to know. Was it a curse? All Yaya could tell me was that my father's sorrows began when he was still in his mother's womb—a relative with whom his father had a land dispute had turned into a python and strangled his father to death. Weeks later, his mother, still in mourning, had died while giving birth to him. With no mother or father alive, his older sister had taken him to her hut and raised him as one of her children. His sister breastfed him alongside her own baby and put him to sleep on her bed, she and her husband nestling both babies so neither child would wake up at night alone and afraid in their new, confounding world.

Everyone I'd met from my father's ancestral village swore to me that his sister and her husband had treated him as if he came out of his sister's womb, but my father, who had cut off his birth family from his life before Malabo and I were born, insisted that their fair treatment of him suggested nothing. He said they'd only been good to him because he was an orphan whom they had no choice but to be responsible for, someone they'd helped so their village wouldn't think poorly of them for having abandoned their own kin— why should he be appreciative of that? Malabo and I ought to be thankful for what we had, he often said, living the life we were born to live, unlike what he had in his early years, growing up without the comfort of belonging, walking around a village where people didn't bother to whisper when telling each other that there were few sadder ways for a child to begin life than the way his had, why wouldn't such a child be unsmiling?

I remember evenings on the veranda, sitting and waiting for bedtime, Malabo telling Yaya and me stories to make us laugh, because if we didn't laugh we would have nothing to do but contemplate our bleak home and our inability to refashion it. How could we think of much else with my father's melancholia in our midst? How else could we handle his worst days, when his never-ending sadness and bad temper converged and he couldn't eat, couldn't do anything but lie in bed for most of the day while other men went to work, and then, after rising, in shame, bark at us for daring to breathe? Once, in my adolescence, in my attempt to understand Malabo so I could be more like him, I asked him if he enjoyed the things he did for others, like going hunting with our father even though he was old enough to avoid the company of a man who sucked dry the joy of others, or visiting Old Bata, our neighbor whom no one cared to be around unless they had to—wouldn't it be easier for him if he only did the things he had to do? Malabo had laughed and said that if everyone only did what they ought to do, who would do the things no one thought they had to do? What did enjoyment have to do with duty?

Marriage and fatherhood only made my brother more of what he was.

I can't forget one night in particular when we were in the village square, having a good time with our friends, the moon brilliant and self-assured, the sky jam-packed with stars, everyone passing around dried ecstatic mushrooms rolled up in plantain leaves, smoking and laughing louder as we got higher, bliss almost as good as a woman's thighs—a visitor would have thought we'd never heard the name Pexton—it was then that Malabo suggested that we stop laughing so loudly, we might awaken the children sleeping in the huts nearby. Don't worry, the children have grown accustomed to sleeping with our laughter by now, one of our friends said, to which Malabo retorted: Wouldn't it be better if the children had a choice in the matter? This was back when Sahel was pregnant with Thula. When Thula arrived, Malabo took a break from smoking during our gatherings in the square so he could be of use to his wife when he returned home, which made us laugh even harder—what help could a man possibly offer a woman with a baby?

Despite my father's failings, Malabo gave him the greatest gift of his life on the day Thula was born, undoubtedly the happiest day of both of their lives. Something about seeing his bloodline extend by another generation, something about holding the child of his child in his arms, a girl, something about it all brought upon my father the deepest and longest, though fleeting, moments of respite he would have from his melancholia. Yaya says that is why Thula was constantly smiling as a baby and a little girl: the first thing she saw in life was a smile her grandfather had long been saving for her.

Our hut never knew joy the way it did in the months following Thula's birth—my father cradling her and not wanting to give her to Sahel or Yaya even when Thula cried; Malabo and I going out at night to laugh and joke with our friends in the square, my brother merrier than any of us even without smoking, laughing the loudest now that his life had been completed by marriage and fatherhood.

After we buried my father, when Thula was six, Malabo became our family head; that was when he became a new man. In a quest to be the father his father never was, the kind of father whose first thought in the morning, and last thought at night, was the happiness of his family, Malabo decided to use his authority to tell us what to do, how to be. He dictated what was best for me, for all of us. Telling me which girls never to bring to the hut again: why waste the girl's time, she wasn't what he envisioned me marrying. He wanted us to live his idea of a happy family, which meant that we had to do as he said, understand that his wisdom surpassed ours. He was determined, also, to give Thula the innocent delights our father's melancholia had deprived us of in our childhood. Yaya and Sahel rarely complained—it was their duty to obey him—but me? I was a man too; I wanted to be listened to. But Malabo didn't believe my opinions mattered—he was older than me, he'd become family head by virtue of being firstborn, so all major decisions were his alone to make. He wanted to go to Bézam, he was going: that was final. His downfall came in believing that, because he loved his family, everything he did for them was justified. Now he and our father are dead. That I'm now the head of our crumbling household is more than I can bear, but I must, otherwise of what import were their lives?

^^^^^^^

WE ARRIVE IN BÉZAM AFTER a day and a half. We get off at the congested chaos of a bus stop in the center of the city, the letter for the newspaperman in my bag. I read the directions Kumbum gave me on how to get to his nephew's office and Tunis guides us as we cross streets, make rights and lefts, cars honking ahead of and behind us, dust flying into our eyes, people speaking in unfamiliar languages, the sun at its highest and draining us of what little energy we have left. We snacked on the bus rides, but long periods of sitting have weakened our legs, so we walk slowly and apart, so as not to call attention to ourselves—we don't know who might be watching us. When we get to the end of the directions, after an hour of walking, there's no office, just an empty patch of land.

We sit on the ground in silence, sweating. Did

the Sick One just dupe us? How could we have been such fools to trust him? From their faces, I imagine Lusaka and Tunis are thinking likewise. How could we have trusted a Bézam man to help us? Before I can say anything, Lusaka stands up and rushes across the street to a drinking spot. He speaks to a man sitting and holding a beer under an umbrella, and he returns to us smiling; the office is not far from here, he says.

We cross an alley, go down a street, and find ourselves in front of a building as high as twelve huts stacked. It matches the description Kumbum wrote down. The first part of our mission complete, we scrape our brows with our index fingers and wipe the perspiration on our trousers. Tunis looks up at the building and asks why people in Bézam make their buildings so tall: Do they want to live in the sky? Are they afraid of something biting them on the ground? Lusaka and I say nothing in response.

I don't think we should go into the building just yet, I say. We've traveled for close to two days; we've taken no baths, and our mouths are unwashed. Tunis agrees—he says we smell like roasted human flesh. I laugh, but Lusaka doesn't join me. He has never been a man who participates in anything because others do, which is why he's always been my favorite of my brother's age-mates. In the evenings of our young-adult days, I struggled not to stare for too long at him when everyone else was loud-talking and laughing and Lusaka, always the contemplative one, observed it all with a smile so faint you could only see it in his eyes.

Once, I joked with Malabo that perhaps Lusaka was our father's real firstborn, not Malabo, and perhaps Thula was Lusaka's daughter. My brother had laughed and said that in a village as small as ours, founded by brothers who had married sisters, it was only by the mercy of the Spirit that we didn't all look and act alike.

Looking at Lusaka now, I can see that this mission, this entire struggle, is changing him, forcing him to reveal parts of himself even the most reticent cannot forever hide. I hope he'll soon be happy, but I've spent enough time around grieving parents to know that happiness is no goal of theirs; seeing flickers of light in the darkness that surrounds them will suffice. Perhaps one of Lusaka's dead sons liked to joke—that may be why he didn't laugh at the jokes Tunis made on the bus rides to steady our errant minds. Tunis's best jokes had involved figuring out which fruit a given Kosawa woman's buttocks best resembled. I'd guffawed when he labeled Sahel's buttocks a pineapple, and Tunis had laughed too, even though Sahel is his first cousin and like a sister to him.

"Let's go in," Lusaka says. "If the newspaperman doesn't want to help us because we smell bad, we'll ask Jakani to turn us into flowers next time."

We head for the door of the building.

There's a man standing in front of it. He looks

ready for a fight, nostrils flared, fists balled, angry about something. I'm not sure what the right thing to say to him is.

"Good afternoon," I say.

"What do you want?"

"How is your day going? My name is Bongo. My friends and I—"

"Don't waste my time."

"I . . . please, we came to see a newspaperman. His uncle sent us."

He assesses us from crowns to toes. "You look like village people." Clearly, it's polite to be rude in this city. "What business do you have with a newspaperman?"

"We need to deliver a letter to him."

"Who?"

"The newspaperman. Could you kindly take us to him? His name is Austin."

"Austin? You're here for Austin?" His smile is unexpected, crooked and broad, revealing black gums. "Why didn't you tell me that already? Are you from his mother's village? He was just telling me the other day about how he still hasn't gotten a chance to visit his mother's village." He opens the door and motions for us to come in. "Wait right there," he says, pointing to a corner of the empty room. "I'll go upstairs and get him."

We're not from Austin's mother's village, but I don't correct the man, grateful as I am to receive preferential treatment based on someone's mistaken assumption about me.

Two women around my age enter the room and walk past us without offering any greetings. They're wearing trousers like men; one of them has short-cropped hair. "So—it's true what I've heard," Tunis whispers. "There are no real women in Bézam, only men who look like women trying to look like men. Look at their buttocks—no shapes." Though our hearts are racing as we stand in a strange room awaiting a stranger, Tunis and I cannot resist a giggle. We quickly cut it off when we see the man from the door coming down the stairs with a woman who looks like a man trying to look like a woman. The man from the door nods in our direction, then goes outside to retake his position. We're left with this person, and I don't know what the person's relationship to Austin is.

"Good afternoon, brothers," the person says in English. "I was told you're looking for me?"

"I am . . . We were . . ." I begin.

I haven't spoken to a stranger in English in years, not since the time I returned to Kosawa after failing to qualify to be a schoolteacher. This was two years after my father died, after my brother told me that he'd heard at the big market that the government was looking for candidates to be trained to become teachers at village schools being built around the country. I was the kind of young man the government was looking for—I'd excelled in school and could speak English better than every other adult in Kosawa; I still enjoy how it feels on my tongue. My love for the language, though, wasn't enough to convince me to leave Kosawa to become a schoolteacher in a distant village. But then I'd told Elali about the program, and she had rejoiced at the thought of becoming the wife of a schoolteacher and living in a brick house.

I soon found myself excited about the possibility too.

I would get to move away from my brother who never liked Elali, because he thought she laughed like a woman without discretion, which he said was telling. He claimed he'd heard from a credible source that Elali was the kind of girl who would spread her legs for any man offering something of worth. According to his source, Elali had been with at least seven men before me. I did not speak to Malabo for days after he said all this to me. He had voiced his disapproval of every girl I'd brought home since our father died—he thought me too focused on superficial traits—and now I'd finally found a woman profound in every way and he'd rejected her too. Elali wept when I asked her if Malabo's tale was true. She asked me, between tears, if I believed the story. Of course I didn't. I loved her. It was for her sake that I applied to the training program, and rejoiced when I was accepted. Weeks later, I moved to a town on the other side of the country, only to fail my qualification exams at the end of the yearlong training, which meant I couldn't be a teacher, I was free to return to Kosawa and carry on as a hunter.

I returned home with nothing but humiliation, my

bamboo suitcase, and four books I'd found in front of the program office one evening. I made the books mine after no one came forward to claim ownership of them; they had probably been left behind by a member of some European delegation that had visited the program to assess it.

The books now sit on a wooden stool in my room, reminding me of how far I traveled, only to return home. They're replete with big words that don't resemble English, so I've read only one of them, a picture book about a place called Nubia that existed before many places on earth, a lost kingdom that had worship-worthy women called Nubian princesses. I used to read the book to Thula, before she decided to stop coming to my bed in the morning and curling up against me, but mostly I read it to Elali, my Nubian princess. She didn't leave me after I returned, but she never let go of her dream of living in a brick house. A Pexton laborer made her dream come true.

All the English words I know desert me. I cannot figure out the polite way to ask this person in front of me if he or she is a man or a woman. The person has long hair, matted into stringy bits and running down both sides of a pretty oval face bearing a straight nose; his or her skin is light and smooth, testifying to an easy childhood in a place where the sun is tender. I cannot make a determination based on the person's clothing, since in this city women wear trousers and men wear blouses. I decide she must be a woman—what I'm hearing isn't the voice of a man, though it isn't quite the voice of a woman either.

"Please, forgive me," I say in English, hoping my enunciation is clear. "I am just confused because we are looking for a man; his name is Austin."

The person chuckles and says, "I'm Austin."

"Oh, Mr. Austin, please, I am so sorry. Please, I was just confused. . . ." I'm about to drop to my knees to ask for forgiveness for my insult, but he grabs my shoulder before I reach the ground, smiling. "Common mistake here," he says. "Don't worry about it. And, please, call me Austin. Did you say you have a letter for me?"

"Yes, from your uncle," I say as I pull the letter out of my bag.

"My uncle?" He looks surprised. "How do you know my uncle?"

"He came to our village, to help us."

"Oh, right, of course, for his job. Is he still there?"

"He was . . ." I hope he doesn't notice the fright in my eyes as my tongue goes heavy in my mouth. How do I answer such a question? How many lies must I tell before this is over?

"When did he leave?" The letter is in his hands, but he's looking at me.

"I . . . I don't remember. . . ."

Why is he asking all these questions? Is he truly a newspaperman, or someone the Sick One hopes will figure something out and turn us over to the government?

"Was your village one of the first ones he and his team visited?" he asks. "I really don't know much about what he does, except that he goes on a tour of villages."

"Yes . . . one of the first," I say. "He stopped in our village, and then he left to go to another village." My heart pounds hard with every word I utter. I fear he will ask me more specific questions. He glances at Lusaka and Tunis as he speaks, but they don't understand much of what he's saying, and in their discomfort they're scarcely blinking, leaving me responsible for presenting a relaxed appearance for us all.

I convince myself that Austin is asking all these questions because American people love to initiate light, meaningless conversations when they meet someone for the first time, so the person will like them and give them what they want; I read it somewhere. Austin doesn't need to know about what we've done to his uncle because there's nothing for him to know. No Pexton men are being held captive in Kosawa, I say repeatedly to myself. I convince myself I've never been inside the back room of Lusaka's hut, and even if I were there, I didn't see anything besides a pile of firewood in a corner.

"I get the feeling he's ready to retire, considering his health issues," Austin says. "But he's got a family, and jobs like his don't come easy."

I don't know what he means by "come easy," but

out of respect I can't ignore anything he says either, so I nod with my head bowed. When I raise my head, I meet his eyes. State your mission, Bongo, I tell myself. Now.

"Our village is dealing with a bad situation, Austin. That is why we came to see you," I say. "Your uncle thinks that you can help us, so he wrote this letter. He wants us to tell you that, please, can you help us?"

I'm sweating as I say this. I urge myself to plant my feet firmly on the ground. Whatever you do, don't falter. Stay upright. My mind collapses still: What if there are soldiers in the building? What if they're hiding somewhere upstairs? I won't be surprised if they walk out any minute now and take me to wherever they took my brother.

"Would you like some water?" Austin asks. My discomfort is obvious. I shake my head, even though I'm thirsty. I can't be so reckless as to ask too much of him.

"Let's have a seat," he says. He starts walking toward a corner of the room where there's a round table and three metal chairs. He tells us to sit on the chairs, then hurries up the wooden stairs and brings a fourth chair. While he's gone, we say nothing to each other. My shirt is soaked. Sweat is running down Tunis's and Lusaka's faces. Tunis starts biting his fingernails. We're about to share our story with a newspaperman.

Austin unfolds the letter from his uncle after he returns; I'd already read it to make sure it contained no betrayal. He displays neither shock nor excitement as he reads. I look at my hands and tell myself to be still—trembling hands never won a battle. Lusaka looks at me and nods at me, to tell me that I'm doing well, I'm not failing.

Austin excuses himself after reading the letter. He runs up the wooden stairs again and returns with a book and a pen. He wants to know more, he says. He wants to know every detail, from the day Pexton first arrived in Kosawa to the day the last child died. I speak, and he writes. One question follows another. How many children have died? I try to remember; too many, I tell him. How many do I think? I ask Lusaka and Tunis. We do a quick count, but we cannot come up with the exact number. I tell him Lusaka lost two sons. He looks at Lusaka, who averts his eyes. Tell me about his sons, he says to me. I tell him how Wambi was the best arithmetic student in his class. I tell him about Lusaka's firstborn son, who, like other mischievous boys in the village, loved to give the family's dog palm wine and laugh as the dog got disoriented. I tell him Lusaka's sons were very close and were looking forward to entering young adulthood together and moving from the room they shared with their little brother to the back room of Lusaka's hut. I do not tell him that his uncle was dying in that same back room a couple of days ago. I only tell him about Woja Beki. I tell him about the size of Woja Beki's house, and the jobs Woja Beki's sons have in Bézam. I do not tell him that his uncle is in Woja Beki's house as we speak, and that I pray his uncle survives whatever is ailing him, for everyone's sake.

I tell him about Malabo. I tell him how Malabo left Kosawa with his best friend and four other men over a year ago and never came back. You must miss your brother terribly, he says. My brother was a great man, I say; he made me angry, he made me happy, the world will never see the likes of him again. Austin says he's sorry for my loss, for all of our losses. I nod, realizing how much it still hurts.

He tells me he has no brothers or sisters, but he has cousins whom he's close to. He ran into one of them earlier in the day, he says. She was running late to an appointment to try on her wedding dress, but she couldn't resist standing on a street corner to excitedly tell him the latest wedding news, most notably that the wife of a government minister would be in attendance. She said her father should be back in a few days to go to the village and pick up two cows for the feast. Did his uncle gush to us about the upcoming wedding? Austin asks me.

He doesn't realize what he's doing. He doesn't know he just told me something I hadn't considered—that the families of our captives have not yet reported them missing.

No one is looking for the men.

Their families think they're still traveling from one village to another.

We have a few days before they're declared missing

and Kosawa and every village they were supposed to visit on their trip comes under suspicion.

I could hug Austin right now—what a revelation for a moment like this. Based on this information, I deduce, we have enough time to return to Kosawa, lead the men into Jakani and Sakani's hut to erase their memories, and send them on their way. By the time the men return to Bézam, Austin will have written our story and sent it to America.

⋀⋀⋀⋀⋀⋀⋀/

THEY LIED TO US WHEN they said that the soldiers would come for us if they didn't return to Bézam after the village meeting. They lied to us because they could. What means did we have to know the truth? How could we have known that they weren't scheduled to return to their homes that evening? That their next stop was another village where they would tell the people that change was coming, something the people would wait for—for how long? Until the day a lunatic tells them to walk out of their wide-open prison gates?

Who sent the two soldiers? Perhaps a government person in Lokunja when the men didn't show up for a planned meeting? Perhaps the overseer at Gardens, because the men were supposed to spend the night in his house but never showed up? But if that were the case, wouldn't the overseer have alerted the Pexton office in Bézam? Why didn't he? Perhaps the overseer told someone in the district office but that person didn't take his concern seriously, thinking the men had decided to abscond from their duties and enjoy some village fun. Is it possible the soldiers believed the story we concocted with Woja Beki? Or could it be that the people in the Bézam office suspect the men are missing but don't yet want to tell their families, lest the incident turn into an ugly drama? Nothing is inconceivable in this country. I'm not skilled enough to untangle the whos and whys, but one thing is certain: everyone hopes the men are doing their job somewhere, no one thinks they're in Kosawa, and if the men were to be declared missing, who would think that the people of Kosawa have the audacity to take representatives of Pexton prisoner?

I tell Austin everything except any of this.

Halfway through the questioning, I pull out the lukewarm bottle of water in my bag and take a sip. I need my voice to be steady as I describe the children's symptoms and the recent oil spills that seeped into the farms of three families. I tell Austin what the big river looks like now, green and flowing sluggishly under layers of toxic waste. I tell him how meager the next harvest is likely to be and how, because of the bad harvests, we use most of what little money we have after paying taxes to buy food in Lokunja.

When I'm done talking and Austin is done writing, he informs me that he'll write the story tonight and send it to America first thing in the morning.

His friends in the newspaper office there will do some research to make sure that, in the absence of evidence, our story can be substantiated by known facts. They might also try to talk to the Pexton people in America, to hear their side of the story, but, knowing what their response will likely be, the people in the newspaper office might decide to print only Kosawa's side of the story and tell Pexton's side separately if they so choose. Ultimately, Austin says, the decision on whether or not the story will be printed will be made by the big men at his newspaper. All he can do is write the best story he can and hope that everything flows smoothly and the story he writes is deemed worthy to be printed. If that happens, the American people might be able to read about us in a matter of days.

I look at him. I cannot speak. I have only thoughts. I'm thinking that the impossible just happened: Our story might be read across the ocean. We will be unknown no more. We will have names. Kosawa will be identified. Our departed children will be heard of—how long before salvation arrives for the children who are still holding on?

I repeat to Tunis and Lusaka everything Austin has said. They cannot believe we just found a champion in someone who wants nothing from us. No baskets of gifts. No kneeling. No pleading. No promises of land.

"When are you going back to your village?" Austin asks me.

I tell him we came to Bézam only to see him; now that we've seen him, we'll be leaving right away. We'll get on the first of four buses in the next couple of hours.

"Can you stay till tomorrow evening?" he asks.

He wants to write the story soonest, send it to his people, and make himself available in the event they want to publish it immediately and need him to do more work on it. Then he'd like to come with us to see Kosawa. He'll bring his camera and take as many pictures as he can, because with pictures he'll be able to write a second, more in-depth story. He wishes he had a place for us to sleep tonight, but he lives with a friend in a small space. I tell him not to worry. We'll sleep at the bus stop and be here to meet him tomorrow. We'll sleep on a pile of garbage if we must, for a chance to reclaim our land.

The Children

WE DIDN'T KNOW HE WAS DYING. NEVER WOULD WE have called him the Sick One if we'd been aware of how infirm he was—half dead, in fact. We'd been sick, we'd seen our brothers and sisters and friends get sick; nothing about it was worth mocking. We only gave him that name because we could think of no better name for a man whose body offered us passing chances at superiority, and we needed it, as a salve for our heartache.

We were playing in our compounds when we heard that a meeting of the men needed to take place immediately. Our mothers looked at our fathers, seeking an explanation for the urgency, but they got nothing. After our fathers had left for the square, we tried to ask our mothers what they thought might be going on, but they scolded us to hurry along and start our evening chores. We were sleeping by the time our fathers returned home. The next morning, on our way to school, was when we learned from our older siblings, who were discussing it with each other, that the Sick One was sick and Lusaka and Bongo and Tunis had gone to Bézam to look for medicine for him.

We had no jokes to make about the Sick One that day—we wished on him every bit of health within the grasp of men. We would even give him some of our health, we agreed, if he promised to return it. All day in class, we daydreamed that Sakani had made a potion for the Sick One, and that it was flowing in his veins, crushing his disease. When we returned home, though, we overheard the women saying that Sakani had refused to go to Woja Beki's house to treat the Sick One.

Why would Sakani refuse to treat a sick man? He was our healer and deliverer from all physical manifestations of malicious spirits; he may have failed in saving our departed friends and brothers and sisters, but with those of us still living he had succeeded. He had lowered our fevers and made ointment for our rashes, given us cough remedies squeezed from leaves, cleaned out poison that had accumulated and was causing pain in our ears. He healed children from villages where the medicine men were mere mortals claiming to be something more—men born in single births, on ordinary days, after routine labors, nothing about them notable. Sakani could heal any sick person except those who the Spirit told him had run out of their allotted time, and even for these dying ones, he offered relief from what might have been an excruciating exit—he gave them a potion that allowed them to go softly and tenderly, unaware they were bidding farewell to this world.

From what we overheard, our men had stood outside Sakani's hut and called for him to come help the captive. He'd appeared at the door and, in as few words as he was willing to waste, told them that he wouldn't do it. We couldn't understand his decision, much as we pondered. Was it because his duty was to heal us, not our enemies? Was that the direction the Spirit gave him when he received his powers at birth? Like his brother, he never explained himself—his ways were not our ways, nor his thoughts our thoughts.

Visiting each other before dinner that evening, we discussed a new detail we'd learned: when young men had arrived at Woja Beki's house with the Sick One on the back of one of them, Woja Beki had a bowl of soup ready for the invalid. We heard Woja Beki had assisted the young men in placing the Sick One on his sofa. He'd taken off the Sick One's socks so his toes might breathe, and unbuttoned his shirt so that air could flow into his chest. One of us mentioned that she'd heard from her sister, whose best friend was a cousin of one of Woja Beki's daughters, that Woja Beki had spent all night at the Sick One's side, rejecting his wives' pleas that he take a rest while they kept watch.

We felt for Woja Beki the more we learned about how well he took care of the Sick One: holding a bucket under his mouth for every vomit, wiping him down with a cold cloth when his temperature rose. We knew he was diligent not because he had any experience caring for a sick man—none of our fathers knew how to care for their sick selves, never mind the sick selves of others—but because he understood what would happen to Kosawa if the Sick One were to die our hostage. We heard the women whispering about it, that Woja Beki could have escaped Kosawa if he wanted to, that if he'd sat down with his family to plot their freedom, they could have found a way to get one of his sons to run to Gardens—surely, there had to be a moment in the deepest hour of night when all the eyes set to monitor them were shut. Once he got to Gardens, the son would have been able to send a message to officials in Lokunja or to Bézam. The government would have sent soldiers to rescue the Pexton men and return Woja Beki to his rightful place.

Our fathers joked about how they'd shrunk him from a leopard to a rabbit, but we knew that couldn't be the sole reason why he'd become so abased. We hadn't seen him since the day he misled the soldiers, but we imagined he was flashing his teeth less, contemplating his love of Kosawa more, a love that years ago evaporated somewhere in his brick house, or was subsumed by the basket of cash we hear sits under his bed, only to return the first night he spent on the floor of Lusaka's back room. This renewed love for Kosawa was at his core now; it was evident in actions driven by a cognizance that his title would be worth nothing if he were reinstated as the head of a village of slaughtered men and grieving widows and dying children. We'd never considered Woja Beki a wise man, but his behavior after his release from Lusaka's hut was the opposite of foolish.

When we asked our older siblings if they agreed with us, they said that, yes, Woja Beki had opened his door to the Sick One because he wanted to be one of us again. They said that days spent isolated in his house, sitting by himself on his sofa—the clock above his head ticking, no one coming to visit, no one for him to visit—had forced him to consider his ways and admit that no amount of wealth was worth the indignity of being an outcast in his own village. A couple of our uncles, though, when we asked them what they thought of this theory, had laughed and said we shouldn't be fooled: Woja Beki had no capacity for such wisdom, he was still a snake. Who knew what he would do or say if the government were ever to find out about what the village had done to the Pexton men?

The government would never find out from any of us, that much was certain—we had sworn an unbreakable oath. The night after our fathers allowed Woja Beki to return home, they assembled our families in our parlors and brought out the umbilical cord bundle. Taking turns, we held it, this clump of our umbilical cords and those of our siblings and our fathers and their siblings and our paternal grandfathers and their siblings and relatives, all the way back to the time when our ancestors first established our bloodline in a valley wherein a big and a small river flowed. The umbilical cords, shriveled and reeking, had turned black and brown through the years and generations, but with every addition to the bundle it appeared even more alive, binding us more tightly to our past and our future. We knew what it signified—the essence of our existence. To hold it and make a declaration was to be aware that our words would walk with us for the rest of our days. Which was why our fathers only brought it out when there was an oath to be made whose keeping would determine the course of our families' future.

On that night, we all took turns holding the bundle and swearing by all it represents. We swore we would never tell anyone about what our fathers had done. We promised we would say nothing to any relative or friend visiting the village. If we were to leave the village to go to the big market, or to visit one distant relative or another in any of the five sister-villages or two brother-villages, we would have nothing to offer them except a smile and conversations about anything but Pexton. If asked about the latest news from Kosawa, we would respond that all was well, except for the usual sorrows, a new illness here, another death there, but of course life intersperses suffering with joys, so there was also this upcoming wedding, and that birth celebration scheduled for next month. We would never tell anyone anything about the captivity until someday in the far future, when the story had spread because it could no longer be contained, the same way a pregnancy was bound to be revealed no matter how well garments had hidden it in the early months; by then, all would be well with us, and the story's revelation would be of little consequence. And if we had to be the ones to tell it, the story we would tell—only if we absolutely had to—would be a story of how our fathers did what the Spirit had commanded them to do.

With the bundles in our hands, we asked the Spirit to curse us in the worst possible ways if we were to break the oath and, in so doing, bring calamity upon our families and our village. If we were girls, our wombs would close up and we would be childless, worthless women for the rest of our days. If we were boys, our strength and manhood would desert us; we'd be the most woeful things that had ever walked this earth.

We passed the umbilical-cord bundles to the next person in our families after we'd said our oath, and we closed our eyes and listened as the next person took the oath.

Everyone in our hut took the oath, even our yayas and big papas, who feared little because the grave was too close for them to care; even our toddler siblings, who hadn't lived long enough to bear witness to lives ruined by curses—lives like that of a Kosawa man named Gombe who became paralyzed three days after his mother cursed him for stealing from her and slapping her when she confronted him. Our little ones made their proclamations slowly, repeating after our fathers. They needed to make the promise even at their age because someday they would learn about the potency of words spoken with conviction, their power to bless and exalt, their authority to uproot and destroy.

But it wasn't only the curses we strove to avoid; it was also the blessings we yearned for. We knew what a blessed life looked like, and though our parents were not living it with Pexton's claws deep in their throats, we knew it was possible when times were good, and that it involved a loving family foremost, good health, an abundance of food, laughter, and sunshine. We made our oaths trusting that keeping them would cause blessings to overflow in our lives. We went to bed that night believing the promise of the Spirit that we would soon be free, and we would flourish, and soar on wings like eagles.

We do not know if Woja Beki passed around his family's umbilical-cord bundle to his wife and children. It is possible he did, because when one of our aunts noticed Woja Beki's third wife, Jofi, a couple of days after Woja Beki was released, whispering and gesticulating near the path into the forest with her visiting sisters, our aunt told one of our grandfathers and our grandfather relayed it to Lusaka, who went to Woja Beki and demanded to know what his third wife was saying to her sisters. Woja Beki had called for Jofi, who swore to the men, upon the grave of her father, that she and her sisters had only been discussing the upcoming death celebration for their grandmother. Woja Beki assured Lusaka that his wife was telling the truth, and that he and his family would never tell the village's secret, not on that day or on a day in the future when people started breaking promises with no concern for consequences. He was still one of us, he said to Lusaka.

The Sick One remained in Woja Beki's house, and every night we prayed for him, and for Lusaka and his group to hurry back from Bézam with the medicine that would put us all at ease. One of us had a dream in which the Sick One was a fat man, smiling as he informed us that he was back at Pexton and preparing for the next village meeting. Hearing about such a dream did not make the rest of us happy—we did not want the Sick One healthy, so he could be free just yet; we wanted him returned to Lusaka's back room, so our fathers could proceed with whatever plans they had. We were desperate for relief from our fear of death, which had been exacerbated when one of our younger sisters died the day Lusaka and his team left for the capital. This younger sister's death had been sudden— neither her rash nor her cough was severe—and from this we inferred that death had grown more ruthless lately. The Sick One needed to live for it to be tamed.

We promised ourselves that we would find a new name for the Sick One, as an act of atonement, after Kosawa regained its freedom. It would be a great name, a name we might even be proud to share with him if we were to happen upon him at a place and time when he no longer had any power over us.

We never did get the opportunity to come up with this new name, for he died on Woja Beki's bed while we were at school. He died in our collective arms.

^^^^^^

OUR FATHERS' TIME IN OUR huts that evening was brief—after returning from the forest, they hurriedly ate and bathed and left for Woja Beki's house, to spend the night with him in his parlor; they couldn't leave him alone with the remains of a stranger. Even if Woja Beki was no longer fully one of us, he still was our blood, and our fathers could never punish him and his family by leaving them to sit by themselves beside a withering corpse.

Our mothers gave our fathers fruit bowls so they would have something cool to eat during the long, hot night ahead of them. As they bade us good night and stepped outside with stools and their bags of nourishment to walk over to Woja Beki's house, our fathers appeared older and sadder than we could recall. We'd never seen them look so lost, so confused. Only when we became older, only when we got close to the ages they were during that period, did we realize that what they bore on their faces that night wasn't grief at the Sick One's death but the deepest sort of dread, not for themselves, not for what would befall them now that a man had died by their doing, but for us, their children, for the ways in which we would suffer for what they'd tried to do for us. Only when we became parents did we realize how we could harm our children in an attempt to clean out for them the smothering decay of this world.

We imagined that our fathers sat in silence around the body all night.

Not knowing the custom of the dead man's ancestral village, not knowing the best way to handle his remains, meant nothing could be said to it all night—our fathers wouldn't dare wrong the corpse of a stranger. If the Sick One were from Kosawa, there would have been singing around him all night, every able-bodied adult present. Jakani and Sakani would have cut off all his hair, and his nails too, which they would burn, the ashes of which they would take to do something we would never know. For this stranger, none of this could be done—his spirit could obey the laws of his land and no other laws. So, in silence, sitting on their stools, our fathers must have waited for the hours to pass, allowing the dead man's spirit to leave his body fully and go where it needed to. When a touch confirmed that his body had lost all its warmth, evidence that his spirit was gone, Woja Beki and the men must have started the conversation on what to do with the body.

We stayed up late that night with the rest of our households. Together with our siblings, we asked our mothers and grandmothers question after question. We wanted them to assure us that our village had done nothing wrong, that our fathers hadn't done to Pexton what Pexton hadn't already done to us, that the Sick One could have died in his own bed, that Woja Beki had done everything he could to heal the Sick One. Perhaps the Sick One's disease was incurable. Besides, was the death of one Pexton man more tragic than the deaths of all our friends and siblings combined? We wanted our mothers to convince us that all was well, that such things happened, and that the Sick One's family would one day stop mourning for him when they realized that they'd never get answers to why he vanished. They'd have to stop crying just as we'd stopped crying for our fathers and uncles who vanished, and even if they cried forever, would their tears ever flow hotter than ours? We wanted our mothers to reassure us, again and again, and they did so, but we couldn't be sufficiently put at ease, for we could see the doubt in their eyes.

. . .

Our sleep that night was only slightly less disturbed than it was the night this all began.

The next morning, while we were struggling to cast aside our fears and do our morning chores, we learned that Lusaka and Bongo and Tunis had just returned from Bézam with a young man with light skin and stringy hair. We could barely eat our breakfasts, fatigued as we were and concerned about what the arrival of this young man meant.

By the time we left for school, our fathers had gone to meet and welcome the visitor from Bézam and hear from Lusaka and his group what had happened on their trip, and, later, to make a coffin for the Sick One.

Walking to school, we discussed what some of us had heard our parents whispering: that the Sick One was the young man's uncle. The news befuddled us. Had the young man come here to save his uncle, or did he learn we had his uncle only when he got here? During recess, few of us went home to eat. We sat on the grassy field and told ourselves that the young man's being the Sick One's nephew did not mean he would kill us in revenge.

After school, we followed the procession to the burial ground to bury the Sick One. There was no singing, only an omen in the form of a coffin. The entire village gathered around the grave, dug in a corner of Woja Beki's section. It was then, as we surveyed the faces, that we saw the stranger with stringy hair for the first time. He was the only one who wept as the Sick One's body was lowered into the ground.

Kindly as he looked, we couldn't understand why this young man, who lived in Bézam and therefore worked for Pexton or the government, hadn't run to Gardens to tell the overseer—a friend of his, most likely, since they were both American people—that we'd killed his uncle. Why was he allowing the men to bury his uncle in Kosawa? Why wasn't he taking his uncle's body back to Bézam? He seemed unhappy to be in our village, his eyes bloodshot and often downcast and avoiding ours, but at no point did he look at us angrily, or in disgust. He was merely alone in our midst.

As one of our grandfathers offered last words over the lowered coffin, telling the Sick One to travel safely to his ancestors and find it in his heart to forgive us for failing to restore his health, we looked at our mothers, our eyes full of tears, our bodies split into equal portions of fright and grief and shame. We could tell from our mothers' faces, and their trembling hands, and how tightly they held our youngest siblings to their bosoms, that they too were in fragments. Had we asked them to explain what was happening, they wouldn't have been able to answer. All they knew was what our fathers had told them, that the Sick One's nephew was on our side, he'd come to see our

so he could tell the world about it and by so
ng us the changes his uncle couldn't. It made
no sense to us why the Sick One's relative was on our
side, but, then again, simplicity fled Kosawa the night
we obeyed a madman and took three representatives
captive.

The young man, whose name we gathered was Us-
things, smiled at us as we were departing the burial
ground. We wished we could hug him and tell him
that all would be well, but Bongo took his attention
away from us, because he wanted to whisper something into Us-things's ear. We hoped Us-things would
stay with Bongo in the back room of the Nangi family's hut, and we hoped that our friend Thula would
eavesdrop, put aside her taciturnness for a bit, and tell
us all there was to know about the American.

We would have no such chance.

Of all the ways we'd imagined on those nights
when we'd lain in bed stiff with trepidation, why did
we never consider that we'd be away when the soldiers
arrived and we'd return to find them waiting for us
in the square, nine guns loaded and pointed at us?
Where was the Spirit on that afternoon? Where were
the blessings we'd been promised?

How fast those bullets came.

How we stumbled, how we staggered, how we
cried, fleeing into the forest.

How heavy the blood flowed—the blood of our
families, the blood of our friends. Why do we hope on
when life has revealed itself to be meaningless?

Sahel

THE WEEK BEFORE SHE LEFT FOR AMERICA, SHE SAID to me on the veranda, Mama, you know I'm going to come back, right, and when I didn't respond, she said, I'll never abandon you, and when I still didn't respond, she started to cry the kind of tears I hadn't seen her cry since she was a baby. She became my baby again, for one last time.

They told me about her new home. They said she would be living at school. When I asked how this was possible, they said the school compound was many times the size of Kosawa, and that at the school there would be houses with books and houses with beds and houses with food, and that once she got there she would simply walk from one house to another, she would no longer need to take a bus to school every morning, like she's been doing the past five years. They promised me that this school was worth her crossing the ocean for, that this was one of the few schools in the world where all knowledge available to man could be found, and that by the time she returned she would have more understanding of everything-worth-understanding than she would need for the rest of her life, which meant that we would all have more understanding too—what could be more important than that? Our people were dying for lack of knowledge, they said, and if a child of ours could go to America and bring knowledge back to us, someday no government or corporation would be able to do to us the things they've been doing to us.

I stood up from my seat and told her that I needed to go check on the meat I was smoking in the kitchen, but I really just wanted to go cry alone. I had no comfort to offer her. I only had my own tears. What use are a mother's tears to her child?

When they came to tell me that she'd been selected to attend this school, I had stared at the news bearer as he spoke—at his huge, chapped lips, made even bigger by his small head. He has a name, but the children call him the Sweet One, since he can't seem to wipe off cheerfulness from his face. He has been the representative from the Restoration Movement to Kosawa since our story reached America and people who share no blood with us arrived, determined to save us.

I'd listened to him speak in the village square on countless occasions, I'd sat down with him to talk abut Malabo's disappearance, I'd watched him help Thula with her homework, but I'd never looked at him like I did that day when he entered my hut, beaming. I said nothing for minutes, gazing at his lips as they moved, incapable of finding comfort in the glow of his eyes. He repeated the news, louder. Maybe he thought I'd detect in the volume what he couldn't say for the sake of respect: How wonderful for you, Sahel; how utterly marvelous that your child will get to travel to America.

When I still didn't respond, he looked at his companion, a man the children aptly call the Cute One. The Cute One asked me how I felt about the news, and if I wanted to share what was going through my mind. I shook my head, avoiding his eyes—being around him and his fine face filled me with longing for things I had no right to long for.

In one of the first meetings these Restoration Movement men had with our village, the Sweet One told us that he was one of us. His grandfather was from one of our sister-villages, he'd said; his father grew up like one of our boys, playing with rubber balls and dreaming of marrying and fathering children and growing old in his own hut. But his father's father wanted a different life for his only son—a life among those who allotted the fortunes of the country, not among those who waited for their portions to be allotted. So the man had found a way to get his son out of his village and into the nation's capital. It was there the Sweet One's father finished his schooling before returning home to get a wife from among his people, and it was there the Sweet One was born. "Still," the

Sweet One said, "my father taught me to never forget where I'm from." On the day he came with the news, as I listened to him detail the reasons why Thula's going to America would be good for her, for me, for all of Kosawa, I wanted to ask him how his grandfather had done it, how he'd gotten his child not only to leave his village but also to find a place in Bézam and climb so high that his grandchild now had a job speaking on behalf of kind American people. I wanted to know what all this had cost his grandfather, and if he was asking me to pay the same price too, but I couldn't find the words to ask.

"It's okay, you don't need to say anything today," the Sweet One finally said, as he and the Cute One stood up to leave.

"Sometimes sleep can help you to come up with the right questions," the Cute One added. They wished me a good afternoon and left, promising to return the next day.

That evening, after Thula returned from school, I told her nothing about where they wanted to send her, but in the morning—as the Cute One had suggested—my questions were fully formed. When the men returned after midday, at a time when Kosawa was quiet except for the faint rumble of gas flaring in Gardens, I sat with them again in the parlor and started talking.

I asked them who would take care of my child in

America, who would cook her favorite meals, wash her clothes, make sure she wakes up on time for school. They told me there would be people to cook for her, and that the meals there, though nowhere near as delicious as ours, were edible, evident in the fact that most of the children who attended the school got fat in their first year. They said the school had machines that would wash her clothes, and machines that would wake her up in the mornings, and if she got sick, every kind of medicine to cure every kind of sickness was available in America.

I wanted to know what the city she was going to live in looked like. They told me that it was a marvel of a place, a city more wondrous than any other that has ever existed or will ever exist. They said that these were not their words, they said men and women of vast knowledge, many of whom had traveled around the world and seen other cities, had said this—they were only repeating what was known.

They told me the name of this great city, but I lost it right after it hit my ears, and on their next visit, a week later, they told me again, but my tongue couldn't hold on to it well. Every time I tried to say it, it plopped off my lips, so when people started asking me to tell them the name, I decided it was better not to struggle, better to tell them that she was going to a place called Great City. When I told the Sweet One and the Cute One of this name, they laughed and said that it was a more fitting name than the city's real name.

We told her the news together.

I let the Sweet One talk. He told her that the Restoration Movement had spoken to schools in America and asked them to help our village by educating our children, and one of the schools had said yes, they would be glad to educate one of our children. The school and the Restoration Movement had looked at the report cards of all the children, and no one had needed to be convinced that she was the one the school should bring to America. Her countenance did not change as the Sweet One spoke. When he was done, she thanked him and the Cute One, but said no, she couldn't go, she did not want to leave me and Juba and Yaya, not at a time when we needed to be together. Then she turned to me and said that if I wanted her to go she would go, but I should think about what I wanted for myself, not what I wanted for her, she only wanted my happiness. She walked out of the parlor when she was done speaking. I knew she needed to cry—it was clear in the way she'd spoken, in how she'd kept her eyes down, that she wanted to go. She yearned, desperately, to better understand the world, but she didn't want to leave us.

The Sweet One and the Cute One made more visits after that, to help us with the preparation for her journey. We decided to tell no one in the village, not even Yaya or Juba, until she had gone to Bézam—with the Sweet One, under the pretense of representing Kosawa in a reading competition—and had all the right papers she needed to travel, and until we had a date for her departure. We knew she would tell no one, because the weight of the journey was severe, and the more she carried in her heart, the less she spoke.

∧∧∧∧∧∧∧/

MY MOTHER ALWAYS CAUTIONED ME against dwelling on the past and the future. What happened will never unhappen, she liked to say; what is to happen will happen—better you focus on what's happening in front of you. But on evenings like this, when I find myself sitting alone on the veranda—Yaya and Juba in the hut; Thula in America for several months now; my friends and cousins busy with their own concerns—I hear no other voices except those of the past and the future. They sit on either side of me, fighting over my mind. Remember what happened, the past says. Consider what might happen, the future says. The past always wins, because what it says is true—what happened lives within me, it surrounds me, ever present. I cannot trust the future and its uncertainty.

I see the past in Juba's eyes, the blankness that appeared within hours after the massacre. He can't unsee what he saw. None of us can. He can't unhear the sound of those guns. None of us ever will. He's a child present but gone, so young in age, so battered in spirit. I hear his brokenness when he asks me to tell him: Do I think his father will ever return? What did Bongo do wrong? Could we please leave Kosawa? He's scared because he's the last male left in our family—Big Papa is gone, Malabo is gone, and now Bongo too—how long before it's his turn? Would Jakani bring him back a second time if he died again? he asks. I hear his anguish when he tells me that he wishes he could understand all that has happened to our family. I've done my best to explain what I can; I've told him that too many things in life cannot be reconciled, though I wish for his sake that it weren't so.

He asks me to buy him drawing books and crayons every time I go to the big market. Morning, afternoon, evening, there's no way of knowing when he'll feel an urge to draw. He has filled a dozen books with pictures. He draws things I don't understand—a man's face with features scattered all over, mouth on the forehead, nose on his cheekbone; fishes and trees in the sky, standing in the place of clouds; the sun and the stars falling down. I ask him why he draws that way, why he can't draw things the way they are. He says he doesn't know. He can't explain, but I know it's grief.

I see his heartache when he goes to Yaya's bed and lies next to her. He's eleven, an age by which every boy in the village has gotten rid of his yearning for affection, busy as they are preparing for their rite of passage into manhood, but Juba is not ashamed to tell his friends that he'd rather not come with them to make new slingshots so they can go bird hunting, he'd rather spend the afternoon with his grandmother. I hear him say it and I know it's the pain. I see it in how eager he is to help me feed Yaya, how he rushes to fetch a cup of water for her, how gentle he is when we roll her from her side to her back at least four times a day so she doesn't get infected with bedsores. I hear it when he asks me if Yaya will ever walk again, why her legs stopped functioning the day we returned from Bézam with the news. I tell him that heartbreak is the worst malady.

^^^^^^^

FOR THE FIVE YEARS BEFORE Thula left, I woke up every school morning and fried eggs for her and Juba, two eggs each. No one in Kosawa eats eggs on a regular basis—chickens lay eggs only so often, and it's best to leave the egg to one day become a chicken and feed an entire family than to break it and barely fill one stomach—but I made sure my children ate eggs, because Malabo believed they were good for the body, and he wanted me to feed them to his children as often as I could. During those five years, I bought the eggs in the big market, using the money the people from the Restoration Movement gave us. It was the money Pexton gave, after the Restoration Movement fought them on our behalf.

The fight happened in America, so we didn't get the joy of seeing the look on the Pexton people's faces when they realized they'd lost a battle to us. But my cousin Tunis told me that he heard from someone in Lokunja that there hadn't really been a battle, that Pexton had gone to the Restoration Movement and given them money to pass on to the people of Kosawa alongside their condolences after news of the massacre reached America. Pexton wanted to show how much our suffering pained them, they wanted to demonstrate their commitment to work closely with the Restoration Movement to improve our lives, but everyone said that they'd only given us the money so that the insults being flung at them on both sides of the ocean would cease, and all the people who had stopped buying oil from them would resume doing so, and Pexton would be able to say, Look at what we're doing, we're helping the people of Kosawa, so how are they not benefiting from our presence?

Pexton claimed they had nothing to do with what the soldiers did that day. They said all they ever did was pay the government for the right to drill our land—why should they be responsible for our government's incompetence? His Excellency must have been furious when he heard that, his people must have made threats, but we heard nothing of that—they needed to be united against us. Pexton wanted more of our oil. Our government wanted more of their money. His Excellency wanted more of the world's finest things. Eight years after the massacre that left

Thula unable to speak for eleven days, Pexton is still on our land.

^^^^^^^

THE FIRST TIME THE RESTORATION Movement came to see what was happening in our village, they were represented by five people—the Sweet One and the Cute One; a man who looked like he could be from our area but was from the neighboring country; and a man and a woman from America, both around my age and wearing brown shorts and hats with strings tied around their chins, their faces approaching the hue of a ripe apple.

They walked around the village and saw the pipelines and the places where crude oil had spilled over the years. We took them into the forest, and they saw farms that had been rendered useless after fires; they examined the shriveled-up products of our soil. They took pictures of waste floating on the big river. They pointed at leaves with holes and said it was from acid rain; they explained to us that our rain long ago stopped being pure water. We led them to see the graves of the children; we saw their lips moving as they counted the smallest mounds. They looked toward Gardens and saw the gas flares.

When we gathered in the square for a meeting, the American man and woman repeatedly sighed and shook their heads while the Sweet One spoke, though they couldn't understand our language. The Sweet One told us that the American man and woman had wanted to see us for themselves: they knew stories like ours existed, because fighting for people like us was what they did, but they'd never seen a case like ours, this magnitude of subjugation. The American man and woman gave our children books and sweets that tasted like honey. They wanted to be hugged, we could tell, the woman especially, her eyes full of tears, but they didn't ask for a hug, and as much as we would have loved to hug them in appreciation, we did not deem it proper to behave as such with Americans.

No one had told us they'd be coming, so we had no food prepared for them. When a few women joined their heads together in conversation and then asked the Sweet One if their group could wait so the women of Kosawa could kill and roast a couple of chickens, the Sweet One whispered to the American people, who smiled and told him to thank us so much, how very kind of us, but they'd already eaten. As they were leaving the square to get into their car to return to Bézam and then America, someone burst into song, and soon all the women and girls, myself included, were singing. I couldn't remember the last time I'd sung, and yet I joined in adding a third part to the melody, every woman swinging her hips and raising dust, our voices soaring, first with a song of gratitude, asking the Spirit to bless our visitors for coming to see us, then the song from the tale our mothers used to tell us when we were children, the one about the three little fishes who escaped the belly of a monstrous creature by itching the insides of its stomach for so long that the monster got a stomachache and vomited them out. The Restoration Movement people swung their hips alongside us, the American woman red-faced and runny-nosed and crying hard. Somehow the drums appeared. As the men beat them in unison, we sang the fishes' plea: **This story must be told, it might not feel good to all ears, it gives our mouths no joy to say it, but our story cannot be left untold.**

A month later, the Sweet One and the Cute One began coming to see us by themselves.

Though they live in Bézam and travel to other villages as well, they always seem to have time for us, staying with us when a new death adds to our sorrow, sleeping on our bare floors if they have to, or at the Sweet One's uncle's hut in one of the sister-villages.

The day they brought the Pexton money, they told us, before handing it to us, that we didn't have to take it. They said that no amount of money could undo what Pexton had done to us, but we took it anyway, because, much as we hated them, we needed their money to help us carry on after all we'd lost. Besides, it was our money, from our oil.

The Restoration Movement men said the money was just for the time being, to help us dry our tears.

They said their people in America would get us more money for every spill that has ever happened. They would make Pexton pay for the toxic waste on the river, and the dirt in the air, and the poison in the well water, and for the farms that might not be fruitful for another generation, and why not for the children who never got a chance to grow up, and the parents whose broken hearts will never heal.

After they'd done all that, they said, they would ask Pexton to clean up our land so Kosawa could return to the state it was in when our ancestors first arrived here. But that would all take years, they cautioned; some of us might not be alive to see a restored Kosawa and a new envelope of money, in which case it would go to our children.

They gave us the money from Pexton in large straw bags.

A straw bag for each of the ninety or so huts of Kosawa, handed to the head of the family. I was the head of my family. What woman dreams of becoming the head of her family? I never wanted such a burden—I'd seen what it had done to Malabo's relationship with Bongo—but there I was, extending my hand and receiving the money, more cash than my husband made in the last three years of his life combined.

Someone started a story that the money we received couldn't have been all the money Pexton had given, that the people at the Restoration Movement office in Bézam must have kept some of it for themselves, and that the Sweet One and the Cute One must have taken their cuts. The rumors flew from hut to hut, some saying that the Restoration Movement was giving us only what they thought would make us happy; perhaps we should go to Gardens and ask a supervisor to tell us exactly how much their people in America had sent us. Tunis is the one who told me about the rumor. He said Malabo's cousin Sonni—who had become our new village head after the massacre—had asked him to help put an end to the rumor. I'd never liked Sonni and his manner of taking too long to think before speaking, and I doubt Malabo would be happy to see that someone whose presentation reeked of weakness had become leader of Kosawa, but I agreed with Sonni on this: If we learned that the Restoration Movement and the Sweet One and the Cute One had kept some of the money for themselves, what would our recourse be? Would we start a fight against the very people fighting for us?

The straw bag sits in a black box under my bed, the same one Malabo used to store the money he brought back from selling his game in the big market. He never brought back much money. Mostly coins, just enough for food and clothes and medicine, things we needed. The only money he left for me before his departure was money his father had left for him—several bills Big Papa had put in an envelope the day Thula was born, which he told Yaya to give Malabo after he died so that Thula would never want for anything.

Big Papa wasn't a man who demonstrated his love in the words he spoke or the looks he gave, but he was a man who, as often as he could, did what love ought to do. Few people recognized that. His own sons struggled to—they couldn't see beyond his inability to be the kind of father they wanted. They did not share my admiration for how he moved to Kosawa as a young man, and how he worked for years on the farm of Woja Beki's father, who gifted him the land on which our hut now stands, in gratitude for Big Papa's hard work. They dismissed the fact that, bamboo by bamboo, Big Papa built our hut and outhouse by himself, every evening, after working all day on the farm. I reminded Malabo of this whenever he came to me grumbling about something or another his father had done or not done because of his mood. I said to him: Your father can do only what he has the capacity to do; surely, it must pain him to fail you. But Malabo couldn't look past his disappointments and the many sad evenings of his childhood. Though Big Papa had stopped his yellings and beratings by the time I married Malabo—he was mostly just melancholic— memories of his transgressions were still fresh within his children. I never spoke about any of this with Yaya. She was Big Papa's wife—I couldn't put her in a position to speak ill of her husband—but I imagine it hurt her more than it did me, how people looked at him as if he were just a level above Konga.

Even children laughed at Big Papa behind his back, calling him Bitter Face and Fire Eyes; they never got to know what more lay behind that countenance the way I did. Yes, it wasn't a pleasure to look at the face, but I rarely thought that the anger on it was directed at me—something in his eyes told me that he yearned to be happy, but he was too consumed with despair and knew of no way to free himself from it. People wanted me to say that living in the same hut with him was akin to eating sour leaves for dinner every night, but I could never say that, because Big Papa was good to me despite himself. No, he never uttered a good morning to me, and when I placed his food before him his gratitude came out as a grumble—many were the times when I found myself alone in the parlor with him and had to find a reason to escape lest that glare of his scorch me—but he went to the forest to hunt food that I would eat. If his mood allowed, he split wood for me to cook with. When my daughter was born, he held her and rocked her to sleep.

^^^^^^^

ON MOST NIGHTS NOW, WHEN all is quiet, I think of Big Papa sitting on the veranda in silence. I think of Bongo singing during his baths, his songs more melodious than ever after he met Elali. Mostly, though, I think of Malabo, my husband, my heartbreaker.

I think of how perfectly flawed life was the day he walked up to me at my friend's hut.

That was back before Cocody and I were friends, when she was just my friend Uwe's friend. Uwe and I were in Kosawa so she could see Cocody and I could visit my aunts who live here. I had just turned nineteen. I remember I wore a layer of anxiety that day—I'd reached marriage age with no one handsome in sight. A man in my village named Neba was my only option, but I couldn't look past his nostrils, which flared like a windswept skirt. "How could you turn down a man because you hate his nose?" my mother had sighed. "How could I not, when I would have to look into the thing every day," I'd replied. When my mother cautioned me to lower my standards, I laughed. Neba would be good to me, I knew, but would that suffice for a marriage?

Malabo showed up at Cocody's hut, looking for his best friend, Bissau, Cocody's husband. I saw his cheekbones, sharp as a spear's edge, and a pointy beard to match. What a face. What a man. Could any man alive be more viciously gorgeous?

Every time I visited Kosawa after that day, my eyes labored in search of him from my arrival till my departure. Cocody and I would walk past his hut at least twice every visit. Whenever I saw him, I pushed out my chest to display the largeness of my breasts, patting dry any sweat on my face as Cocody laughed the laughter that everyone knew belonged to her only: ka ka ka oh. My efforts, though, had no effect on

Malabo—he wouldn't notice me until the day he was ready to.

It wouldn't happen till several months later, one afternoon when we were laughing on Cocody's veranda—me, Uwe, Cocody, and her friend Lulu. Malabo appeared from nowhere and stood in front of me. "I just want to say that I've never seen teeth as beautiful as yours," he said. I died. I came back to life and died again. Weeks later, he would tell me that the whiteness of my teeth must make the clouds feel inferior, and I would tell him that the sharpness of his cheekbones made knives envious, but on that afternoon, there would be no words coming off me. With the full brightness of his eyes on me, I forgot how to produce sound. Embarrassment would have killed me if it were a disease. He told me that he'd seen me around the village and had wondered what I did to keep my teeth so white. Palm kernel oil, I wanted to say; I swish with it every morning. "Whatever you're doing," he said, "keep doing it."

I forced a smile.

"Say something," Cocody and Uwe whispered, adding to my mortification.

I widened my eyes at them, hoping they'd read in it: Say what? I'd spent hours fantasizing, but I hadn't planned for the moment when Malabo would put his cheeks close to mine and ask me to go for a walk with him. I found myself lifted off the ground, unable to touch it again. Float away with him I did, from that moment till the end.

We were happy, Malabo and I.

I try not to forget that, but the nature of our last days together threatens to smear all memories of our spirits uniting as one. After that first walk around Kosawa—hand in hand, footsteps synchronized, me beaming—no one could convince me that the days I waited for him to come visit me in my village or for me to visit him in his weren't worth the torment. I could have waited for ten dry seasons and ten rainy seasons to feel the beat of his heart for one minute. My friends laughed at me. "Sahel finally got the cheekbones of her dreams," they said. I laughed with them. When it came to Malabo, everything made me happy. Even my friend Lulu's annoying questions made me happy— Lulu asking me if I really wanted to marry the son of the most unhappy man who ever lived, what if I gave birth to children as unsmiling and despondent as their grandfather, could I imagine how uncomfortable it would be to live in the same hut as someone who grunted whenever you wished him a good day. I'd responded that, of course, I'd considered it all and who wouldn't want to marry Malabo, the firstborn of the unhappiest man who ever lived? Who wouldn't want to have his semi-smile directed at her every day? That semi-smile started vanishing when children began dying. By his departure, it was all gone.

But did it ever glow for me.

Did it glow that night when he took me into his bedroom, on a day when his parents were at a funeral in one of our brother-villages and Bongo had gone off in order to give Malabo all the space he would need, just as Malabo did when Bongo had a girl. Did it glow when, without his asking, with him merely sitting on his bed and looking at me, his eyes glimmering in readiness, I began undressing, beads of sweat appearing on his forehead as I pulled off item after item, slowly, until I was left with nothing but my body in its bare state, begging for him to stand up and hold it, which he did, rising with hands outstretched, lips parted, his eyes never leaving mine. I did not beg him to lay me on his bed, and he did not me ask if he could—we had talked about it, and laughed about it, how in not too long we'd be married, and once the children started arriving our only chances would be in the darkest hours of the night, under our sheets, as silently as we could, and there'd be so many things we wouldn't be able to do with them in the bedroom, so we had to do it all now, as often as we could, while we were young and free.

I'm certain Yaya and Big Papa heard us the night of our wedding, excited as we were to lie side by side on our marital bed with no child yet in sight. Our clothes were on the floor even before the women from my village left, the ones who had carried my belongings on their heads and, with my mother leading the procession, sung and danced from my aunt's hut to my new family's hut, where they placed everything I owned in the parlor and pushed Malabo and me into our bedroom and closed the door, laughing and shouting from outside that we'd better not step out until I was pregnant. How happy were we to oblige? At least once I said to Malabo, in between sessions, that we needed to do a better job of being quiet, because we didn't want to disturb Big Papa's and Yaya's sleep, but Malabo laughed and said that Big Papa and Yaya were probably not sleeping, they were most likely doing the same thing we were doing, and that the only reason why we weren't hearing them was because they'd learned how to do it quietly, after decades of experience. I found it hard to believe this, considering the looks Big Papa gave me in the morning, an acknowledgment that he'd heard me, coupled with something I couldn't decipher. I wished he hadn't given me those looks, but it didn't stop us the following night. Nothing stopped us until I was huge with Thula, and Yaya, one day in the kitchen, said to me that there were certain things a woman had to stop doing for the sake of her child. Nodding, I told her I understood. Malabo protested. He said that his friends had told him that it was not true, that their children had all come out fine, and that the important thing was to know how to maneuver around the fetus, but I told him we needed to do it for Yaya, and he agreed; it hadn't been easy for us, but we'd done it, though when I was pregnant with Juba I was insatiable, which thoroughly thrilled Malabo.

My desire was, and remains, its own beast, rabid and untamable.

In those early days of our love, it was no punishment. It was a gift to my husband, this wanting and more wanting, every night. Cocody and Lulu laughed at me whenever I yawned in the middle of the day and told them that we couldn't stop, it was too hard to stop. They said no woman should have an appetite like mine, that their husbands would send them to Sakani to be given whatever I'd drunk if they somehow discovered that it was possible for a woman to be as desirous as a man. "I hope Malabo isn't telling Bissau any of these things you guys are doing and giving him ideas," Cocody said. "I don't want any trouble with him coming to me in the middle of the night and asking me to open my pot so he can cook some crazy meal in it." At which Lulu sighed, pressed her tongue against her gap tooth, and said, "My own pot, for two months now, I haven't felt like taking off the lid. I don't even want to think about how many cobwebs have accumulated inside it." Lulu swore that most of my insides had to be male. She said I probably had invisible hair on my chin and a lump on my throat that nobody could see. Cocody had agreed and laughed, ka ka ka oh, and they'd slammed their palms together. In those days I'd laughed with them, because Malabo was around to honor me and my voraciousness, but after he left and never came back, what was there to laugh about?

In the first year after his disappearance, I cried many different kinds of tears. The tears I cried in the morning were different from the ones I cried at night. At night, I thought of our nights together. I thought of my palm on his cheek, his on mine. I thought of how much he loved my breasts. I cried with longing, alone under my sheets. I cried because no one had touched me since the day he last touched me, and to this day, no one has touched me.

Like every woman who has lost a husband before me, like every woman who will lose a husband after me, I am doomed to aloneness. My days of being cuddled and fondled have come and gone. I hear my mother's voice in my head from back when I was a child. Like me, she lost a husband, though she was much older than the twenty-nine I was when Malabo left. I hear her say to her friends: I lost the one husband life gave me, I have no right to ask for another one, not when there are other women waiting their turn. I see her friends nodding sadly: what is the point in questioning a broken heart?

I was eight when my father died and, with my five older sisters married, it was just my mother and me in our hut. It was clear to me that she did not resent her fate—she never complained—but I prayed the Spirit that I would never become like her. Malabo promised never to leave me husbandless. Why would I want to leave this body? he said.

There is an abundance of women like me in Kosawa and throughout the sibling-villages—wives with dead husbands. Men marry us young and die before us, taken away by nature or disobedience to our wisdom. At their deaths, we cry, we dry our eyes, we prepare to spend the rest of our lives taking care of the very young, the sick, and the very old. Desire becomes of the past. We'll never be afforded the same privilege given to husbands with dead wives. For these men, there will in all certainty be another companion, thanks to the Spirit's design that our women out-number their men. For grieving men, there'll quickly arrive someone younger and willing to take over the mothering of their children, someone eager to add to their lineage. Unless they're so old that only the grave wants them, they will never know what it's like to have a body begging for just a little touch at night. They will never be ashamed to announce that they have found someone to take their wives' place, because everyone would agree that a man should not be alone.

You can be alone, the men say to us. You're a woman, you're built to endure.

In that first year after Malabo vanished, I prayed the Spirit to cause another woman's husband to wan-der into my bed. Some nights I prayed for a young man who hadn't yet picked a wife to keep me as a placeholder, take this used-up body and enjoy it until a fresh one came along; even then, he could retain me for the months when his wife was pregnant. I'd do what I hear some women in my position do: meet him deep in the forest, under a tree, with only the birds and beasts watching, or in a barn late at night. I'd let him do to me all the deeds he might not be so bold as to ask his wife to engage in.

On our worst days, Cocody and I cried together in my bedroom.

Where once we'd been happy to marry best friends who did everything together, now we wept that we'd married best friends who did everything together. In between our tears, we joked that perhaps we should marry each other. One evening, Cocody's younger cousin Aisha was with us when I said this. She joined us in laughing at the idea, before adding that maybe women marrying each other wasn't such a bad idea, it might even be the best thing to ever happen to humans. This made Cocody and me laugh hard—Aisha was an adolescent, she could get away with saying such ridiculous things.

Cocody doesn't want a man the same way that I do. She wants a man to help her guide her sons, since she has no male kin in Kosawa whom she's comfortable discussing her sons' progression to manhood with. She worries about her youngest child, born two months after our husbands went to Bézam and vanished. She and I had both been pregnant at the same time; my child would also be running around the village today if all had gone well, but I thank the Spirit that I alone suffered that loss and my friend was spared. I agree with Cocody that her youngest boy would need a new father to teach him how to grow up to be like the father he never knew, but I have no need for a new father for my children. I have my husband's family and my cousin Tunis, who, though he too is suffering—who in Kosawa isn't suffering? who in the world hasn't just suffered, is suffering at the moment, or soon to suffer?—is still the brother the Spirit never gave me.

One evening, about a year after Malabo disappeared, Tunis came to check on me and found me sitting alone on the veranda, staring into nothing. He sat next to me and whispered in my ear that he'd heard some men in the big market talking about my buttocks; the men had said that my buttocks looked like a sweet pineapple. I slapped his head in jest, though I wish it were true, so I could go search for the men, pick one of them, bring him to my hut, and unleash my lust.

With my cousin sitting next to me and making me laugh, I spent little time wondering what happened to Malabo. After Tunis went home, I wondered all night how Malabo had died. If I had a grave to sit on and cry I would do so, to soak up whatever solace is present atop the mound under which a beloved lies. But the dust with which my husband's flesh was formed has already merged with the Bézam soil. Or maybe a river there took his blood away. Perhaps his burnt bones were long ago blown away by a cruel gust. I'll never know. I speak to him daily, often when I'm outdoors, hoping that birds flying toward Bézam will take my words with them, and even if my words aren't what he wishes to hear, the sound of my voice will cause him to be less alone. Perhaps he's not alone anymore.

Perhaps Bongo is with him, brothers for life and in death.

^^^^^^^/

THE AFTERNOON WE RETURNED FROM Bézam without Bongo, Thula went straight to Bongo's bed and curled up under his old clothes. She remained there all day and all night. She did not answer when her friends came and knocked on the door, begging her to open it because they wanted to be with her and comfort her. She did not come out when relatives started arriving to wail with us in the parlor and tell us to be strong. She was not there when my aunts did the unbearable duty of telling Yaya what had happened in Bézam. Thula was not there when we held Yaya's hands as she was told that Bongo was dead.

I'd collapsed not from my grief, but from seeing Yaya's devastation at the news, the way she started shivering and hyperventilating as if life was leaving her. I couldn't bear to watch; the Spirit has no right to punish a good woman this much in one lifetime.

Thula wasn't there when the women revived me and I opened my eyes to see that Yaya was no longer Yaya, just a breathing object awaiting death. Thula remained alone in Bongo's bedroom, lying on the sheets we hadn't changed since the day they took him to Bézam. She avoided us, as if her grief and ours were parallel rivers.

After that first day stuck in a gloomy fog, when I'd gathered whatever strength I could, I sent a message for my cousin Tunis to come help me break down the door to the back room so we could get Thula out—I couldn't let her stay in there with no food or water. Tunis came over and called out to Thula to please unlock the door so he wouldn't have to break in. Thula stayed on the bed and ignored us. Tunis found a way to open the door without causing much damage and left. Quietly, I entered the room.

I found her lying under Bongo's clothes, her face tear-stained.

She was clutching to her chest the book Bongo used to read to her, the one about a place called Nubia, that place Bongo loved to talk about: Did we know that in Nubia women were as powerful as men? he liked to say to Malabo and me on the veranda, at which Malabo would give him a blank stare and I'd laugh and ask him to tell me more.

I knelt by the bed and pleaded with Thula to get out of the room. She turned her face to the wall. I told her we needed to preserve the room in the event Bongo's spirit wanted to roam there for a while before beginning its journey to be with the ancestors. She ignored me. "You're too young to sleep here alone," I said, still kneeling by the bed. No reaction. I told her that as a girl she couldn't make the back room her bedroom;

Bongo could do so because young men can handle the danger of sleeping in a room with a separate entrance. Still no reaction from her. I stood up. Letting go of the tenderness in my voice, I told her I would no longer put up with her insolence; I hadn't killed her father or her uncle, my patience with her wasn't going to last forever. Still she made no effort to rise. My cautions turned to threats. "I'll never let you back in the hut if you don't come in right now," I said. I could have been speaking to a rock. Determined to get a response, I yanked her off the bed. It was then I noticed how wet the pillow was, drenched with her tears.

What could I do? Our parlor was full of women sitting on the floor around Yaya, singing to her in her numb state; I didn't want to announce to them that Thula was compounding my grief by defying me. So I went into my bedroom and closed the door and window. In the darkness, I sat on the bed and bowed my head. I asked the Spirit to tell me where I'd gone wrong. I wanted to know where all of us, as a people, had gone astray. Surely, our ancestors had committed an offense, and their punishment was being visited upon us, for no hut in Kosawa had been spared this desolation wrought upon us. I wept for Bongo, I cursed Malabo. I wish I didn't detest my husband for dooming me to a life of being solely responsible for a broken girl and a lost boy and an old woman, all of them laying upon my back their anger and grief, with no one to bear mine but me, because it had to be so.

I screamed into my pillow. I told Malabo I wish

I'd married Neba in my village, the first man who'd asked me to be his wife. I wish I hadn't told my mother to tell Neba that she couldn't accept any gifts from him because another man had already requested her permission to marry me. I'd joked and laughed about the lie with my friends, because I believed that I'd someday find a man I wanted who wanted me too; I was confident that waiting for this man would be worthwhile. And he was worthwhile, my husband, my dream, who with a semi-smile brought low the clouds and laid them for me to walk on, who with a single touch left me floating face downward on the stillest, cleanest water, everything about him so worth the damnation of being born. In our youth and freedom, our exhilaration seemed as if it would last forever. Look where my lie landed me.

Before drying my eyes and rising, I told Malabo that I hoped his journey from this world to the next would take a hundred eternities so that he would forever be alone, never with us, never with his ancestors. I cursed him for choosing me only to make me pay for his foolhardiness, for loving me only to pass me off to a life I loathe, for giving me everything I ever wanted only to leave me wishing I'd never prayed for the things I got.

For most of the nights since the day Malabo refused to heed my advice and left for Bézam, sleep has lost its

battle against my fidgety mind. I pass the hours waiting for the roosters to tell me it's dawn so I can find
respite from my regrets and ruminations. The past is
past, and yet I can't stop thinking that I could have
stopped him if I were a better woman, a better wife, a
better mother, a more persuasive person.

I try not to punish myself with such thoughts, but
I can't stop counting all the sorrows that have befallen
our family because Malabo did not listen to me. I list
them, from the moment I began feeling the pain in my
belly though it was too early in my pregnancy for me
to feel such pain, to the moment, a week later, when
the baby came out and I screamed and closed my eyes
because I did not want to see it, to the afternoon when
the soldiers arrived with guns and I saw a wickedness
worse than I'd ever imagined possible, to the evening
we returned to Kosawa from Bézam with Bongo's
death notice.

"You're acting as if this problem is yours to solve," I
said to Malabo the night before his departure.

"Whose problem is it to solve?" he said.

"Are your children the only ones drinking the
water? Why do you have to do the fighting for
everyone?"

"Is that who you think I am, Sahel? The kind of
man who sits back and waits for someone else to take
action? Is that the man you married?"

"Juba returned to us," I cried. "That's an omen.
Can't you see? It means he's not going away any-

time soon. Nobody dies and comes back only to die again soon after."

"How many people have you known who died and came back?"

I did not respond; we both knew the answer.

"Juba was the first person in Kosawa in a generation to be brought back to life," he said, as if I didn't know. "Of all the sick children, the Spirit chose to spare ours. Why? Have you wondered? Don't you think we ought to play a bigger role in ending all this, considering how much we've been favored? Have you even thought for a second about Juba's adulthood, how his coming back to life is going to affect him as he gets older?"

"We're not talking about when he gets older. We're talking about now. He's fine now. Isn't he?"

"What about Thula? What about when she too gets sick?"

"Thula never gets sick. I'll boil their water for ten hours if I have to. Please, don't go to Bézam. Cocody is right now begging Bissau not to go with you. Lulu and her family are begging Lobi to stay home. There's no saying how the government will respond if you show up in their town making demands—that city is full of wicked men."

"I don't understand: how can you not think about the future?"

"We're surviving," I cried. "By the goodness of the Spirit—"

"You want me to not fight for my children's future because you're afraid."

"I'm begging you to not make a mistake. . . . I don't feel good about this. . . ."

"You're pregnant. You never feel good about anything while you're pregnant."

"This is not the pregnancy talking."

"Sahel, please."

What did Malabo ever ask me to do that I didn't do for him? He said, "Sahel, this is what I want to eat today," and I cooked it. He said, "Sahel, wear this dress and not that one" and I said, "Of course." I was following tradition, yes, but between him and me marital rules were useless—my spirit yearned to please his. And then I made a single request to him, and what did he say? He said, No, I won't do it. He went to Bézam and he failed, and Bongo tried to undo what he'd done and he too failed. Now the people of the Restoration Movement are trying to undo and redo everything.

I don't know what the outcome of the Restoration Movement's fight on our behalf will be, but Thula, from the first time she heard them talk, believed that with them by our side, we will prevail over His Excellency and Pexton.

I noticed the calm that appeared on her face days after the Restoration Movement people first came to visit us, a couple of months after Bongo was taken to Bézam. I could see from the light returning to her eyes that they had convinced her when they promised us that they would help us reclaim and restore our land and water and air. After that meeting, the other children had fought over the sweet things the American man and woman brought, but not Thula; she had picked up the books they brought and taken them home. That day was the day she began living in books and, in effect, living in America.

Six years later, on the evening after the Sweet One and the Cute One informed her about the invitation from the school in America, she came to me in the kitchen as I was boiling yams and told me again that she'd go, but only if I wanted her to go. I told her she had my blessings to go, only if she wanted to go, only if her spirit was telling her to go. We sat in silence, watching the wood beneath the iron pot turn to crimson coal.

∧∧∧∧∧∧/

THE SWEET ONE AND THE Cute One were the ones who brought up the idea that the children of Kosawa would benefit from advanced schooling. They said it would be good for our village and future generations if our older children started attending the school in Lokunja, where the district officials send their children. Upon completing the Kosawa school, rather than the boys picking up spears to hunt and the girls becoming apprentices for their mothers, they would learn things that some of our village schoolteachers didn't even know. The Restoration Movement men said we could plead with the government to improve our school and send us more qualified teachers, but the government would argue that Kosawa was too small to be deserving of a better school. Given that, the men said, our best chance at preparing our children for a future that might be far from Kosawa was to send them to the superior school that already existed. The Restoration Movement would pay for a bus to take children twelve years old and over to the Lokunja school.

What did we think? they asked us at the village square.

Rain had fallen that morning, but the evening was sunny and hot; it was as if we were living through two seasons in one day. The Sweet One and the Cute One were sitting next to our new village head, Sonni, under the mango tree. It had been two years since the massacre; grass had sprouted and covered the heaps beneath which the slaughtered lay.

Sonni stood up to speak, counting every word in that manner of his that makes me want to pull his tongue and force it to hurry up. He thanked the Restoration Movement men for their offer, saying that it would be good if our children could have better schooling. There would need to be another meeting of the men, he said, for fathers to talk about all this, to gauge everyone's openness to the idea. . . . But voices of mothers and fathers had already drowned his to say that no additional meeting was necessary, it would never be a good idea for our children to be taken on a bus to a big school in Lokunja every day; such a price could never be worth paying for the sake of further learning. What would be the purpose of the added schooling? We had fallen into the trap of animals: how would the children learning beyond how to read and write and do simple arithmetic cause our captor's hearts to change so they might look at us and see something of worth? Though we trusted the people from the Restoration Movement, many said, though we were thankful for all they'd done for us, we simply couldn't hand over our children to strangers in Lokunja. Our eyes wouldn't be on them over there—if the government could kill them in our presence, what would it do in our absence?

The Sweet One and the Cute One said that they understood our concerns, but that, though the school was owned by the government, the bus would be owned by the Restoration Movement, paid for by the same American people who had been giving money to the Restoration Movement to help in our fight against Pexton ever since Austin's story appeared in their newspaper. The representatives said these people who would pay for the bus were the same ones who had given money to fight for the release of Bongo and Konga and Woja Beki and Lusaka—they'd been on our side then and would always be. Still, the voices of dissent rose. If the Sweet One and the Cute One had seen the things we'd seen, several parents shouted, if they had been here on the day of the massacre, they would understand why we now feared even the rustling of leaves.

^^^^^^^

THE POSSIBILITY OF ATTENDING A school in Lokunja was what got Thula to start talking more often, three years after Malabo vanished.

She was still the same girl, saying only what she needed to say, but her anger at the massacre and all that had happened to our family was no longer holding her in chains, or at least the chains had grown looser. Perhaps it was the hope the men from the Restoration Movement brought every time they visited, and the news that the children now had a chance to acquire knowledge that might save us from future suffering. Or it could be that she finally recognized we were all in chains and that her pain was unique but in no way greater than others', so what choice did we all have but to carry on? She didn't return to smiling with ease, or laughing like she used to with her father, but her face brightened daily, highlighting the lovely largeness of her eyes.

Whenever I happened upon her and her friends

sitting somewhere in the village, I lingered for a bit to hear if she would laugh, and if she did, a thousand bountiful harvests wouldn't have made me happier. Without my asking, she started coming to sit by me in the kitchen to help me cook. On days when Yaya needed extra attention because she was having a very bad day—perhaps because one of her sons had visited her in a dream—and I had to roll her over repeatedly for a better position or wipe her face because she couldn't stop crying, Thula cooked for the family. It nearly made me laugh whenever she reminded me to eat, considering how little she ate—no more than half the food on her plate, often less, despite my pleas for her to eat more.

I worried about her weight. I worried about the fact that her bleeding hadn't started though she had reached the age for it. I worried that her friends' breasts had grown past the size of oranges and hers weren't up to that of a cashew. The competition for men with potential to make great husbands was fierce in all the eight villages, and Thula was at the age when girls needed to start sending signals and flaunting whatever wares they had. Her friends already had buttocks that men gaped at; beside them, Thula looked like a child trailing her mother and aunts. Malabo loved to boast that, with her sublime eyes and abundant smiles, his daughter was going to grow up to become the most beautiful woman the eight villages had ever seen. He said it even when Thula proved herself incapable of gaining weight. As a father, he could be blinded to certain things, but as a mother, I had a duty to stay attuned to all the challenges my daughter would encounter. Stunning as her face was, I could tell that her thinness and flatness, coupled with her impenetrable nature, would lessen her in the eyes of wife-seeking men.

When I lamented to Cocody and Lulu about this, they laughed and asked me why I couldn't carry to-day's load today and take on tomorrow's load when I got there. Couldn't I see it was pointless to agonize about Thula's breasts and bleeding when my only choice in the matter was to wait for them to arrive when her body was ready? "Have you ever met a woman who has not bled and has no breasts?" Lulu asked me, laughing. Why was I wasting time think-ing about the moment when Thula would see her first blood and run to me for comfort? What made me think she would even tell me when it happened? Cocody and Lulu, daughters to mothers and mothers to daughters, understood why all these things mat-tered, but they preferred to use their minds for things other than imagining, as I often did, the celebra-tion of a daughter's first bleed—the happy evening when our older female relatives and friends would gather to give Thula an account of all the wonders in store for her now that she was a woman. I smiled whenever I pictured her face, caught between dread and confusion, as the women whispered to her that, in the hands of the right man, the pleasure would more than make up for the pain, and that, the sweeter the pleasure that accompanied the conception, the greater the pain at the child's delivery, and wasn't that one of the most wonderful things about being a woman?

One evening, in Lulu's kitchen, while Thula and a friend were watching Yaya, Cocody and Lulu told me about the evenings after their first bleed, when their mothers had called the women of Kosawa to celebrate them. We laughed as they reminisced about the women, most long gone, who told stories from their journeys through womanhood, stories that they must have passed back and forth in smoky kitchens but which they just had to share again, for they relished telling them over and over: accounts of how they had spat into their husband's soups in moments of spite, and how they knew which position to use to conceive a girl, and which to use for a boy, and how they'd faked illnesses when they didn't feel like cooking and their husbands had served the children fruit for dinner, and if only their husbands knew how many steps ahead their wives always were, but what use was that cleverness for the wives who discovered from a foe or a friend that their husbands had visited a woman's bed in another village? What could a wife do besides sigh and carry on after she confronts her husband and his response is that none of it is true, why was she asking questions, leave him alone. The stories never lacked for flavor, Lulu said, and they made her at once proud and furious to have been born a woman.

THULA ENTERED MY ROOM FOUR days after the Sweet
One and the Cute One suggested the Lokunja school.
"Mama," she said to me as I was folding clothes on the
bed, "I'd like to take the bus to the school in Lokunja."

"No," I said. She turned around and left.

The next morning, she came to me in the kitchen
after she had bathed and put on her blue uniform.

"Mama, please," she said. "I really want to go to
the school in Lokunja."

I continued frying her eggs; I said nothing.

After the eggs were ready, I put them on a plate
alongside some fried plantains. I handed it to her and
told her to go eat on the table in the parlor, away from
the smoke.

She left, and I plated Juba's breakfast and brought
it to him on the table, just as he was about to finish
putting on his blue shirt and khaki shorts. I watched
them eat, like I did every morning—Thula eating
four slices of plantain and a couple bites of eggs; Juba
eating all of his food plus Thula's leftovers. After they
were done, they went into Yaya's room, to hug her
goodbye. Yaya didn't sit up from her lying position;
only her mouth moved as she told them to make
sure to obey their teachers. They nodded, left Yaya's
room and hugged me before heading off, Thula
holding Juba's hand and walking only as fast as her
little brother's legs could take him. He still needed

her protection. He only started going to school after Bongo died and their great-uncle Manga went to the school and begged the headmaster to allow Juba to start in the middle of the term because, though his age-mates were still running around naked, Juba's right hand could go around his head and touch his left ear, evidence his brain was large enough for school.

I checked on Yaya after the children were out of my sight. I brought her a pot to spit in, or urinate, or excrete, whatever she needed to do. I still do this daily. Some days she cannot sit up to use the pot, so I lay a plastic sheet under her buttocks and place a cloth over the plastic so she can excrete lying down, after which I clean and dry her.

If her feces has a smell, I don't smell it. She's my mother. Whatever suffering she has to bear, I bear it with her. Until the day she leaves me, or tells me to leave her, I am hers and she is mine. She has lost all her teeth, so I mince her meat, and chew her cocoyams before putting them in her mouth, the same way she once chewed food before putting it in the mouths of my husband and my children. When she needs to cry, I sit on her bed and we cry together. I wipe her eyes and I beg her to stop crying—while she cries, I too must, I can't let her cry alone. Other times we just let our tears silently roll until we run dry. We mourn the men we've loved and lost, and, some moments after, we imagine the beautiful day when we will reunite with them in the land beyond.

. . .

A week after Thula first heard about the school in Lokunja, she comes to me again to beg me to let her go there. I'm sitting on the veranda; one of my aunts has just left after a visit. Thula comes and sits next to me. She asks me if I can talk to the Cute One and the Sweet One on her behalf, let them know that she loves their idea of the village children attending a better school. I sigh and turn my face away. She changes seats so she can look into my eyes.

"Mama, please," she says.

"You really want to go to this school?" I ask her.

She nods.

I tell her I'll sleep and think on it. I wake up the next morning worrying for her.

From the day she was born, she's wanted what she's wanted. If Thula wanted to see her father before going to sleep, her eyes wouldn't shut until he returned from smoking with his friends in the square. I remember one evening, when she was five, I told her that Malabo had gone to visit a sick friend in another village and would not be back till the next day, so she could come sleep with me in the bed. When nighttime came, I couldn't find her. Yaya and I were about to panic when Bongo ran out of the hut and returned minutes later dragging Thula—he had found her on the path to Gardens, planning to catch the bus to go spend the night with her father, wherever he was.

. . .

I call her into my bedroom after she returns from school and ask her to sit next to me on the bed. I tell her that I understand why she wants to go to the better school—having more knowledge could never be a bad thing—but that going to Lokunja would not be good for her. I tell her how tiring it would be to take a bus for an hour every morning, an hour every afternoon. She says she would be fine doing it. I remind her that her friends would not be there in the new school, most will likely be married in no more than four, five years. And if she were to go to school in Lokunja, a town where we have no family, if something were to happen to her, who would bring us the news? She asks me what I think might happen to her there. When I don't tell her about all of the horrid possibilities that circulate in my head every day, all the ways in which life could conspire to take my children away from me and leave me empty-handed, she tells me that I can't think of anything because there's nothing that could happen to her there that won't happen here. "Who will you share the bus with every day?" I ask her. "No mother or father in Kosawa is going to allow their child to go to that school." Did she expect the Restoration Movement to send a bus for her alone?

She leaves my bedroom, returns to Bongo's room, gets on the bed, and turns her face to the wall. She does not rise when Juba stands at the door and asks her to take a look at what he's drawn—does she like it? Juba enters the room, pokes her in the ribs jokingly, to force a reaction. She does not turn, not even to glance at the drawing and tell him he's done well. Juba pokes her once more, shrugs, and returns to the parlor to draw something else.

In the morning I make her eggs and plantains before she goes off to school, but she refuses to eat. I make a dinner of sweet potatoes and pumpkin leaf sauce and she looks at it as if it's a pile of mud. I sigh and sit on the bench in the parlor. I am tired, the child has wrung me out, I have nothing left with which to break her and remake her. I stand up and, between clenched teeth, tell her that she's ungrateful and selfish and the most spiteful child ever born to a woman. She stares at me as if I'm an empty vessel making a loud noise, as if my disappointment is no match for her resolve. I'm about to accuse her of having neither scruples nor shame about adding to my anguish when Yaya calls for me. When I go to Yaya, she tells me to please give Thula what she's asking for.

It was on that day that I began going from hut to hut, trying to convince fathers to allow their children to ride the bus with Thula to the school in Lokunja.

Over and over, I hear that a girl does not need to ride a bus to get more knowledge than what the village school is offering. I am given a summary of what the government has done to us, what it is still doing to us. I am told, lest I've forgotten, that the children of Kosawa are still in danger, that they're still dying even though the Restoration Movement has shamed Pexton into providing us bottled water for the babies. I am lectured that no one in Kosawa should ever trust the government even if the Sweet One and the Cute One tell us that we can in some instances, that we should never enter a building owned by the government unless we must, and that, even then, we would need to grow eyes in our ears and eyes in the back of our necks; we should never think the government wants anything but our demise—the government is not made up of people with souls and hearts of flesh.

I listen to all this and more.

I say, Yes, Papa, to every father, and Yes, Big Papa, to every grandfather.

They ask me questions and I respond in a manner that suggests I don't know much about what I'm trying to say. I nod while they speak, limiting eye contact. They have to see how much I revere their wisdom. They want to know why I'm doing this, why I can't just tell my daughter no. Isn't it time my daughter learned to understand her choices in life? Why haven't I advised my daughter that the most important knowledge she will ever need as a woman is how to find contentment with whatever life offers her?

I cannot argue or defend my choice; I'm not allowed to, for the sake of respect.

I only tell them that a mother's love compels me.

A couple of times, Cocody's younger cousin Aisha, who's become like a little sister to me, comes along to help me in my persuasion. Once, when a grandfather tells us that in the olden days women wouldn't dare walk around the village taking up the precious time of men for the sake of girls, Aisha, with only the slightest hint of humility in her voice, tells the grandfather that in the days to come the world will function the way women want it to. I'm too shocked to laugh.

After weeks of entering and exiting every hut in Kosawa, four fathers tell me they'll allow nine of their sons to ride the bus with Thula to Lokunja. None of them share with me the reasons behind their decisions; they simply tell me, when I show up to their huts for a third or fourth time, that I don't need to repeat myself, their sons will be taking the bus, but not for my daughter's sake. The rest of the fathers find a reason to avoid me when they see me approaching—Papa just left to go visit his uncle, a child says; he went to the forest to check on his trap, a wife tells me, though it's dark outside. I sit and wait while children play around me. I force chats with wives I'm not friendly with, women to whom I say little more than a hello around the village. After doing enough of these, I decide nine boys will be plenty to share the bus with Thula.

On the night I tell Thula that I went earlier in the day to the Restoration Movement's office in Lokunja and spoke to the Sweet One and the Cute One and they agreed to start sending the bus when the school year ends and the next school year begins, she jumps for joy, wearing the biggest smile she's worn in years. She runs over to me and hugs me, her thin arms tight around my neck. I hold her close and arrest my tears.

I think of Malabo.

That was how she used to hug him, when he walked around with a semi-smile and she was often happy, back when she was just a ticklish toddler, not a soon-to-be woman with thoughts she didn't share, back when my life was mostly lovely and no heartache was more than I could bear and I strove daily to do what was right, to speak no unkind words, to think no wicked thoughts, so that the Spirit would not, in wrath, wreck me.

⌃⌃⌃⌃⌃⌃⌃

THE BOOKS THEY GAVE HER at the Lokunja school became her pillow and her blanket, her plate of food and the water that quenched her thirst. By the time I woke up in the morning, she was up, in Bongo's room, sitting by the lamp, reading as if she lost the books in a dream and woke up to find them. She read while she was putting on her uniform and while she was nibbling on her breakfast. She read as she sat on the school bus to Lokunja.

In the evening, while she read, I looked at her and wondered what she saw in those books. She seemed to be in a trance while reading; sometimes a tear ran down her cheek. When I asked her what was happening in the books, she told me that it was hard to describe, it was more than she could put into words. When she set a book down and stepped out of the parlor, I looked at the cover. I cannot read, but I still remember my letters from school. I can recognize words like "of" and "the." One of the books was called P-E-D-A-G-O-G-Y "of the" O-P-P-R-E-S-S-E-D. Another was "The" W-R-E-T-C-H-E-D "of the" E-A-R-T-H. The one she most liked to read was a thin one called "The" C-O-M-M-U-N-I-S-T M-A-N-I-F-E-S-T-O. I once asked her if these were books her teacher wanted her to read, if all the children at her school spent as many hours reading them as she did, and she said that no, these three were Bongo's, the ones he brought back from his teacher-training program. She could read most of the big words in them now, something her uncle couldn't.

Those three books were her closest friends. She loved her schoolbooks too—once, I overheard her telling Juba a story from one of them, about a young woman in Europe who commanded a bad man to cut another man's flesh in a way that no blood would spill, and the bad man couldn't do it. When Juba said the young woman sounded crazy, Thula said she didn't think so—when she grew up she wanted to be like that young woman.

She still went to visit her friends, a book in one hand.

Older boys lingered around them, and Thula would sometimes converse and smile, but she did not put down her books. It was as if she was trying to send a message to the boys: If you want to get to me, you must prove yourself worthy of my putting down my book for you. Even as an early adolescent, you could see on her face that she found it all to be a sort of debasement, this desperation to be found worthy by a man whose brain was no match for hers. Sometimes I thought she would prove me wrong and be the first of her friends to get married—a woman who's uninterested is often the one men want. On quiet days, I amused myself by fantasizing about men arriving in Kosawa to fight for her. She knew she was beautiful, because Malabo told her so every day, and I saw no sign that she shared my worries about the burden of her size. Perhaps she wanted a man to run after her and offer pigs and goats for her hand, just like girls the world over dream. Whatever it was she wanted as far as marriage was concerned, she didn't say. All she allowed us to see was her and her books, loving each other. There was no semblance of sadness on her face during the hours she spent doing schoolwork, or reading while her friends giggled and ogled at shirtless young men. Perhaps her books sang lullabies to her at night after she put them on Bongo's bed, right on the pillow, next to her head.

IT WAS IN THULA'S FOURTH year of school that my young friend Aisha came to tell me that a date had been set for her to marry a man from one of the brother-villages. She had just turned eighteen and was in no rush to leave Kosawa, but her soon-to-be husband, on the brink of thirty, couldn't wait any longer to bring her home. She told me the news with no joy, as if she hadn't just achieved something spectacular.

"Try not to wear that long face when everyone is dancing and singing to celebrate your marriage, okay?" I said to her as we sat in my kitchen.

"Stop sounding like my mother," she said. "I didn't come here to get the same nonsense I get from her. I wish I could just run and hide until this whole thing is over."

"What whole thing?"

"The thing where you all dance and take me to his hut, he climbs on me, I give him children, he dies, the children grow up and have their own lives, and I'm free again."

"May the Spirit shut its ears to that wicked prayer," I said. "How could you call a curse upon yourself by wishing for the best days of your life to quickly pass you by?"

"Best days of my life? What part of serving others from morning to night every day for the rest of my life is going to be so wonderful?"

"Please, enough with your woe-is-woman song. You're not a child anymore."

Aisha scoffed. "You must be feeling very wonderful-is-woman these days, with the Cute One whispering cute things in your ear," she said.

"What?" I wasn't sure whether to laugh or to scold her for her disrespect. "Me and the Cute One—"

"Please, just stop it, Sahel, it's too late to pretend. I've seen you and him flirting."

"Me?"

"From the way he smiles at you I can tell you've shown him your moves."

I started laughing in confusion, which must have made her think she had cornered me, because she said, "I knew it. . . . I can't believe it—"

"Aisha, you're speaking rubbish," I said amid my laughter. "That mind of yours—I hope your husband tames it. The Cute One? Don't make me vomit. The very idea—disgusting."

"Right. But tell me one thing only, Sahel: where do you and him prefer to do it? In the barn, or deep in the forest so you can moan as loud—"

"Get out of my kitchen right now before I kill you with my cooking spoon," I said, raising the spoon as she ran off laughing.

The morning after my conversation with Aisha, I woke up thinking about the Cute One. I thought about him all day, wondering what he looked like naked. If someone had told me when I first met him that I would someday lust for him, I would have wept in shame. I'd never flirted with him—what Aisha said was her attempt to switch the conversation from her impending wedding—but now that Aisha had put the idea in my head, I started thinking: why not him? He was nowhere as handsome as Malabo, and his large belly carried the threat of suffocating me, but his hands were massive and his buttocks firm. Most important, his wife was in Bézam. She'd never know. I'd never wake up in the morning to find an angry woman on my veranda, demanding answers.

By the third day after my conversation with Aisha, knowing that the Sweet One and the Cute One would come to my hut to check Thula's schoolwork during their next scheduled visit, I picked out the outfit I would wear for the Cute One. I chose a dress I reserved for trips to the big market. I told Lulu I'd need to redo my hair in eight days. My breasts were no longer what they were when I flaunted them for Malabo years ago, so I stitched my sole brassiere to make it smaller and give my bosom maximum elevation.

If the Cute One was surprised to see me so radiant when he stepped into my hut, he did an excellent job of showing it. His eyes widened. He couldn't stop looking at me and smiling. When he asked me about the occasion I was dressed for, I told him that life was the occasion. He laughed louder than I'd ever heard him laugh. He seemed to notice my teeth for the first time when I smiled—he stared at them, the way Malabo once did. It thrilled me to do this again, falling all over myself for a man to see me.

While the Sweet One checked Thula's homework, I sat on a bench next to the Cute One in Yaya's room, pretending to touch him by accident as he asked Yaya questions about her health, and as she responded to his questions with short phrases about how she had no new complaints, every old person should be so lucky as to have someone like me. I smiled at Yaya's words, not because I needed to hear the praise, but because I hoped the Cute One would realize that I would take care of him too, in whatever way he wanted me to.

When he left that day without asking to see me in private, I did not fret. Nor did I fret the next time, or the time after. I didn't always dress up for him, but I could tell, from how he smiled at me, that it wouldn't be long before we made our first arrangement.

I could not read Thula's report cards, but I attended every parent-teacher meeting, always the lone mother in attendance on behalf of a girl. Her teachers told me every time what great intelligence she had, what a hardworking student she was, the best they'd ever had.

Everything I heard about her passion for knowledge, all the evaluations I got of her report cards, made me happy, because it made her happy. Still, I was aware of what a waste all her reading would amount to in Kosawa. All the hours spent doing homework—what good would it be after she finished her schooling at seventeen and became even more peculiar, an eagle among domestic animals? One of her teachers once said she could go to Bézam and attend a higher school so she could get a job with the government. I was not sure whether to spit in this man's face or to heap upon him every curse for suggesting that my daughter become a servant for the same people who killed her father. But then the Sweet One and the Cute One came to me at the beginning of her fifth and final year at Lokunja with the letter from the American school, and even though I still don't understand how going to America will help her after she returns to grow old alone in Kosawa, I agreed to hand her to them, because knowledge is what she seeks, and knowledge is what they'll give her there.

I worry for her every day and night. What if she needs me and I'm not there to help her? What did I think I was doing, letting a child of seventeen go alone to America? Will I ever see her again? When will I see her again? The Sweet One said how long she stays in America will depend on her, on how much schooling she wants to get before she returns home. I dream of her homecoming. I tell myself not to worry, and then I worry even more. I can't stop worrying for my children. But if I were to spend ten thousand years worrying about all that could happen to them, what difference would it make?

. . .

Aisha got married not long before Thula left for
America. How I danced that day. I couldn't remember the last time I so enjoyed myself. I was up before
the rooster's crow to make breakfast for Yaya and the
children, after which I hurried to Aisha's family's hut
to join the women of Kosawa in cooking. We sang as
we sliced vegetables, swapped stories as we diced and
fried. At some point, one of Aisha's uncles brought his
drum, and the preliminary dancing began, women
twirling buttocks and mincing spices to the right,
grating cocoyams and stamping feet to the left. From
the corner of my eye I saw Thula, peeling plantains in
a circle of friends—even she who didn't love to dance
was swinging her tiny hips in delight. By the time we
returned home to take our baths and dress up I was
tired, but my fatigue disappeared when Aisha was led
out of her hut, veiled and clothed in white.

In front of all of Kosawa and her relatives from
the sibling-villages, her father asked her if he should
accept the bride price that had been offered for her
hand. "Remember," he said, "once I eat these animals
and drink these bottles of wine, I cannot return them.
That means you cannot come to me and say you no
longer want to be married to this man. Once you go
with him, there's no coming back. Do still you want
to go?" When Aisha, in a soft voice, said, "Yes, Papa,"
her husband stood up and pulled off her veil, and we
all shouted for joy. We danced till the dust rose to the
sky. We ate and we sang and we danced some more,

till the moon appeared and Aisha left Kosawa, never to return.

By then, I'd spent close to a year waiting for the Cute One to do more than smile at me. I'd moved from dressing up for him to offering him and the Sweet One food, meals I made with the Cute One's enjoyment in mind. For my efforts, all I got was words of profound gratitude. Still, I persisted. Only after a random conversation, during which he mentioned his wife's name three times, did I decide to pour water on the fires of my yearning. I decided it was time to stop flirting with the Cute One and all the men I laughed too loudly with whenever their wives' backs were turned. I decided I could no longer be a part of the shameless competition—I would live with my plight for the rest of my days. I asked Malabo to forgive me for the infidelity of my thoughts and promised him I would be only his until we meet again.

I told Aisha this a few days before her marriage celebration, while we were lounging on my bed on a rainy evening. I told her to cherish these days when she had a man to herself, her own man, not another woman's she'd stolen. I told her to protect her man, because potential man-stealers like me abounded. She laughed, and sighed, before saying that it really was about time women started marrying each other. When I tried to laugh, she told me she wasn't joking.

She asked me to think about it, think about what bliss would envelop Kosawa if all the husbandless women like me met in barns at night and paired off and did to each other what we no longer had husbands to do to us.

And why shouldn't we do it? she went on. We'd lost husbands and children and our youth. We spent all day caring for family members who couldn't reciprocate. We were powerless against forces that considered us unworthy of being caressed again—what evil would we commit by indulging in one of the last avenues of rapture at our disposal? Why not celebrate our battered bodies, massage and stroke and tenderly release whatever desire was left in them? If we wanted men and there were none available for us, why shouldn't we do it for ourselves? Because we had no right to? Because the women who came before us and the men who lived among us said we dared not? Don't you think, she said to me, that the time has come for you to start living by your own rules?

THE PEOPLE FROM THE RESTORATION Movement promised me that they wouldn't stop asking questions till they found out the truth about what happened to Malabo, and where Bongo is buried. The Sweet One and the Cute One said it the first time they sat down with me, the same way they sat with everyone who had lost a child or a husband in Kosawa, going from hut to hut in those first months to compile the names and ages of those who'd been killed for the sake of oil. In a letter sent to us from America, which the Cute One read aloud, the Restoration Movement people told us that when they saw the pictures of the massacre they knew that ours had to become one of the villages around the world whose dignity they fought every day to restore. They would be the spear of Kosawa, they said.

Their full name, we learned, was the Movement for the Restoration of the Dignity of Subjugated Peoples. According to the Cute One, after Austin's first story appeared in the newspaper in Great City, the Restoration Movement people had held a meeting in their office to talk about the report; they'd long harbored suspicions about Pexton and its deeds in places where no outside eyes were upon them and no laws existed to compel them to do what was just. Austin's story had proved them right.

On the same day the story became public, the Restoration Movement people called the Pexton office and asked them for the truth: Did Pexton know what its oil exploration was doing to the village of Kosawa? Was Pexton doing anything to help the villagers affected by their spills and toxics wastes? The people at the Pexton office had stammered—they couldn't figure out how our story, so inconsequential, had ended up in an American newspaper. Pexton must have been very angry, because, from what we gathered, by the next morning the Pexton people in Bézam were meeting with His Excellency's men. There must have been quarrels and blames at that meeting. In the end, everyone likely calmed down and agreed that they had to find out as soon as they could why Kosawa was spreading lies about Pexton and, in the process, hurting His Excellency's image. I imagine it was at this conversation that the decision was made for soldiers to be sent to Kosawa—someone had to be held responsible for the smear.

I was at the back of the group that day as we crossed the small river. The death and burial of the man the children called the Sick One had so drained us that the warmth of the soft sun in our faces after a rainy morning did nothing to uplift us. Bongo was in front of me with Austin, who seemed in danger of falling from the weight of his shock and grief; it was clear to us all how much he yearned to escape whatever he'd walked into.

Everything in Bézam had gone far better than planned, Bongo would tell me months later, when I visited him in prison. Even before they left the city, Austin had sent the first story to his newspaper in America. When they arrived in Kosawa, Austin would take pictures and question as many people as he could, in order to write a second, longer story.

But while Austin was in Kosawa, every care would be taken to ensure that he knew nothing about his uncle's presence in the village. Bongo, Lusaka, and Tunis had debated this, how to tell the newspaperman not only that they had his uncle in their custody, but that the last time they saw his uncle the man was sick, after having slept on a bare floor for days. How much honesty did they owe Austin, considering the good he was about to do for Kosawa? If they told him, would he understand why they had to do what they did? What if he decided to write a story about it? Then the people in America would think of us not as a feeble lot throwing a desperate punch at their captors—simply doing what they must—but as people as unscrupulous as the ones against whom they were fighting.

No, they couldn't tell Austin anything.

All Austin would know was that his uncle had passed through Kosawa. Yes, that would be sufficient information. As soon as Austin did what he needed to do and left Kosawa, the Pexton men and their driver would be rushed to Jakani and Sakani's hut, where their memories would be erased, after which the village would bid them farewell. They would get in their car, Austin would take the bus, and uncle and nephew would not meet again until they were safely back in Bézam. If Austin, upon visiting his uncle, as he was likely to do soon after that, mentioned the letter his uncle had sent through Bongo, his uncle would have no remembrance of having written it. Because Bongo would keep the letter, Austin would have nothing to show his uncle as evidence that his uncle had indeed written a letter asking for help for Kosawa. Austin wouldn't understand why his uncle couldn't remember, but that would not be our concern. The next time we met or heard from the Pexton men again, they would be telling us not about what Pexton couldn't do for us, but about the date when Pexton would start making changes that would benefit us.

Bongo had closed his eyes and shaken his head ruefully after telling me all this.

As they were departing Bézam the evening after meeting with Austin, Bongo went on, he and Tunis snickered, whispering and elbowing each other once the bus was safely out of the city. Could the Spirit have been more benevolent in making their trip so seamless? At that same moment, back in Kosawa, the Sick One was a day away from death. Beside him, Woja Beki was praying. In the bus, to the right of Bongo and Tunis, Austin slept next to Lusaka, the American's head against the window, his face tranquil.

By the time the group arrived in Gardens, the Sick One's grave had been dug.

Sonni went to meet them before they entered the village; a child had spotted them approaching, a man of fair skin among them. Sonni pulled Bongo and Lusaka aside and told them everything. Right there, by a dried tree trunk, along the path that connects our huts to the Pexton oil wells, Bongo sat Austin down and told him the whole truth.

Austin had laughed at first, Bongo told me. He

thought Bongo was making a tale to amuse him. It couldn't possibly be true that he'd taken a bus with people he'd just met to a remote village only to learn that the people had his uncle's remains. But when he went with the men to Woja Beki's house and saw his uncle's body, he had screamed and dropped to his knees beside the mat on which the corpse lay. He had taken his uncle's hand and wept into it, saying: I don't understand, I can't believe this, what happened? Bongo said his cry bore the agony of a child realizing that the world was not going to fall into place for him. Everyone left the parlor so he could mourn in private.

When he came out of the room, red-eyed and runny-nosed, he walked out through the corridor to the backyard. Bongo followed him, but he said he needed to be alone. He found a rock behind Woja Beki's wives' kitchen and sat there, crying softly. Woja Beki's first wife brought him a plate of peanut sauce and rice; he didn't touch it.

When he finally stood up, he told Bongo that he was too stunned and in too much pain to think clearly: this was the stuff of nightmares. He needed to get out of Kosawa as soon as possible. Whatever we'd done, he said, how we thought it was going to help us, now wasn't the time for him to understand. He began crying again, his shoulders quaking. His uncle was a good man—how could we do this to him? How could Bongo have lied to him? Was it naïve of him to think Bongo was an honorable man because he'd presented himself as such? It didn't matter. All he wanted now was for Bongo to take him to Lokunja so that he could arrange for his uncle's body to be transported to Bézam.

Bongo never got to tell me how he was able to convince Austin to stay, or how he got Austin to agree that it was best his uncle be buried in Kosawa. Austin must have realized that something about his writing our story, and then being in Kosawa right after his uncle's death, would make the government suspicious of his involvement in our operation; years later, we would learn that not long before Austin arrived in Kosawa, the government had sent him a letter threatening him with expulsion from the country if he didn't cease writing things His Excellency did not like, and if he didn't desist from attending clandestine meetings where people talked about how to create "a better country." I never found out if Austin's surrender to the idea of his uncle's being buried in Kosawa was driven by grief, or fear, or a calculation that had nothing to do with Kosawa, because Bongo did not have the time to enlighten me.

On the day he told me the story, the prison guards, without giving any reason, informed all visitors, upon arrival, that they would be allowed only thirty minutes with their loved ones. By the time Bongo finished the food Thula and I had brought for him and got to the middle of the story, the prison guards sounded the bells and commenced barking at the women and children to give their final hugs and gather their bowls and utensils and finish their crying outside. The next time I visited Bongo, we had things more pertinent to discuss—Juba's nightmares, Yaya's health, the Restoration Movement's ongoing battle to free him. He never stopped believing he would be free again. None of them did. None of them imagined, on that afternoon of the Sick One's burial, that the day would be the last time they would ever see Kosawa.

∧∧∧∧∧∧

AT EVERY PRISON VISIT, WE sat on parallel benches in a room abounding in misery, the wives and children on one side, the prisoners on the other. All around, people spoke in whispers. Woja Beki always sat at one end of our men's bench, his face puffy and covered with a rash he'd contracted. Who could believe that the man in the dirty brown outfit that all prisoners were made to wear had once worn new American clothes and sauntered around Kosawa, a mighty rooster among sickly chicks? Who could imagine Woja Beki in a brick house upon coming across the crumpled old man? Even his gums and sparse teeth no longer seemed notable in a room of such unqualified destitution.

Lusaka, though he looked not much better than Woja Beki, always spoke in a firm voice, asking his wife and daughters about the farm, telling them never to cry for him, never to let anyone in Bézam see them cry. When the time came for us to say our goodbyes, Lusaka, smiling, always reminded his family to clean the boys' graves. A man who had once been rare of emotions, a man who awed us in how he kept every sentiment tucked in, had become a man unbound in prison, cheerful as if he were lounging in his parlor and his sons were alive. I wasn't ever sure whether to believe this new persona—if prison had truly freed him—or if it was all an act for the benefit of his family.

On my first visit to the prison, which I made with one of my aunts, every woman in the room had jumped up when the guard opened the door to let in the men. I ran to Bongo and held him, feeling the bones that had taken prominence now that much of his flesh had thinned off. He looked worse than I'd feared, more than twice his twenty-eight years. His lively eyes had turned cloudy and shriveled into a permanent squint. After he and I had hugged and cried and hugged and cried some more, we dried our eyes. My aunt led us to the bench, cautioning us that we didn't want to spend the entire visiting hour standing in one spot crying, and, besides, did we want the other women to take news back home about how suspicious our extended hug had looked and how odd it was that a woman would hug her dead husband's brother for so long? Bongo had burst out laughing, but quickly stopped, perhaps at the remembrance that said brother was Malabo. I told him about Yaya, after we'd sat down and wiped our eyes again and blown our noses—I told him how Yaya wasn't eating. He wept. I gave him the food Yaya had made for him. He laughed when he saw that she had put mushrooms in the chicken stew, even though Yaya thought mushrooms were bad for one's health; she'd done it to give him what little joy she could.

All around the room, I heard wives urging their husbands to eat, eat, there would still be enough left-overs for the coming days. Bongo and Woja Beki and Lusaka always shared their food with each other, and we all made sure to bring a bowl for Konga, though the prison guards never allowed us to see him. We hoped the guards would give him the food, but if evidence had existed that they didn't give it to him, we wouldn't have stopped bringing it anyway—Konga was one of us; we couldn't not try to feed him.

Out of spite, or out of fear, the prison guards kept Konga in a shed at the back of the prison, a structure that used to house the prison dog until it died. Bongo told me that, though all the prisoners lived in one expansive room, eating and sleeping on mats lined from end to end, dressing in each other's presence after bathing in the prison yard, Konga stayed alone all day and night in this shed, a chain around his neck, chains around his legs, chains around his waist, chains wrapped so tightly he couldn't do anything but drink water and eat whatever the guards tossed to him if they were moved to be merciful. Their generosity never rose to the level of letting him step outside the shed, not even to feel the warmth of the Bézam sun for a clipped second. It was in the shed that he urinated, and it was there he excreted, in a hole they'd made Bongo and Lusaka dig on the opposite end from where Konga slept on the deceased dog's blanket.

Day after day, Bongo told me, Konga begged to be set free. On the nights when the guards couldn't enjoy a good rest because of Konga's unrelenting pleas to have the chains taken off, the guards stormed into his shed. Every prisoner could hear Konga crying as he asked the guards, while they kicked and stomped on him with their heavy boots, who they were, why they were doing what they were doing to him, questions that only made the guards more determined to break and tame him, teach the foul-smelling fool a lesson. When Konga sang, however, the guards did not strike him—they seemed to find pleasure in his songs, songs that were always about a faraway place he'd never been to but had heard of, a place where the rivers tasted like honey and the grass grew so green it could be eaten raw; a place where the laughter of children echoed and voluptuous women made stupendous meals; oh, if someone could show him the way to that place. As he sang, his voice rising in rapture, it was clear his spirit was already arriving in that place. The guards, amused, would taunt him, telling him that they knew the place, but as a prisoner he couldn't visit it—if Konga was as powerful as they'd heard, why wouldn't he free himself and go to the place and get himself a fine woman and some sweet water?

I HAD KNOWN, WITH THE Sick One's death, that our situation was about to get dangerously complex, but I'd also hoped that Austin's arrival would cause something incredible to happen and absolve us of our role in the death.

As I was walking back from the burial ground with most of the village, I sent a silent prayer to the Spirit to spare my children and me, whatever might befall. My eyes were lifted up to the hills when someone toward the front shouted: Soldiers.

Quiet descended.

Children ran and hid behind their mothers.

Soldiers were in the square. Nine of them. Nine guns drawn and pointed at us. One of the soldiers shouted for us to approach.

We walked toward them, into the square. We stood in front of them, all of us except Austin. While we were still frozen, he had managed to escape their watch and dashed off to observe from behind a hut. It was from his hiding place that he took off the camera he'd been carrying around his neck. With this camera he began darting from the back of one hut to another, clicking, clicking. Only later, after the burials, would we learn he had taken pictures of everything, pictures he would send to America.

The pictures would show that Bongo and Lusaka went to the front of the crowd to speak for the village, though they wouldn't show what was said—Austin would write that down, what he heard. Austin would tell the American people how Bongo and Lusaka had informed the soldiers that our village knew nothing about this newspaper story the soldiers were referring to, they did not know why lies were being spread in America about what Pexton was doing to us. Austin would tell of how Bongo and Lusaka had stammered when asked which of them was the village head, before saying that neither of them was, officially, but the village had recently undergone changes in leadership. Austin would write about the moment when the spokesman for the soldiers—a man whose forehead was so large a hut could be built on it and there'd still be space for a front yard—had interrupted Bongo and Lusaka and barked for the real village head to come forward, demanding to know who he was, at which point Woja Beki had stepped to the front and said he was the former village head, his was the name the government had in its books, but things had recently changed. "What things have changed?" Soldier Forehead barked. Woja Beki was in the midst of mumbling a response when the Leader and the Round One and their driver, still in the back room of

Lusaka's hut, began shouting, calling for the soldiers to come rescue them. It was then we knew the end had arrived.

^^^^^^

IT'S THE BLOOD I'LL ALWAYS remember. When I lie dying, I may forget the sound of those guns as they went off, or the shrieks of mothers fleeing with babies on their backs and dragging by the arm any child they couldn't carry, but I'll never forget the blood of our people. Jakani's and Sakani's blood, the first to spill. Would the bloodshed have started if they hadn't come running toward the soldiers? Why didn't the twins stay in their hut? Two spears each, one in each hand. Spears faster than bullets. Spears that knocked four soldiers dead at the moment bullets entered the twins' skulls. Their blood shot upward before their bodies went downward. Four soldiers gone, and only two of us down. The soldiers had to at least even the numbers. Bullets began flying, felling children like little trees that did not deserve to grow. Felling mothers through their backs. Felling fathers as they attempted to save their families. Five children. Four women. Five men. We did not know who they were then.

Where was Thula? Juba was home with Yaya, but where was Thula? I cried out her name as I ran. Thula,

Thula. Only later would I learn that my child had lain on the ground at the village square through it all and acted dead; she had tried to run but had tripped and fallen. Afraid that her legs wouldn't be able to carry her fast enough, she had stayed still, hoping her death would be quick if they found her out. Only after eleven days of being unable to speak would she tell me that she had opened her eyes to see the soldiers reload their guns as her tears mingled with the blood of the slain around her: an age-mate one of them, a cousin another.

I ran past the burial ground. Some ran up into the hills. I found a hiding spot behind a tree. Thula, I cried out. The sounds of many others, calling different names, drowned out my voice. We heard more gunshots. We ran farther into the forest.

But Bongo could not run. Lusaka could not run. Woja Beki could not run.

The soldiers grabbed all three of them before we could say goodbye. They seized them and freed the Pexton men while we quivered in the forest.

The Pexton men told them everything; they must have.

I can imagine the Leader's face as he told the soldiers of the ordeal he'd been put through. Lusaka was the mastermind, Bongo his lieutenant, Woja Beki the great betrayer. There's one more, he must have told the soldiers. The crazy one, the lunatic, the brainless idiot. The soldiers went around the village looking for him. Come out, they shouted to Konga. Come out or we'll hunt down every single person in this village and finish them off. In our hiding places, we dared not breathe. They went into our huts and pointed their guns at the old and the sick. Where's the madman? they said. Tell us or you'll die. Yaya, on her bed, said nothing. Juba knelt before them, crying. Please, he said, I don't know. They went into the next hut, and the next. They came after us in the forest. Fast as they might have been, they couldn't get us—we knew the forest better, how to disappear in it.

They grabbed my friend Lulu's sister, whose limp made it hard for her to run as swiftly as the rest of us. Take us to the madman, they said. Lulu's sister took them to the school compound, where they found Konga snoring. They hit him in the head with their guns. Wake up. Konga woke up to feel his blood flowing from his crown to his mouth. Austin had trailed them there. Crouching behind a classroom, he took a picture of Konga's face, dazed; the Leader's expression, disdainful; he's pointing at the madman, undoubtedly telling the soldiers, that's him, that's him. Austin took a picture of the Leader's palm pressed hard against Konga's chest, his nostrils flared, his eyes gleaming with contempt as he all but said, I thought you were untouchable, go ahead, show everyone what will happen to me now that I've touched you.

The soldiers put their dead friends in their truck and took them away along with our men: Bongo, Lusaka, Woja Beki, Konga. When we were certain the truck had left, we started coming out of our hiding places. Some of us collapsed, running down the hills. Thula rose up from among the dead, covered in blood. From the forest and hills we all returned, to cradle our dead. Our wails reached the yonder world when we saw who the dead were, all of them lying around Jakani and Sakani. Eyes open. Mouths open. Blood oozing out of pierced bellies. One of my friends and her only child. A neighbor whose daughter was recovering from a long illness. Thula's age-mate had a hole in her chest. Children held their dead parents' heads and wept. Girls fell upon their siblings' bodies. Mothers buckled in shock; the rest of us held them, drying their tears while we cried, begging them to be strong, even though there was near to zero strength left in any of us.

The men carried the dead away, two or three men for each body, blood leaving trails from the square to every hut wherein a departed had once lived.

Jakani and Sakani were the last bodies to be carried away.

They died next to each other, hand in hand. Inseparable from birth to death, their blood flowed from their heads and down between them, parallel at first, before linking and flowing past their feet, diverging and turning upward, toward their heads, thereafter meeting at the top to encircle them. In that red circle they lay until six men came to carry them away, taking care to ensure that the twins never stopped holding hands.

We slept nothing that night.

We needed to wash our dead. And sit with them until their spirits fully left their bodies. Then bury them the next afternoon. How could we make coffins for everyone? We didn't have enough planks. No one could run to the big market to buy more planks on such a day. Someone said we could bury the children without coffins, but the mothers wailed their dissent—how could they fail their children in life and in death? We had to use bamboos. Coffins made of smooth planks and ragged bamboos. Ugly coffins, but at least our dead had a home in the ground, a semblance of safety before the maggots came.

Did we sing on that procession to the grave? Maybe others did; I did not.

From one end of the procession to the other, coffin after coffin sat atop shoulders, twelve in all. Plus the first twin coffin Kosawa ever made. If only I could be free of these memories: The volume of our collective wailing that afternoon. The sight of mothers and fathers and brothers and sisters and husbands and wives still wearing clothes stained by the blood of their lost ones. Thula walking behind them, still wearing her bloody clothes too, weeping, her three books in her hands, clutching them as if they were the source of her breath. My cousin Tunis in a daze, his oldest child in one of the coffins, a girl whose first bleed we had just celebrated—what does death gain from such cruelty?

We were returning to the burial ground only a

day after leaving it, no longer wondering what our punishment would be for what we'd done to the Sick One. We buried our dead side by side, paying little attention to who owned which plot. We placed the coffins in the earth and asked the Spirit for forgiveness for where we'd gone wrong—surely, we'd gone wrong somewhere; surely, we'd brought this upon ourselves. If not us, then our ancestors—which one of them had committed the wrong that doomed us?

We did not think we would have any tears left by the time we got to Jakani and Sakani's coffin, but that day we learned that within us lies an ocean. The twins lay side by side in their coffin, their hands still clasped, in the largest coffin our village had ever made. They would walk together to the other land. We would have no one to cure our ailments or intercede with the Spirit on our behalf, not for many years, not until a new spirit child was born unto us; who knew if, who knew when, that would ever come to be?

Austin took pictures of everything: The bullet holes in the dead as they were being washed. The twins' clasped hands. Parents kneeling by their children in parlors for a final goodbye before the sealing of the coffins. Thirteen coffins waiting in front of thirteen freshly dug holes. Children clinging to their parents' coffin before they were lowered into the ground, begging them to please don't go, please come back.

Our families from the other seven villages ran to us when they heard of the news. They came a day after the burials. Austin captured their faces when they went to the square and saw red patches of land where the earth had drunk the blood of our people.

^^^^^^^^
ᴡᴜᴜᴜᴜᴜᴜᴜᴜᴜᴜ

AUSTIN WENT BACK TO BÉZAM two days after the funeral and returned in a truck with his uncle's eldest son and other relatives. The men dug up the Sick One so he could go rest in the land of his ancestors. Austin had a message for us from Bongo; a friend of his in the government had helped him get into the prison to check on Bongo. When Austin came to the hut and told us that Bongo was alive and hopeful of his freedom, Yaya's tears flowed in silence; she ate for the first time since Bongo's arrest. We'd been certain that the soldiers had taken the Four to a place where they'd be handed the worst possible death, but Austin told us to eat well and sleep well and try not to worry, Bongo would be home again before long. He looked into Yaya's eyes as he spoke, Yaya's hands in his. Though Yaya did not understand his words, she understood his countenance of certainty.

Austin called a quick meeting of the families of all the captured men and told us to be strong—help was coming soon. The moment his pictures appeared in the newspaper in America, our story would be news there, and Pexton would be put to shame.

He was right. Two months after the massacre, the Sweet One and the Cute One, along with the man from the neighboring country and the man and woman from America, arrived for that first meeting.

The Sweet One and the Cute One—we can never forget their goodness. How they kept coming to visit the families of the dead and the imprisoned. How they sat in silence in every hut, knowing that no words could accomplish what their presence had. When we cried they looked to the ground, and when we offered them food they ate it.

Their dedication convinced us that the day of our restoration was nigh.

⁓⁓⁓⁓⁓

THOUSANDS OF PEOPLE IN AMERICA read our story. Hundreds called the Restoration Movement office in Great City to find out how they could help us. That is what we learned, based on the report the American man and woman brought during that first meeting. Mothers called, crying, after they read about our children. Young people marched around Pexton's office, shouting: Shame on you, Pexton; shame on you, murderers. We were no longer alone. Many stopped buying oil from Pexton. Money flowed to the Restoration Movement for our salvation. People who had seen Austin's pictures told other people, and those other people passed the story to their friends and neighbors. The Sweet One told us that the American people were like us, they passed stories from mouth to mouth, and that our story was spreading faster than a fire set off by a dry-season spill.

Pexton swore they had nothing to do with the massacre, but Austin's story in the newspaper had pictures of documents that proved their alliance with His Excellency. The more Pexton tried to argue that their business relationship with His Excellency did not mean that they endorsed the slaughter of peace-seeking people, the more people believed our story and the more money poured in for our salvation.

The Restoration Movement would use some of the money to cover all expenses related to getting our men out of prison, the Sweet One told us. They would allocate part of it to pay for a bus to take us to Bézam every three weeks to visit our prisoners. After their release, the Restoration Movement would use the rest of the money to hire the best American lawyers to fight Pexton until it met our demands. We cried our first tears of relief during those meetings, though so mingled was our hope with our sorrow that we couldn't exhale.

The Sweet One and the Cute One took us to Bézam every three weeks, as promised. Yaya, with her last bit of strength, went to the kitchen on every one of the early mornings before the trip to supervise the food I was cooking for Bongo. We packed for him fried meat and smoked chicken, things our relatives in other villages had brought to us, to share in our suffering. We packed fruits we had dried under the sun, so he could eat them when he ran out of his leftovers.

The trip took one day, since we didn't have to change buses. Sometimes on the ride, the Cute One read letters American people had written to us, willing us to be strong, reminding us that our battle was theirs too. He showed us pictures children there had drawn for us. One of them was of a little man and a big man, the little man standing and smiling while the big man was tumbling because the little man had sent his little spear into the neck of the big man. The Cute One told us that the child's teacher had taught him in school that, every so often, little men do triumph. We forced ourselves to smile: we had learned no such thing in school, it had never been so in our lives.

We reached Bézam in the early mornings. No matter how tired we were upon our arrival at the prison, the sight of our men, and the realization that they were still alive, strengthened us. We slept on the bus ride back to the village, exhausted in every way.

THE LAST TIME I SAW Bongo, he wasn't feeling well.

Just a cold, he said, but his eyes told a different story. He ate little of his food. Please, eat more, I said; otherwise, I'll worry, and I'll tell Yaya and she'll worry too. He forced a smile, knowing I wouldn't ever add to Yaya's suffering by telling her of his condition. I pleaded with him, scooped it up for him, but he wouldn't eat. Beside us, Lusaka listened to his wife telling him a story. Lusaka's daughter tried to make conversation with Bongo, asking him how he had slept, but Bongo avoided her eyes, which surprised me, Bongo never having been one to be shy around girls. Farther down the bench, Gono took notes while Woja Beki spoke between coughs. We had heard that Gono was running a separate endeavor to free his father—in addition to the one the Restoration Movement was running—but we had no way of knowing if it was true, or if it was true that Gono had angrily quit his job at Pexton after Pexton told him that they couldn't do anything to help him get his father out of prison. We also heard that Gono and his mother were no longer speaking to his two other brothers who worked for the government, because the brothers had refused to quit their jobs to show solidarity with their father. The brothers had supposedly said that they had families to feed, and Woja Beki had neither reprimanded nor frowned on his sons for their choice: everything he'd done was for his family too. We believed these rumors, though we had no way of confirming them—Jofi, Woja Beki's third wife, who had been our source of intelligence about that family, had fled Kosawa with her children the day after the massacre.

"Yaya will never survive if anything happens to you," I said to Bongo.

He held my hand and promised me nothing would happen to him. In that brief moment, I heard Malabo saying those same words. "I'll be all right," Bongo said, and Cocody, sitting next to me, nodded. Things were moving well, he reminded me; the Cute One had said that His Excellency had promised to set a date for the trial as soon as possible. He wiped his eyes and forced another smile. Tell Yaya not to worry, he said.

On the day the Sweet One and the Cute One told us that a trial date had been set, we rejoiced. We prayed the Four would get sagacious judges before whom they would prove their innocence. If any of them had committed a crime, then all of Kosawa had committed a crime, and we would pay for our crime as one people. We would never allow our own to suffer singularly for our collective deeds.

The elders decided to send a delegation to the trial, to serve as witnesses for the Four and argue that we had all seized the Pexton men, and we had all held them captive, and we had all killed the Sick One, and we had all stood by and watched as Jakani and Sakani thrust spears into the four soldiers. We would accept any sentence. We would ask only that it be fair, that the crimes of those who had pushed us into our transgressions be considered first if those who judged us were to call themselves just.

∧∧∧∧∧∧/

THE TRIAL DATE WAS SET almost a year to the day after the massacre. We took this as an omen from the Spirit that this cycle of dry months and rainy months in which we'd nearly run out of tears would soon be over. We'd had other years of suffering more than we thought ourselves capable of bearing, and we knew more tough years lay ahead, but this year that had almost made us believe we were objects masquerading as humans—how desperately we wanted it gone. Despite comporting ourselves for decades, despite never resorting to beastly deeds, we hadn't succeeded in persuading our tormentors that we were people deserving of the privilege of living our lives as we wished. But the trial—it could give us a major chance to convince them to rethink us, get to know us for who we are, and in the process find us worthy of reclaiming the pleasure of quiet existence we'd lost.

We woke up that morning and put on our best clothes.

On the way to Bézam, we beseeched the Spirit for mercy, and thanked the Spirit for promising us justice in unspoken ways. Thula came with me—I wanted never to forget the moment when she and Bongo walked out of that prison, hand in hand, smiling.

When we got to the courthouse, a guard met us in front. He led us through a corridor and showed us an empty room in which to sit.

He left the room and shut the door.

We sat there in silence: Thula and I; Lusaka's wife, two of his daughters, and his sole surviving son; Gono and Woja Beki's two remaining wives and four of his younger children; five elders to speak for Kosawa. The guard hadn't permitted the Sweet One to enter the courthouse, saying that for circumstances like this only one representative was allowed to come inside the building. The Sweet One had wanted to protest, but the Cute One told him to go back to the office and to report to Great City what was going on.

In the bare room we sat, dreading the verdict and desperate for it to arrive.

We avoided each other's eyes, our hopes so fragile we dared not break them with a whisper. But we couldn't stay quiet forever. We were just starting to converse in low tones, wondering if the trial would be held in that waiting room, when the door opened and a different guard walked in. Without a word, he handed the Cute One a letter and hurried out of the room. The Cute One read the letter. His hands shook as he held it. He dashed out of the room. We soon heard him shouting at the guard. The guard shouted back at him, but their words were indistinct to us from the other side of the walls.

We looked at each other.

"What's going on, Mama?" Thula asked me.

Woja Beki's first wife looked at her son and asked him to go find out what was happening. Gono went outside. He remained outside with the Cute One. From the silence, it appeared they'd gone to another part of the building. We waited for over an hour. When they returned, Gono read to us what the government had written in the letter:

We wish to inform you that the four accused were hanged to death earlier this week for the kidnapping of four employees of the Pexton Corporation and for the death of one of the employees, Kumbum Owawe, and for their complicity in the murder of four soldiers of the republic. Our fair and balanced team of judges, representing the people of our country, deliberated for hours after listening to all witnesses, including the kidnap victims and the accused, before finding the accused guilty of kidnapping and murder and accessory to murder. The judges concluded that the accused did what they did in an attempt to extort money from the Pexton Corporation, a corporation that has done nothing but bring opportunities to the village of the accused and our country. The judges determined that the accused must pay for their crimes, for all those who seek to hurt the republic must be made to pay a price. They were hanged after they'd each made a statement asking Pexton and the people of our country for forgiveness. They asked that their families learn from their mistakes and choose to live wisely. Because of their ignoble deeds and death, they were buried in a shared grave in a location we wish not to disclose. We hope you will learn from their lives and go forth and live in peace.

The Children

WE WERE PARALYZED, GROUND TO BITS FINER THAN dust. When the bus returned from Bézam that day with the news that we had little left with which to fight, our bravest having been dumped in one grave, we knelt and banged the earth. We begged the Spirit to forgive our growing doubt of its existence, for though we had seen proof of its supremacy, we'd also seen evidence of its weakness, and we couldn't reconcile this, its inability to do no more than stand by and watch them destroy us. We had no Sakani for guidance, no one to help us comprehend what we were living through, so we crawled from one day to the next, too weakened to rise. How could we have been so reckless as to dream? Why did we for so long refuse to lie prostrate before the inevitable? Because we carry the blood of men who stood on a land between two rivers and received it from the Spirit? Because they told themselves that this land was theirs, to be passed to their children and their children's children, generation after generation? If our forefathers had known of the oil beneath their feet, would they have so gladly bequeathed it to us? They thought we'd never know such degradation, because we carry the blood of the leopard, but if they had seen the extent of our enemies' powers, their beliefs would have turned to ashes.

IN THE EARLY MONTHS OF the Four's imprisonment, the Restoration Movement had gone to dozens of newspapers across America with our story. Some of the newspapers sent men from Bézam to take pictures and ask us more questions about what we had endured at the hands of His Excellency's government and Pexton. Every time the Sweet One and the Cute One visited, they assured us that we had growing multitudes of supporters across the ocean. They showed us pictures of people in America shaking their fists in front of the office of Pexton. People all over America wrote letters to Pexton, begging for the Four to be released. Pexton told them that they had nothing to do with the men's arrest, it was up to His Excellency. The American people asked their leaders to speak to His Excellency, to threaten him if necessary, to say they would no longer help his government in times of crisis, they would eject him from groups he ought to belong in, they would punish our country so severely a recovery would be years-long. The American leaders said these things and more, and leaders the world over said the same, because people in their countries wanted no association with evil. Corporations in Europe that often gave His Excellency loans to create shared wealth told him that if he didn't release the Four they'd stop lending to him, they couldn't condone the unjust treatment of any human, but everyone knew that these lenders wouldn't stop making the loans—keeping countries like ours in their debt was why they existed. That is why His Excellency had laughed at their threats. He'd proceeded to show the European and American people how irrelevant their opinions were to him, for on the day he decided to hang the Four, he'd done exactly as he wished. Pexton had condemned what he'd done, and governments worldwide had done the same, but His Excellency had merely laughed some more and told Pexton that if they were so disappointed with him they could leave his country. But Pexton couldn't leave. There was still so much oil under our land—why abandon it because of a conscience?

Our village took the money Pexton gave as a token of solidarity, though, simultaneously, we cursed everyone who worked there. Alas, our curses can only harm those with whom we share blood, so no harm ever befell our foes because of the words of our mouths.

Indignant as our parents were, when the Restoration Movement began sending a school bus that Pexton had purchased as a gift to us—the Restoration Movement paid for the driver and the maintenance of the bus—they put us on it. In that first year, only a few of us went; most of our parents were distrustful. By the time the school year ended and none of us had been killed in Lokunja, more parents began putting children on the bus. Before long, the Restoration Movement needed to use its own funds to buy another bus, because all the parents wanted their sons over twelve to go to the school in Lokunja.

WE KNEW THE DAY WAS bound to come when our bonds as age-mates would start to fray, and we'd depend less on each other for friendship. We'd seen it happen to age-mates born before us. We'd noticed our older siblings' circles of age-mates dwindle when the girls' bodies started showing signs of womanhood, leading them to prefer the company of young men capable of giving them things their boy age-mates didn't yet have. By the time most children in Kosawa got to eleven or twelve, they'd decided that a shared birth year need not be the paramount basis for mutual closeness, leading to a rise in friendships with older adolescents. That is what happened to us when the boys continued going to school while the girls stayed home. The girls began spending more time with older girls and women: going to the farm, doing laundry, going to the market, taking care of babies, gossiping in kitchens. The boys went to school and spent their evenings hunting or playing football. Thus, it so happened that even before the end of our second year of taking the bus to Lokunja, we were no longer a pack of boy and girl age-mates traversing life together—just seven boys who got together often to do homework, and Thula.

By fifteen, three of our girl age-mates, all of them Thula's good friends, had found husbands. The girls who hadn't yet done so were attending every wedding they could in every village, hair braided and faces painted, hoping to meet a man in search of a wife, marriage celebrations being better than any other place in stirring within the unattached a longing to be lonesome no more. One of our age-mates became the woman of a soldier in Lokunja and moved into his house, which hurt and betrayed us, but the girl hadn't been blessed with sense to begin with. We tried not to speak ill of her, because we all needed to find love and move on to the next phase in life, hardships aside. Fate hadn't given us numerous chances to be children, but we'd grabbed every occasion we could; though now, as we went further into maturity, few traces of our childish ways remained. Still, no matter how far behind the past was, we saw its face with clarity even when we weren't looking for it. We couldn't speak of the future without segueing into a lament for the bygone days of our ancestors, those simpler days the likes of which we feared we might never see.

One of our age-mates had died in the massacre, when a bullet turned her years of daydreaming about a wedding day into a vile joke. Two of our age-mates died a few years later—one from the years of the poison that had accumulated in his belly, causing it to swell so high he looked like a pregnant woman on the brink of birthing, and the other in an accident, when the bus he had taken from Gardens swerved off its path and shattered against a tree. Though three laborers had also died in that accident, we had cursed Pexton as we dug our friend's grave—how could we separate anything happening to us from what they were doing to us?

Several of our age-mates left Kosawa in our mid-adolescent years, forced to bid their friends and cousins farewell by parents who had once sworn that they would never surrender to the gas flares and oil spills. One of our age-mates needed to leave the village because of a condition that caused her monthly bleeding to last for weeks, accompanied by blood clots and backaches and severe cramps. This friend had followed all the directions the womb doctor gave her and drunk the prescribed herbs, but relief never came. In the absence of Jakani and Sakani, she had no choice but to leave Kosawa in search of a cure. Other friends of ours had to move to new villages because a father had died and a mother deemed it best to live among her people, or a mother had buried more than one child and knew that the burial of another would be more than she could endure.

In their new villages, our friends crammed into the huts of relatives, sleeping on their floors, or in back rooms that had been vacated by married sons who had decided that it would be better to build new huts and keep their wives and mothers in different corners of the village. Our friends lived like vagrants until one relative or another gave them a piece of land on the village's periphery. There, they built huts that they worried would never be filled with the warmth of the ones they'd left behind in Kosawa.

Whenever they visited Kosawa, our escaped friends looked around wistfully at all that was once theirs. But when one of us talked about how the smoke blowing from Gardens seemed blacker than ever the other day, or when we sighed about how the amount of bottled water Pexton was sending for the babies was not enough, and how some babies still drank boiled well water, we saw our age-mates' yearning for home dissipate like dew. Sometimes they took some of the empty plastic water bottles with them, to serve as fuel for their fire—something we also did—or to bring their own drinking water upon subsequent visits.

Their gratitude for the hills between us was evident, the separation of our suffering from their new serenity. But nothing Pexton did could compel the parents of the rest of us to leave Kosawa. Most huts in Kosawa remained full and boisterous, and young women from other villages continued marrying Kosawa men and moving here to add to our numbers. Now that we were getting closer to manhood, we could have left of our own accord, we could have fled for a poison-free life, but we were determined never to give up our land, not then or ever, and the Restoration Movement and Sonni reminded us of this, that it was our land, come rainy season or dry season, it would always be ours.

^^^^^^^

SONNI WAS NOT SUPPOSED TO be our new village head. Woja Beki's firstborn son, Gono, had been next in line. If Gono did not want the role, any of his brothers could have taken it, but none of them wanted it—after learning about what our fathers had done to their father, none of Woja Beki's sons wanted to ever breathe Kosawa's air again, or concern themselves with whatever might befall us. After the hanging, Gono made a final trip to Kosawa to pack up his family's things and take his two youngest full siblings. Exactly how he was going to fend for them and his own family in Bézam, being that he no longer had a job at Pexton, we would never know, but we had better things to do than occupy ourselves with that. The women of Kosawa, however, made it their concern. They analyzed the family's situation from every angle and decided that Woja Beki must have given Gono some of his money to hide, which meant that the family was never going to lack, thanks to the government's and Pexton's money.

Gono moved everything from inside his father's brick house into the truck he had arrived in, everything from his father's bed and rug and clock, to his mother's mortar and pestle. All he left for his father's second wife was the house itself, nearly bare but still grand. Woja Beki's second wife, in her inherited house, had shed no tears—her co-wives and their children were gone; her children would now all have their own bedrooms in a brick house. We suspected that the woman knew—she had to know—that the day was bound to come when one of Woja Beki's older sons would return to take back the house; that family had never been known to be givers. Still, as we watched Gono leave in the loaded truck, we knew that the family would be gone from our lives for a long time. Indeed, it was so. None of them returned to Kosawa for the death celebration of the Four.

Though we did not know the date of the Four's deaths, we celebrated it at a three-month mark, and also a year after, using the date on which the courthouse guard had delivered the letter. We celebrated with the hope that the Spirit would not frown upon us for picking a date that, though not arbitrary, was far from precise, and nowhere in line with the exactness we needed to apply to ensure that the departed arrived safely in the next world. As we offered prayers to the ancestors on their behalf on the three mornings leading to the celebration—at the sound of the rooster's crow, kneeling in the parlor with our families if any of the men were our immediate kin, otherwise sitting alone on our beds or mats; eyes closed, our palms on our chests—we tried not to imagine how arduous their journeys would be, after having been tied by their necks and left to choke and dangle, then tossed into a pit, one body atop another, all still in prison garb, none of the bodies washed, their spirits forced to travel to the new world with the filth of the old.

For the first celebration we killed four goats and four pigs and sixteen chickens, as per the Spirit's dictate. We dressed in white, and wore no shoes. A medium from one of the sibling-villages poured libations and we softly played the drums, wishing the men the peace this world couldn't give them, a peace we would find when we joined them.

After this three-month celebration was when we made Sonni our new head.

One of our grandfathers, Pondo, had wanted to become village head. He said that, having been a counselor to Bongo and Lusaka, and also being a relative by marriage of Woja Beki, he knew what the slain men would have done if others had been hanged and they'd been left to create something out of our loss. Pondo said he could imagine the ways in which Lusaka and Bongo would have worked with the Restoration Movement to keep aflame the anger of the American people so our story would not be forgotten there. Manga, another one of our grandfathers, had stood up and reminded everyone gathered that he too had been a counselor, and that on the day of the massacre he had coordinated the carrying of the dead to their huts and made sure every corpse had a coffin. Manga argued that his son Sonni had no less wisdom and calmness than he did, and thus should be our new leader. Even more, he added, Sonni had the right to the position, given that he was first cousins with Bongo. With Bongo dead and having left no son or brother, and with Sonni the oldest male of all Bongo's cousins, the inheritance of Bongo's position should be his; Bongo wouldn't disagree if he were present, considering how much he admired Sonni.

We hadn't been allowed at the meeting where Bongo was anointed leader, but our fathers allowed us to attend the deliberations on who would be Bongo's successor, even though we were only a year older. They agreed that we were old enough, not in years, certainly, but in what we'd seen, for we had seen far more than our lifetimes were capable of digesting. Still, on that late evening, when the men gathered under the mango tree to talk about the way forward, we only listened, for we weren't deemed wise enough to contribute—we still had at least two more years before we would begin our entrance into the age of wisdom.

We watched as Pondo and Manga argued, and then as our fathers began taking sides because they shared a stronger blood relation with one man or the other. In the end, all the men agreed that arguments and side-takings would never give us a new village head. They resolved to come back three evenings later to declare whom they each wanted—whoever the most men wanted would be our new woja.

Such a thing had never happened since our ancestors arrived here—blood was the only means by which power was transferred—but we also knew that many things had not come to pass for us the way our ancestors had imagined, so, when the evening for the declarations came, the men who wanted Pondo to be their leader arrived with twigs, and the men who wanted Sonni arrived with stones. When they'd put it all down and counted it in the sight of the assembly, the number of stones was found to be more than the number of twigs, and so Sonni became our new head.

Pondo said no more on the matter, not even when gossip began leaping from hut to hut about how Manga and Sonni had visited some men late at night to convince them that Pondo was too old to lead us. Pondo was realizing, perhaps, that the village now belonged to the young, the old would soon depart, why argue against that? But if the Spirit were to be merciful, he might live long enough to see the day of our restoration.

^^^^^^^

WE SPOKE ABOUT IT DAILY, from the time we were seventeen, about the day we would repay Pexton in full. On verandas and in the village square and on our way to the forest, we spoke of what we would do to the Pexton people. What we would do to His Excellency. We fantasized about burning down buildings at Gardens, killing laborers, acquiring guns and going to Bézam and killing high-level government people. Such thoughts soothed us, the mere idea that we could make them fear us. We kept these fantasies to ourselves, for, though our heartache was no greater than everyone else's, we knew that, unlike us, our families and friends were clinging to the idea that there was no virtue in hurting our enemies. The massacre had so broken the village that Sonni and the elders had decided that our only recourse was to leave ourselves in the hands of the Restoration Movement, believe them when they said that they'd never cease fighting for us. Sonni repeated this during meetings, that help was on the way. But we didn't want to wait for kindly Americans. We doubted that their hatred for Pexton burned as fiercely as ours did.

We were talking about such things one evening in early 1988, on the veranda of one of our huts, when Thula came to tell us, with her very own mouth, that she would be going to America in a few months' time. If anyone else in the eight villages had said it, we would have laughed—Go to America to do what? we would have said—but because it was Thula, and because her countenance did not change after she said it, we did not doubt that it was true, that Thula was going to America, to read even more books. We hooted and hugged her and asked her if she would come back to us with a new skin color. She chuckled, and said that would be impossible.

We sent the news to our friends who had left Kosawa.

They were all there, three days before her departure, when Sonni gathered everyone in the village square, just after sunset, to rejoice for Thula Nangi, our Thula, who was going to America. We roasted three porcupines in an open fire, the women brought trays of fried ripe plantains, the men brought palm wine. All evening long we sang and danced. One of us was going to soar, and someday we'd all soar because of her.

Our fathers and grandfathers took turns pulling Thula aside to tell her what she needed to know about life in America, intelligence that we had no idea how they came upon. Thula listened to all of them, nodding—"Yes, Papa," "Of course, Big Papa." When one of them told her never to look directly at the moon in America, for it contained a magic that could shrink her nose and make it hard for her to breathe, she bowed her head and nodded, saying, "I won't look, Big Papa; I don't want to ever have a small nose."

We couldn't all get on the bus to Bézam with her—there were not enough seats—but two nights before her departure, we went into her bedroom, the back room of her family's hut, which used to be her uncle Bongo's. All of us age-mates who were still alive were there—girls who had become wives and mothers, some with second babies growing inside them; boys on the verge of becoming men who would one day lead Kosawa.

We sat on the bed and the floor and remembered the times we had lived through. We talked about our lives before Wambi died, those days when we used to bathe naked in the rain, when there wasn't much worth fearing. We mourned Wambi, and all of the others now gone, the latest the month before in childbirth. We went through the list, name by name, story by story, and we dabbed at our tears. Then we laughed about the morning we'd put a dead rat on Teacher Penda's chair. And all the mischief we'd done. We took turns hugging each other, and hugging Thula as she cried—we'd never seen her so happy and sad at the same time. We sang to her, and she promised us that she would never forget us, though we told her that we didn't need her to say it, we knew in our hearts that she would take us with her wherever she went. At the night's end we shared one long hug, as we prayed that we'd someday be together again in Kosawa.

^^^^^^^
ᴜᴜᴜᴜᴜᴜᴜᴜᴜᴜ

HER FIRST LETTER TO US arrived three months later. In it, she told us about her flight, how the airplane was much louder and bouncier than our textbooks had suggested. She talked about how the people in the Restoration Movement office had made a welcome meeting for her, in their office—they all wanted to hug her, and she'd hugged them. She said that though the food they'd served had little flavor, she'd been happy to eat with them, to be among people who knew her through the story of her people.

About Great City, she wrote:

I find it hard to imagine that New York City and Kosawa exist on the same earth and that I've been in both of them and lived such different lives. If it weren't for my memories, I'd swear that the previous days of my life were a dream, as there is nothing around me to confirm that I am who I think I am. The cold is enough to make me forget that I've ever been warm. What can I compare it to? Imagine being so cold that the hearth in your mother's kitchen, a bowl of vegetable soup with cubes of smoked meat thrown in, and the laughter of your family are not enough to give you warmth. Every time, before I step outside, I brace myself. One breath and all warmth is gone. I long to run back to Kosawa, but I didn't come here to flee. I take in the air slowly. I tell myself that, one day, I'll be warm again.

It's not only the cold that baffles me. This is a place where people stand in lines for everything, those who arrived first standing at the front, no one paying attention to who is oldest or neediest. The faces are of so many colors; sometimes, when I look past the colors, I swear I see a young man who looks like one of you, and it makes me happy. Yesterday, I saw this woman—she had the same smooth, skinny legs with feet pointed in opposite directions as Old Bata. Seeing such things brings me great joy. I wish it happened more often. There are afternoons when I remain in my room for hours because the thought of the distance between here and home is more than I can bear. In my bed, with my eyes closed, there is no distance. But then I rise and I remind myself that I did not come here to wish for what I'd left behind. I came here to find what I'm searching for, and I get it every day, in my classes, and in the books I'm reading, and in a meeting of students who believe they must do something about the things they cannot accept. It is there I've made some friends. Together we talk about what we must do for our peoples.

Some of my friends come from far away too and are as lost in this city as I am, even though they've been here for three, four years. Some of them are from America. They left their towns and came here to be lost and to be found, because there's no better place to feel as if you belong, and yet feel terribly alone, than New York. It's a sad feeling, wanting to be part of a strange, new world, while looking at it from a distance, watching those who've conquered it walk with high shoulders. Sometimes I take a bus from school to see what the rest of the city looks like. I look out the bus window at happy children and trash cans stuffed with the wastes of people with little time to spare. There's a great deal of speed over here; everyone seems to need to be somewhere sooner than is possible.

The roads here all have names, and the houses have numbers. I laughed when I first saw it—I couldn't imagine why we would ever need to put numbers on our huts. The names of streets are written on green boards, perhaps for the benefit of newcomers like me, those who need signs to help them navigate the city so that they may one day find their way out of it. The people around me seem to have no appreciation for this distinct orderliness of their world. I've never yearned for such order, since we have no need of it, but now that I see it—houses built in straight lines, streets as parallel as bamboo poles, everything with a name, days structured from sunrise to sunset—I recognize it as beautiful in its own way.

There's also a river here, running along the city's east side and past its southern tip. On the riverbanks are tree-shaded benches on which sit men lacking homes and women hoping for husbands, and people like me, gazing at the water. It is to this river that I go when I long for the quietude one can only get from the place of one's birth. It is where I'm sitting as I write this to you.

I must go back to my room now. The schoolwork here is harder than we had in Lokunja, but it's good for me. In a class I'm taking we're studying one of my uncle's books that I loved, the one called **The Wretched of the Earth**. I'm rereading my old copy and finally understanding it, thanks to all the lectures and class discussions. What this man has to say about what people in our situation ought to do, I'm in awe of it—my friends and I spend hours dissecting his ideas. I hope all Kosawa children will one day read this book; it's a whole new way of thinking. Tomorrow a friend is taking me to a meeting. It's in a part of the city called the Village, but my friend says that this Village is nothing like Kosawa. I'm fine with that—to be in a place named for the sort of place I'm from is enough.

Thank you for continuing to take care of my mother and Juba and Yaya. I know you do it not for me but from the goodness of your hearts, but

I thank you still. When you reply to this letter, please ask my mother if there's anything she would like to say to me that she wouldn't be comfortable dictating for the Cute One to write down. I don't think she has anything to say to me that she can't say to him, but I don't want her to ever worry that she can't tell me certain things. I know that you will relay to me honestly, and completely, all the news that I need to know.

Have there been any births since I left? Marriages? My welcome in this place has been good, and while I won't stay here a day longer than I need to, I'm glad I'm here now. Every day I learn new things. I don't know how, but I'm convinced this knowledge I'm acquiring will do something for our people.

I'll always be one of us,
Thula

What gladness her letter brought us. We could see, even on paper, that America was changing her. She was using more words, allowing us into what was going on behind her eyes. Perhaps being surrounded by friends who were like her in ways we weren't had set her free to talk about things she couldn't in Kosawa. Perhaps living alone had created in her a longing to talk more. Whatever the case, she could no longer be the inscrutable Thula we knew if she hoped to survive the life of an outsider. No matter the cost, the time had come for her to let in the world if she hoped to return home with what she sought.

We didn't have much to tell her in our response; little had changed for us.

We were still the seven of us, waiting for the rains to come and go, hunting antelopes and porcupines and taking them to the big market. We still got together in the village square and we attended death celebrations and birth celebrations and marriage celebrations, keeping our eyes on the girls we'd decided to marry, making sure they were still proving themselves worthy of our love and protection. The father of one of us had recently died, and we knew it wouldn't be long before all of our fathers left to meet the ancestors and we'd have to bear children to fill up our huts, and then become our fathers, and someday our grandfathers, though the thought of that did not delight us.

The village still met with the Sweet One and the Cute One. They rarely had much to report except for the fact that things were moving, slowly but certainly. They claimed that as soon as discussions between the Restoration Movement and Pexton were completed, the pipelines would be fixed and the waste swept off the river and the gas flares reduced. For now, though, they said, it would be best if we focused on the fact that children were dying less often, thanks to the bottled water, and buses were taking boys to

Lokunja to acquire knowledge. Before we knew it, Kosawa would be Kosawa again.

When we had asked them, at the last meeting, when they thought Pexton would leave, would it be years or decades, they had replied that, well, that was a tough question to answer. Our best option for now, they said, was to learn how to be good neighbors with the corporation. We told them that Pexton could never be our neighbor because the land wasn't theirs. The land was our land. It would never be theirs, no matter how often they said so. The Sweet One responded that he understood and completely agreed with us, but the ownership of the land was now a matter of law, only the government could determine who owned what land. He told us that, the previous week, His Excellency had declared that just because our ancestors claimed the entire valley as theirs did not mean the valley was theirs and ours as a result. Which meant that the land belonged to all the people of the country; the government, as the servant of the people, had the authority to give some of the people's land to Pexton so Pexton could use it to better the lives of all citizens.

At this revelation, we stood up, our voices raised in pained incredulity, this being the first time we'd ever heard such a thing. The Cute One begged us to calm down. He said the entire world agreed with us: no government had the right to make such claims. But until the day His Excellency agreed with us, he added, Pexton would not be leaving.

We told Thula this in our letter.

We told her that, based on the Sweet One's statement, we did not believe Pexton would ever clean up or leave our land; our children and their children would in all certainty live forever amid their poison. We told her we did not understand why the Restoration Movement was regurgitating such nonsense to us—the fact that they were doing so made us wonder how much our suffering pained them. How hard could we trust them to fight for us, considering that their most powerful weapon was words? Wasn't it time we stopped using words and tried something else, something altogether new?

We did not receive a response from Thula for several months.

The day we finally did was a rainy day when we'd all stayed home. She told us, in her letter, that the cold season had left the city and it was now close to warm, though not as hot as she wished. She'd done better in her classes than she had hoped. Then she said:

Remember that meeting I told you I was going to attend in my last letter? The one in the place called the Village? My friend was right, nothing about the place reminded me of Kosawa, but I cannot tell you how much the meeting energized me. The moment I left there I began writing this letter in my head, eager to tell you everything I'd witnessed. The people at this meeting were there to talk about what we could do about corporations

like Pexton. These people were not like the ones at
the Restoration Movement, talking about how we
can peacefully bring about change with dialogue,
negotiation, common ground, more dialogue. No,
these people were angry. One man stood up and
spoke of a place many days' travel by car from
New York, this place has pipelines too. The pipelines are not spilling like ours, but the people there
do not want them crossing their land, they say
pipelines are a calamity waiting to happen. Their
government disagrees, so these people have to live
with the pipelines just as we have to. Pipelines, in
America—can you believe such a thing? The pipelines here run under the ground, but the people say
it doesn't matter—simply having them deprives
their land of its sanctity. But their government is
not concerned about the sanctity of their land. In
this country, governments and corporations are
friends too. Over here, governments also sit back
and do nothing while corporations chain people
up and throw them in bondage.

And there's another place, on the other side of
the country, where children are drinking poisoned
water. The government knew the water was poisoned and did nothing about it. Listening to this,
I thought I was in some bizarre dream in which
America had revealed itself to be Kosawa. The stories were endless. There's also an area south of here,
where land is disappearing into the sea. Every day
land the size of a small village is lost, all because oil

corporations have the liberty to do as they please and the government chooses to do little while its citizens watch helplessly. I could hardly breathe as I listened to these stories about small corporations and big corporations, about government offices that said one thing when something else was the case, about representatives who told people nothing was wrong though they knew disaster was approaching. We knew we were not the only ones in our country, but could you have ever imagined that such things are happening to people in great countries too?

I'd long thought that our problem was that we were weak, lack of knowledge our greatest incapacity. My father, my uncle, all those who stood up for Kosawa and lost their lives, I thought they failed because they were unschooled in the ways of the world. I promised myself after the massacre that I would acquire knowledge and turn it into a machete that would destroy all those who treat us like vermin. I badly wanted to grow up so that I could protect Kosawa and ensure that children of the future never suffer like we did. Knowledge, I believed, would give Kosawa power. But these Americans, with their abundance of knowledge, how could they be powerless too? How is it that their government, which is supposed to be their servant, is acting as their master? From the books I read in our last years at Lokunja, I'd come to believe that if we could design a democratic government, just as is the case in America, our country would be a wonderful place to live in. But now that I live here I'm realizing that something far more complex is going on all over the world, something that binds us to these beset Americans and others like us in villages and town and cities in nations big and small. Whatever it is, we'll figure it all out, and nothing will be the same after we do.

I wanted to stand up during the meeting to tell our story too, but I didn't know if my voice would hold steady, and I wanted nothing of putting myself up for pity, this being my first time speaking in a room full of strangers. It was while I was urging myself to stand that I saw a slim man get up to join the line that had formed for those who wanted to speak. I saw that stringy hair moving toward the front, and I knew it was him. Austin.

He greeted the crowd good evening when his turn came. He said it was only his second time coming to this meeting; he'd lived for several years overseas and had attended dozens of meetings of this nature, and from them he had learned a great deal. He didn't know what he would do if such meetings didn't exist, opportunities for solidarity with the likes of us. If not for them, what would we do with all our anger? Put it in a bottle and light a fire in it and turn it into a good bomb, someone shouted. The room roared in laughter. Austin chuckled. He'd been to many places and seen the extent of human depravity, he said, but he still didn't know what he could attribute it to—greed seemed too trite a reason. All he knew was that there was much that we still needed to understand about ourselves before we could find solutions. There was one village he'd been to, he went on, he didn't know what the solution for the people there might be. He wanted to share their story still, because it was a story some people in the room might have read in the newspapers, but none had likely been to that place, except for him.

After the meeting, people gathered around to ask him questions about this village. I waited my turn, my heart pounding—it was all too strange. My turn came. I greeted him, smiling. He smiled back but said nothing, perhaps waiting for me to ask him a question. Unsure of what to say, I blurted out that I was Bongo's niece. His brow twisted; he seemed to be struggling to remember Bongo. Bongo, from Kosawa, I said. He remained confused. I repeated it, and whispered that I was there on the afternoon when the soldiers came. It was then that the look on his face changed to a blend of astonishment and something tender I can't describe.

I can't tell you how tightly he hugged me, or how much I'd longed for a hug like that since the day I left Kosawa. After we separated, I saw his face clearly—he was still prettier than any man I've ever seen. His hair was still as long as when we first saw him and some of the girls had giggled as they wished they could have hair as plentiful as his. Where he once had the residual softness of boyhood, though, he now had hard lines of manhood running around his face. It occurred to me that he had to be around the age my father was when he vanished.

We found two chairs at the back of the room. He asked me how I was settling in New York. He apologized for not having contacted me; the Sweet One had written to tell him that I would be arriving and ask if he could help me if I ever found myself in need of assistance. Austin said he told the Sweet One he would do whatever he could while I was here, but his newspaper job had him traveling all over the country; rarely was he in his apartment, in an area called Brooklyn. He'd actually forgotten that I was in the city; he didn't mean to be rude when I came up to him, he was only trying to understand why a stranger was talking about Bongo.

I nodded, averting my eyes from his, which were aglow with gentleness.

I asked him if he'd left our country of his own volition or if he'd been forced to flee. He told me his uncle's death and the massacre still haunted him, but he would have remained in our country given the chance—he loved its people. The decision to leave or stay, though, wasn't his. Two weeks after pictures of the massacre appeared in his newspaper in America, soldiers arrived at his door to escort him to the airport. They told him that His Excellency did not want in his country any newspaperman who made up fake stories— doing so meant that Austin was His Excellency's enemy, and thus the enemy of his people. Austin would have been glad to tell me more that night, I could see, but I knew I would meet him again, so I didn't ask if that meant he could never return to our country again. Besides, he had to leave to meet someone for a story. So we had another hug, and he held my hand as we walked out of the building onto the street, letting go only at the last moment. Watching him walk away, I couldn't decide whether he'd held my hand because he had a history with Bongo, or because the Sweet One had asked him to watch over me, or because he wanted to, for his sake, not for anyone else's.

We've seen each other twice since that day— he's come to visit me at school. We mostly talk about Kosawa and about how he wishes he could have done more for us. Not since my evenings on our veranda with my father have I sat down and spent so much time with someone else pondering life's whys. He and I will be seeing each other next month. He'll take me to this place called Brooklyn—I hear I can find food as good as ours there, I'm desperate for a tasty meal. But for now, what I'm eager to do is to return to the Village Meeting. I want to meet someone, a man who spoke at the previous meeting. This man, named

Maxim, said something that opened my eyes, something I must tell you.

Maxim was the last person to speak at the meeting. He was an old man, around the age of our grandfathers—he'd needed a chair to sit on while onstage because his legs wouldn't allow him to stand for long. There were over one hundred of us in that room, and none of us had made a sound as Maxim told the story of when he was a young man in a poor, cold country in Europe, how he and a group of his friends had burned down a government office building. He told us how they took oil and matches and just burned the whole thing down. His eyes lit up as he recounted the magnificence of the flame and smoke rising on that dark, frigid night. No one ever found out it was them. Months later, they went to another government office and ripped up documents and broke cabinets and sprayed paint all over. Afterward, they sat down on the floor of the office and drank alcohol. Then they urinated on the tables and chairs, laughing. Maxim laughed when he said this last part, and we all burst out laughing too, and clapping. We didn't stop clapping until he told us that it wasn't long before the government figured out who was responsible. The government arrested him and his friends; they spent a year in prison. That year was the proudest of his life, he said, because instead of sitting and talking and waiting for someone to do something,

he'd done what he could. He'd done what he believed he had to. He'd shown those bastards that
he could fight back, and that as long as he had
breath in him, he would never stop fighting back.

You should have been there at that moment to
see this man's pride, his fearlessness, how in awe of
it we all were. We stood up and clapped for so long
the sound of it must have echoed all the way to the
west end of the universe. My eyes welled up. Was
Maxim's message for me? For us? I remember all
the times when I listened to you talking about it
in the village square, saying we ought to hurt
Pexton. I didn't agree with you then. Burning a
building seemed so futile. Even burning ten buildings seemed futile. Pexton could rebuild Gardens
in a day. But perhaps the point isn't for us to hurt
them in a manner from which they'll never recover.
Perhaps the point is merely to let them know that
we're here. And we're angry.

Yesterday my friends and I were discussing
Maxim's story in my bedroom. There were six of us,
and only one person agreed with me that destroy-
ing our enemy's property could lead to anything
good. It's just not effective, was the consensus. I
argued that we can't decide based on the notion
of effectiveness—how can we know that a strategy
won't prove itself worthwhile generations after
being deemed a failure? Our duty is to do what we
can now. That is what Sonni and the elders are too
blinded by fear to see. Waiting for the Restoration

Movement to free us is safe but cowardly. I admit that the more I think about it, the more the idea of damaging someone else's property leaves me uneasy. But my father used to say we can't do only what we're at ease with, we must do what we ought to do.

Forgive me the length of this letter. What I most want you to know right now is that I'm open to listening to your ideas about making it clear to Pexton that it's not over.

I'll always be one of us,
Thula

In our response, we reminded her of the story about the ants that killed the growling dog, bite by bite. We could do such a thing too. There was no better time to start biting Pexton than now. Kosawa was in danger of becoming uninhabitable. We were about to start getting married, after which children would follow—how could we allow our children to suffer like we once did? If we tried something and failed, wouldn't it be better to one day tell the children that we'd done everything within our capacity? Thula agreed, writing:

Yes, if we are to be conquered, let it not be because we never fought. Our fathers, brothers, uncles, friends—what did they die for? They died so that we could live peacefully in Kosawa, and if not us, then at least the next generation. No one has the right to make us prisoners on our land. No one has the right to take from us that which the Spirit gave our ancestors. Across America today are pockets of people who were made prisoners on their land. The land of their ancestors was taken from them, and now they live at the edge of society, a plight worse than ours. At least we still walk the paths our ancestors walked, but who's to say that one day all of our land won't be taken from us like it happened here? The ancestors of these trampled people in America fought hard and they lost, but what's most important is that they fought. Much as the story of their defeat saddens me, it heartens me also, because I realize that, like them, we're not weak, a ferocious creature gave us its blood. The government and Pexton have left us with no choice but to do what we must in order to be heard. They speak to us in the language of destruction—let's speak it to them too, since it's what they understand.

Do it, knowing you have my blessings. I only ask that you harm no humans; we'll never become killers like them, because the blood of noble men flows in our veins. I'll send you what money I can to help, and I'll pray the Spirit to watch over you.

I'll always be one of us,
Thula

Yaya

IF THERE IS ONE REGRET I HAVE ABOUT MY MAR-
riage, it's how little I laughed. So much to laugh about
in life, and yet I deprived myself. Why? Because my
love for my husband demanded that I not bask in
bliss while he tottered in sorrow? Because, what really is there to laugh about in this world? But there's
so much to laugh about. Only now, as I lie on this
dying-bed, do I realize it: life is funny. People fighting
over a piece of land that none of them can take along
when death comes—how is that not funny? Everyone
wanting something to make them happy, only to realize once they get it that they want something else to
make them happy—how is that not funny? Life is a
chase after the wind, meaningless, ridiculous. How
could that have eluded me? Why did this world
become amusing only when I realized I was about
to leave it? Perhaps it's because I now have nothing
but time to spend thinking about how sad it is that
I didn't long ago realize it and laugh more. Alas, it's

too late for me to start doing so—the closer death gets, the less I care about the present. My thoughts are mostly of the past, the things I've seen. On sleepless nights, as I await a new day exactly like the old one, I think of the events that laid the setting for what would happen to my family, to my village. I think of stories my husband used to tell me on his better days, like how he once spent two weeks on a beach.

He was young back then, several years before we met. Three men from Europe were passing through Lokunja, on their way from Bézam, heading to the coast, where they would get on their boat to sail back home. They had lost one of their guides and were looking for a hard worker to serve as replacement; my husband heard about the opportunity from someone who knew about his discipline and thought he'd be good at it. This was long before he moved to Kosawa to work for Woja Bewa, taking care of his farm. He knew a guide job had its benefits but, like the rest of us, he was wary of men from Europe, these men who had come to make themselves masters over us. Soon, though, he found out that the men were going to pay him well and that his duties would take him to the ocean. He'd never been near the ocean; no one from our area had ever seen it. We knew it existed a great distance away, but not many of us wondered about it—we had streams and rivers, they were sufficient. But my husband wanted to experience more than was sufficient. So, fearful though he was of what unstated dangers might be involved in the guide job, he agreed to do it for a chance to see the ocean.

The day he set out with the men was the first time he'd ever been in a car.

He and the other guide traveled in the open space in the back of the car. In those days our country was mostly a landscape of densely packed trees, an odd village here and there, not much to see. My husband made a fire and cooked for the European men whenever their group stopped to spend the night in villages along the way or, if there were no villages in sight as darkness approached, in whatever seemingly safe spot the group settled in along the forest paths. His co-guide was from the Bézam area and had a sharp ear; the man had learned English and served as the Europeans' interpreter throughout the trip. The co-guide instructed my husband on how warm to make the men's bathing water, how long to roast whatever creature he'd spotted and killed for them, how to prepare and serve the dried fruits and sweet things the Europeans had brought from their country. The guide told my husband that the Europeans and their friends, stationed in towns around the country, were people of great curiosity. He said that the Europeans had traveled here to understand what kind of people we were, why we behaved the way we did, how they could help us so we could live better lives.

My husband let the other guide talk for most of the trip; it made the hours spent bobbing in the back of the car more bearable. Besides, the man couldn't have been silenced—he seemed incapable of keeping to himself the wonderful changes these European men had brought to the country. In his estimation, the Europeans' arrival had carried the brightness of dawn. Despite there being much he didn't like about his masters—how they spoke to him as if he were a dog, for example—he loved that they were giving him a chance to separate himself from his age-mates. His eyes shone when he talked about strolling around his village wearing clothes his masters had given him, the looks of envy his friends gave him, close as he was to becoming a European man himself. Though he missed his wife's cooking when he traveled, he enjoyed eating his masters' leftover food and drinking whatever alcohol they couldn't finish, even if the drink was nowhere as good as palm wine. He hoped the masters' mission would be successful. If everything went according to their plans, he said, people in every village in our country would soon be speaking English and wearing fine clothes and reading books and eating sweet things and owning cars, and maybe, he added wistfully, a child of his would one day own a car too, and he would get to sit in the front, no longer in the back.

. . .

My husband couldn't recall how many days it took to arrive at the coast; he had stopped counting after Day Two, deciding it best to be mindless of how far he was from the only world he knew. When he finally entered the coastal village of the European men's departure, everything about it was like his birth village except for one thing: the smell of its air. It was distinct, a scent he couldn't describe to me because, he said, it wasn't sweet, not exactly, it wasn't delicious in the way a pot of stewed chicken smells, but he could taste it and swallow it. It was an entirely new sort of pleasure for his tongue, this air the ocean was directing his way. He'd inhaled it, savored it, eyes closed, over and over.

He ran to the beach as soon as he was done helping the masters get settled in the village head's hut. The horizon was the first thing he noticed, its curve and expanse. "How can I describe it?" he asked me. "How can I help you conjure such an enormity?" Looking at it, he was suddenly aware that he was a mere speck in life's infinite wonders. He realized he was everything and nothing. He sat down on the sand, open-mouthed, slack-armed. He remained on that beach for hours, while the village's children swam in front of him, splashing water against each other. He was still there when fishermen began returning with their catch. Some of the fishermen looked at him on the sand with his mouth agape and laughed—they'd seen the likes of him before, one of those from the hinterland who had never seen blueness without end. That evening, he saw the sun enthroned at the horizon. He watched it bow before the earth. When he touched his cheek, there was water on it; that was the only time he ever cried as a man.

He slept on that beach for two weeks, while the other guide slid into the bed of a husbandless woman with whom he had an arrangement (the masters left on the third day; the boat that took them brought new masters, four Europeans who wanted to stay in the village for a while). Some of the men from the village offered my husband space in their huts, but he thanked them and said no—he'd soon be returning to sleep in huts for the rest of his life, but he would never again sleep on a beach once he left. In the evenings, he took beach strolls and bought dinner from women selling freshly caught grilled fish marinated in salt, pepper, ginger, and garlic; covered with sliced red onions; served with fried ripe plantains and a peppery dipping sauce. After the descent of darkness on full-moon nights, when the villagers came out to the beach to sing and dance, he helped the men beat their drums. For the first time in over twenty years of life, he was happy. But he knew that he couldn't remain in that village: a man belongs with his people, among those who share his ancestors, not with strangers, no matter how beautiful their land.

I REMEMBER STILL, WHEN I was a little girl, a day when two Europeans and their interpreter came to Kosawa. They came to tell us about their Spirit. They said their Spirit would bring us out of the darkness we didn't know we were living in. We would see the light.

The men were covered in mosquito bites and sweating, though it was a cool day, no sun in sight. One of them was old enough to be a grandfather, and yet there he was in our midst, saying he couldn't die until he'd told us the truth. We later found out that this man had been traveling across villages since he was young, convinced he'd someday meet fertile hearts on which the seeds of his words would germinate and grow. He hoped that the fruits born of those seeds would in turn travel far in our part of the world, causing all spirits to bow in surrender to his Spirit.

We gathered in the village square to hear them talk, not because we cared to but because our woja at the time believed all European men had guns—why risk being killed if we could simply lend them our ears for an hour? Their interpreter, a young man from the third of the five sister-villages, began the meeting with a song. Clapping his hands, he sang with his eyes lifted to the sky about someone who once walked on water, a man who had twelve friends who followed him everywhere—the song made no sense. When he was done singing, the European men delivered a message of how we would live a better life after we died if we turned our backs on our Spirit and chose their Spirit. "You have no ancestors waiting for you in the next world," they said to us. "Your ancestors are burning in a fire—do you want to join them there?" They did not tell us why their Spirit would throw us in a fire when we hadn't done anything to offend it. We wondered, as we listened to them, why their Spirit was so bitter and irrational. If we closed our eyes and said some words in prayer, the men said, their Spirit would become our Spirit. After we died, instead of joining our ancestors in the fire and burning with them for an everlasting night, we would spend our afterlives in a place where there was no night, just one glorious morning, a place where the roads were straight and shiny, and the gardens had the most beautiful flowers. Everyone loved each other there, and a choir in shiny white robes never stopped singing.

You should have seen how hard my father and the other men of Kosawa laughed after that meeting. This wasn't the first time they'd listened to such talk, but it never ceased to tickle them. They laughed even harder whenever news reached us of how someone we knew in another village had chosen the Spirit of the European men after considering what life in the fire would be like—no water to drink, everyone crying, no one sleeping. One relative, desperate to avoid these European flames, had thrown his family's umbilical-cord bundle into a fire, believing its power to be false, convinced that the only true power in the world rested with men from Europe and their Spirit. Though the likes of him were few, it revealed to me even then the fickleness of the heart of man.

I remember my father and his brother wiping their eyes after a long laugh. They couldn't understand how any man whose head bore a large enough brain could believe such nonsense as an everlasting fire. But they wouldn't have laughed if they'd recalled that, for generations, a different sort of fire had been burning down our way of life.

KOSAWA WAS SPARED WHEN MEN began arriving from the coast looking for humans to snatch and sell, but we should have known we wouldn't always be spared calamities coming from afar. The snatchers came generations before I was born. My grandmother told me about them—the story had been passed down to her of the time when men and women from distant villages appeared in Kosawa bloodied and in tears, bearing accounts of how young and old alike had been thrown into chains. The sick had been left behind to die alone, babies flung on the ground so their mothers could be dragged away with warm milk flowing down from their breasts. Those who had escaped had run for countless days before stumbling into Kosawa, their clothes turned to rags. Many more of them made it to one of our sibling-villages. Still in shock, they told our ancestors that they ought to be prepared—Kosawa or one of the sibling-villages was bound to be next.

Our ancestors fed the escapees, and allowed them
to make a home among us; their descendants live in
our midst to this day, though their blood has long
since been diluted by ours. From what my grandmother told me, our ancestors sharpened their spears
and created flight paths in the forest. They told their
children what to do if the time did come. But the
snatchers never arrived. Still, the fear of it happening
remained across the eight villages. With every arrival
of a new group of escapees presenting stories of villages
emptied out by snatchers, our ancestors made more
spears and machetes, though the escapees told them
that such weapons would be of no use, the snatchers
had a thing that spat fire and could fell a man with
one click. Even after new escapees stopped arriving,
men rarely went alone into the forest to hunt. Mothers
told their children to be good boys and girls, lest the
snatchers come for them. Few were those who slept
soundly through the night. For many years, Kosawa
was shrouded in disquiet.

Today I hear children joke about it as they play;
they say, Do this, or stop doing that, otherwise the
snatchers will come for you. Their friends laugh, and
I know they do so only because we were spared. In
my girlhood, young women even had a song about a
maiden who could find no husband and prayed that
the Spirit would send a snatcher for her, a man who
would seize her out of her father's hut and, upon seeing her face, make her his and cast off the chains of

her unweddedness. The young women giggled when they sang this song. I loved its melody, but now, in my old age, I wonder, what song would they be singing if we'd been stolen and displaced and no one was left to tell our stories? The ones who were taken, where are their descendants now? What do these descendants know of their ancestral villages? What anguish follows them because they know nothing about the men and women who came before them, the ones who gave them their spirit?

I once asked my husband why he thought Kosawa and the seven villages were spared. Was it because the Spirit had a fondness for us? The story given to us was that the most powerful mediums who'd ever existed walked among our ancestors at that time, and that these mediums had made a burnt offering of newborn pigs, and it was thanks to this sacrifice that the Spirit had caused the snatchers to never find any of our villages. The snatchers, if they'd walked past Kosawa, would have seen nothing of its huts or its inhabitants; they would have seen only the trees and shrubs. My husband had sighed at my question and said nothing, but I'd pushed. With another sigh, he asked me why those who were stolen had been punished for not having powerful mediums in their midst. Why couldn't the Spirit have shown them mercy in the absence of sacrifice? Besides, he said, we weren't spared, merely set aside to await the descent of another sort of terror. Which was true. Nowadays young people talk about the oil as if it's our first misfortune; they forget that, long before the oil, the parents of our parents suffered for the sake of rubber.

The young men who went to work in the rubber plantations did not leave Kosawa or any of the other seven villages with chains around their necks, but it might as well have been so. They numbered in the hundreds, my relatives among them, all taken away by law. Unlike the snatchers from the coast, who had arrived in darkness, these Europeans and their interpreters arrived in daylight. Guns pointed, they declared that every village had to volunteer men to work in rubber plantations—the new country they were building needed all available manpower. The Europeans picked out whatever number of able-bodied young men they needed. Those who resisted were shot dead. They assured families that the men they were taking would return as soon as they delivered their quota of rubber.

Only later would our people learn that, while at the plantations, their sons and husbands were beaten and starved and made to work long after the sun had set. If a man fled without delivering his quota of rubber, the interpreters came for his family. Children were pulled from their huts and beaten in village squares because their fathers had escaped the rubber plantations. Wives were raped. Mothers punched. No one was spared. Rubber was needed in Europe, and it was incumbent upon our ancestors to meet the demand. For the sake of rubber, a generation of our young men was wiped away. How many men from Kosawa died on those plantations? In their absence, the European men took little boys, whom they whipped because the boys couldn't tap the rubber fast enough. Through it all, though, Kosawa remained standing. Not every village the rubber men visited lived to tell its tale; we heard stories of some that were entirely eradicated.

By the time I was born, there seemed to be signs that peace would return to our area, albeit nothing like what once was. The stories of the snatchers now seemed like legend, and the hunger for rubber in Europe had abated enough that our people's blood no longer needed to be spilled for it. Still, the fear never left our mothers and fathers that some new demand would arise in Europe and their children would be taken away. As we entered adulthood, though, we saw no signs of a new affliction descending. The European men had been around long enough that we'd begun to fear them less, though we never forgot that they came not to befriend us but to make us do whatever it was that they wanted us to do. They introduced us to money, not because we needed it but because we had to learn how it worked for their sake. They forced their Spirit upon the weak-minded and built a church in Lokunja, not because we had any use for it but because they wanted us to believe that our Spirit was evil, our ways immoral. If they were to make us a part of their world, we had to integrate into our lives the principles by which they lived.

A few years after Bongo was born, we learned that the masters had decided to return to Europe. What a day of rejoicing that was. We would have no more masters. Our children would have no masters; they would spend their lives walking tall on their own land. Looking at my children growing up in a world that seemed in a hurry to distance itself from the one in which I'd grown up, hearing the chants coming from the village school in another man's language, I'd begun fearing that our ways would vanish in one generation, a shallow river besieged by a ruthless drought. Now I needed to fear no more. The ways of our ancestors could live on for posterity. Though it was too late to go back to living the way our forebears had lived under the laws of the Spirit, and though the departing masters did nothing to undo what generations before them had wrought upon us, we would at least no longer have them chipping away at what was left of our inheritance.

Through Woja Beki, the masters told us that Lokunja would remain the seat of the government for our district—the people who would govern there, from the district officer to the least of them, would be from our area; we would have an understanding with them. The seat of the government for our country, the masters decided, would be in Bézam. The masters believed that the Bézam people were the most intelligent of all the people of our young country. I always wondered how they came to that conclusion. We knew little about these people in Bézam, besides that they lived in the direction from which the sun rises. We did not think we belonged with them any more than we belonged with other people in other parts of the world, but the decision on that wasn't ours to make. Nor did we have a say in the Bézam man the masters picked to be our president. When that president died—we heard that the Europeans engineered his death after they decided he wasn't an obedient servant—we didn't have a say in the man chosen as our next president, the one who now rules us these decades later, the man we call His Excellency.

One night, a decade into His Excellency's reign, I turned to my husband in bed and asked him which he thought was worse: the European masters, or His Excellency. The madmen who created this farce of a nation, or the servant who took over the task of making sure it never fell apart. My husband shrugged and said he couldn't decide. Maybe the masters were better, I said. He did not respond. He turned around and went to sleep.

In every office and in every classroom across the district, a picture of His Excellency hangs on the wall:

right-leaning leopard-skin hat on his head, a vertical mustache running down his philtrum as if to grab snot before it dropped. We hear he was a soldier who became a minister by virtue of the ease with which he slaughtered. We hear he is responsible for the death of our first president, that he killed the man by making him step on poison—he was ready to be president and couldn't wait any longer for his turn. From the story that reached us, the masters had gone to His Excellency after they fell out with our first president, hoping that together they could devise a plan to oust their common foe within a year. His Excellency had told the masters to leave it to him; he had done the job in a day. Some say he went to a medium in his ancestral village and gave his manhood in exchange for power so he could rule over us for the rest of his days. Once a year, apparently, he goes to Europe so his blood can be drained and replaced with the blood of a younger man—everyone in this country will be dead and gone and he'll still be here. We hear that he does not sleep in the same bed as his wife, that his children do not carry his blood. He does not eat meat, they say, because he's a beast and cannot bear to eat the flesh of his brethren. We know little about his wife except that she hates her hair. It grows tight on her head like millipedes, exactly like ours, but this woman detests her hair so much that she shaves it all off, and her husband pays European people to make for her new hair, yellow in color, like the overseas women's, but high on her head, and wide and long, which makes us wonder why a woman with a rich husband would think it a good idea to walk around with a bush on her head. They say it's what His Excellency prefers.

We've never seen his face in the flesh; ours is a remote village, too far for him to leave his palace to see. We only hear stories that have traveled from Bézam through countless villages before arriving in ours. I cannot swear that the stories are true. What I can attest to is that, the day he ascended to the top in Bézam, this country became his property. From it he harvests whatever pleases him and destroys whoever displeases him. With our sweat and blood paid as taxes, he has built houses in Europe grander than we can fathom. He has hired European men to paint pictures of him dressed like one of their kings. He has bought boats on which he dines with Americans. They say his shoes alone cost more money than a hundred men make in a year.

Whenever I saw one of his soldiers walking around Lokunja, ready to shoot, I was reminded of his iron fist around our necks. With the power vested upon them by His Excellency, the soldiers needed permission from no one to mete out punishment. Laws were for us to obey, not to question. I have relatives in the sibling-villages who had to give up lands so offices could be built and roads that connected our district to the rest of the country could be widened. One of my cousins, they took his hut and left him with nothing. The soldiers said that if the government wanted someone's land, the government had the right to the land. My cousin went to the district office and cried, but all he was told was that nothing could be done: the orders came from Bézam, from His Excellency.

Then came Pexton.

They didn't arrive bearing guns. No, the men who arrived were a smiling group. It appeared as if, for once, something good was coming out of Bézam. The men told us about some people who sold oil overseas and called themselves Pexton. They said these oilmen did not operate under the orders of His Excellency, they answered only to the people who bought their oil. When we heard "overseas," many of us weren't sure what to think—what good ever came to us from overseas?—but the men from Bézam assured us that the masters and the people from Pexton came from different parts of overseas. They said Pexton was not from Europe, they were from America; they said Pexton had no relationship with our former masters. If we needed to know the truth, they added, American people were far better than Europeans. American people liked to mind their business and only do good—we would soon get a chance to see that for ourselves.

The one thing we had to know, they went on, was that if oil was found under our land, Pexton would take over most of the valley—they'd need a lot of land to do their work. We wouldn't have to give them the land on which our huts stood, but Pexton would need to pass equipment over the big river and through our farms; the equipment wouldn't bother us. We didn't understand how oil got under our land, but did it matter? All we had to do was sit back, let Pexton do its job and hand us our share of the money.

I remember someone at that meeting asking the representatives how long it would take for Pexton to take all the oil it needed and leave the valley. The representatives looked at each other and stammered that it wouldn't take long, not long at all. Of course it wouldn't take long, we thought—how much oil could there be under the ground? We imagined Pexton would spend months, no more than a few years, in our midst. In that time they'd pull out more oil than they would need. Then they'd be gone. When we asked if our thinking was right, the men did not tell us it was wrong. Nor did they tell us that Pexton would channel all of its production water and toxic waste into the big river. They did not tell us that poison might travel through the soil from their site and shorten the lives of our children's children. Why wouldn't we be excited when the truth was so artfully withheld? It was all too easy to believe the sincerity in their eyes. We began dreaming of how splendid our lives would be. Everyone did, except for my husband.

He did not believe any of it.

He told me it was unfathomable to him how we could all believe such tales after what generations of men from overseas had done to us, after what men in Bézam were doing to us. I tried to remind him that the men had said that the people coming for the oil were not His Excellency's people, and that they were not related to our former European masters, but he pushed my hand away when I tried to hold his. He said he never knew he'd married a fool for a wife. I was tempted to get angry, but I reminded myself that this was who he was—he couldn't rejoice at good news, he had to find some fault in it.

My husband went to see Woja Beki the evening after Woja Beki had gathered all the men of Kosawa and everyone had agreed that Pexton and its mission were no less than a gift from the Spirit, an answer to a prayer we hadn't even uttered. My husband told Woja Beki that he disagreed with the entire village; he said he did not believe this story about people from overseas sharing profits with us—why would they do that now, when they'd never done it before? He wanted Woja Beki to send a message to Pexton that we did not want them on our land, but Woja Beki laughed at him. You need to learn how to be happy once in a while, Woja Beki said. Wasn't being a perpetual woebegone painful? Why be so unbendingly glum when everyone was celebrating our good fortune?

What Woja Beki didn't tell my husband, what not even he knew then, was that His Excellency had already given the land to Pexton before those men came to see us; we had no say in the matter. We would learn this only years later, from a supervisor at Gardens who accidentally spilled the truth to Woja

Beki. We would discover that the men with tales of prosperity only came to see us because Pexton wanted them to do it for the sake of propriety, and because a man in the government, a man familiar with our customs, had suggested it. This government man had told the Pexton people that they needed to do whatever they could so we would rejoice at their arrival. In our joy, the man had said, we would call upon our Spirit to bless Pexton and prosper them in order that we would, in turn, flourish through them. It wouldn't hurt for Pexton to have the favor of our ancestors if they were to drill our land, the man had advised. The American people must have laughed at the mention of our ancestors: What can dead men and women do for us? they must have said—but, then, what would it cost them to send men here to tell us lies? Once we said a prayer for Pexton, the man went on, we wouldn't be able to take it back, for a prayer said is an eternal plea, and even if we changed our minds about Pexton, the prayer would stay answered and Pexton would remain on our land, blessed by our Spirit.

And, indeed, it happened so. In our delight at the news, we poured libations to our ancestors. We regarded the coming fortune as atonement for the centuries of pain and devastation upon which we'd built our lives. We prayed that Pexton would forever soar.

I TRIED TO TELL MY husband, years later, that he was right when he said all those things, that I should have been the one person not to make him feel as if he was a madman for having a singular opinion. He didn't want to hear it. He was angry still, because no one was noticing what was obvious to him: that Woja Beki was going to betray Kosawa. How did he figure it out even then? What about the young woja so differed from Woja Bewa—his father and our previous woja—whom my husband had trusted? Was it because, even as a boy, Woja Beki's affected pleasantness was discomfiting? My husband refused to attend the celebration of Woja Beki's marriage to his second wife, convinced that our village head was already in the process of swapping our blood for oil money. How could he have seen, even then, that our deliberate blindness would someday cost us every-thing?

What would he say now if I were to tell him how much this has cost me?

Would you still love me, dearest husband, if I told you that our sons are both dead, gone in part because we dismissed your words? Would you turn your back on me, or dry my tears for me? What would you do if I told you that there's no grave for our sons, because they were killed and tossed aside to rot like garbage, your own flesh and blood?

I don't need to tell—you know already, our children are with you.

They've told you by now what happened to them in Bézam.

You know better than I do the things that were done to them in that city of brutes. Things I do not let my mind dare conjure. Dreadful things I would never have imagined would befall them in those nights when I cradled them and shushed them back to sleep, beautiful as they were, life's most perfect creations.

You are together there. I am alone here. The worst kind of curse that could befall a woman happened to me. Do you cry for me from over there? Do you wish death would be merciful to me and hurry up?

I yearn to join my husband and sons, but Sahel doesn't want me to and I don't want to leave her just yet. I hope to stay with her until someone comes to take her away from this hut. Someone may be coming soon. A Bézam man. He wants to take her to Bézam. I've told her to go. I've begged her. She has cried and said she can't ever leave me, she can't leave behind what she had with Malabo. I tell her she must; this village, it's dying. I want her to take my grandson and go to Bézam—take far away from here the only person left to carry the Nangi name and make sure that my husband's bloodline does not disappear.

The day before Thula left for America, she, Sahel,
Juba, and I spent all day in my bedroom, entertaining
relatives and friends who weren't sure they'd be in the
village to give her a final hug before she stepped onto
the bus. Between visitors, we sat in silence, trying not
to think about the meaning of the next day. In the evening, Sahel brought the dining table from the parlor
into my room and we all ate our dinner from the same
bowls. Juba slept on the bed with me that night, and
Sahel and Thula slept on a mat across from us. When
the bus arrived the next afternoon, before leaving with
Sahel and Juba for the airport, Thula came and knelt
by my bed. She said, "Yaya, when I come back I'll do
everything to make sure Kosawa is back to the way it
was in your childhood."

My poor, sweet child.

I wanted to tell her, no, please, don't worry about
Kosawa, we have to let Kosawa go. But I could see in
her eyes that she wouldn't let it go. Determination
is her name; never have I seen her resolve broken.
Even as a baby, no matter how hungry she was, she
would push away everything until she got exactly the
food she wanted. As a little girl, if she didn't want
to wear a certain dress, she would fold her arms to
prevent her mother from putting it on her. Many
parents would have beaten that willpower out of her,
but Malabo refused to; he said children should be allowed to be the way the Spirit created them to be. So
all I could do on her departure day was lay my hands
on her head. I prayed for the Spirit to bless her and

keep her, watch over her comings and goings, now and forever.

Everyone said that Thula was a replica of my husband, his face on a girl's head. My husband's eyes shone whenever he heard this—he wanted the world never to forget that she was his. I still recall the day of her birth, the moment I brought her out of the room and handed her to Malabo, who passed her to his father. Has one human ever looked at another with more wonder? Whenever he held her, even when she cried, his pride was laid bare. He reserved for her most of the few smiles he was willing to give to the world.

I remember one night when I woke up and went outside to use the toilet—Thula was just past four months then. I heard the start of her cry as I approached the toilet, but I didn't hurry back, though she cried on; I figured Sahel had picked her up and was changing her soiled napkins. When I got back to our room, though, it was my husband who had her. He was singing softly to her. He'd figured out that Sahel and Malabo were not in their room—they were married people; it was never our place to ask them why they liked leaving the hut to go wherever they went in the darkest hour of night—so he had gone into the room and picked up the baby. I sat down next to him on the bed, and he continued singing until Thula quieted down. Her eyes soon became heavy, and she went back to sleep. My husband wiped away her tears. He rose and took her back to her sleeping basket at the base of Sahel and Malabo's bed. He didn't need to, but he stood there watching over her for close to an hour, until Sahel and Malabo returned home.

By the time he died, Thula was a girl, no longer a baby in need of being sung to and watched over, and yet my husband's spirit returned on many nights to sit by her bed. Malabo had put a little bed in my room after his father's funeral, so Thula could spend nights with me on occasion. Whenever Thula slept in my room, my husband returned. He wore a yellow shirt every time, his skin as smooth as if it had never combated elements. The anguished look he'd carried for most of his days in our world was gone; his new demeanor was of serenity beyond any I'd ever seen. He left in the morning, before the rooster's crow, and I spent the day eagerly waiting for Sahel to ask me if Thula could come sleep in my room again. Sometimes Sahel asked me and I agreed but Thula refused to comply, wanting to be in her parents' bedroom. I never pushed for it to happen—I wanted my husband to come for a visit only when life designed it to be so, not because I'd manipulated it to placate my longing to see my beloved's face. Sahel was pregnant with Juba at that time, and I knew that after the baby's birth my husband would stop coming, since the spirit of the newly arrived and the spirit of the recently departed cannot dwell in the same space, coming from and heading to lands at opposite ends of time. As Sahel's belly grew, I found it hard to sleep each time he visited, not wanting to close my eyes and miss a thing. I couldn't have enough of the joy on his face as he watched Thula, or the tranquillity that enveloped him, evidence to me that he was finally free.

The day Juba was born, I cried as I held him. Everyone thought my tears were for gratitude—one man gone, another come to replace him—but I alone knew why.

∧∧∧∧∧∧

PEOPLE ASKED ME OFTEN, IN the early years of our marriage, why I'd married him. How could I be happy with an unhappy person? Wasn't it tiring to always feel as if I needed to give him reasons to be happy? Wasn't it a burden, striving to be cheerful for both of us?

I gave them one response only: I saw in him things no one else could see.

To them he was cursed—dead father before birth, dead mother at birth, joyless spirit—but to me he was that bird sitting alone on a separate tree branch, singing a different song. How could such a bird be anything but beautiful? I remember the first days of our marriage, when it was just the two of us in this hut. He said to me only the things that had to be said, preferring the sound of silence. We could sit on the veranda for hours without saying a word to each other and I would feel as if I'd had the most enchanting conversation. Only with him did I come to realize how much noise there is in the world, and how marvelous it is not to be a part of it. In those days, his display of anger was muted; it was after he became a father that his temper began to run short. It seemed to me that there was something about having children to protect, little ones for whom he had to do everything in his power so no harm would befall them, something about making them happy when he couldn't make himself happy, something about doing all that in a world that to him was perpetually covered in darkness—there was just something about it all that was too much for him to bear, and he simply couldn't.

Malabo hated it when his father threw on the floor the food I had cooked because he wasn't in the mood for that particular dish, or it was too spicy, or not spicy enough, whatever it was that he had to complain about that day. Malabo insisted that I never pick up the food, that I let him do it for me; it was his way of atoning for his father. Whenever Malabo came to sit with me after such an episode, he'd ask me why I allowed his father to treat me like that. Wasn't I afraid that one day he would raise his hand and hit me? Never, I told him; your father's battles are with himself, not with me or anyone in this world. I always let him know that his father was suffering more than all of us combined. I did not tell Malabo much else, because a child need not be privy to the intricacies of his parents' relationship. I did not tell him how, lying in bed, my husband often pulled me close, held my hand, and asked me to look into his eyes as he thanked me for everything I'd ever done for him, and all the loads I daily took on for his sake and the sake of the children. I told Malabo nothing about how, on nights after his father had railed against my food, or a missing shirt, or a friend of mine who came for a visit and stayed for too long, he told me that he was sorry, and asked if I could forgive him. How long did it take for him to hurt me again? And yet I loved him still. And yet I pray the Spirit to take me to be with him.

How many people have I loved and buried? I wouldn't dare count. Which do you think is worse, to be the first to die or the last? You got the best of it, dear husband—you left after your parents and before your children. How many humans will be so favored? Yet I am thankful that I'm the one living with this sorrow—better me than you. Sometimes I try to imagine what your days would be like if our sons and I were gone and you were here alone. I wouldn't rest easy in the next world knowing this. You can rest easy for me. I take comfort in the fact that Sahel needs me, that she begs me to stay for a while longer.

Days come and go and I can no longer tell you how soon before the rains return. Juba doesn't come

to lie on my bed anymore. Thula is overseas. Sahel
hardly leaves the hut now, afraid I'll die in her absence. I want to live for her, and I want to die to set
her free. How can death be so sinister and stupid,
devouring children and leaving old people begging
for their end? If it's flesh the grave is hungry for, why
not take those who offer themselves and spare the
ones eager to drink up more life? Isn't flesh as good
as flesh?

I worry for Sahel, her loneliness. We are now two
women without husbands, singing songs of mourning
on moonless nights. But me, when I turn around to go
to sleep, the empty space beside me does not despair
me as much as it does her. How can she, in her prime
years, have no one to warm her? Did Malabo worry
about her future, or just his children's? Now she has
to spend her nights alone, never to be held by a man
again.

But why?

Who made this law? Did our forefathers allow
our foremothers a say when they designed our tradition? Why must Sahel's destiny be of selflessness and
sacrifice? Because she has me. Because she has Juba.
Because she has Malabo's memory. Because she's allowed one man per lifetime. She accepts it. She says
she has to. But I don't have to. I won't accept it. Let

other women do as tradition dictates; I won't let her join them.

I won't stop asking her to move to Bézam. Thula is far away. I'm dying. What is she staying here for? Her friend Cocody has moved to the second of the five sister-villages; Cocody's brother came and took her and her children away after her youngest child got so sick he almost died. Before she left, Cocody came to tell us goodbye, crying. She wanted to leave but she didn't want to leave. Sahel cried only after Cocody left. They'd been each other's everything after their husbands died: bringing each other food, taking care of each other's children, wiping each other's tears. But Sahel has other friends here. Lulu came over last night and made us laugh with a story about how her son came home from school in Lokunja and said that his teacher told them that our ancestors used to be monkeys—what other crazy things do those overseas books have to say about us?

Sahel has her cousin Tunis too. He comes often to split her firewood and help her dig holes to plant yams and plantains in her small backyard farm (she won't leave me to go to her farm in the forest). She also has her aunts and younger cousins, but her sisters—we never see them. Ever since her second sister was caught in bed with the husband of her oldest sister, her family has not known harmony or the joy of togetherness. Sahel was only a little girl when all this happened, but that didn't stop her from getting caught in it, since

she was living with their mother. Their mother had refused to take sides with either of her feuding children,
and it wasn't long before they all stopped speaking to
each other for a jumble of reasons no one outside their
family could untangle.

My husband was still alive when Sahel's mother
died. He told her, while she wept, that she shouldn't
fear, his family would always be her family, she would
never be in need of people with whom she could
have a total sense of belonging. But her mother was
her strongest link to her village, and Sahel knew
that, with her mother's death, the life she once had
would exist only as fragments in her memory. If she
were to wonder whether something had truly happened, there'd be no one to answer her questions, no
one to talk to about the way things were. These days
she sees her sisters only when she goes to a celebration
in another village. None of them came here after what
happened to Malabo and Bongo. She heard that two
of them have reconciled but neither they, nor the others, to mourn or to rejoice, come to visit. Who will she
have left here after her aunts are gone and her female
cousins have settled into their own lives?

⌃⌃⌃⌃⌃⌃⌃

I NEVER IMAGINED THAT THE situation in Kosawa
would get worse in my final days, but it has. This past

year, soldiers have arrived in the village more times than I can count. They go from hut to hut asking questions, searching for those responsible for the destruction of Pexton's property. When they come here, Sahel lets them check under my bed to make sure no one is hiding there. They don't believe that no one capable of sneaking around at night to burn and destroy lives in our hut.

The first time it happened, we had woken up to hear that a building at Gardens had been burned to the ground. We were not sad to hear the news, and it never occurred to us that the fire might have something to do with Kosawa. Weeks later, a pipeline exploded over the big river. I heard people rushing to see it for themselves. Sonni went to Gardens and begged the supervisor to send men to fix it before the riverbanks overflowed. The laborers closed it, but not because of us—we later learned that they had a new overseer who did not want a drop of Pexton's oil to go to waste.

A few days after this happened, a supervisor came to talk to Sonni. My brother, Manga, came to visit me after the supervisor met with his son. Manga said the supervisor believed our children were behind the recent fire and explosion. I shook my head. No, I told my brother. Not the children of Kosawa—they're not those kinds of children. Not long after that evening, a friend came to visit me. She had lost her remaining two teeth since I last saw her, but she could still speak a hundred words to my one. She told me that the gossip going around the village was that Sonni's wife had seen their son leaving their hut late one night, and that the next morning there had been another fire at Gardens. Someone from Gardens reported seeing Sonni's son there, though the boy denied it and said he was in bed all night. That is how we began to suspect that these children, born the same year as Thula, were the ones burning and breaking at Gardens.

The American overseer sent word that he wanted Sonni to come see him.

Sonni went to Gardens with the two men who have been helping us, our Bézam friends, the Sweet One and the Cute One. They went to the overseer's house, which stands a far distance from the houses of the laborers and the supervisors.

Manga told me that Sonni said the overseer's house was as cold as well water in the rainy season. It had white carpet all over, and more chairs than any one house could possibly need. Three men from the district office were there. When everyone had been seated in the parlor, Sonni was given one task only—to make sure that the vandals from his village stopped what they were doing; otherwise, Kosawa would have a lot to regret. But did the young men listen when Sonni brought back the message? No. They insisted that they didn't know what Sonni was talking about, that they'd never done anything at Gardens, that Pexton had enemies all over the world, it could be anyone.

Nobody believed these children—their intentions were evident in the ashes. Two of them had recently gotten married; their wives went to their new fathers and cried and pleaded for them to ask their sons to stop getting out of bed in the middle of the night to look for trouble. What could the fathers do? Their sons were grown men, with ownership of their own lives. My husband liked to say a man's feet can never stand on his head, but these children, they reminded the elders that, though that might be so, the feet could go wherever they wanted, and there was nothing the head could do except come along.

Pexton recently hired armed watchmen, but that only seems to serve as an enticement of sorts to these children. Today it's a pipeline break. Tomorrow it's a fire. Two months ago, they waylaid and beat a laborer walking along the big river in the darkness; a supervisor came to speak to Sonni, because the laborer had been so pulped he needed to be taken to Bézam for treatment. The laborer hadn't seen any faces: his attackers were wearing masks. When questioned, the young men swore they had been in their huts.

Sonni has held meeting after meeting to beg for an end to the destruction. Sometimes these young men don't even attend village meetings; Sonni's pleas mean nothing to them. Their mothers have implored them to stop; they've threatened to walk around the village naked so everyone can shame their sons for caring nothing for their mothers' dignity. Some fathers have said they'll bring out the umbilical-cord bundle. No parents have yet carried out their threats—aren't we all suffering enough from our collective curse?

In one of the village meetings, the Sweet One and the Cute One begged the young men to find other ways of expressing their anger; they encouraged them to write a letter to the government, tell the government how afraid they are for their futures.

The young men laughed in their faces; they don't care what anyone who does not share their zeal has to say. They say Sonni is an old man, and that neither the Sweet One nor the Cute One is one of us. They believe Kosawa is theirs, their heritage. They say it's their duty to fight for its restoration any way they want. But where has all the burning and breaking gotten them? Has Pexton picked up and left? Will they ever?

~~~~~~~~~

EVERYTHING GOT WORSE LAST MONTH, when a child in Gardens disappeared. The soldiers were here before dawn. They went from hut to hut and dragged out every male from the age of ten, barking at them to sit on their verandas and not dare take a step. I heard mothers and wives crying out for mercy, saying their men were innocent. Before I could scream for Juba to run, the soldiers were banging at our door. Sahel opened it. They shoved her aside and pulled out Juba as he screamed. From my bed, my hands stretched out. I cried, "Juba, Juba, please don't hurt him, he's only a child, he's a good boy." Did anyone hear me? Stand up, and run to the square, the soldiers shouted. The boys and men began running. Women ran alongside their sons and husbands. I could single out Sahel's voice, pleading for her only son's sake.

In the square, Sahel later told me, the soldiers made all of the boys and men kneel down and clasp their hands on their heads. The soldiers pointed guns at the backs of their skulls and asked for the whereabouts of the missing child. No one said a word. They asked again. No response. If the males remained quiet, the soldiers said, they would start shooting. Sonni, made to kneel alongside all the others, finally spoke. In his trembling voice, he told the soldiers that no one in Kosawa knew anything about this child, that he was telling the truth. He swore on his mother's grave. A soldier walked over to him and put a gun to his temple. Sonni closed his eyes, his hands still clasped on his head. His lips quivered as he struggled to prevent the entire village from seeing him cry. He swore to the soldiers that if he got any information about the child's whereabouts he would come to Lokunja. The soldiers asked him to swear again, on the graves of all of his ancestors. His father, my brother, old as he was, he was kneeling too, beside his son—the soldiers had deemed him strong enough to commit a crime, even though he walked with a cane. Sonni swore three times, louder every time. His own son was kneeling not too far from him—the son who was one of the young men heaping this new tribulation upon Kosawa.

The soldiers, guns still pointed, told everyone in the square to consider their ways. They said that if they deemed it necessary they would gun down every living thing in the village, babies and animals included, and no one would lay a hand on them.

They got into their cars and left.

Sonni pulled himself up. He was shaking.

"Why?" he shouted, looking at the young men beside him, his arms flung wide in frustration. "Why are you doing this to your own people? Haven't we suffered enough? We're so close to putting an end to all this and having the peace we've long been waiting for. Why ruin our chances when we have good people in America fighting for us?"

"Where are the results of their efforts?" one of the young men shouted.

"Let the soldiers kill us if they want to," another young man added. "Is it death you're afraid of? If we're not afraid of death at our age, why should you be at yours?"

"But why entice death when there's still a chance at life?" Sonni cried.

No one was listening. Angry voices, including his own son's, were drowning his, shouting back at him that the Sweet One and the Cute One were saying useless things, they were weak talkers. Wait, wait, patience, patience—that's all they've ever said. How long should Kosawa wait?

It was clear that morning that, even though few in Kosawa would have left their beds at night to burn and break, many got satisfaction from what the young men were doing. Anger that should have been levied upon these young men was directed at Sonni, for whatever choices Sonni had made that had forced the young men to take matters into their own hands.

When Sahel recounted this story to me, I wished Manga had said a word in support of his son instead of keeping his head bowed throughout the lambasting, but Sahel told me that Sonni was not without his supporters—men of his father's generation and some from his own had also rebuked their sons, telling them that they were idiots to believe that Kosawa could singlehandedly defeat Pexton, that they must have forgotten what happened where they were standing, on that afternoon a decade ago.

Last week Sonni and the Sweet One came to see Sahel.

They took a seat in my room, on the bench across from my bed. For a few minutes we tried not to talk about anything heavy, but few topics in Kosawa are soft in nature these days. During one pause, the Sweet One asked Sonni if the child who had disappeared from Gardens had yet to be found. Sonni shook his head. The Sweet One asked no more questions on the matter. We were silent again, until Sahel came to join us.

The Sweet One cleared his throat.

He said he wanted to tell Sahel something but he needed to say it in front of Sonni, so that Sonni could be his witness that he had told Sahel the whole truth. What he'd traveled from Bézam to talk about, he said, was very important: the young newspaperman from America, Bongo's friend, had written a letter about Thula.

I still remember the young man from America and his pretty face—he was good to Bongo, he was good to all of us. The Sweet One said the young man wanted us to know that he liked Thula. I looked at Sahel. We were both trying to suppress our laughter. This was confirmation of what we'd talked about after the last letter from Thula that the Cute One had read to us. In it, Thula had mentioned this young man several times, talking about how he made America feel like home to her. We did not want Thula to marry a foreigner, but if this man did not marry her, who else would? We knew her marriage to him would be fraught with mis-understandings, considering the different traditions that had shaped them, but we'd still thank him for saving Thula from the life we oftentimes feared might be hers. Thula, with a husband. Imagine such a thing.

But the Sweet One hadn't come to tell us that Thula might be getting married.

After clearing his throat, he told us that the young man had written to say that he was worried about Thula—she wasn't eating well, she wasn't sleeping well, she was spending too much time helping organize fights against governments and corporations and not enough time thinking about her own well-being.

The young man said Thula had recently traveled with some friends to another area of the country to be part of a human wall meant to prevent government workers from throwing poor people out of their homes and taking their land; the poor people and their supporters believed the money the government was offering for the land wasn't enough. Some days, he said, Thula did not go to class, instead spending long hours in one of the city's squares, chanting words of outrage. The young man said he admired Thula for what she was doing, there was nothing wrong with it, he had done some of it himself at Thula's age; he was actually the one had who introduced Thula to the organizers of some protests. The problem was that Thula did not seem to have a sense of balance. She appeared to have forgotten that she came to America to go to school, not to involve herself in matters that might undermine her well-being. There were nights when she and her friends stayed out in the cold protesting. She'd gotten sick once; right after she got well, she went back to doing it, to show her anger about the fact that a small group of people in the country had too much money while millions of families barely had enough food to eat and it just wasn't right. Once, the newspaperman said, Thula had spent a night in jail for her actions; he was the one who went to the jail and paid for her release.

Sahel and I were drying our eyes by the time the Sweet One was done talking. We wished we hadn't heard what we'd heard, that Thula was going around America tempting death. Is that why she wanted to go there? To bring upon herself the same fate that had befallen her father and uncle? Did she care nothing for what we had already endured?

The Sweet One wanted Sahel to dictate a letter to Thula to beg her to stop doing what she was doing, implore her to focus on her schooling and return to us safely. Sahel had to touch Thula's heart in a way only a mother could.

And could Sahel also ask Thula to stop writing letters to her friends encouraging them to break and burn Pexton's property? Sonni added.

Before Sonni was done saying this, Sahel had jumped off her stool.

"What are you talking about?" she said.

Sonni seemed taken aback, as if he'd only made the simplest of requests.

"How dare you suggest Thula has anything to do with that?" Sahel said.

"Everyone in this village knows it, Sahel," Sonni replied.

"Shut up."

If someone had told me Sahel had such rage in her I would never have believed it, but I saw it that evening. It was as if she was finally ready to scream out her pain for the world to hear. Her eyes alone could have sliced open Sonni from the top of his head to the part where his thighs join. She was pointing, pumping her fist, yelling, telling Sonni to get out of her hut, never come back into it if his intention was to accuse her daughter instead of recognizing his own uselessness as a village head. Sonni was too stupid and blind to see what his son was doing, too weak to do anything about it, and he thought it easier to blame Thula. Thula was not the problem. Sonni was the problem.

Sonni stood up and quietly walked out of the hut.

The Sweet One followed him.

It was then that Sahel sat down and wept.

Watching her, I knew I could never tell her that I agree with Sonni; that, like everyone else, I believe Thula has a hand in Kosawa's new wave of woes. The entire village knows that Thula sometimes sends money to her friends through the Sweet One. She sends us money too, whatever little she saves from working at school, which isn't a lot in America but a great deal to us. Sahel never keeps all of the money—there are too many people in Kosawa who need it. That may be why nobody ever talks about Thula's role in the destructions around her mother. But Sahel has to know it. A mother knows her child, even an enigmatic one. If Sahel refuses to believe the whispers, it's only because certain truths are too bitter to swallow.

Sonni hasn't come to visit me since that day, but Manga, having recovered from a recent fall, came two days ago to see how I was feeling. He didn't ask me if it's true that Sahel swore she would never speak to Sonni again. If he'd asked, I would have told him that Sahel's anger wasn't at Sonni, or at anyone among us. I would have told him that Sahel is angry because there's nothing else a woman in her position can feel besides fury. Which was why, that evening, I begged her once more to move to Bézam.

⌃⌃⌃⌃⌃⌃⌃

THE MAN IN BÉZAM, HE'S not a young man, but he's younger than my husband was when he died. He is the uncle of the Cute One, who is the same age as Sahel.

It was the Cute One who said to Sahel—and I don't know how it came up—that his uncle was searching for a new wife. The Cute One said his uncle was not a man who liked being alone; his wife had died eighteen months before. The man and his wife never had children—his wife had been unable to keep her pregnancies—but this man had never considered replacing her with a fertile wife. Now she was gone, and the man was alone in his brick house in Bézam, working at a government job.

The Cute One said that his uncle was a good

man, and that when they had spoken about his loneliness and his getting a new wife, the first person the Cute One thought of was Sahel, not one of the young women in Bézam. The Cute One told Sahel, in my presence, that he'd seen how well Sahel took care of me, and he knew Sahel would take good care of his uncle too, and his uncle would take good care of her and Juba in return.

Sahel looked angry when the Cute One made the proposal, as if she deserved something better. I didn't like the way the Cute One said it either: it sounded to me as if he wanted Sahel to move to Bézam to spend a few good years with an old man, followed by many years of cleaning him and feeding him and helping him die. But then I thought about how wonderful those few good years might be for her. Besides, who's to say the man doesn't have a decade of vigor left in him? My husband's hands were strong till the afternoon he felt pain in his chest, and was gone in hours. Even if this Bézam man is gone within a year, Sahel and Juba moving there will keep them safe from what's surely coming to Kosawa.

Last night, I called Sahel into my bedroom. I asked her for the seventy-seventh time to say yes to the man in Bézam.

"I can't, Yaya," she said to me.

"Why?"

"You know I can't. . . ."

I told her to do it for my sake, and for Juba's sake, but mostly for her own sake. She sighed. I could see she had been thinking about it.

"At least go with the Cute One to Bézam for one night and see the man for yourself," I said. "If he's too old, you can pass him on to me."

I'd intended for her to laugh at my joke, but she didn't. "How could the Cute One suggest such a thing to me, knowing I can't leave you?" she said.

I told her not to blame the Cute One. Men, thinking too highly of their intelligence, sometimes come up with ideas without considering the different sides of what they're talking about, but there's no use in our pointing that out to them. Besides, it didn't matter if the Cute One ought to have been more sensitive in making the suggestion, I said; it was a great proposal.

"If I go—not that I want to—but if I go, will Malabo forgive me?"

"That's not for you to worry about," I said. "Leave it to me. I'll handle him when I see him again. He'll be older than me in death years, but I'll still be his mother."

She chuckled. It was the first time we'd laughed about death. The lightness wouldn't last, I knew; our tears are still too close by.

"I promised him in my grief," she said. "I said that if he never returned from Bézam I'd never unite my spirit with another man's."

"When Malabo was alive, he told you what to do,

what not to do. You obeyed him, because you loved him," I said. "I sat here and watched you do as he wished, and you were never unhappy about any of it."

"Making him happy made me happy."

"Yes, but now he's gone and you're still making decisions based on what you think will make him happy in the next world. I'm old and dying, so I can say things now that I would never have said when I was your age. I don't care if anyone calls me crazy, so I'm going to ask you to tell me, Sahel: When will it end for us women, this doing what we have to do for the sake of husbands alive, husbands dead—when will it end?"

She shrugged, as if to suggest my question was irrelevant.

"Why are you punishing yourself? Because it's what you're expected to do?"

"But, Yaya, if Big Papa had left at a younger age, would you have remarried?"

"No," I said. "And I would have regretted it."

She was quiet. I knew she believed me; why would I lie, standing at death's door?

"I hate Bézam, I hate government people, but this man sounds like a good man," she said. "And I think Juba would be happy to have a new father."

"Don't do this for Juba. Do this for you."

"What about you? I'm not going without you. Will you be happy in Bézam?"

It was then I told her my plan.

. . .

You won't be happy when I tell you where I'm going to, dearest husband, but I must go.

You left that village long ago and came to the place where I was born and made it your home. You told me, often, that my people were more of your people than yours had ever been to you. Why did you leave? I asked you when we first met. You said you never belonged there. I pondered your answer—was not belonging ample reason for a man to visit his ancestral village so seldom? Was your all-consuming sadness the reason for your cutting your relatives off, or a result of it? I didn't understand why you were so determined to have none of your sons know much about your kin when there was no visible quarrel, no obvious falling-out involving you and your siblings and their children. I asked you repeatedly. Again and again you told me that there was no story to tell.

But there is, my dear husband. There is a story.

Why didn't you tell it to me?

Why did you choose to bear your pain alone, when you had me to share it with?

How could you not have let me hold you, and weep for you?

My husband's grand-niece, a woman named Malaika, was the one who told me the story; it was her grandmother who raised my husband after his parents died.

Malaika has been visiting me since Bongo was taken to Bézam. We had never met before my husband's funeral—she came to it along with his living siblings and several relatives whom my husband hadn't spoken to in decades. When I asked Malaika why no one in that family ever came to visit us, she said my husband had made it clear that he didn't want them to have anything to do with his new family. I told her that I understood, and that, now that my husband was no longer around to dictate to us, we could see each other as we pleased. She returned only once after the funeral to visit me, but when she heard about the massacre and Bongo's arrest, she began coming more often. After they killed Bongo, she came and she slept on the floor next to my bed, alongside other relatives from all eight villages. She helped in feeding me and bathing me; she was the one who made the mixture that allowed me to sleep for a few hours and escape the torment of the realization that my children, both of them, were dead.

One evening, not long ago, she came to visit. Somehow, we started talking about her grandmother, my husband's sister. Malaika told me that her grandmother, before she died, was desperate to talk to my husband one last time and tell him that she was sorry.

"Sorry for what?" I said.

"For everything that happened," she replied.

"What everything?"

It was then she told me the story my husband's sister told her before she died, a story the sister had never told anyone. A medium had told the sister, while she was wasting away with a large mass in her belly, that she needed to tell someone the darkest secret in her stomach in order for death to come, so she had told her granddaughter days before she died. She revealed what happened when my husband was seven years old.

You went to her one evening and told her what an uncle had done to you. How the uncle had asked you to go hunting, and how, once you were both deep in the forest, only bugs and birds in view, under an iroko tree, the uncle had untied his loincloth, spread open his legs, and said his manhood was itchy, could you please itch it for him? When you shook your head and averted your eyes from the swollen organ, he said he couldn't believe you wouldn't help him after all the gifts of fruits and nuts he had given you, he hadn't shown any other boy in the village as much generosity as he had shown you, he thought you were friends, how could you not help him in his time of need? When you started crying, he told you that if you didn't take the manhood in both hands and start rubbing it, he would leave you alone in the forest for beasts to feast on your flesh. That was how he got you to do to him things a boy should never do to a man.

You sobbed as you told your sister the story.

When you were done speaking, she asked you no questions. She merely told you never to repeat the story to anyone. When her husband, the man you called your father, came back from a family visit, your sister made you repeat the story to him. He too said what your sister had said, that the story must not be told. Not in their lifetimes, not in your lifetime. The uncle who had taken you into the forest was one of the heads of your family. He had two wives and nine children. No one would believe your story. Even if someone believed you, your sister and her husband said, what would they do about it? Would they undo what the uncle had done to you? They believed you, they said, because they knew you were a good child. But they also knew that the uncle was a good man. Whenever there were conflicts between family members, your uncle was the one who resolved them. He was a dear friend of the village head and one of his counselors. The village was what it was, safe and prosperous, because of men like him. Did you want to see the village fall into disarray because he'd done something you did not like? Wasn't it more important that everyone bore whatever they could for the sake of the family and the village? Your sister's husband told you to wipe your eyes, show them that you were a strong boy. Look at your body, your sister's husband said, did the uncle leave any scars? You shook your head. So there's nothing for you to dwell on, then, your sister said. As soon as you let go of the whole episode, there would be nothing worth talking about.

I pulled my blanket to my face and cried when Malaika was done talking. Even after she left, my tears wouldn't stop flowing. I wept for my beloved—him as a child, alone in his shame; him as a man, alone in his torment. She sacrificed him, his own sister. Made him suffer for her honor. She sewed up his lips so others would not speak ill of her for allowing him to tear apart the village with a vile tale. I spent days wondering why my husband felt compelled to hide this story, and then it occurred to me: even if he had revealed it in his adult years, how many among us would have believed it, or understood what it was like for him, a grown man, held captive by someone long dead?

And his sister—I feel so many things toward her, malevolent things, but I also force myself to imagine her suffering. How it must have devastated her to do this to him. How she must have fought with her husband to do something, anything, to which her husband must have told her that nothing could be done. Sacrifices, her husband must have told her, they must be made in life. He must have reminded her that everyone needed to make sacrifices for the sake of their families and villages and countries, to keep them together, to move them forward, to prevent them from falling apart from within.

How I wish you'd told me. How I wish you'd allowed me to keep you company in that darkness. I would have cried with you on the nights when your gloom thickened. I would have understood why you raved and yelled and insulted whenever you thought someone wasn't rising up and saying what needed to be said, or doing what needed to be done. You fumed at even the most inconsequential of events—an older child taking a younger child's toys and the adults doing nothing. We thought it was all just a part of your miserable disposition, your inability to simply let the world be the way it was, but now I hear the things you used to say, and I hear them differently. When we reunite, not long from now, I will lay your head upon my bosom and let you curse every form of wickedness for as long as you want. I won't tell you to stop. I won't beg you not to get too angry, such is life, these things happen. I won't tell you to calm down, let it be.

Oh, dear husband, I fear that, like you, Thula walks around consumed by all the ways the world has failed to protect its children. Like you, she seems doomed never to find peace until a new earth is born, one in which all are accorded the same level of dignity. How I ache for you both—you for the joy you never had, Thula for the disappointment that is surely coming her way. Why was she, of all the children, chosen to be this way? This longing to right all the wrongs she can, where does it come from? Did you, on the nights you visited while she slept, tell her never to accept that which is not the way she believes it ought to be? Please come back and visit her again, dearest husband, and tell her that it's all right, she can let Kosawa go. Please do it, for Sahel and for Juba.

My beloved and I will be reunited before the rains come, I can tell. I want to fly away on a dry, breezy day. I see his face already—him as a young man again, is he smiling at me? My journey from here to the land of our ancestors will be the fastest there ever was—I won't stop running until I arrive in that marvelous place and see my husband and children again and join them and my ancestors in blessed oneness with the Spirit for all eternity.

As soon as Sahel is ready to move to Bézam, Malaika will come take me to go live with her; we'll keep each other company. All three of her daughters have become wives and moved to their marital homes. Her own husband died long ago, and her only son did not make it past childhood, so she's alone in her hut now, with a bedroom across from hers, empty and waiting for me to move into it.

A gust of energy entered my body today. I may soon be able to take a few steps if I need to, but Malaika assures me I won't need to do much walking in her hut. She'll feed me and help me to the bathroom and the veranda, where I'll breathe the first clean air I've breathed in so long I can't recall. I would have preferred to die here, in this hut my husband built with his own hands, on this bed where we spent the best nights of our lives, but Kosawa might be dead before me, and I want no part of its end. I hope he'll forgive me for moving to the place of his birth. He left it and said he wanted nothing to do with his people, and for all those years I said we should visit them and introduce the children to them, so they could know their kin, but he said no, and I begged him, and he yelled at me. Now I'm going, after what was stolen from him there, but where else can I go?

The Children

WE WENT TO BÉZAM TO WELCOME HER BACK HOME, the five of us who were left. Death wasn't the reason our numbers had decreased once more, and for that we were thankful. Still, we wished, as we rode the bus she had sent us money to hire, that every single one of us who had ever lived could be there the moment she walked toward us, a decade since we last saw her, the thinnest and most quiet of us—who could have imagined she would one day become our leader?

Six years before she returned, we were still seven, but two of our friends later decided to leave for the sake of their families. One of them told us he wanted to be a part of us no more after an evening when we'd gone to set a fire at Gardens. Nothing about that operation had been far from the routine—we had once again outrun a watchman who fired shots in our direction as we disappeared into the darkness—but the next evening, while we were laughing about how close we'd been to our demise, deliberating what actions to take next, this one of us had sighed and said he couldn't do it any longer. Bravery wasn't his paramount virtue, clean as his heart was, so we did not try to reason with him. We did not ask him to consider the future when he told us, eyes on the ground, that he couldn't continue putting himself in such close danger of lying faceup in a coffin, or sitting in a prison, leaving his wife and young children more destitute than they already were. He argued that nothing had changed despite the pipelines we'd damaged, the fires we'd set, the tanks we'd destroyed. None of it had done anything besides force the government to get tougher on lawbreakers and double the capacity of the prison in Lokunja, a prison in which three of us were currently sitting. The three of us who were free gave our friend our blessings to be a part of us no more, thanking him for everything. We told him we couldn't put an end to the assaults, not until Pexton met our demands, which they appeared willing to do the following month, when they asked the Sweet One to tell us that a new overseer would soon be arriving at Gardens, and the man was eager to start a dialogue with us.

The new overseer came to meet with us within a week of his arrival at Gardens. On one side of him stood his interpreter; on the other side Sonni, the Sweet One, and the Cute One. The interpreter began the meeting by telling us the overseer's name—Mr. Fish, which made our children giggle and our wives cold-stare them down—the American town in which he was born, the many parts of the world he had traveled to, the years he had spent learning about our country. He said Mr. Fish was eager to start working with us so he could get to know us better and find ways in which we could live in harmony.

Our ears stayed with the interpreter, but our eyes rarely left the overseer's face. For more than an hour he stood before us, dressed in a wax-print shirt, ignoring the seat reserved for him despite the heat that was flooding his face with sweat. His constant smile gave him the air of a human with an open heart, the kind of heart we rarely saw from overseas or Bézam, the kind Bongo and Lusaka once hoped they would find in the capital.

From the moment this American arrived in Kosawa, having walked from Gardens in the evening of that hot dry-season day—he left behind his car, we later learned, to show us that the distance between us was small—we could tell he was no ordinary oilman. The brightness in his eyes was a balm for our disintegrating spirits.

When he entered the village, waving, young children—some of them ours, none of them acting differently from us when we were that age—peeked at him from behind their mothers' skirts. Several cried, finding the stranger frightful, never having seen a man with skin and hair so bright. But when our wives tried to take them home, they begged to stay so they could stare for many more minutes at the curious face.

We sat on stools close to the front at that first meeting with Mr. Fish, our older brothers and uncles still in the very first rows, alongside our fathers. Now that we were married, having child after child, we'd become the fathers, and our fathers had become the grand-fathers, and our grandfathers had joined the ranks of the ancestors, leaving us to be the ones whose words and deeds would determine the future of the next generation.

Our wives waited with our children under the mango tree. The women did not cry as much as our mothers used to in our childhood, but their faces bore little hope that the simple things that make a life content would be abundant in the lives of their children. Most huts in Kosawa were still full, but there were constant whispers about who might soon be leaving, who couldn't bear it any longer. Even if children were no longer dying as often as they did when we were younger, they were still getting sick. Pexton was sending less bottled water with each passing year, knowing there was little we could do to make them keep their word. Our air was getting dirtier, despite promises. They spilled their oil on our land with recklessness; we spilled it in vengeance. No new envelopes of cash had touched our hands, not even Sonni's hands—all we had was more of too little.

The interpreter told us that Mr. Fish had met the previous week with the district officer in Lokunja about releasing our imprisoned friends; the meeting had gone well. No mention was made of the truth about why our friends were in prison—the interpreter said nothing about the fact that the government's official story was as false as a snake walking on four legs. Our friends weren't in prison because they'd been caught at the big market without their tax receipts. Their tax receipts had been taken out of their pockets by soldiers who proceeded to rip them up in front of the entire market, their eyes declaring: We did it, what can anyone do to us? What could our friends have done as the soldiers handcuffed them and dumped them in cells? Who in Bézam cared for the truth that our friends had been framed because the soldiers suspected we were behind the attacks on Pexton's property?

We seethed, but we could say nothing.

At our friends' trial, no one who'd seen the tax receipts being ripped had been willing to step forward in their defense, so the judge levied a sentence of one year in prison and six months of taxes. We told our friends, as they were being led away by the prison guards while their wives and mothers and daughters cried out for them, that days might be long, but years were seldom slow. Once more, from what little she had, Thula sent us the funds to pay the fines.

During the year our friends were in prison, monthly, sometimes weekly, as often as we could, the rest of us burned a parked car here, dislodged machinery there, sent a letter threatening to kill everyone at Gardens if Pexton did not leave. Twice, we accosted a bus full of laborers on the road between Lokunja and Gardens. Our machetes pointed at them, we demanded all the money they had. We showed them no compassion, though they pleaded, saying Pexton paid them too little, they needed every bit of money for their families—could we find it in our hearts to be merciful to them for the sake of their children? How could we respond to such drivel except with slaps? Pexton's whores talking about children—nothing disgusted us more.

We made the bus drivers give us the oil from the engine, so we could use it to burn something else owned by Pexton. With raffia bags covering our faces—soiled and oily bills in another bag—we asked the laborers to listen up. We told them that it was time they thought about returning to their villages. We let them know, in case they'd never considered it, that they were our enemies by virtue of eating the scraps off the plates of our enemies. None of them would survive the reckoning coming for Pexton, we warned.

IT MUST HAVE BEEN THE Sweet One who told Thula
about the attacks and threats on the laborers, for we
made no mention of it in our letters. Zealous as she
was, she was still a woman incapable of inflicting
bodily harm, and we'd worried that our going after
the laborers would cause tension between us. And, as
certain as sunrise, it did. Every time she heard about
it, she wrote asking us to stop, saying that was not
the plan, the plan was to get their attention, let them
know that we mattered and we were angry, the plan
was never to kill—what were we thinking? We assured
her that we'd kill no one; we merely wanted to instill
fear in the laborers, cause panic in Gardens, make
them think we'd stop at nothing. She would not be
convinced. What if we'd killed the laborer we'd badly
beaten? she said. Blood on its hands was the last thing
Kosawa needed. The laborers are not our enemies, she
argued, Pexton is. In some letters she threatened to
withdraw her financial support from us. And there
were indeed months when the Sweet One brought us
no envelopes from her. Then, just as we were about to
start wondering if she had changed her mind and was
no longer one of us, we received an envelope, along
with pleas to remember that the laborers were fathers
like us, men with families for whom they were making hard sacrifices.

. . .

In the third year of our attacks, Pexton informed the laborers that it would no longer allow them to bring their wives or children to Gardens. The directive was late and inconsequential: the women and children had begun leaving more than a decade before, after three children passed away around the time our friends started dying.

We had heard of the Gardens children's deaths when they happened, but we never considered that they were for reasons similar to the death of our friends. For years, we'd believed that, between the clean water the children there drank, and the American medicine Pexton had for those living in the settlement it had created around its wells, no one at Gardens would ever suffer our fate. The Sweet One and the Cute One were the ones who told us the truth that no American medicine, no matter how potent, could cure a child of years of accumulated toxins.

There was no way for us to have known that in Kosawa.

No one from our village ever held a proper conversation with a laborer. In our childhood, we never spoke to the children in Gardens, not even when we sat next to them on the bus, full as we were of hatred for them, partaking in the scorn our parents had for theirs. They looked and acted like us, but they weren't children like us—they were Pexton children. Only these years later did we learn that, though they hadn't died as often as our friends, they had died still, and their parents had wept too.

The Cute One told us that, after the first half-dozen or so deaths in Gardens, mothers began packing their belongings and fleeing whenever any of their children started coughing. Following the mysterious disappearance of a child a year after we started our assaults, the women and children who remained were gone within days.

By the time we went to Bézam to welcome Thula home, Gardens contained only men, broken and longing for home, yet still holding on to visions of wealth for the sake of those they loved. The school sat empty, teachers gone alongside the children. The only teachers left there were the teachers for the Kosawa school, all of whom were freshly out of their training program. Even Teacher Penda had fled; he left with a goodbye neither for us nor for our nieces and nephews, whom he was teaching at the time. We couldn't blame him for acting as if we were his enemies: given a chance to burn Gardens to ashes with him in its confines, we wouldn't have held ourselves back to spare his life.

The laborers' tribulations became increasingly evident to us after all their wives left. We heard them coughing on the bus, the exact cough Wambi used to have. We saw their eyes watering, like ours used to. We heard about rampant drilling accidents, which resulted in deaths so gruesome body parts had to be packed in plastic bags. Many were the men who survived accidents and returned to their villages with missing arms and legs. We heard reports of their nonaccidental deaths too, but if these deaths were because of the men's proximity to the poison, we never knew—Pexton would never have wanted us to know. What we knew was that, for every dead laborer at Gardens, there were ten men in distant villages waiting to replace him, raring to partake in the riches from America. Gardens was always full of men dressed in oil-stained uniforms, covered in dust, dreaming on.

In the months after we escalated our attacks, we saw in these men's eyes how acutely they feared us. They might not have recognized our faces, which we always masked during our incursions and ambushes, but they had to know it was us—no one else in the eight villages hated them as much as we did. If our eyes caught theirs—say, at the bus stop—we looked downward and pretended to examine our fingers. Yet they struggled to breathe around us. How could they not? Their woes were many: they had Pexton standing above them, barking at them to drill to the last drop or go home; we stood in front of them, hiding nothing of our detestation; toxins swam within them, preparing them for a death they could only hope wouldn't soon arrive. Their wives and children were afar, waiting for money for sustenance, praying to their ancestors to make the men as prosperous as those who had worked at the oil field decades before and returned to build brick houses. Until then, though, their wives lived husbandless lives, their offspring grew up like fatherless children, their parents died without a farewell.

How often did the laborers question the value of their lives? Did they cry at night in regret? Whenever we saw one of them at the bus stop with a packed trunk, having decided that the prospect of riches was no match for a simple life of love and quiet, we knew not whether to admire the man or scoff at his weakness in fleeing.

⌃⌃⌃⌃⌃⌃⌃

A MONTH BEFORE THAT FIRST meeting with Mr. Fish, the men of Kosawa had an assembly. The Sweet One and the Cute One had called for it, telling us that there was an incredible development they wanted to inform us about, the breakthrough we'd been waiting for.

They told us that the Restoration Movement people in New York, having grown tired of Pexton's broken promises, had filed papers with an American court to force Pexton to clean up our land and waters and start sharing its profits with us; the Restoration Movement intended to argue that because Pexton was profiting from our land, we were entitled to a portion of whatever the company earned from the oil it sold. But Pexton was under a new leadership that was determined to show the world that fairness was at the core of their business. The new leadership had decided it wanted no court case—they were ready to work with the Restoration Movement to finalize an agreement. Under the agreement, we would not be receiving an envelope of cash, as had years ago been given to our mothers and fathers. We would receive, instead, a percentage of all the money Pexton made from our land from that day forward. We'd get a percentage every single year.

At that first meeting with Mr. Fish, his interpreter confirmed all of this.

He said that, though the two sides had not yet agreed on what the percentage would be, there was no doubt that everyone would agree on the right percentage.

"Approximately how much would it be?" someone shouted.

The interpreter whispered something into Mr. Fish's ear. Mr. Fish nodded and whispered back into the interpreter's ear.

"Mr. Fish says it's hard to know what the percentage will be," the interpreter said. "You have to remember, Pexton has a lot of people who want its money. The government in America wants some of it. The government here wants their share. All the people who work for Pexton, they need their monthly salaries. But your share is also very important, because together we inhabit this valley, and we must do so peacefully."

Questions came from every direction: Did the

people in Bézam know of this pending agreement? What did they have to say about it? Were they going to tax our percentages? Why weren't they present at the meeting?

"Pexton wants to do what's right by you," the interpreter responded. "Sharing profits with communities is not something corporations do, but we're going to do it, because that's who we are. We don't care if the government of this country supports or does not support our plan. Governments do whatever governments want to do, that's just life. At Pexton we believe our duty should be to people first, not to governments."

"What's that supposed to mean?" one of us asked. "Isn't it the government who gave you our land?"

"Yes, of course, in a way," the interpreter said. "But Pexton is Pexton, and His Excellency's government is His Excellency's government. We operate by our own principles. As a company, our mission is to do what's best for the world—that's why we're here today. After this deal is final, if you need help from us on how to use your money to improve your lives, we'll gladly send people to help you. If you'd like to move to Lokunja, or buy land in one of the other seven villages—"

"Move to Lokunja?" several shouted in unison.

"Buy land?"

We did not need to hear any more.

We stood up and lifted our stools. We signaled to our wives that it was time to leave. Some of them appeared reluctant to obey; one look and they knew it wasn't the right time to attempt to defy us. The interpreter called out to us as we walked away, saying we didn't need to sell our lands and move to another village unless we wanted to. We heard Sonni calling too, saying we should give Mr. Fish a chance to explain.

A few of our fathers lingered to talk to the interpreter, to find out what it was that Pexton truly wanted, but we knew there was no need to ask—they wanted the entire valley. They wanted whatever oil was below the ground on which our children played. They wanted to search for oil beneath our huts. They wanted whatever oil sat idly under the kitchens in which our wives cooked. We would die before we let them have it.

The next day, Sonni made a round of our huts to extend an invitation from Mr. Fish: the oilman wanted to sit down with us in his house. It was certain to be another waste of time—what more could he have to say?—but we went anyway, a week later, along with the Sweet One and the Cute One, who insisted we owed it to our friends in prison.

In a room full of books and pictures of a long-haired woman and three boys with leaf-green eyes, Mr. Fish's interpreter told us that Pexton absolutely did not expect us to sell them our lands. The only thing Pexton wanted, the reason they'd sent the previous overseer back to New York and brought Mr. Fish to us, was that they truly wanted peace. If we wanted the same thing, why didn't we all shake hands and start anew? Pexton was ready to make a deal with us, a preliminary deal to set the basis for the bigger deal: if we stopped breaking and burning and instilling fear in their laborers, they'd continue working on the agreement regarding our percentage with the Restoration Movement. But first our friends in prison would be set free, as soon as we all shook hands as men.

The three of us in attendance excused ourselves and went outside.

On Mr. Fish's porch, looking at the expanse lying before us—the laborers' conjoined houses and the empty school; the oil fields with structures jutting into the air delivering black smoke; pipelines running in all directions; our huts in the distance, undignified and slumped on their knees—we deliberated on whether we should accept Mr. Fish's terms. We wished Thula were there, but we couldn't write to her and await her counsel: our friends in prison longed to sleep on their beds, eat warm meals, wrap their legs around their wives, and watch their children do homework by the bush lamp. It was for their sake that we agreed to walk back into the house and shake Mr. Fish's hand, and lay down our matches and machetes. We would give Pexton three months to start giving us our percentages, in cash, delivered on the same day of the month, every month. We would give them a year to start cleaning the river and the air and the land, and if they couldn't fully clean them, at least stop poisoning them so they might recover by themselves.

The overseer agreed to everything. Of course, he said, smiling. We smiled back. One of us laughed. Was it truly happening? Were we really making a deal with Pexton?

The interpreter took a photo of us shaking hands with Mr. Fish as the oilman beamed, grabbing our hands with both of his. We looked at each other, flattered and amused at his excitement. The fact that we had the power to make an important man from America so happy surprised us. After the handshakes we took a group photo, Sonni and Mr. Fish in the center, shaking hands, the three of us and the Sweet One and the Cute One on either side of them. The interpreter, as he took the photo, said it would be sent to newspapers in New York to serve as a testament to the power of dialogues.

Mr. Fish rang a bell, and a servant, dressed in black and white, appeared.

He nodded as Mr. Fish spoke. In less than a minute he returned with a tray of glasses, all filled halfway. We each took a glass. Mr. Fish held his glass up in his hand and said something in his American-accented English that sounded nothing like the English we'd spoken with our teachers at the Lokunja school. His interpreter laughed at whatever he'd just said and we all laughed too. We lifted our glasses high, to imitate the American, grinning like giddy goats. Mr. Fish clinked his glass against Sonni's, and we began clinking our glasses against each other's. Mr. Fish drank whatever was in his glass in one gulp. We looked around at each other and did the same. The taste made us crunch our faces, which made Mr. Fish burst out laughing, and soon we were all laughing hard, forgetting we were in the house of an American oilman. We walked out of the house that evening with three bottles of the drink, his gift to us. That night we shared it with all the men of Kosawa as we recounted the story of the meeting, enjoying this moment of unity that had long eluded us. We told ourselves not to celebrate quite yet, but we were prepared, finally, to exhale.

That all happened about six years before Thula returned home.

In that time, we did nothing to hurt Pexton. Oil spilled on our land and we did nothing. Our children coughed and we did nothing. We sat on the bus to Lokunja with the laborers and we did nothing to them. We'd given Pexton our word. We kept it.

We waited for them to keep theirs.

^^^^^^

IT WAS WHILE WE WERE waiting that one of us was awakened one night by the groans of his pregnant wife. She did not respond when he asked her what was wrong. Her eyes were wide open, though her mouth was tightly shut. Our friend hurried to his mother's room and roused her. When his mother also failed in imploring his wife to open her mouth, our friend ran to get the womb doctor, who, with one touch of the belly, said that the baby was coming. The womb doctor touched the belly again, and corrected herself: the babies were coming. His mother began boiling water. Our friend pulled his spear from under his bed and started sharpening it on the veranda, eager to go hunting when the sun rose, grateful for the chance to be far from his hut when his wife finally opened her mouth.

He thought about his babies throughout the day in the forest, and we ridiculed his sudden inability to engage in conversation. On our way home, he imagined, as we all did, that when he returned the babies would be there and it would be a long night of drinking in his hut. But the babies hadn't arrived when we returned. By dusk, his wife's silence had turned to groans, grunts by the next morning, shrieks by the time he returned from the forest the next evening. It was then we realized, even before a medium arrived from the first of the five sister-villages to confirm it, that Jakani and Sakani were returning.

We don't know why the twins chose the womb of our friend's wife over the wombs of all the other fertile young women of Kosawa, though we imagined it had something to do with the fact that she was copiously busted and extra wide of hips. Those hips were not of much help, however, as the babies elbowed and kicked and pressed in an attempt to clear a path through her to re-enter our world. The volume of her cries was evidence that the discomfort she was in was not one a body made of flesh was meant to sustain. Just as one of our grandfathers had told us was the case when Jakani and Sakani last arrived, the woman stayed in labor for seven days and nights, her pain rising daily, so that by the fourth night no one in Kosawa could sleep, not the crickets or the birds or the beasts of Kosawa, not any creature with a singing voice, most of whom joined the laboring woman after every sunset, a whimpering chorus around her anguished cries, which came accompanied with her blood spilling, dripping off the mattress and forming the shape of a face as it touched the earth, the shape of Jakani's and Sakani's faces in the days when they went around healing and interceding for us.

Come out the twins finally did, holding hands.

We'd never doubted that they would return to us—extraordinary humans never stay dead, not as long as the world continues to need the likes of them—but we were awed nonetheless that they'd indeed returned, and that our years of living without a channel to the ancestors were over. At last, we could return to experiencing the fullness of the Spirit in our midst. It would take them some time to start healing and interceding for us, we knew, but as we filed through the hut to see them, all the men, women, and children in Kosawa awaiting their turns, we felt healed by their mere presence; a sense of wholeness descending upon us, courtesy of the hope they'd brought to grant us.

A week after their birth, their father told us that he wouldn't be able to join us if we decided to revive our battle against Pexton; that was how our numbers decreased to five. Our friend said that he needed to dedicate himself to guiding the twins to becoming the men they were born to be. We did not try to convince him otherwise, though we knew that the twins, whom he had renamed Bamako and Cotonou, wouldn't need guidance from their human father, for they were born ready to be what they'd been created to be; they could grow up to be nothing else. Still, we gave our friend our blessings to be one of us no more, knowing that his burden as the father of children living in two worlds would be one he would need all of his strength for. Someday, a descendant of ours might have to shoulder the duty, for it was certain that the twins would keep on returning as long as men lived on earth, and that, no matter how they died, they would return together. Generations before our time, they'd lived in another place, but now they were in our midst, because a woman whose womb they'd chosen to be carried in on one of their returns had married a man from Kosawa. Here they were now, ours, we hoped, forever.

Nightly, we contemplated this in the village square, shaking our heads at the wonder of it all. Not even bullets had been able to end their lives. We talked about the time in the not-too-far future when people from other villages would start arriving on the bus in search of wisdom and healing from the best medium and medicine man in the area. Aware of the truth that Kosawa could one day become a beacon of light in the darkness of our nation, we affirmed our resolve to stay in it even if everyone else fled.

⌃⌃⌃⌃⌃⌃⌃

WE TOLD THULA OF THE twin's return in a letter. We told her of how their hands had never been separated, not even at the moment they re-entered the world. They'd died hand in hand, thus returned hand in hand, and it appeared they would live out this return hand in hand, for they slept as such, and crawled as such, and when guests arrived to visit them, they had to carry both of them at once, careful not to separate their hands, because everyone had agreed that their hands should never be separated until they decided to separate the hands themselves.

In her reply, Thula told us that she'd shared the good news with her friends in New York City and they'd been confused: they couldn't understand how Jakani and Sakani could return after being buried. She had lacked words to explain it to them, she said; unless people had lived in our world and seen the things we had seen with their very own eyes, they could never understand how weak the laws of nature truly were.

For the next several years, with nothing to do regarding Pexton except wait and hope, our letters to Thula were mostly about ordinary happenings in the village—births, the size of harvests, deaths, spills and cleanups, relocations, silly gossip that our wives insisted we pass on to her—and her letters to us were about new experiences she was having, protest movements that she was involved in, the progression of her studies. In her eighth year away, she informed us that she had started making plans to return home in 1998.

She had finished one level of schooling by then, worked for a couple years, and was in the process of completing the most advanced level of education in her field of study, thanks to a scholarship that allowed her to study and teach. With the date of the completion of her education set, she had started turning her mind even more toward Kosawa, eager to continue the dialogue we'd started with Pexton. She was hopeful she and Mr. Fish would find common ground that would benefit Pexton and us. She was confident, also, that the coming years would be an auspicious time for us to negotiate with Pexton. Apparently, Pexton had had other stains on its reputation in the years since the massacre, one of which happened when an American newspaper exposed maneuvers Pexton was using to avoid paying taxes to the American government. Though Pexton had defended itself against all accusations, they'd realized that their future profits would depend on showing the world more of their moral side. Based on what we'd told Thula about Mr. Fish, she believed that moral side was already revealing itself.

It heartened us to know that eight years had done nothing to diminish her love for her birthplace. In her first year away, we had fretted that America might do something to make her forget Kosawa, perhaps by offering her things we couldn't. In her second year away, despite her letters and the money she sent, we worried still, for we could see Austin had entered her heart and altered it. In one of her earlier letters, she'd written:

The other night he and I went to a party at one of his friends' apartments. He knows dancing is not my thing but he still led me to the dance floor, saying I needed to learn how to dance my way through life. Before I knew it, I was dancing, and enjoying it. I can see the shock on your faces as you read this. Thula, dancing? Turns out in this country, unlike in Kosawa, dancing does not have to be done a particular way. You can move your body any ugly way, even the way I do, and nobody's going to tell you to please sit down lest you hurt yourself. Even though I did have that thought while looking at one man at the party. He was a heavy man, but his size was of no matter—he was banging his head and spinning and smiling as if the world were boundless with bliss. When I pointed him out to Austin, Austin chuckled and said everyone alive should be that uninhibited. He said the man reminded him of a colleague of his uncle's who was just as fat; the colleague was one of the best dancers he'd ever seen—any party this man was invited to was destined to be unforgettable; the man was full of jokes and crazy stories; people like him were what he missed the most about Bézam. . . . He would have gone on reminiscing if I hadn't told him that I did not care to know any more about this person, certainly not in the midst of my fun. He stopped talking and spun me around, laughing hard as I shook and twirled in all the worst possible ways.

I never dreamed that I'd become one of those people who count down to when next they'll see their beloved's face, but here I am, Austin makes sure of it. He's perfect for me. Every day with him is as if the world has conspired to make me happy. He sings to me. He takes me to try all kinds of foods across the city. Last weekend the weather was warm, so we laid a blanket on the grass in a park and spent the day reading to each other. After that we bought and ate food on the street, then strolled hand in hand to a river to watch the sun set. The next day, he took me to see the ocean for the first time. I'd love to tell you about it, but I would need a whole book to describe its beauty and majesty, how it felt when the waves crashed against my feet.

In every way our spirits are one, except when it comes to Kosawa; he has no sense of loving a place the way we love our village. He doesn't understand how Kosawa is the beginning and end of everything we've ever had. I try to explain to him that I cannot give up on the struggle for which Papa and Bongo gave their lives, and he says he understands, we should never forget our people, but when he begs me not to leave him, I know he doesn't understand. How could he, when he didn't live our brand of fragile innocence? When his childhood didn't end with friends dying in succession? When he never went to sleep wondering if he'd live to see the next day, wondering if soldiers or drinking water would be his demise? How can he appreciate our resolve to give to the children what Pexton stole from us?

He says he doesn't need to have experienced what we went through to see our viewpoint, but I don't believe him—no one who had a childhood like ours could ever be at home in another man's land. Even those who, unlike me, cannot physically return home, do so with their spirits—their sanity demands it. No matter where they go, they carry their birthplace, never apart from all that it gave and took away from them. They seek its warm air on cold days, imagine its sunshine when clouds cannot be subdued. They see long-lost faces in a sea of strangers. They hear a voice and remember a story from a distant evening. A love song breaks their heart, for they yearn for their motherland to hold them, caress them, whisper in their ears. It will never be so again; those days are far gone. But the nostalgia, it makes crybabies out of grown men on the darkest of nights—many of them will never be whole again. They'll be forever poorly patched and existing in a world that has little time to ask them to tell their stories—who cares for their stories? I don't want such a life for myself. I want my spirit and body to dwell for all the years to come in the place where my ancestors once proudly strode.

Sometimes I fantasize that Austin will return with me. He speaks often of how his years spent in our country were his happiest after his mother died and before he met me—his uncle was good to him, he made great friends in Bézam, he loved writing about our country. But it's unlikely he'll ever come back. After he dug up his uncle in Kosawa, and once his uncle had been reburied and his uncle's wife had accused him of being complicit in his death and some of his cousins had stopped speaking to him, he began packing his things to fly to New York for a few months to take a break, only to have His Excellency's soldiers show up to deport him to America and make his trip permanent. All these years later, though, he finds no comfort in his homeland.

Much as we hoped Thula wouldn't give too much of her heart to Austin, we wished him well. If a man couldn't find solace in his own birthplace, what chance did he have at happiness? When we asked Thula the source of Austin's unrootedness, she wrote:

I think being born to parents from two different parts of the world made him a man from somewhere and elsewhere but sadly from nowhere. Worse still for him, the parent he most loved as a child, the one who molded him into who he is today, was the one from elsewhere, who died young and left him to navigate a life of perplexity alone. He speaks often of how beautiful and wonderful his mother was. The only woman I've ever met in her league is you, he's said to me. From the stories his mother told him before her death, her marriage to his father was one of life's funniest jokes. She loved her life in her village, not far from Bézam; she never aspired to leave it. Austin's father was in our country simply to preach about salvation, not to find a wife. But when his father saw his mother's beauty, and later heard her say she believed his message of one eternal glorious morning, he swore he wouldn't return to America without her. She always laughed when she got to this part, he told me in his recounting, and his father laughed with her.

His mother's parents did not need much convincing to give their daughter in marriage to an American missionary—his mother was the ninth of fifteen children and the preferred child of neither parent, so the parents had taken the bride price Austin's father gave, thrown a small wedding, and made the groom promise he would keep their daughter safe. A week later, the couple was married again in an office in Bézam, and they left for America not long after. He said his mother never loved America, but his birth, ten months after her arrival, meant she only had time to think of her love for him. They did everything together, from cooking to singing songs from her village to sharing a bed when his father traveled for his new job as a medical device salesperson. When she was killed in a car crash one afternoon while he was in school, he thought he would die of grief.

It appears that little about his childhood after that was worth being nostalgic about. He and his father moved to a new town, where he attended a school for boys from rich families during the day and spent his evenings with a woman his father had hired to take care of him, since his father's job took him away for most of the week. The other boys in his school found him odd, his skin too dark, his hair too high. In the silence of his father's house, in a town in the middle of America, he read books that questioned the purpose of life, the futility of it all. He began writing, and it was in writing that he found the joy he feared he'd lost with his mother's death. When it came time for him to further his studies, he told his father that all he wanted was to study the essence of existence, identify the reason for his birth. His father gave his encouragement—acceptance was the least the man could do to atone for all the things he couldn't give his son.

When he was twenty, while living alone in an apartment his father had taken a loan to buy for him in Brooklyn, he decided to become a news-paperman, hoping to find a measure of purpose in writing about the lives of others. Wouldn't his days brim with resolve if he were to spend them mak-ing known the stories of the deliberately unheard? Words written by others had shaped his world; why wouldn't his shape the world? He laughs now when he thinks about it, but in his first years of being a newspaperman he loved it. He enjoyed chasing stories he believed the world needed to know, writing them, rewriting them, beseeching his supervisors if they weren't keen on his ideas. Now, though he travels to different parts of the country to unearth specifics, though he holds on to scraps of hope that a story he's written may entice his countrymen to reconsider their ways of thinking and being, he can't dismiss his weariness with it all, what little difference his work makes, what a longing for the moon to come down it is.

He regrets writing the story about Kosawa. He says Bongo would be alive today if he hadn't been so determined to expose Pexton. Was it worthwhile? I know it was worthwhile, we all know that, but it's not my place to force him to believe so. I tell him that the Four, even if they hadn't been hanged, would have died either way, and he agrees—we can escape the hangman for only so long, the noose is coming for us all. Still, he's not certain much is worth fighting for anymore. Certainly not a battle like ours against Pexton, given its lopsidedness. He wants us to win, of course. He says if we defeat Pexton we'll be the rare story he's written to get a happy ending. Did he once truly believe that newspapermen could right the wrongs of the world? He scoffs at the memory. Folks read the stories he and his fellow newspapermen write, he says, and they sigh. They carry on with their days, leaving the words soggy and lonely at the bottom of trash cans. Sometimes readers write letters to groups that might change the situation. Other times they march. Or stop buying from a corporation. Or they change governments. But too much remains the same. They carry on—what else can they do? Change may come when it's ready to come, he says, or it may never.

. . .

We found it hard to understand how Thula, with her zeal, could be so bonded to Austin and his sense of resignation. The hearts of women are fickle and easily altered by love, which is why we prayed often for the Spirit to grant our friend wisdom. Before she left, she had promised us that she would write in her letters all there was to write so that we could keep her accountable; thus we were compelled to ask her, after recognizing that Austin was making her into a new creation, if, when the time came, she would leave Austin for Kosawa. If she were to decide to remain in America for the sake of love, we told her, we would accept it. We would rejoice and wish her well. To that she responded:

How could you ever doubt me? If I'm telling you about Austin, it's not to make you wonder if I'll return. I tell you so that you may know why I must return even though my heart cries out in protest. Yes, I want to be with him up to the moment when I have just one breath left. I want to lie next to him and cry about Papa and Bongo and a world gone so thoroughly mad I want to rip it apart and free the universe from humans. He wants the world re-created too, but not in the way we seek to do it. He believes in dialogue, in people sharing their stories, hearing others' stories, enemies gaining new perspectives on each other. I'm tempted to laugh at his naïveté in thinking stories alone can do that. When I told him about your first attack at Gardens, he was aghast that we'd gone in that direction. He and I had a quarrel about it; we didn't speak for days. I find it hard to discuss anything about the struggle with him. Still, I do, he's my best friend. But if he doesn't understand my vision, how can I let him stand by me in the years to come?

Over and over he tells me that what we need is patience. He says His Excellency and his government will sooner or later crumble under the weight of their reckless greed and Pexton will flee with them. It infuriates me when he says it. Patience, be patient. What we need isn't patience. What we need to do is fight. But he doesn't believe in hostility; he says every single conflict in the world can be resolved by dialogue. I told him ours hasn't been—that's why we'll fight on.

But how were we to fight on when we'd put down our weapons? we asked her.

By the time of that letter, it had been four years since our agreement with Mr. Fish, and still no percentages were forthcoming. We were not eager to pick up our machetes again, but we could not let them take us for imbeciles. We told Thula that perhaps the time had come for us to revive our late-night visits to Gardens. We needed to remind them that our farms were still producing shriveled crops, our well was still full of toxic water, our children were still breathing poisonous air.

Thula agreed. "It appears keeping a promise means nothing to them," she wrote.

She did not, however, want us to resume our attacks immediately. She wanted us to wait until after her return, which she was in the process of planning. She wanted to sit down with Sonni and the elders and convince them that while she was determined to engage in dialogue with Pexton, she also believed that we should not wait for Pexton indefinitely—it was important to her that the elders and we were in accord that if Pexton failed to meet our demands, we would reinstate our former tactics. She wanted to explain to the elders that the Restoration Movement would likely at some point move on from Kosawa to another place, and that wouldn't be unkind of them, it was how these things worked; we had to start planning for the day when we would have little outside support.

We agreed with everything she said. We told her we would wait for her return before reigniting the battle, for we knew that, with her back, our tenacity would grow.

In her next letter, she told us about another idea she had been pondering.

Think about it, Pexton isn't acting alone. They only have power over us because our government gave them power over us. The government gave them our land. The government sent the soldiers that afternoon. The government hanged our men. If we were to get Pexton to leave, wouldn't the government return in another form to continue smothering us? Which means that our ultimate enemy is not Pexton, it's our government. That is not to say we shouldn't take a stand against Pexton, it only means we need to take a stand against the government too. I know this is going to sound outrageous, you'll probably think it's far beyond our capacity, but what if we started a movement to bring down His Excellency's government? What if we were to send a message to Bézam that we won't take it anymore?

I believe we can do it. We may be the only village breathing air poisoned by Pexton, but their pipelines pass through other villages and spill in them too. Soldiers are menacing innocents everywhere. The entire country is suffering under the yoke of His Excellency. Millions want him gone. That's an opportunity right there. We can join forces with people who are as ready for change as we are. Rouse them to get out on the streets and demand a new country. I've studied such movements; they have happened in America and Europe. People have gone out onto streets and changed their countries by marching. It'll likely take us months or even years to get multitudes of people marching, but with proper planning, we can do it.

We'll start in Kosawa and the sibling-villages

and travel as far across the country as we can. I'm confident that, once word starts spreading, people will start realizing that they don't have to accept anything, they have choices, they can do something about their government. That'll be the most crucial element for the movement, because only the people can uproot His Excellency. Only the people can free themselves. We need to open their eyes to their power.

Do you agree with me? I desperately hope that you do, as I've been musing on this idea for years, but it's only now that I have total certainty that the Spirit has called for me to do it, for us to do it together.

I've discussed my vision with my friends here, and they're excited about it. We've talked about past movements and the lessons I could gather from them. They've recommended books for me to read. One of them introduced me to his uncle, a man who was involved in a movement in America that led to the passage of laws that gave everyone in the country the right to be treated equally. The uncle said to me: if it can happen here, it can happen there; humans are mortal and so are the systems they build. Then, in a manner that reminded me of Teacher Penda trying to demonstrate how Americans talk, he added: you gotta never stop believing, baby. Change's gonna come.

But Austin, whenever I discuss my ideas with him, tells me that I need to ignore the history of movements in Europe and America and instead closely study such efforts in countries that resemble mine.

What you're proposing isn't a small movement, he said, it's a revolution.

Movement, revolution, I don't care what it's called, my country needs it, I replied.

But look at what revolutions have done to countries all around yours, princess, he countered. Look to the south of your country, a land where power once lay in the hands of a few. Good men rose up and fought so that wealth might be spread evenly. Did it happen so? Didn't wealth simply pass from the hands of a few to a new set of hands of a few? Look at the country to the east of yours, where rebels stormed the presidential palace with guns given to them by their overseas backers. They desecrated the palace, sent its inhabitants into hiding. They put bullets in the chest of the man who for long had trampled upon them. They lifted their guns and cheered their new freedom: victory at last, victory at last. What happened next? Didn't tribes turn against tribes, villages against villages, no strong man between them to force a peaceful accord? Look at how the children of that country are now wasting for scarcity of food. Look at how the women there have been turned into slaves for men who once fought for the liberation of all. If you were to ask these people, would they sing the praises of a revolution?

What makes you think your revolution will produce different results? he says. Why add to people's woes with a pursuit that's all but bound to fail?

It hurts when he says such things. It hurts more to know he's saying it to keep me in America. I see the desperation in his eyes when he holds me and tells me that he can't let me go. We've been together for almost eight years. It's been wonderful, but he's known from the very beginning that the part of my heart that belongs to Kosawa belongs to Kosawa only, though if any man could steal it, it would be him. I don't allow myself to think of the day I'll say goodbye to him. Just listening to him trying to dissuade me in an effort to protect me, wrong as I know he is, causes my tears to build up. But I can't shed any tears. There will be no tears until the struggle is over.

I know what I'm suggesting in this letter sounds like a mission that will consume the remainder of our lives, but I'm willing to dedicate my life to it if you are. We might not live to see the day Kosawa or our country comes out of its darkness into light, but we'll forge forward believing, because there's no other way to live.

There's no other way to live, we wrote back to her. What she was suggesting indeed sounded daunting, we said, but we'd rather fight and die than live as cowards. We would follow her and trust that whatever plan she had in mind would give us new lives—that was why she had gone to America, to bring back for our benefit what she had learned. We cautioned her that it was unlikely people across the country would share her enthusiasm for toppling His Excellency, not wanting to call his wrath upon their towns and villages, but we wouldn't know until we spoke to them.

In her response, she said that she'd learned from Austin to focus not on what was or what might be but on what is. Still, she admitted that she had moments when she thought about her father and her uncle and all those whom Kosawa had lost, and she couldn't help being afraid that our village might lose many more before this was all over. But the memory of our departed also gave her strength. She said:

Last week, Austin read me an essay he'd written as homage to men like my father and my uncle. In it, he spoke of how brave men were falling all over the world, the sacrifices of their lives going to waste as new forms of greed and recklessness overtake the old ones. What will become of those who rise to take the place of the likes of my father and my uncle? Flickers of progress are brightening lives in isolated corners of the world, yes, but a universal solution eludes us.

As much as Austin and I argue on how best to free ourselves and those around us, we agree on everything else. We agree that too many humans are losing awareness of their true nature, leading the most rapacious of us to see the rest as feasts to be devoured. I am consoled, and further broken, by what I've seen in America, by the awareness that Kosawa is only one of thousands of places to be so thoroughly overcome; that places mightier than us have been broken far more severely. I still attend meetings in the Village every week, and at every meeting we ask ourselves: What do we do now? What do we do after we've done all we can and seen no change? What will our children do after they've done what they can and failed, just as our fathers failed before us?

Austin won't stop begging me to stay in America. He says I could make money and send it to you. He thinks it might actually be better if we sold Kosawa to Pexton. How can he understand? Money will do what it can, but what we want isn't just to be left alone. What we want is to own our lives and strut like the sons and daughters of leopards that we are.

After we received that letter, whenever we thought of her words and her belief that we had every right to dignity and respect, our chests puffed out and our shoulders went high. Later that month, the entire village echoed her when we all gathered to celebrate the rite of passage of a generation of boys entering manhood.

The manhood passage was always one of our favorite celebrations, because it reminded us of who we were as a people and the kind of life we were created to live. We laughed whenever we reminisced about the night before our passage, when we were taken deep into the forest by male relatives and left there. Some of our age-mates had tried to follow their relatives back home, and the relatives had whipped them and threatened to tie them to a tree. None of us were allowed to return home till the sun rose. We spent all night calling each other's names amid inexplicable noises and smells, struggling to find one another in the darkness, scared we'd step on a snake or a scorpion. Those of us who found friends huddled with them against a tree, shivering; we weren't allowed to take a blanket, though the rituals always took place in the rainy season. If we couldn't find a friend, we climbed on trees for safety, or sat up all night hugging ourselves, too scared to lie down alone. By morning, we were covered with mosquito bites but proud that we'd proved ourselves fearless. Walking to the village, laughing, we interrupted each other and shouted to be heard, eager to share our tales of survival.

We returned to the village to the sounds of our mothers' cheering, though they had no reason to fear that we wouldn't return—no Kosawa boy had ever failed to return to the village the night before the celebration. Still, the drums beat hard, and aunts and older sisters sweated in the kitchen as they cooked. But we couldn't eat yet. We couldn't hug our mothers. We weren't even allowed to go to our huts. We were ushered directly to the square by our fathers and the elders. There, we sat on mats under the mango tree. We were not allowed to move or to speak, because manhood would require us to practice stillness. Only hand gestures were allowed if we needed to go use the toilet, after which we returned to our sitting position, hungry and cold. We sat there all morning and afternoon, until the hour the village was ready to commence the celebration.

Our last test began after all of Kosawa, plus friends and relatives from the sibling-villages, had gathered around us, a crowd of hundreds.

Every eye on us, we stripped down naked to walk on hot coals.

We had to take forty steps across the coals, displaying no shame or agony, because as men we would need to hold our heads high despite the world's gaze, and channel our pain wisely. Our fathers had advised us to walk fast on the coal, but when the time came, few of us could; most of us ground our teeth with every step, and at least a couple of us leaked urine. At the completion of this test, our mothers and other female relatives wrapped loincloths around us, and our fathers and other male relatives carried us home, where our burnt soles were cleaned and bandaged after we took a bath.

When we returned to the square, dressed in red,

it was to the sound of the village anthem, everyone dancing and singing: **Sons of the leopard, daughters of the leopard, beware all who dare wrong us, never will our roar be silenced.**

Before the eating and drinking began—the part we'd been dreaming of all night in the forest and all day sitting in silence—we knelt before the elders. They laid their hands on our heads, poured libations, and anointed us the next generation of leopards. When we arose after the anointing was when we entered manhood. We knew, though, because our fathers had told us, that the rite of passage alone did not make us men. We knew we would only become men the day we became responsible for other lives, when we acquired wives and had children and looked at them and realized we were worth nothing if we couldn't give them everything. Now that we were men, we repeated this often to the younger generation, that the rite of passage was merely the door being opened for them to enter manhood—they would need to remind the world over and over of the blood of the leopard within them; otherwise, they'd be forever boys.

When we told Thula about the latest ceremony's success, she was stupefied that babies she'd carried around the village had now entered manhood. "I'm glad I'm coming back soon," she said. "I don't want to return and discover my friends are grandparents." In that letter, which was her final correspondence from America, she told us of an impromptu farewell party her friends had thrown for her, how her friends had made her cry as they spoke about all the adventures they'd had together, the places they'd traveled across America. For most of the letter, though, she told us about her own recent passage:

Two days ago I went to Austin's apartment to have dinner with him. We had decided that it would be best if we stopped talking about the fact that I'm leaving in three months, better we just enjoy ourselves as if we'd always be together. Sometimes we succeeded, but I could tell from his sullen demeanor the moment I entered his apartment that it wouldn't be so that day. While we were eating the fried ripe plantains with beans and mushroom stew he'd learned how to make in Bézam, he took my right hand and told me that he had to tell me something.

Princess, he said. I'm dying.

I scanned his face, words refusing to leave my tongue.

What do you mean, you're dying? I asked him finally.

I'm dying, he said again. I don't know when, I don't know what my cause of death will be, but today, tomorrow, next week, next year, I'll be dead.

What's going on? I said. Were you at the doctor's? He shook his head. My heart quieted; I decided he was just in one of his contemplative moods.

Are you writing a story about death that's upsetting you? I asked.

Every story I write is about death, he said. It dawned on me today that life is death, death is life—what's the point of it all?

So you're not sick? I asked him. He shook his head. A drop of water spilled from my eyes, and he wiped it with his free hand.

We sat there for I don't know how long, looking into each other's eyes. Water started rushing out of my eyes, I couldn't understand why. My body felt heavy, fatigued after a turbulent life. And yet I felt an awakening of my spirit. I began sobbing, and Austin started wiping my tears, which made me sob harder.

He said to me: You're dying too, princess. We're all dying. I haven't been able to stop thinking about it all week, how close death is. Doesn't it make you want to change the way you live? It makes me want to. I want to float through life, untethered from human vanities. It's unbelievable, you know, what a blip our existence is in the infinite expanse of the universe. It's baffling, so humbling and liberating, don't you think? We don't even matter.

He chuckled and lifted my hand to his lips, to kiss the back of it.

You know what I'm realizing? he said. Living is painful. That's why we so often forget that we're dying, we're too busy catering to our pains. I think it's one of nature's tricks—it needs us to not dwell on the fact that we're dying, otherwise we'd spend our days eating low-hanging fruits from trees and splashing around in clear rivers and laughing while our pointless lives pass us by. Nature makes sure that pain awaits us at every turn so that in our eternal quest to avoid it, or rid ourselves of it, we'll keep on wanting one thing after another and the earth will stay vibrant. We feel pain, we cause pain, a ridiculous endless cycle. All the misery we cause others, what is it but a result of us dumping our pain on them? I don't want to do it anymore, living my life by the dictates of my pain. This pain I'm feeling at your leaving, I want to channel it into love. I want to love and love and love, no conditions. I could be dead before you get on the plane, I could die tonight. I don't mean to be macabre, I'm just trying to learn how to hold on to nothing in life. My entire life has been a game of holding on tightly, and wanting to never let go, and yet losing. It's painful. . . . My mother, today is the anniversary of her death.

That was the first time he told me the date on which she had died.

How could I rebuke him for never sharing it with me when her passing still so deeply grieved him? His father recently had a fall. Austin flew to see him and spent two days with him at the hospital. I think all of that was on his mind, the thought that, with his father's passing and me returning home and His Excellency not wanting him back in our country, he might live and die alone in America.

If my mother were here today, he said, she would tell you to just love, and be kind to everyone. That's what she used to say to me every day, and I saw her practicing it. I saw how she smiled at everyone. She smiled even when the weather was cold. She smiled when people in stores stared at her because she didn't look and talk like them. When her time came, she died with a smile on her face. These past years, the world has tried to tell me that there's a better way to live; I should act on my pain, because people like my mother are misguided. The world is wrong.

I spent that night at his apartment, sleep elusive, my mind unquiet. It was as if I was living through one of those dreadful nights of our childhood, only this time I wasn't afraid of death, I was just hyperaware of it, listening to it say to me, I'm coming for you, Thula, get ready. It all forced me to consider: What if Austin is right about life being an endless cycle of feeling pain and causing pain? I don't want to partake in such a cycle anymore either. All night, I couldn't stop asking myself: Is our fight against Pexton driven by pain, or by love? Could it be driven by love? Should it?

Yesterday, back in my room, I lay in bed and imagined myself in a space full of beautiful things made of glass. The space was vast, the size of

Kosawa. There was nothing in it but me and plates and trays and glasses and vases, colors of every kind, adorned with flowers, row after row of priceless, breakable things. I yearned to break them. I closed my eyes and screamed. I began running around the room. Pulling things off shelves. Smashing them on the floor. Flinging them against the wall. Kicking them. Crying as I broke them. I toppled the shelves. Destroyed until there was nothing left in that room but me and my brokenness. I then sat against a wall and wept until my head ached and my cheeks felt numb. I dried my eyes. I stood up and saw a broom in a corner. I swept the pieces out of the room. There, they dissolved into nothing. I closed the door and I was alone in the empty room. I started crying again, but this time I wasn't just crying. I was crying and dancing, then just dancing, laughing, my joy abundant.

I hope the love that dwells today in my heart remains forever, but if it doesn't, may this letter serve as a testament that there once was a day when all I wanted was for peace to reign. Tomorrow I may wake up in pain with a mind crowded with images of what we've suffered, and I may want nothing more than to punish Pexton. I may wish I hadn't sent you this letter, but it'll be too late. You may have read my words and decided to join me in freeing Kosawa without causing pain to anyone; without any word, thought, or action that destroys another. You may have vowed never to break or

burn again, because you would have come to wonder if I was wrong, if we were all wrong to believe
that we could seize freedom through destruction.

Or maybe you'll read this letter and toss it into
the fire, considering it nothing but the ramblings
of a lost woman, wondering why you'd ever given
so much credence to my words. I ask you only to
search your hearts, ponder the idea of reclaiming
our land with the love that flows in our blood.

I see it clearly as I write this, what we must do.
I see us marching to Pexton, singing, dancing in
front of soldiers. We may cry, or get angrier, but
our fury will be from a place of love for ourselves,
for our birthplace. From this love we'll demand
our rights, and we shall win.

If we should die, let it be that we died for peace.

I'll always be one of us,
Thula

IN OUR RESPONSE AND FINAL letter, we told her it
would be better if we discussed what she was suggesting in person. We revered her intelligence, but we
recognized her words to be those of a woman about to
bid farewell to her beloved, having been so altered she
can only speak of love. None of us believed we could

win this fight with talks of kindness and singing and dancing. The time for friendliness with our enemies had come and gone.

One of us had recently been approached by a soldier who whispered to him that he could help us get guns. Guns would allow us to do more than break and burn—they would make Kosawa safer. We had pondered the soldier's offer and decided that it was an investment worth making. Still, we thought it best to wait and ask Thula for the purchase money in person. That was why we said little to her in our final letter; we merely told her that we'd heard all she'd said and were thankful that she had found peace.

We confirmed to her that we'd be at the airport to welcome her on the day of her return, and that we'd already told our wives to starch and iron our best outfits. When she visited Kosawa a week after her return, to truly be home again, our friends who had long ago left the village would be there to join us in celebrating her homecoming.

Our wives had already decided who was going to cook what. A couple of goats would be slaughtered, the village square swept. Our children who were born after she left wanted to know everything about her, their Thula. What rejoicing there would be that day in Kosawa.

And it was, though our joy began sooner than

everyone else's, when, at the airport in Bézam, standing next to her family, we watched her come out through the gates and into our arms. She had left as a seventeen-year-old and was now on the verge of twenty-eight, a woman in years lived but not in looks, for she still looked girlish, her face smooth and free of creases. She was as thin as ever, though the largeness of her eyes was more apparent, her smile bigger and brighter, her hair stringy and long, all of which made her beauty more uncommon and alluring. She cried as she hugged us. Her mother and brother cried. It had been so many years, ten years, a lifetime.

When she and her family arrived in Kosawa a week later, we beat the drums hard, and Sonni and the elders poured libations, and we all marveled at how she had returned so unlike the girl who had left Kosawa and yet entirely like the girl who had left Kosawa, still in possession of the worst singing voice, but no longer of few words, happier, dancing with the women, playing with the children, free, a bird back in its nest.

WE BROUGHT UP THE NECESSITY of acquiring guns on the second day of her visit. It was at night, after one of our wives had fed us and we had moved to the village square so we could be just the six of us, sitting under the mango tree, above which a half-moon looked terribly lonely. A few days before we went to Bézam to welcome her home, we had argued about the best way to present our request to her—as a group or one to one, considering the amount of persuasion that would be needed. Ultimately, we decided to do it together, confident that the transformation she'd written to us about was temporary. How long could she sustain the belief that we could love our way to freedom?

It didn't take many minutes for us to realize we'd been mistaken in doubting her.

There was nothing but conviction in her eyes as she spoke about great men whose lives and works she'd been studying closely, men who had changed their countries without committing acts of destruction or shedding blood. We could do it too, she said, by bringing our enemies to our side, breaking down the wall that stands between them and us, showing them that our children are their children, their children are our children; that was what her father died for, to tell people in Bézam that truth.

She would have talked till morning if one of us hadn't interjected to say that, though we agreed with what she was saying—and we'd certainly join her in uniting citizens to oust His Excellency—we also believed that it was time for Kosawa to acquire guns.

Who are you going to kill? she asked after a long silence.

Only those who seek to hurt us, we said. Soldiers had arrived in Kosawa and slaughtered our families and friends, and we could do nothing. They threatened our lives, and we could do nothing. They had humiliated us countless times in front of our children, and every time we could do nothing to them, because they owned guns and we didn't. They swaggered into our village, and we had no power to tell them to leave. Didn't she think that it was only prudent for us to be able to stand up against them in the future?

She shook her head.

No, she said. We can't do it. If we are to stand for peace, we are to stand for peace at all times. How can we speak of making peace with them while planning to kill them?

We're not planning to kill them, we said. We won't resume any attacks on Gardens. We won't threaten the laborers. The guns will be solely to protect ourselves in the event of another attack. We cannot keep on speaking of peace while we remain defenseless—that would be reckless and absurd. His Excellency and Pexton have no qualms about spilling our blood for their gain; why should we not seek to combat that? We hope the day will never come when we do likewise to them, but we have to be prepared for it.

We promised her that if she provided the funds for the guns we would do all we could to see her vision of a revolution come true. As soon as she gave us the word, we would start meeting with village heads in our district and nearby districts to listen to the stories

of their people's woes of mudslides caused by government mass deforestation; lands under seizure by
decrees; dying children; raping soldiers; schools with
collapsed roofs. We would ask the village heads if they
wanted to join us to defeat our common enemy. It's
possible some of them would dismiss us after hearing
us say that we hoped to bring down His Excellency
by marching. We imagine elders laughing in our face
and saying: Oh, you young people, you still have the
strength to be angry, what a luxury—wait and see
how much angrier you'll be when your teeth start falling out. But we would persist, no matter the ridicules,
because we believe, as she does, that victory is possible. Without the guns, though, we couldn't commit
ourselves to her ideals.

Whatever joy she had brought to Kosawa was gone
from her face the next morning.

Still, she forced herself to smile during the meeting
she had with the entire village just before she left to
return to Bézam to start her government job. Standing
in the square, beside Sonni, she told the gathering
that the time had come for us make our final push
to save Kosawa. She said she would need everyone to
join in the efforts as much as their bodies allowed—
the village stood a chance only if we were united. She
promised to come back as often as she could.

After she was done talking, before she got into the

car with her mother and brother, our wives and children took turns hugging her. She stooped to receive blessings from the elders, who assured her that they were behind her, the ancestors and the Spirit were behind her, all of Kosawa would add their strength and hope to hers.

^^^^^^^

SHE RETURNED FOR A VISIT a month later, but she had no response for us about the guns. We got no response the next month either. Eager as we were, we did not pressure her, for it was obvious in her demeanor how torn she was on the matter. The state of Kosawa only compounded her indecision—the graveyard had doubled in size in her absence; a few huts that had once been crowded with families now stood empty and derelict; so much oil had spilled into the big river that the little ones no longer called it the big river, they called it the sad water. Thula did her best not to reveal her despair; it was important to her that the village see her optimism at all times. Repeatedly, she asked everyone to believe. But what use is mere belief? Without us, she could do little for Kosawa. She had the vision and funds, but we had the muscles. Our friends and siblings were fleeing, or praying for miracles, or resigned to whatever fate His Excellency had drawn for them—they all wanted better lives, but none of them were willing to pay the utmost price for it.

We were the ones who had no fear of death, the ones who recognized that, whether we chose to sit back and do nothing or stand up and fight, we'd end up dead, so why not fight? Sometimes we wondered what it was that separated us from the others, why other men our age with ample vigor were unwilling to risk their lives in pursuit of that which is paramount and just. We could only surmise that it had to be something in our spirits, a thing the Spirit had decided not to give all humans for reasons we didn't attempt to conjure. But this thing in our spirits, it couldn't protect us from the agony of waiting, year after year, for our suffering to reach its finale.

Kosawa had been fighting Pexton since we were children; our land was poisoned even before we were born. Few were the days of our lives that weren't nestled between oil spills and deafening gas flare roars. Countless were the hours when we spoke of little else but Pexton. We had worried and hoped and gained small victories and endured many losses, yet little was changing. The Kosawa of our dreams remained a mirage. During our student days at Lokunja, our teachers had spoken often about the approaching new millennium, how the world would be different then, and we imagined it would be so, because in the eighties the year 2000 seemed seventy-seven lifetimes away, but now it was only eighteen months away, and instead of strutting into it, we were crawling.

Only the mercy of the Spirit kept us from losing our resolve, for it gave us reasons to smile in the laughter of our children, the appearance of rainbows that left us in awe, the birth and marriage celebrations that filled Kosawa with gladness in the days before and after, the euphoria on full-moon nights when we took out our drums and our children skipped around the square while the elders cheered and our wives twirled their hips, causing our groins to stiffen.

At times like these, we thought little of how many years of waiting still lay ahead; we thought mostly of how blessed we were, what boundless promise life bore. Such moments reminded us that, no matter how long the night, morning always comes.

We thought often, also, of how blessed we were to have Thula.

We never feared she'd toss her hands in the air, forget about Kosawa, and return to Bézam telling herself that she had done her part and failed. That was never who she was. She had the fortitude of the sun—no matter how dark and thick the clouds, she was confident she could melt them and emerge in full glory.

⌃⌃⌃⌃⌃⌃

SIX MONTHS AFTER HER RETURN was when she gave us the money for the guns.

She did it without ceremony. She simply took out

an envelope while we were sitting in one of our huts. In it was the full amount we had requested to buy five powerful guns and sufficient ammunition. She said nothing as we stood up, one after another, stooped next to her, bowed our heads, took her hand in ours, and expressed our gratitude. When she did speak, her tone was stern. She told us that we were not to use the guns without her permission. We were not to use them for anything but the defense of our lives and those of our families and friends. No one was to know that we owned guns until the day it became imperative that we use them. We were never to say she gave us the funds to buy them. If we were to kill anyone with them, may the Spirit be her witness that she never gave us her blessings to take the life of another human. We gave her our word.

The next morning, one of us went to Lokunja to meet with the soldier who'd approached him about the gun sale. The soldier agreed to get us five guns, though not before making it clear that if the government found out that we had guns we'd be dead. He'd also be dead, he said, and he'd rather not die for our sake; he was merely a broker, doing what he needed to do to supplement his government salary and take care of his family. One mistake from us and he would be ruined. We assured him we'd be careful.

On the day he brought us the guns, we met him deep in the forest.

When he took the guns out of his bag, our mouths dropped open in awe. There they were, at last. Smooth-skinned. Perfectly weighted. Blacker than crude. We turned them in our hands. We held them upside down and sideways. We looked at each other, the look of men who in an instant had been born again. The soldier showed us how to use them. How to clean them. How to prevent jams. The magic of the weapons' telescopic sight. He told us how, with the telescopic sight and suppressor, we could kill from afar, soundlessly, leave no trace of our culpability. We never knew such a thing was possible. The soldier told us his dealer in the neighboring country had personally altered the guns for us; he'd explained our situation. We had the best guns for our money.

We marveled at how good it felt to hold them. Killing suddenly seemed the most natural thing. Imagine: one pull of the trigger, one less enemy. Four, five bullets in one body; four, five layers of pain shed from our hearts. Their blood spilling, someday no drilling. Their children fatherless, our children free to live. That evening, in the forest, we received our ordination as slaughterers. The Spirit was there. We felt it. The spirit of the Four. The Six. They were there at the moment it dawned on us that the battle would no longer be fought on uneven terms. When our chance arose, and it would, we would slaughter them the way we once feared they'd slaughter us. Soldiers, laborers, His Excellency's people—how many would we kill? While they remained on our land, would we get tired of killing them? It seemed unimaginable that we, who were once trembling children, had gained the ability to stand supreme over other mortals, but we were not unworthy of it. No, we were deserving of the thrill of inflicting on them the suffering they'd exacted on us. But we wouldn't do anything just yet. We'd given Thula our word. We'd await our opportunity. The weapons would have to stay hidden in the forest.

After the soldier left, we dug a hole and buried the guns and ammunition.

We left the forest that night excited about joining Thula to start laying the groundwork for a revolution, for we knew that if marching and singing and dancing failed, we would have a recourse. How glorious it felt to be powerful.

^^^^^^

OVER THE NEXT THREE YEARS, Thula came from Bézam as often as she could, and we traveled with her to other villages to talk about her vision. Everywhere we went, men seemed perplexed that an unmarried woman—a girl, judging by her size—could be so bold as to tell them that their lives and their children's future would be brighter if they joined her in her mission to free our country. Once, an elder asked her how many children she had. When she said none, he asked her when she intended to have them. When she said never, the men burst out laughing. The American books in your head, one of them said, look what they've done to you. You know, my son is looking for a wife, another added; he likes them small like you, so that if you do anything stupid one good slap is all it'll take to straighten you out. His friends collapsed in giggles. A third added that he'd gladly take Thula as a fourth wife if she was still single in a year. It was evident to us that they resented her, a woman who thought she could be happy without the likes of them—how dare she? But Thula, our Thula, if she was humiliated, she did not show it. Not even her brow twisted in perplexity. She let them talk, and when they were done laughing, she told them that when our country was finally free she would gladly take on three husbands.

Strangers were not the only ones asking her about her plans for her womb.

Our age-mates, the women especially, never ceased to let her know that they could help her find a good husband. Her former relationship with Austin was known to all, evidence that, at the very least, she had desires common to other women. Whenever she visited, in smoky kitchens across the eight villages, in parlors and on verandas, rocking her friends' children on her lap, she sought to explain to them that she was married to her purpose. What do you mean, you're married to your purpose? they asked. She couldn't explain except by saying that she was at peace with the life she had.

. . .

Her vision for the revolution was for it to begin officially on a day we would call Liberation Day. On that day, men and women from towns and villages in our district and surrounding districts would gather in Lokunja. She would invite a newspaperman, the man who had taken over Austin's job. The newspaperman would take pictures and chronicle the rebirth of our country. If Liberation Day went well, we would have more rallies in other towns and in as many districts as we could, until we were ready for men and women to march in protest on a single day, in every town, in every village, all across the nation, fists clenched up and chanting, until the walls of the regime fell down flat.

She believed it was possible, far-fetched as it seemed. She was aware that it might take more than one revolution, or more than one century, to change our country, but that was no deterrent to her, only a motivation to continue the work the past generation had started so that future generations might complete it and never stop building upon it. She said to us often: America and the prosperous countries in Europe did not become what they are today without generation after generation of people fighting and dying for peace.

During those years of laying the foundation for Liberation Day, our weapons remained hidden. There were occasions when we were tempted to retrieve them and head to Gardens, often on days when Kosawa seemed devoid of joy because of death or worsening sickness or a bad spill. At such times, it appeared morning would never come. Conforming to the darkness around us seemed to be our only choice. Whenever our wives showed us the meager harvest from their farms, whenever we looked at the gas flares and imagined toxins coming for our children, we spent long nights fantasizing about putting holes in laborers' heads. Our faith became the thinnest of threads, in danger of snapping at any moment, but we hung on to it as hard as we could. We prayed to the Spirit to keep us from falling, because we couldn't fall; if we hoped to soar again, we couldn't fall. And for Thula's sake, we could not bring out the guns. Our day will come, we told each other when we got together late at night to dream while all of Kosawa slept.

IN BÉZAM, THULA TAUGHT AT the government leadership school during the day and, in the evenings, invited her favorite students to her house to talk about revolutions. They were her new Village Meeting, she told us. With them she discussed her favorite books; and to her they swore that they would join in fighting for Kosawa. We were happy that she had devotees in Bézam, but we doubted that these students' interest in our struggle came from a pure place. None of them came from a village like ours. They had gained entrance into the school by virtue of their connections to powerful men—when did people ever rise up to put an end to their own privilege? Still, the idea of ending the reign of the man whose servants they were about to become, the monster their fathers bowed to during the day and cursed at night, must have been what lured them to Thula.

Three of these students were with her when, four years after her return to the country, she went to meet with Pexton's managing director for our country, the man whose orders everyone at Gardens and the Pexton head office obeyed. Before the meeting, Thula had submitted countless requests for an audience and made numerous impromptu visits to the Pexton office complex, only to hear that the director was in a meeting, out of the country, or otherwise unavailable—would she like to leave a message?

The day she finally got the chance to meet with him was the day we learned why the Sweet One and the Cute One rarely visited Kosawa anymore, and what the true reason was for the delay in us getting our percentages: Pexton had decided to allow the matter to go to court, hoping to contest the Restoration Movement's claim that we deserved a percentage of its profits. The case was waiting its turn in an American court. It was bound to make its way slowly from one American court to another. Because the American court system moved at the pace of a corpulent snail, our children would likely be parents before the time came for a judge to listen to both sides and make a final decision.

Pexton's managing director leaned back in his chair and clasped his fingers behind his head as he told Thula that the Restoration Movement might as well give up on their fight for now: they did not appear to have the funds to wage such a long, costly battle. They already had dozens of open cases against a wide range of corporations and not enough resources to fight every case to completion. It was unlikely Kosawa would ever see its percentages. The director said there was nothing he could do to help us.

When Thula brought back the news to Kosawa, none of us understood why the Restoration Movement men had withheld the truth from us. Sonni, frail and leaning on his cane, gathered the men of Kosawa in the square and asked us what to do.

Several men thought we needed to summon the Sweet One and the Cute One to answer for themselves, but many more argued that it would be of no use—why shame them when they were likely only hoping to spare us the bad news? We need to go talk to the overseer directly, one of our fathers said. No one opposed him, nor did we need much debate before agreeing that it was time for us to move on without the Restoration Movement. Though Thula had been back for four years, we had still depended on the representatives to be our intermediary with Mr. Fish, because the Sweet One had suggested to Thula that it would be best if he and the Cute One concluded a promising conversation they already had under way with the overseer, it wouldn't be a great idea for Thula to start a parallel dialogue. Thula had agreed. But now, given the news, and with Thula having a channel to the biggest Pexton man in the country, the time was right to start doing the discourse differently. At the time Thula met with the managing director, we hadn't seen the Sweet One and the Cute One in nine months, so it didn't take us long to come to a consensus that Sonni would ask Thula to lead a delegation to meet with Mr. Fish. She would speak to him in the way she'd learned how to speak to American men while living in their country. We had no better bridge between them and us than her.

We were not part of the delegation sent to Mr. Fish. The elders decided that, because Thula was a woman, the oldest of the village's able men should accompany her, to give the delegation respectability. We would learn from her, after the visit, that in the absence of an interpreter she and Mr. Fish had chatted freely and at length about their times in New York, laughing when they discovered they'd both loved a particular store that sold old clothes. Thula's elderly escorts, clueless about the conversation, had laughed too.

Yes, it was true that Pexton had decided to let the courts decide whether it owed Kosawa anything, Mr.

Fish told Thula when the time came to discuss the reason for the visit. Pexton had said nothing of this to us because it wasn't their place to inform us, it was the Restoration Movement's.

"If I had the power to help Kosawa I would," Mr. Fish said. "But I don't. As you well know, this is all in the hands of the legal guys in New York. I did what I could to help broker a temporary deal when I first got here, but I can't overstep my bounds."

"We've been keeping our end of the deal for years," Thula said. "Our situation is dire; it's getting worse by the hour. We can't wait indefinitely for a court decision."

There was nothing Pexton could do about speeding the case through the courts, Mr. Fish said. All he could do, personally, was speak to his superior, the managing director; he could ask him to check with New York on the status of the case. Not that that was going to make a difference, but it was worth a try. It might also help if Kosawa was no longer represented by the lawyers for the Restoration Movement, he added.

"If your village were to speak for itself with you as their spokesperson," he said, "it might make the guys in New York excited about wrapping things up."

"Right," Thula said, "because, with the Restoration Movement gone, there'll be less of a chance of any new blunders by your company getting to the media."

"I'm simply trying to do what I can to help your people."

"I don't doubt your sincerity."

"Here's what I can suggest: You and I and a couple of your village elders will go to Bézam to meet with the director. See what can be done about hastening things in New York. The director may have come across to you as cold, but he's a good man; he has young children. Hearing about the children in your village is upsetting to all of us."

"I'm open to the idea," Thula said.

"But you have to understand that the director and the folks in New York are only going to be interested in talking to you if I tell them in advance that you're willing to sign an agreement accepting whatever payment Pexton deems to be the best restitution for the deaths and damages, and you're open to making a joint statement."

"Absolutely not."

"You have no leverage. There's no basis for the suit the Restoration Movement lawyers filed. A judge is going to dismiss it—Pexton has no contractual obligation to Kosawa. I can't make a fool of myself by asking my bosses to waste their time discussing an agreement with you if you're going to walk in making outrageous demands. They don't have time for that. Without a court verdict in your favor, you're entitled to nothing. I'm offering you a chance, in good faith, to at least get something for your people."

"And what if we say that a monetary compensation is not enough?" Thula asked. "Money is just a small part of the issue. We deserve to live in a safe environment."

"I'm not in a position to make any promises on that."

"And we're not in a position to keep waiting year after year."

"I'm sorry" was all Mr. Fish could say in response.

THULA'S VISITS TO THE VILLAGE multiplied after that meeting. With the possibility of a peaceful accord through dialogue gone after three more meetings with Mr. Fish yielded no compromise, Liberation Day became more vital. For five days of the week she was in Bézam—spending half of her evenings with her Village Meeting, the other half with her mother and new father and her brother—and for two days she was with us, chauffeured from Bézam in the car in which we traveled to other towns and villages. No more than two of us accompanied her on any given trip; we took turns hunting and tending to our families, and planning the revolution.

In every town and village we visited, though men and women our age and older looked at her in befuddlement, the young people were enthralled. They came to sit with her, to hear her talk about her vision. She amused them with her stringy hair and how she sat with her legs crossed, as if she were an eminent man. They were curious about what she had seen and learned in America. Why would anyone travel to America and return to this ugly country? they asked her. The question always made her smile. Don't you want our country to one day be as great as America? she would respond. She did not need to lecture them on the assured gloominess of their future under His Excellency. She did not need to tell them about how, much like their parents, they would have little ownership of their lives because the country wasn't theirs and would never be, not when one man controlled it. What she needed to tell them, what few outside the capital knew, was that His Excellency, aging and anxious, had recently been growing even more ruthless.

Thula heard the talks around Bézam, about how His Excellency could sense the end of his reign was near—that was why he showed no mercy to friends and enemies alike. He had survived multiple coups, and executed all those who had plotted his demise, yet his enemies were still plentiful. Which was why he reshuffled his Cabinet every two years, sending former subordinates to prison for the slightest grievance lest they start having ideas. The prison where the Four had been held now contained the same men who had facilitated their entry there. Around Bézam, rumors circulated about how the president never slept in his bed, how he never told anyone where he was sleeping, lest a coup arise in the middle of the night: the first coup he survived had been orchestrated by the captain of the presidential guard. What worried him most, people claimed, was that he had no way of knowing all who hated him—Bézam was full of vultures masquerading as doves.

The entire city worshipped at his shrine, sang his praises at the annual celebration of his ascendance, and yet virtually every one of those worshippers longed to see him dead. He trusted not even his cook, according to the stories, which was why the cook had to bring a member of his own family to taste every meal in His Excellency's presence before His Excellency would eat it. His most obsequious Cabinet member, with the backing of a European government that wanted no more ties with a lunatic, had plotted his death, schemed to have his plane shot down in a manner that would look like a crash; the scheming went on while His Excellency's daughter was getting ready to marry the son of this Cabinet member. His Excellency had found out about the plot days before the wedding. The Cabinet member's immediate execution had taken place on the busiest intersection of Bézam, hundreds watching at noontime, everyone afraid to cry.

At the next celebration of his reign, while soldiers and government workers and schoolchildren of all ages stood at attention, sweating on a scorching afternoon, His Excellency gave a speech christening himself the father of the nation, the lion whose mere presence causes all creatures to lie prostrate. Anyone planning to kill him was attempting to hurt his children by rendering them fatherless, he said. Their punishment would be singular. They would be sliced and stewed and served to him in a silver bowl.

You rise up against me, he declared, and you'll never rise again.

◆◆◆◆◆

SIX YEARS AFTER THULA'S RETURN home, we had yet to set a date for Liberation Day. We still went on trips to inform and awaken, traveling to some places multiple times, but few people, outside of packs of intrigued youths, showed strong interest in our cause. Our time will come, Thula said to us as we drove back to Kosawa enervated, but her words did little to assuage our doubts and our fears that nothing would ever change.

There were months when we visited no villages, our belief in the mission floundering wildly, but hers never did—she was born a missionary for fairness and could live as nothing but a believer. Her earnings from her job, whatever she didn't spend on her expenses and on her mother and her new father, went to helping her friends and relatives care for their children, and funding our travels. She bought books for our children, and let the little ones climb into her car and honk the horn on the steering wheel. Never forget that it's for them we're doing everything, she told us. When we asked her how long we'd keep at it before giving up on the revolution dream, she said: We've planted seeds in minds, the seeds are bound to germinate and spread; we only need to be patient, people will awaken. When she said such things—often, as we sat in one of our parlors, pondering all that had come to pass since Konga asked us to rise—she seemed a new version of herself. A soft aura of madness encircled her, as if something of Konga's now lived within her.

Our guns might have remained hidden in the forest forever, awaiting Thula's blessing for us to use them, if one of us hadn't returned from visiting a relative in another village to find his son dead.

We could not say if this child died of Pexton's poison—he didn't have a cough or a high fever, but he had been vomiting for two days. What we could say was that he might have been spared if Pexton's poison hadn't caused the herbs used to cure stomach ailments to wither. We could say, without equivocation, that Pexton killed him the day our soil became too toxic to sustain the medicinal herbs that once grew in abundance.

Our friend wept like a child as he sat in the graveyard watching us dig his son's final resting place. During the burial, we needed all of our strength to hold his wife back so she wouldn't jump into the grave after her little boy's coffin had been lowered in.

The evening after the funeral, our friend decided his wait was over.

Possessed by an evil long lying dormant within him, he went into the forest. He dug out his gun and headed into the bushes at the edge of Gardens. From behind a tree, through his gun's telescopic sight, he observed three laborers smoking pipes in the late evening's breeze, chatting about one thing or another that had transpired during their day.

He killed them all.

Shot the first in the head. The second man's bullet entered his chest before a scream could get off his tongue. The third man he shot in the back as he turned to run away. No one in Gardens heard anything; the gun's silencer made sure of that. The bodies would not be found until after our friend had fled to the guns' hiding place. There he stayed as darkness descended, weeping, with the weapon in his hand.

After reburying the gun, he came to one of our huts to tell us what he had done. He was still crying and trembling, his eyes bloodshot. His son was his first child, his only son. His name would die with him if his wife did not give him another boy.

Two of us had already buried children, all of us had carried more miniature coffins than we could count, but something about watching our friend undone by grief made us realize that our time to kill had come. We'd had enough. We'd wept enough. We'd buried enough. Our enemies needed to start paying for our suffering.

We decided on that day that we did not need Thula's blessing to do what we ought to do for our families. We would continue traveling with her to convince people to come to Liberation Day, and we would start avenging every child Kosawa had lost.

For days after the killings, we waited for soldiers to arrive. They didn't. Pexton, we later found out, had decided not to make the killings public, afraid of what the news might suggest about its oil field. We later heard that supervisors told the murdered men's families that the men had died in a drilling accident, that their deaths had been so grotesque their bodies weren't suitable for viewing. We heard the families were given the remains in coffins sealed by Pexton so that the true cause of the men's death would never be found—how would Pexton have explained its laborers dying of gunshot wounds when the only people who owned guns were soldiers?

How the news leaked we never knew, but in no time, across the district, people were talking about the killings. Some said one of the laborers was sleeping with a soldier's wife and the soldier had killed him and his friends in revenge. Others said Pexton had paid soldiers to execute the men for something they'd done to offend the overseer. One of us heard a woman in the big market telling her friend that it was the spirit of someone one of the laborers had betrayed: spirits now had guns. This was closest to the truth, for it is what we'd become: phantoms leaving dead bodies in the dark.

A month after the killings, knowing of a house where two soldiers lived, three of us went there and put holes in their heads while they slept. A government worker at the head office in Lokunja was next, together with his wife, in their car. We knew none of these people. We executed them only to pass a bit of our pain along to our tormentors.

After every kill, those of us who had taken part in the act accepted palm wine from the others. While the killers got drunk, the sober ones pondered whom to kill next.

We were now the spears of our people.

The soldiers came hunting after our twelfth kill. In all eight villages, they searched for guns under beds and in kitchens, ransacked piles of dirty clothes looking for bloodstains. They gathered males in village squares and ordered the murderers to surrender. Their warning was clear: if the murderers did not surrender and were later caught, all the men in the village would be executed. They got no confessions, only silence.

In some villages, they forced dozens of women into their trucks at gunpoint and drove them to Lokunja. There, at the prison, the women took turns lying on their backs in a dim room as the soldiers interrogated them, demanding every detail on the whereabouts of their husbands and sons on the night of the latest killing. Old women, who'd heard only rumors, were struck in the head and promised a protracted death if they did not give detailed enough answers. Young women returned home with accounts of how their underwear was ripped off, their legs pried open by three or more soldiers—some women couldn't recall how many soldiers had mounted them. The sister of one of us was among them. A cousin, barely out of girlhood but with the body of a woman, was left bleeding for days, her womb in danger of becoming useless. Our wives cried, as did our mothers, fearing their turn would inevitably come. Sonni met with the wojas of the other villages to search for a solution. They went to the district officer, who told them that until the murderers were handed over he couldn't promise that our people would be left alone.

Thula came from Bézam with a newspaperman. She took him to all the eight villages to talk to the women who had been beaten and raped. The newspaperman asked the women if they thought the killer was from our villages. The women shook their heads; they swore upon their ancestors that no man among our people could do such a thing. Thula swore too, even though she knew. She'd figured it out after the first killings. She'd pleaded with us to stop it, and we had asked her what evidence she had that it was us— wasn't it possible there were other men in the eight villages with guns? We couldn't confess the truth even to her; we couldn't expect her to understand why we had to do it.

When the newspaperman left, Thula wept while describing to us the face of a raped woman she'd visited, how it was still swollen from the punches she'd received, her eyes still shut. Being raped was her worst fear, she confessed. "For the women's sake," she cried, "please, stop it. For the sake of your wives and daughters, I beg you to end it."

We'd had the talk among ourselves already—for whom were we killing if our actions left our children motherless, our sisters childless, our parents daughterless? We hated our enemies even more for taking away from us this chance at blood reparations, but we knew we had to pause. We vowed to resume with new and better tactics.

As if the Spirit was in agreement with our cease-fire, no one died in Kosawa in the next six months, so our regret at laying down our arms was abated. Whatever rift had developed between Thula and us as a result of the killings began to narrow. Whereas in the days of the killings she seemed afraid to look into our eyes, now she hugged us, and commended us on jobs well done, as if we were wayward sons who had returned home.

It must have been around the seven-year anniversary of her return home that she announced to us that she had selected the date for Liberation Day. When we told her that the date was only three months away, too soon, she told us that it was fine, we would have to proceed with however many people had thus far heeded our message. We did not think this to be a prudent move, and we cautioned her against it—if we were to start a movement with a scanty rally, we would become objects of ridicule. We needed more time; an explosive revolution could not be ignited with a feeble spark. Also, in the aftermath of the killings, the soldiers were not wont to show mercy. Did she want to provoke them at a time when they were eager to use their guns? There would be no guns, she said. She'd used her position at the school and her privileges as a top government worker to get a letter from the presidential palace giving her permission to rally young people in Lokunja to celebrate the country. The district office would have a copy of the letter; any soldiers at the rally would be there for our protection. We could have laughed at the irony—soldiers ordered to protect us—but we didn't, concerned still, as we were, about the turnout, about whether she was ready to address a crowd and tell them to get ready for a revolution. And what would the government do when they learned of her true motives?

We believed Liberation Day needed another year or two of preparation. It had become wholly evident to us that, deep as hatred for His Excellency ran, desperate as many were for change, few, if any, would join a movement led by a woman, worse still an unmarried, childless woman. We couldn't ask people to look past her lack of a family. We couldn't tell them that it meant nothing—it meant everything. It meant her deficiencies were many, too many for a man to take on. We hoped that, with time, she'd find a husband, someone with whom she'd have a child so that she could become a real woman, because nothing could make her respectable besides motherhood and marriage.

We couldn't hurt her by telling her this, nor could we tell her that we were having enough of a struggle explaining why we were followers of a woman—we'd already come to terms with the mockery—but neither could we let the resistance fail because our leader was determined to remain unfathomable. Still, after listening to her argue that we couldn't keep waiting for the perfect moment, it might never come, we agreed to her date after consulting with the twins, Bamako and Cotonou.

Though they were still boys, the twins were already in possession of skills almost as good as those of Jakani and Sakani, and we knew we couldn't proceed with Thula's plan without going to them to seek the Spirit's favor.

After we made a payment of smoked bushmeat to them, they agreed to intercede on our behalf. Days later, they came to us with the message that the Spirit was in agreement with the date Thula had selected for Liberation Day. The Spirit had also instructed them on the ritual they would need to do to prepare Thula.

. . .

On Thula's subsequent visits to Kosawa, we started putting together the groundwork for Liberation Day. Now that our belief in the movement had been renewed, thanks to the hope given to us by the Spirit's approval, our enthusiasm grew as the day neared. The elation that carried us through those weeks enlivened all of Kosawa. Without our asking, our families began disseminating the news across the other villages. Old and young alike were talking about Liberation Day, counting down to it, to the day when the light we'd long been dreaming of would begin emerging. Word spread to towns and villages in the surrounding districts. We busied ourselves thinking of the speeches we would each make, organizing our children into a choir for entertainment, persuading friends to bring their drums so that, after Thula had declared a new day, we would all dance till the stars came out and the crickets joined our chorus and we had nothing left with which to rejoice.

THULA RETURNED TO KOSAWA SIX days before the Day, having taken off time from her job to be present in the area and be of help with the final details. She was sleeping in one of our huts, late one night, when the twins arrived and told us the time had come for the ritual.

The twins began by sedating her, spraying something in her room, and closing the door. After that, one of us carried her on his back into the twins' hut and exited with no memories of what he'd seen. He did not need to see anything—the twins had told us what they'd do to her, and we'd agreed to help them do it, though only after a quarrel.

It was the worst argument we'd ever had: two of us were against the idea, three were for it. The night we met to decide on the matter was laden with pleas and blames and threats. The two of us opposed to the idea believed that it was not our place to make a decision about her body—we were neither her father nor her husband. Though we trusted the twins that the ritual would be for the best, that it would fortify the movement, we nonetheless thought it best that she be informed about the procedure so she could decide whether she wanted it to be performed on her. We were adamant that we would not partake in doing such a thing to her. But one of the three of us who supported the idea, in a long talk two nights before the ritual, argued that we had to help the twins. He said we couldn't trust Thula to make the right decision on this matter; Thula was willing to die for a better country, but she'd never give up her right to control her body. We needed to make the choice for her, for her sake, for her dreams.

By the time the night of the ritual arrived, we were

all in agreement that we had to do it for her sake. It brought us no joy to have to do such a thing to her, but sacrifices had to be made—hadn't she often said so herself?

The twins, speaking to us as if we were children and they the adults, had told us what they would do to her. The semen would be that of a young man in the village, someone the Spirit would cause to sleep-walk into the twins' hut, spill his seed into a bowl, and return to his bed still unconscious. Though the semen would be this young man's, the child in it would be the Spirit's, for the young man would only be a vessel.

In Thula's sedated state, the twins would undress her from the waist down. One of them would spread her legs apart and keep them open while the other inserted the semen inside her, rubbing her belly as he chanted to the ancestors, declaring her victorious, proclaiming that the child of the Spirit within her would make her a woman above all men, anointing her the Mother of a people ready to be reborn. After the procedure, we would carry her back to her bed and lay her on her side to stop the semen from leaking. In no more than two days, all who looked upon her would see what the Spirit had done.

We were the first to notice the change, eager as we were to see the results, so much hinging on it. She was still the same size, and yet there was something about her, a glow and a majesty that could only be from the child growing within her. She was a woman, finally, beyond woman even, and everyone could see, though they could not tell why, they could only conclude that she was deserving of their devotion. She was no longer a childless old-girl whom loutish elders could laugh at, or the enigma her friends wanted to marry off; through the power of the Spirit-child living within her, she had transcended her body and become sublime.

The twins had told us that she'd never know anything of it, and we could tell it was so. The seed within her would stay dormant, and she would never question why she'd become a recipient of greater deference and admiration from men and women, old and young. When we asked the twins about the child she was carrying, they told us that the child was in no rush to depart the host of the unborn. On a day of the Spirit's choosing, they said—it could be months or years away—whenever it was that Thula woke up in the arms of a beautiful man, the Spirit would cause the seed within her to start growing.

THE REVOLUTION BEGAN, AS SHE'D dreamed it, on a November evening in 2005, at the field of our former school in Lokunja. We set up stools for the old to sit on, and tables on which we would stand to speak. Our brothers and sisters and friends, mothers and fathers, relatives we would never have supposed cared for our message, arrived from all corners of the eight villages. Young men took buses from distant towns; young women dressed as if for weddings, hoping to find husbands. The enterprising brought one thing or another to sell. At one end of the field, drummers practiced for the finale while little children danced. We hadn't planned for a festival, or a day for relatives to reconnect and for friends to meet to pass gossip, but that was what we got in the first hours. The entire district seemed to be there, the crowd spilling past the school compound. In the distance, soldiers stood with tight faces, their guns pointed. No one feared them; our bliss made them invisible.

In our welcoming remarks, we told the crowd that this day was their day, the day for them to declare their readiness to take back their lives. Their roar could have caused all our dead to rise. Our children had rehearsed a song for weeks but decided that they no longer wanted to sing, so one of our wives led the crowd in a chorus about how magical it was to be alive, everyone clapping as they moved in rhythm. Three of us climbed onto the table to introduce Thula

Nangi, our sister, back from America, ordained by
the Spirit to lead us to victory over our adversaries.
The people shouted for joy as we lifted her to the table
and handed her a bullhorn.

"Power to the people," she cried with her fists
clenched up.

"Power to the people," the crowd cried back.

"Who are the people?"

"We are the people."

"Yes," she said, "we are the people, and our moment has come."

The multitude roared. With every declaration she
made, they roared louder, raising clenched fists alongside hers.

"This land is our land." Roars.

"We'll take it back whether they like it or not."
Roars.

"We'll no longer be slaughtered, poisoned, or trampled upon." Roars.

"Let those who stand in the way of our peace and
happiness be warned. Let them know that we'll march
through the streets of Lokunja and district capitals
around the country. We'll clench our fists until we get
to Bézam. We'll roar until they give us back our dignity. Our voices will be the fire that will burn down
every system of injustice, and from the ashes we will
build a new nation."

"Fire," someone shouted.

"Fire," the crowd sang.

"Yes," Thula cried, "we are the fire that will leave

nothing immoral unburned. My brothers and sisters, mothers and fathers, we have seen the light. There will be no return to darkness for us. We have awakened, and we will not stop raising our voices until every man, woman, and child in this country is free."

Juba

WHAT DOES IT MEAN TO BE FREE? HOW DO HUMANS behave when they start believing that their definition of freedom is at hand? I saw how, that day in Lokunja. I saw men standing tall, strutting as they headed home. I saw little girls waving and smiling at soldiers as if to say, Hello, look at my pretty dress. I saw women throw their heads all the way back when they laughed. I sensed the air around me vibrating from the burdens that had momentarily been cast off shoulders. Possibility was written on the faces of the multitude, an unguarded anticipation of the future. I saw it over and over as I followed my sister to the next rally, the next district; as we traveled the western part of the country. I heard it as people lifted their voices and demanded a democratic election, demanded that His Excellency give them the right to choose their own president so they could create their dream country. I saw freedom on my sister's face, as she stood before crowd after crowd.

Her fists never unclenched. Her resolve never wavered. She never stopped believing that Kosawa would one day be whole. She took her people to Gardens, to Mr. Fish's front yard. They demanded reparations. They demanded to be treated with respect. When guards lifted their guns, Mr. Fish asked that they lower them, chanting never hurt anyone. This land is our land, they sang. Some days they sat at the center of Gardens. Mothers with babies on laps. Grandparents on stools. Many who had fled returned to fight. They shared stories about Kosawa's lost days of splendor. They sang: **Sons of the leopard, daughters of the leopard, beware all who dare wrong us, never will our roar be silenced.** The oil was their inheritance, they said—they had the right to occupy Gardens. One week they occupied it nonstop, taking shifts. They wouldn't relent. Even if Pexton continued to ignore them, they said, an American court would one day grant them victory.

I WAS WITH MY SISTER the first time she spoke to Kosawa's new lawyer. She had written to a former professor asking for advice after her talks with Mr. Fish stalled. The professor told her about a nephew of his, a man named Carlos, who was a partner at a prestigious New York law firm. Carlos's firm represented the likes of Pexton, the professor had said, not the likes of Kosawa. But it would be of no harm for Thula to talk to him.

Half an hour before Carlos was to call her at her office, she was already settled behind her desk, going through her list of prepared questions and consulting notebooks in which she had jotted down thoughts and ideas over the years. The container of food I'd brought to her for lunch was unopened. It was possible she hadn't eaten all day.

"Have a few bites, at least," I said.

"I'm not hungry," she replied without looking up.

"There are other lawyers in America," I said. "If he says no, you'll find—"

"I don't want another lawyer. There's no way we can put up a real fight against them unless we bring one of the big New York guys. Carlos is our best chance."

The phone was in her hand even before it finished its first ring. For most of the conversation, she listened. When she hung up, the look on her face was of neither relief nor excitement. Carlos had merely given her more to worry about.

Kosawa's case against Pexton was weak, the lawyer had told her; based on his preliminary research, Pexton's agreement with our government was that Pexton would extract the crude and our government would be responsible for all negative externalities. What this meant, he explained, was that if the case ended up in a trial, Pexton wasn't going to deny that its practices led to spills that famished Kosawa's soil. Its lawyers wouldn't try to dispute that the waste on the big river was from their oil field. They wouldn't even need to argue that the children's deaths had nothing to do with them. All they would need to show was evidence that our government had relieved them of any responsibility to the land and people in exchange for splitting the oil profits.

"Does that mean he won't take the case?" I asked her.

"He needs time to think about it."

"What about his fees?"

"That's another thing. He doesn't do contingency fees, and he knows we can't afford him. He's going to talk to his partners and see whether someone can do it pro bono. We'll have to find a way to pay whatever expenses come up."

A few weeks later, she received a phone call from Carlos saying that he had decided to take the case on a contingency-fee basis. First, though, Kosawa would have to drop the case brought on by the Restoration Movement; Thula would need to talk to the Restoration Movement and inform them of the village's decision to hire Carlos and start a new lawsuit. Once the old suit was dropped, Carlos would file a new one, accusing Pexton of conspiracy under something called the Alien Tort Statute. His argument would be that Pexton knew, going into a partnership with His Excellency's government, that it was a government that cared nothing for the welfare of its people. Pexton took advantage of this and violated international laws, causing untold damages to property and lives in Kosawa.

Pexton was certainly going to ask the judge to dismiss a case they'd label frivolous, Carlos said, but he would request that the judge subpoena their internal documents related to Kosawa as far back as when its workers first appeared in the valley. At trial, Carlos would ask the court to impose substantial compensatory and punitive damages. None of this was to suggest that the battle was going to be easy or pretty, the lawyer cautioned—it'd likely take years, suits against powerful corporations were nearly impossible, Kosawa's chance of victory in an American court was infinitesimal. He didn't want the village to rest all their hope on it, though he was going to fight hard for them.

My sister had never been someone who jumped for joy at many things, but as she updated me in my living room, she couldn't stop skipping around and saying, I can't believe it's happening, it's finally happening. She'd lived in America, she knew what its courts were like, yet she put Kosawa's fate entirely in its hands, because where else could she put it?

When she gathered the village in the square to tell them about their new lawyer, they cheered, and hugged each other, some even shedding jubilant tears, amazed that a mere four years after her return from America, Thula was already on the verge of saving Kosawa. She did not attempt to curb their celebration—their joy was her strength—but she nonetheless told them that the odds were against them, Pexton had armies of lawyers, but Carlos was fearsome too; he'd never lost a big case, and he was in this to win. One of the Five stood up and gave a stirring speech about how Pexton had been cornered at last, by the time this was over they would wish they had never stepped foot on our land.

After the village meeting, Thula informed the elders in a closed-door meeting in Sonni's hut that, though Carlos would be working on a contingency-fee basis, he'd still need money for expenses, including payment for the experts who would be coming for a reconnaissance trip. Carlos couldn't file any papers without a large amount of money up-front, so he had referred Thula to someone who could lend the village the money, someone at a place called a hedge fund. The hedge fund would give Carlos the money he needed, and if Kosawa won the lawsuit, they would give the hedge-fund people a percentage of what they got from Pexton. After giving Carlos and the hedge-fund people their percentages, Kosawa would get to keep less than a third of the awarded damages.

"How much money will we get, then?" one of the elders asked.

"I don't know," Thula said. "Carlos says there's no

way of knowing. But if these hedge-fund people are open to lending us money, it's because they believe we have a strong case and they're confident their percentage will be many times what they lent us."

Everyone was silent for several seconds. "Do these people in America understand that money is really not what we're after?" another elder asked.

"Money is the only thing the courts in America can force Pexton to give us," I said before Thula had a chance to speak. She never seemed to feel it was a burden to explain everything to everyone, but I longed to relieve her of this task whenever I could.

"Juba is right," she said. "The American courts can only make Pexton give us money, and then we can decide whether to use the money to clean the village. If we get a big enough sum, we can pay for people in America who know about cleaning lands and waters and air to come and look at the village and tell us what our options are."

"But why can't the courts just make Pexton leave?" the first elder said. "I know you said it doesn't work that way, but there has to be some law in the American books that says that people have the right to live peacefully on their lands. Can't this man Carlos look for this law in his books and ask the judge to apply it to our situation?"

"I'll ask him, Big Papa," Thula replied. "Carlos understands that restoring the village is what we're most after, and I trust him to do his best to see that that happens."

"If you trust him," Sonni said, "give him our permission to do what he must."

The day that Carlos filed the new lawsuit passed
with less fanfare. I picked Thula up from a classroom
after her lecture, and she showed me the fax from
Carlos telling her to buckle up for the ride. I hugged
her; we drove to see our parents, who hugged her
and told her to get some rest—who knew how long
it would take for the lawsuit to drag itself from court
to court? They asked her to try not to think about the
lawsuit, or the country.

She couldn't. There was too much to do.

After Liberation Day (which she spent every spare
minute preparing for, and spoke about nonstop, in the
three years after Carlos filed the lawsuit), she formed
a political party to pressure His Excellency into holding an election, the first presidential election in our
country's history. She named her party the United
Democratic Party, though her devotees called it the
Fire Party, for how often she shouted "Fire" with
her clenched fist raised high. Her hope was that she
would find enough supporters across the country to
form local chapters of the party, ultimately result-
ing in a strong national presence. From within the
ranks of the party, someone would arise who would
stand up against His Excellency and defeat him in
a democratic election. Elections in the country were
still a fantasy—His Excellency retained the right to
have the only political party—but my sister believed
it crucial to declare her movement a party, albeit an

illegal one; it was imperative that her party be ready to go against His Excellency when he finally called for an election.

Together with the Five and her Village Meeting students, she held a rally in a town outside Bézam, exhorting people to join her in being the fire that would burn down the regime in the voting booth. She spent her vacation time that year, the entire month she was off, doing similar events around the country. But her party would never take root outside the western part of the country. At some stops in the north and the east, no more than a dozen people attended. Imitators were springing up nationwide, many hoping to gain a popularity as large as hers and use it to enrich themselves. In Bézam and throughout the southeast, few people dared to align themselves publicly with her for fear of His Excellency. The eyes of other tribes were also opening; they wanted one of their own to be their leader, a man with a familiar name, not a woman they barely knew. Wasn't it time every tribe started looking out for itself? they wondered. My sister tried to argue against such thinking. She tried to contend that the country might be made up of dozens of tribes but it was still one nation, a garden with flowers of assorted shapes and colors and fragrances, in unison forming an exquisite beauty. Few listened—unity seemed too vulgar a notion.

Mama and I worried for her daily. Sometimes I slipped cash into her driver's pocket when she was leaving for a trip. "She's my only sister," I said. "Please, watch over her." The driver nodded. He had seven daughters; worry was all his wife did.

I teared up in fear, with pride, whenever I watched her in front of an audience, telling them to dream with her. We traveled with her as often as we could—Mama, our new papa, my girlfriend and I. A couple of her friends from America visited; others sent cards with encouragements. She was a dove forging through a fire, burning yet soaring.

^^^^^^^

CARLOS AND HIS TEAM OF three arrived in Bézam a couple of years after Liberation Day. He told Thula, right at the airport, that there was something he'd been dying to tell her but he wanted to say it in person. He'd recently bumped into an old friend who worked at the Justice Department and told the friend about his Pexton lawsuit. The friend had confided in him that the Justice Department had a file on Pexton; they'd been gathering evidence on them since the massacre, evidence that showed Pexton breaking American laws by giving bribes to foreign officials. The department hoped to bring charges against them under the Foreign Corrupt Practices Act. What this meant, Carlos said, was that if the department won, the judge might force Pexton to make restitutions to Kosawa.

When Thula repeated this, while our family was

having dinner with Carlos and his team in Mama and Papa's house, we all cheered.

It was a long shot, Carlos cautioned—the odds of Kosawa's getting anything out of it were minuscule— to which Thula, her face illuminated with euphoria, said, "You never know; impossibilities happen, that's the great beauty of life." We toasted that night as we ate pepper soup with goat meat, and land snails in tomato sauce with rice.

After dinner, while everyone else watched American sitcoms on our parents' television, I sat with Carlos on the porch to finish our beers and catch the late-night Bézam breeze.

"I can't remember the last time I saw so many stars," the lawyer said, looking up.

"You can move here and see them every night," I said.

He chuckled. "I'm not cut out for this kind of life," he said.

Clearly, I wanted to say, glancing at him. If someone had told me that he'd just walked out of a movie, I would have believed it, considering his flawless profile and heavy stubble, an overwrought handsomeness highlighted by his sleek hair. He had an expensive-looking watch on his wrist, and a wedding band on his finger, though from the way he looked at my sister, and the number of times he complimented her during dinner and leaned over to rub her shoulders, it was evident to me he'd gladly forget his vows if Thula gave him a chance. He would find out, if he tried, that neither he nor any man alive stood a chance with Thula while Austin still lived. One story from Thula about an experience she and Austin once had would be enough to tell him that his cause was lost.

"I know you don't need to hear it from me," I said, "but I still want to thank you for taking this case. Kosawa means everything to my sister."

"My uncle told me," he said.

"Professor Martinez?"

He nodded. "He can't stop talking about his star student who is going to change her country. We're sitting together at family dinner—him, my parents, the whole family—and he says, 'Hey, Carlos, what do you say about helping this village?' And everyone starts talking about all the terrible things happening in the world, and how I could do something about it—'Come on, Carlos, just help this one poor village.'"

"So you're here because your family pressured you?"

He laughed. "Of course not," he said. "Defending the big guys is what I enjoy doing, but I thought I'd fight for the little guys for once, do something different. It'll make my parents happy. My dad drove cabs fourteen hours a day so my siblings and I could go to college, and when I got into law school he told their friends that I was going to become a lawyer to put bad guys in prison. I don't ever intend to make a career out of that, but at least, the day Kosawa wins, my parents can show the news clipping to their friends."

. . .

I didn't see Carlos and his team before they left for Kosawa, or after they returned, but Thula told me their trip was successful—they flew to America with an abundance of videotaped interviews, and photos, and soil and water samples. Their presence had also enlivened the village. They had shared stories about the America of 2007, how a woman just became the third most powerful person in the government there; and how some men were fighting for the right to marry each other, which made the elders laugh so hard they nearly lost the rest of their teeth. The evening before they left, palm wine had flowed and the Americans had played the drums while the children danced and the adults clapped.

The next day, Kosawa began a new season of waiting. Women continued trekking for hours to find fertile lands. Mothers boiled water for babies. The forest supplied bushmeat, which brought in money for basics. Children died because of Pexton, and for reasons that had nothing to do with Pexton. Newborns arrived to replace them. Families fled. Families returned, often for the sake of grandparents who wanted to die where they were born. Days of serenity intermingled with days of despondency.

Through it all, Thula never wavered, even as years came and went and her students from her Village Meeting graduated and new students came in and graduated. Even as she received a promotion and became head of her department, which led her to suspend her party activities so she could focus on her students, who remained one of her best chances at realizing her vision.

She still traveled the country, to speak to occasional gatherings of her supporters, the young people who walked with high shoulders even in the presence of soldiers and greeted each other by raising clenched fists. She traveled also in response to letters she received asking her please to come and speak to one community or another because, emboldened by her story, they'd decided to stage protests in front of government offices and corporation factories. She exhorted the protesters never to stop believing that change was going to come. Whenever she arrived somewhere, women welcomed her with joyful dancing. "Look at what one of us is doing," they sang. "Look at what a woman can do."

She knew many were those plotting her demise, but she did not fret. Not even when she sensed she was being followed around Bézam by a man in dark glasses whom she'd spotted sitting in a car outside her house; shadowing her in the supermarket; lingering around her office with a cellphone to his ear. It did not surprise her—of course Pexton was going to try to scare her. But they misjudged her. They didn't expect she'd smile at the man whenever she saw him, wave at him sometimes. She told Carlos and the Five about the man, and they all agreed that she should take cautionary measures for her safety. But my sister was never one to slow-dance with fear; she refused to hire a private bodyguard. Once or twice when I was with her, I saw the stalker and begged her to be careful.

She laughed and told me to stop worrying. One day, the man stopped following her. When she told Mama that she could relax, the man was gone, Mama cried in relief.

.^^^^^^/

WHEN THULA FIRST RETURNED HOME from America, Mama often took me aside to remind me that I mattered too, that everything wasn't about my sister, I shouldn't feel compelled always to put aside my needs for the sake of Thula. Mama could see, as only a mother could, that around Thula I often forgot that I had a story too, that Mama and I both had stories and dreams unrelated to Thula's vision for Kosawa and our country.

Sometimes, in her kitchen, Mama and I reminisced about the time after Thula left for America, when it was just Yaya and us in the hut, Yaya unable to get out of bed, Mama and I sitting on the veranda, enjoying our last days in our hut. We both cried the morning we closed up the hut and set out for Bézam to live with my new father. We left after we'd buried Yaya within a week of her moving to live with Malaika. We gave away our possessions to friends and relatives; the hut we abandoned was as bare as it was the day Big Papa built it, likely to stay forever vacant now that Kosawa was emptying.

We arrived in Bézam with a bamboo trunk stuffed with old clothes, smoked meats, sun-dried vegetables, and spices wrapped in leaves. Mama had carried it on her head from one bus to the next, wary of trusting the city's food too soon. On every prison visit to see Bongo she had brought along food—never had she eaten food not from home.

Our first night in the city, after my new papa had hugged us and fed us and given us water with ice cubes in it, he asked us to tell him everything about our trip. Then he said to us: This is your home, now and forever. Mama nodded. She told me to thank my new papa, yet she whispered to me before I went to sleep, "Never forget your old papa." I said, "Yes, Mama." I swore to her that I'd keep Papa in my heart always. I was ashamed to tell her that I'd already begun to forget Papa, Bongo too. My memories of them were waning, much as I wanted them never to.

One week after my arrival, my new papa held my hand and walked me to my new school. He guided me around cars green, red, and yellow; bought me sweet things to eat along the way. He gave me money for lunch and wiped the sweat off my face with his handkerchief. He'd never had a child; his heart was full of love he was desperate to share.

Years came, years flew. The faces of Kosawa faded away, my old papa's among them. My new friends, when they came over to play, could see that Mama still lived in Kosawa, dressing as if she'd never left. She couldn't speak English, unlike their parents, most of whom worked for the government. Mama thought often of her former life, asking me if I remembered this or that person, or the day such and such happened, making up songs about the hut in which we once lived with my old papa, sad songs that ended whenever my new papa returned from the office. When she heard my new papa's footsteps, Mama's melody abruptly turned joyful. Her voice rose as she set his food on the table. She did to him as she used to do to my old papa—she pulled out a dining chair for him and watched, smiling, as he ate and said a more delicious meal had never coated a man's plate. She brought him water to clean his hands at the table, and helped him settle on the couch after his meals, so he could be as relaxed and content as a man ought to be.

Papa made sure Mama's purse was never light. He gave her all she would need to keep the house clean, the food abundant, and retain for herself enough cash to travel to other parts of the city and laugh with women from her area, women she had overheard chatting in the market not in any of the lingua francas of our country but in the language unique to Kosawa and its sibling-villages. That sufficed as a basis for friendships.

After her visits to friends, Mama got off buses stuffed with brash city people to find Papa waiting for her, his trophy, in the living room. He stood up every time to kiss her, his eyes aglow. Even though his hair was gray, he could still lift her, which made her giggle as he carried her to the bedroom, telling me to go to sleep as he shut their door.

^^^^^^^

ALONE IN MY BEDROOM, I thought about the night I had returned from the dead. I lost something that night; I don't know what. I gained something; I don't know what. I remember everything about the journey except what I lost and gained. My old papa handed me to Mama after my eyes opened. He needed to hurry to the back of the hut to hide his tears—he couldn't contain his pain. Mama held me as she cried from relief. Yaya cried. Thula cried. They caressed me, asked me how I was feeling. I gave them no response as I looked around the parlor, searching for the thing I'd brought back from the forest yonder. I wanted to tell Mama about another thing, the thing I'd left behind, but I couldn't recall dropping anything before jumping over the river everlasting. It seemed plausible that I'd traveled with nothing but my body and returned with nothing but my body. Yet even now, decades after that day, I twitch and sweat in my sleep, searching. During the day, I'm overcome with worry, a suffocating urge to look for it, this thing I brought back. It has to be somewhere, the thing I lost, what was it? How could I live without it? I've accepted, after years of pondering, that I'll always be dead and alive, both and neither.

I wanted to ask my old papa to help me understand what happened that day, how Jakani managed to find me and guide me back home—Papa had a way of making the inexplicable logical—but he left for Bézam soon after I returned. I honor his sacrifice, dying so I might live long, but I wish I'd told him before he left that if Jakani hadn't called me back I would have gladly continued walking toward the ancestors. I'd beheld their hilltop city, glimmering in the distance, and I was eager to get there.

As a child with few friends, a burdened mother, an oft-distant sister, a broken grandmother, I watched life carry on around me after Papa and Bongo died. In a corner of the parlor, I sat and filled notebooks with drawings. The urge to draw came upon me not long after I returned to life. I'd never drawn before, but one evening I picked up Thula's pencil and a piece of paper. Images took form as my hand moved over the page. After the massacre, I felt no urge to cry, only to draw what I'd seen.

I wish I could spend my life drawing and painting the world around me.

Were it not for the duties love has placed upon me, I would find a way to move to Europe, where my favorite artists are from, and see what sort of life would avail itself to me. Only when I sit down to draw do I find answers to my questions, answers language cannot relay. Only in my illustrations does it make sense to me, what happened in Kosawa, the absurdities of humanity. It is my sole escape from the senselessness of existence, rendering the world as I see it. A world where real turns surreal before my eyes—that is how I began experiencing life the day I returned. At work, a colleague's head morphs into glass while we're chatting. A book flies off my shelf and burns in the air. A crown descends on Mama's head. My beloved's skin turns translucent, I see her blood flowing. None of it frightens me, though I developed a fever the first time it happened, when Woja Beki was speaking at a village meeting and his tongue turned into a dog's tail. These days it happens at random, but when I close my eyes and attend to my breath, all is real again. I can tell no one, not even Mama and Papa, not even the woman I love—they might consider me deluded. I accept it as the price I have to pay for two lives.

My best nights of sleep in my adult life were the four nights before my sister returned from America. I was finally ready to tell someone about my affliction, and it could only be Thula, the one who had fed and bathed me after our father vanished and our mother could do nothing but mourn for him and the baby who had died in her womb.

I imagined Thula would laugh at my confession and tell me that my condition was ordinary, all humans lived in a land between life and death, the world was just too chaotic for most people to notice. Perhaps she wouldn't say anything. It wouldn't matter. I just wanted to sit beside her again at the dining table and finish her leftovers. I wanted her to recount to me the conversations she used to have with our old papa about the whys of the world. I wanted to walk next to her, in awe of her singularity, like I used to in Kosawa.

I still remember our embrace at the airport the day she returned.

She looked at my bearded face, laughed, and said: Hey, what happened to my handsome little brother? It was for Mama and me that she left Austin and America. For Kosawa, yes, but for her family too. It was for us she took the job teaching at the government leadership school, though she had rejected their offer time after time, wanting nothing to do with people she deemed soulless. The government persisted, promising her she would have the freedom to teach whatever classes she wished—brains like hers were rare, and the sciences she'd studied would be vital to the well-being of the future children of the republic. They offered her a car and a driver and more money than she would ever need, money Kosawa needed, money her movement would need.

So, just as Papa joined forces with Woja Beki and went to Bézam though he hated Woja Beki and Gono, just as Papa did what he did not care to do, my sister shook hands with the government and went to work for them after she returned from America.

We lived and worked in different parts of the city, but we were together on many evenings, especially in those first years after her return, when she needed me to introduce her to the city. She had stopped eating animal products in America because Austin did not eat them, but in Bézam she began eating fish again. On some evenings, she and I would drive around the city in my car, searching for women roasting fish on street corners. My sister enjoyed our evening visits with Mama and Papa in their house—she loved how they fawned over her and asked her please to eat more, a mighty wind would be the end of her with so little flesh stuck on her bones—but she also relished Bézam street food. She loved the roadside banter with the other roasted-fish customers, conversations about the heat, the proliferation of stray dogs on the streets, the country's football team, which had just won a match—finally, something to be proud of about our country. Sometimes, if the roasted-fish lady had a boombox, my sister stood up and danced to the music with other patrons, her moves as unsightly as they were in Kosawa, her spirit unburdened, if only for a few minutes. Once, as I was dropping her off, she said that she hadn't thought she'd ever say this, but she loved living in Bézam.

Just not enough to forget Kosawa.

In the months after Carlos filed the lawsuit, she talked about the struggle daily.

I listened to her and tried, as gently as I could, to tell her that she'd done her part to save our village, no one would blame her if she decided to step back and just await the verdict from America. She did not agree with me: fighting for Kosawa was her birthright.

Fighting for Kosawa was not my birthright. Which is why I made up my mind, after Liberation Day, to start disentangling myself from my sister's dreams. I was weary of it all, the traveling, the waiting, being away from my beloved, my sister's constant agonizing over strategy, the seesawing of hopefulness and despair. I'd done everything I could for Kosawa. I'd done everything I could to help her. I could not make my life one of service to another human's cause, not even if that human was my sister. I never explicitly said anything to her—we still went to eat roasted fish, I still visited her in her office, she was my sister— but I knew I couldn't be part of her revolution anymore. I wasn't her; I would never be like her; I had to go my own way. I found solace in the fact that she had the Five, and her devotees from her Village Meeting, which I never attended. Looking at her on days when she couldn't get off her couch from exhaustion, I wished she'd chosen another way of life. I wished she'd chosen Austin over Kosawa. I wished she wasn't sacrificing so much for others, not after what our family had endured.

^^^^^^^^

IN A LETTER I SENT her months before her return from America, I told her how happy I was that she was coming home. We would get to be a complete family again—she and I, Mama and our new papa. I told her I was certain she and my girlfriend, Nubia, would love each other. She was enthralled by the prospect of loving my girlfriend, the idea that she would have someone akin to a sister. She enjoyed the story I'd told her about the day Nubia and I met, how I'd said to Nubia, "Is your name really Nubia? Unbelievable, my uncle and my sister, when I was young, they used to read a book about Nubia, they showed me pictures in it." Thula had sent Nubia a card thanking her for loving her brother. Just before Thula returned, she wrote Nubia saying how eager she was for their meeting. When they finally met in person, though, and saw the full extent of each other, it was clear a friendship would never be—they were as alike as a mountain and a valley.

It did not change what I felt for Nubia.

I'd made up my mind to travel the remainder of my life with her the day she said to me, by way of telling me her story, "Fathers—doesn't our pain begin and end with them?"

Nubia's father had a dream for our country and he named her after that dream, so her name would serve as a reminder to him, to everyone, that, as surely as the ocean's waves are born and reborn, gentle and mighty, everything that once existed would return to take its rightful place, be it where it was before, or wherever it finds suitable upon return. By naming her Nubia, he declared his belief that no ends exist, only new beginnings, like the seeds that fall and bear trees that drop seeds that bear new trees, like the water that falls from above only to be pulled up from below and sent back whence it came. Nubia was, Nubia would return.

When she was a child, her father told her of the land of Nubia, and a time too long ago for her to comprehend. He said the women of Nubia rode black panthers on streets covered with rose petals, and men there walked with high shoulders. He told her these stories sitting by her bed, on nights when she couldn't sleep. He spoke to her in English—the only language they spoke at home, so she and her brothers and sisters would be ready when the time came for them to go to America. "Why did our people leave Nubia, Dad?" she asked him. "They were men of zeal," he said. "They wanted to create a new Nubia, spread wide our greatness." "Why did they fail?" "They never failed," he told her, "they forge on through us."

One day, when you wake up, he said, we'll be back

in Nubia. You'll be a Nubian princess. You'll live in a kingdom.

He was gone by the time she woke up, to work in the presidential palace. He was one of a dozen men tasked with guarding the life of His Excellency under the leadership of the Captain. It was from the Captain that he had learned about Nubia; it was for the Captain's vision that he would lose his life. Did her father ever ponder how ridiculous that tale was? She doubts it. On the night when the Captain stormed the palace to kill His Excellency, take his place, and rename our country Nubia, her dad was there, a guard turned traitor. He killed two men as he searched for His Excellency alongside the Captain, a man who, having seen enough madness in the palace, had decided to rewrite our nation's story and free us from our abductor. Nubia's father and the other five guards wanted the same thing. For a new country named Nubia, they were willing to lay down their lives. Lay them down they did, all seven of them. They were captured and executed by the palace gates, their bodies left for crows to feast on, for His Excellency to smirk upon during his comings and goings. The bodies remained on display for days, so that every soul in the nation could see the folly of coups. Nubia saw her father's body, though not with her eyes—her family shut themselves up in their house. She sees her father's body still, in her mind. She hears his voice every time His Excellency appears on television to speak.

It all ended that day, their lives as America-bound children with skins glowing from wealth. Their lives as a family hanging in the highest circles of Bézam, lounging by swimming pools. Her dad's relatives arrived from the village with a message: her mother had to leave the house, which now belonged to her father's eldest brother, the head of the family. Her mom did not beg. She did not tell them that His Excellency had taken all of her husband's money, so they had nothing, only the house. Her mom packed her children's things, hiding her tears. She took them to a friend's house and listened as the friend explained why she couldn't let them stay. The friend said everything but the truth about why she could no longer associate with them, the family of an enemy of the republic; she couldn't say she had privileges to safeguard, a husband's job to protect, children whose bright futures she had to ensure. To the next friend they went, and the next, until they had no one, until Nubia learned that the world abounded in women who were afraid to be bitches. She promised herself she'd never be like them.

The only woman who offered her family a pot to lick was a woman her mother once met at a party. She saw them waiting at a bus stop as she was driving by and stopped. Since she was in need of a new servant, she offered them her servant's room, a shed at the back of her house, one room for them to share, a mother and five children. Their food would be free, but her mother would have to cook for the household—husband, wife, a daughter Nubia's age. Nubia's mother would have to go to the market, clean the house, hand-wash clothes, serve meals, wash and dry dishes, do what servants once did for her. Her mom said yes. In the shed they lived. They slept on a single bed, lying horizontally to fit on it. That is what her father condemned them to the day he gave his life for a dream.

She told me, crying, of the night when she was seventeen and the wife and daughter of the house had traveled to visit relatives and the husband was alone at home. How she entered the husband's bedroom and shut the door behind her, took off her clothing as the man's eyes bulged. How she did to him things she'd read about in steamy novels. He grunted so loud she feared his wife would hear in the next district. She returned for three more nights. They did it again when he found a reason to send his wife and child away for two weeks, during which time she went to him after school, telling her mom she had to study. In his ecstasy, he promised to do anything and everything to help her and her mom and her siblings. He kept his promise and got her into the leadership school, where I was waiting for her to walk beside me on my climb to the top of the government.

When she was done telling me her story, she swore that when she had children she would burn down cities to give them everything and rip out the hearts of anyone who dared try to take anything that belonged to them. I knew then that she would one day become the rock upon which I would build the next generation of the Nangi family.

. . .

Mama began telling me when I was a boy that the Nangi family name was mine to carry forward; she said I had to do all I could to extend our bloodline. Yaya reminded me often too that I would have to one day marry and have children, and that I would need to tell my children about those who came before me. For nodding at everything Yaya said, she blessed me with good fortune.

My new papa had his own dreams for me.

He believed I was destined to become a great man, which was why, though he wasn't rich, he sent me to the finest schools. I never told him that I wanted to spend my life drawing—with Thula wedded to her mission, I was my parents' only chance at a joyful and proud old age, and I longed to give it to them. Papa spent hours helping me with my homework, and when I passed my tests he gave me cash gifts. When the time came for me to get into a career training program, he went to the biggest men he knew in government, seeking help for his gifted son. He couldn't do it alone, being that he was but one of thousands of small men sitting at the bottom and striving for their sons to get to the top. Mama cooked and assembled baskets of fruits, and Papa took them to these men in their homes, along with bottles of alcohol, goats from the open-air market, and stuffed envelopes. That was how I got into the sole government leadership school in the country.

During my days at the school, I wrote to Thula about what I was learning, the conversations I was having with my classmates. I told her about all the ways my being in government could help villages like Kosawa. What the country needed was a government made of people like us, those who had suffered the consequences of bad policies and knew how things ought to be. We needed a leader who would put citizens first, place all businesses under state owner-ship. We needed to direct all funds from exports into the nation's coffers. If we put in measures to prevent the coffers from being pinched, they would eventually overflow. We would use our abundant wealth for healthcare, for education, jobs creation. There was no reason why citizens should lack when the country had bauxite to the north, oil to the west, timber to the east. With a visionary leader, a prosperous country was possible. Wasn't it evident, I asked her, that good government was the solution to the ills of our nation? I told her I believed we could do it, our generation. We could be the ones to uplift and equalize, no citizen greater or lesser than another. We could create a beautiful country. But first we had to wait our turn; the older generation's turn was not over yet. Our current leaders were men for whom the word "change" elicited chuckles, but there wasn't much we could do to force them and their archaic mentalities out, we had to wait for their eras to end. The past would soon be gone, and the future would be ours to design.

Thula did not dismiss my hope, though she said it was unlikely a country like ours would transition effortlessly from a wretched government to an upright one. She said our nation did not have the foundation for such a progression, because it lacked a constitution; what every country needed was a declaration made by the people, all the people, about what sort of country they wished to live in so that they could build it together. If you look at countries with a history of stable governments, she wrote, you'll see that they have solid foundations created by those who came before them. The Americans are standing on a foundation created by their founding fathers. European monarchs created foundations for the kinds of countries their descendants would live in. Who created a foundation for our country? No one. We were different tribes thrown together with no common dream. We were forced to build upon sinking sand, and now we're crumbling from within.

Despite my sister's wariness, I harbored hopes during my years at the leadership school for what I would do in government. My classmates were like me, convinced that we would never be corruptible like the older generation, determined to hold steadfast to the ideal that the emphasis on the title "civil servant" should be on the second word.

It did not take me long to realize, after I began

working, that my hopes would not come to be. I could see, even from my first day of balancing budgets, that the past and the future of our country would be identical. Repeatedly, I was told my job was to clean up numbers, not to ask questions about why large sums of money could not be accounted for. When I asked what would happen if the deficit was discovered, I was told that the problem was for another day—my responsibility was to worry about the present.

I learned, within my first year after leadership school, that political theories and their applications existed in separate realms. And that Thula was right—ours was a country with no foundation upon which a better country could be rebuilt. I slowly began to accept, just like my colleagues, that, ultimately, we had to do whatever suited us best. Only I didn't know in those days what suited me best. I didn't know what I really wanted.

Nubia knew what she wanted—five children who would one day study in America, health and prosperity, happiness for herself, for me, for our families. The country meant nothing to her. What good is this country to anyone? she asked me often. In our school days, I used to argue that the country stood a chance if we gave it a chance. Then I went into government and realized that no one in my office, from my lowest-ranking colleague to my biggest boss, gave the country a chance. They diverted all the money they could into private accounts, took whatever supplies their children needed for school, sent the office driver to chauffeur their wives around town, came to work as late as they could, left as early as they wished, because they deemed themselves entitled. My classmates from the leadership school, when we got together, laughed about the impunity, how much worse it was than they'd expected, but in the best possible way. I refused to join in. For years I worked and collected just my salary because I believed in my sister's dream, because I believed it only took one upright man to remake the world. But I knew my salary would never afford Nubia and me a life of great comfort. Many nights, I considered the ways in which I was failing my wife and future children for the sake of a better country.

By the time Liberation Day came, I'd spent years helping Thula with her mission, and Nubia had spent many evenings alone at home, because she understood that I longed to support my sister, and nothing was more sacred to her than familial love. She still thought it all futile, Thula's fight, which was why when I told her, a couple of months after Liberation Day, that I was ready to let Kosawa go, she kissed me and told me she was ready for us to start anew.

I'd traveled across the country with my sister, I'd borne witness to how little was changing despite her zeal, and I'd realized—while some men were heckling Thula at a poorly attended rally in the east—that my

Nubia was right all along: our nation was decaying with us inside it, all one could do was abscond with whatever one could. But we're not absconding, Nubia likes to say, we're only taking what's ours; we have the right to do so. She calls herself the Great Bitch, my beloved. She speaks in an American accent and prefers European fashion designers for both of us. For me she's done whatever a bitch needs to do to get her man what she believes he's entitled to.

To move me to the top in the government, she has arranged trysts with young women for my married bosses; she gives the trysters our bed and serves them dinner afterward. She has paid friends of friends in government offices to change my birth certificate so I wouldn't have to stop working at the mandatory retirement age of fifty-five—why stop working so young when there is wealth begging to be accumulated?

Together, she and I have amassed riches from payoffs I take after she tells me how much a requested favor is worth. She doesn't let me settle for anything but the max; she reminds me to stop thinking about fairness. We own lands nationwide given to me as gifts by companies and local rulers seeking my assistance. Our coffers are bloated with funds she helps me channel our way, now that I'm the head of the national taxation office.

We've bought a house for Nubia's mom and her siblings. We bought a car for her mom, and another car for her albino brother, so he'd no longer have to stay long under the sun waiting for the bus; we got him a high-paying job so young women would overlook his skin color. We bought a gated, two-story house for Mama and Papa, and found a woman to care for Papa now that his old age has become a sickness. We've built our own house—seven bedrooms, one for our relatives when they visit, the rest for our children, the first arriving any day now. Mama and Papa picked the baby's name for us. I cried when I heard it. I rubbed Nubia's belly that night as I whispered: Malabo Bongo.

Thula came to see Nubia during the month the doctor ordered Nubia to stay in bed. She sat with Nubia till the hour I was to come back from work. She told Nubia that Malabo Bongo would live in a better world, people were awakening to the truth. Thula knew about Nubia's father; she'd lived longer than Nubia, seen more, and yet she believed still that goodness would triumph. Nubia saw no use in telling her that the world operated under laws Thula could never change, and that our sole obligation was to ourselves, to our happiness and the happiness of the ones we loved. After Thula hugged Nubia to head home and prepare for a trip to Kosawa, Nubia turned around and lay back in bed, in a bedroom bigger than the one she had imagined during the nights she slept in a shed. She gazed at her closet, at clothes I'd bought for her on my last work trip to America, from a store on Madison Avenue. It was then I returned from the office, got into bed, and wrapped my arms around her as, downstairs, our servants prepared our dinner.

Even though our paths have diverged, I still give my sister counsel whenever she asks for it. And she gives me what she can—her acceptance that, though my ways are not hers and hers are no longer mine, we will someday meet at the same place again, a place where my focus on family and her focus on a better country will bring us all contentment. Will that ever happen? Why do humans fight when we all want the same things? What will my child, Malabo Bongo, arrive wanting? Mama says it will be a boy, a happy boy. How I wish for a world abounding in happy boys. We've all suffered, I said to my sister. Why choose to keep on suffering? Why not grant yourself more of the world's pleasures? But Thula doesn't believe that the world's pleasures can satisfy her spirit the way her purpose does. She says her purpose in life is to do as she must, even if it means suffering.

In my mansion, I suffer still.

I wake up daily before dawn to sit by the window with my drawing book. Sometimes I reread my old, worn copy of Nietzsche's **Beyond Good and Evil,** but most often I sketch images from my dreams, the faces of Papa and Bongo and Yaya. They're smiling at me always, happy in the next world. Or so I force myself to believe in order to attain what measure of peace is available for me. I'm certain true peace would be mine if I hadn't become what I once loathed, but I no longer yearn for peace like I once did. I have accepted that, just as I live in the space between the dead and the living, I'll always be whole outside and broken inside. I have let go of any hopes of ever being free.

Why won't Thula let go? I ask this question of Nubia. She has no answer to offer me. We each carry our burden, she says, searching for a place to lay them down—smart bitches know how to carry their burdens with style, and how to lay them down. She said she knew she could lay down her burdens only by returning her mom and brothers and sisters to the life her dad had cost them. Only then could she give the finger to His Excellency and the women who had turned her family away. And she knew she had to stick it to them wearing red stilettos and apparel off the racks of European designers.

^^^^^^

YEARS AGO, WHEN NUBIA HAD just become my girl, I found out that the father of one of her friends was the Leader of the team Kosawa had held captive. Nubia and I went to the man's house once. I shook his hand, we exchanged words, but I did not mention that I had been there that night at the village

meeting, and that afternoon when the soldiers res-
cued him and slaughtered my friends and relatives. I
told Nubia about it after we left the house, but asked
her never to tell her friend. It was then that Nubia
told me the story of how the Leader's wife and two
oldest children had died, eleven months before he
started coming to the village meetings. She told me
about how the car in which the wife and children
were traveling had fallen into a river. The bridge
under them had collapsed; government men responsible for maintaining it had misallocated the funds
for the repair of the bridge, putting it in their own
bank accounts. Some of them had been the Leader's
friends, people he had laughed and drunk with. They
consoled the Leader at the wake as his children and
wife lay side by side in matching coffins, dressed in
white. The Leader, when he returned to work after
the funeral, stopped thinking about the right things
to do for the sake of others. He thought only about
his surviving children.

He worked hard for them, to send them to America,
convinced that there was no hope for our country, a
country cursed at its birth, beyond salvation. He traveled to villages, doing his work for Pexton, parroting
what he was paid to parrot. Whenever he returned
home, he hugged his children, ironed their clothes,
fried eggs for their breakfast every morning. He never
remarried, choosing to cook for his children and clean
the house himself. Nubia's friend told her about how,
one evening, she'd entered her father's bedroom to see

him lying on the floor, weeping, clutching a photo of her and her surviving sister.

I'd sighed after Nubia recounted this, and she'd asked me why I'd sighed. I told her that on all sides the dead were too many—on the side of the vanquished, on the side of the victors, on the side of those who'd never chosen sides. What good were sides? Who could ever hail themselves triumphant while they still lived? Perhaps someday, I added, after all the dead have been counted, there will be one number for the living to ponder, though the number will never tell the full story of what has been lost.

I thought about that conversation last night.

I thought about Kosawa. How much longer will it remain standing? Mama reminds me that our people carry the blood of the leopard, but she seems to forget that leopards are disappearing; few remain in our part of the world. It's been twelve years since Thula returned, five since Liberation Day, yet the village remains poisoned.

I watched on the news the other day how Pexton's profit has increased by double digits from last quarter. His Excellency is expected to appoint a new Cabinet next week. He finally allowed our nation's first presidential elections last year; his European backers had insisted on it, saying he needed to demonstrate that he cherished the ideals of democracy. Opposition parties formed overnight to contest. Thula dismissed it all as a charade. No one was surprised when the results were announced.

Earlier this year, Carlos called Thula with the news that the Justice Department would not be indicting Pexton under the Foreign Corrupt Practices Act. Thula did not tell me why when she informed me; she barely wanted to talk about it. Carlos had hoped that an indictment by the department would bring publicity to the village's pending lawsuit based on the Alien Tort Statute and force Pexton to make a settlement—an ideal scenario, since Carlos did not think that the village stood a good chance at trial. And Pexton had indeed gone to Carlos with an offer, but Carlos did not consider it to be enough. No longer in danger of a Justice Department indictment, Pexton took all talks of a settlement off the table. Kosawa's only chance at restoration now rests on a judge's decision.

My sister is approaching forty. The toll of the struggle is finally visible on her face—soft lines are appearing on it, her cheekbones are protruding. Seldom do I call upon the Spirit, but last night, as I thought about Kosawa, my journey from there to here, and everything in between, I prayed for my sister, and for all who still live in our birthplace.

The Children

WE ARE THE AGE-MATES OF THULA AND THE FIVE, THE ones who had long ago moved on from the group and gone silent. This part of the story can only be told by us.

Some of us were still in Kosawa the day we learned of the judge's verdict, but many of us had left by then. We had left for new husbands, for our families, for no longer wanting to hear relatives rebuke us about our complicity in the deaths of our children, the same words we would later heap on our family and friends who remained in Kosawa. We had built new huts, had children, leased lands from relatives on which to farm.

Those of us who remained in Kosawa did so with pride.

Our enemies underestimated the depth of our resolve. They never appreciated to what extent we would go to protect that which our ancestors had passed down to us.

When we had begun marching, all they did was send soldiers to observe and report. The reports must have said our actions were harmless, because they let us be. What could marchers do to a regime? Did raised voices ever bring down a system? When Thula got a newspaperman to spread news of our movement overseas, when she took delegations from villages burned down by soldiers to meet with big men in ministries, the people in Bézam sighed. The woman was a nuisance. They never threatened to take away her job if she didn't stop. When she taught her students things the government didn't wish its future leaders to be taught, they ignored her, leaving her to do as she pleased—American-educated women were sometimes hard to control. They would have preferred she teach only what she was paid to teach, but they had to grant her the leeway; her educational accomplishments were matchless. Standing before rapt students, she flung insults at His Excellency, at his senseless cronies, their ineptitude, their shameless disregard for morality. The government yawned when they heard about her Village Meeting in her government-provided house. They said: What can one angry woman do?

One angry woman did everything, and she failed.

Did she cry alone in her house the day the lawyer from America called with the news that we would not be getting justice from an American court? Or did she go to her parents' house for a hug? Did she wish she had chosen Austin over Kosawa?

The judge who made the final verdict did not deny that Pexton had ruined our land, Thula told us when we gathered in the square to hear the news. The judge said it was likely Pexton and our government had colluded to commit countless crimes. But she also agreed with Pexton that American courts had to stay out of the matter and let the courts in our country decide whether Pexton and our government had done us wrong. She said it would be unfortunate if we did not get justice in our country's court, but America had to respect other countries' boundaries. What the judge meant by this, Thula explained, was that a man could not go into his neighbor's house and beat him up just because he didn't like the way the neighbor was running his household.

We did not know whom to feel sorry for the most when we heard this—ourselves, or Thula. Our friend's lips quivered as she spoke, but she would not allow herself to cry. This is not over, she said repeatedly. But we knew it was over. We had lost our last chance at restoration. Filing a lawsuit against the government and Pexton in a Bézam court would be ludicrous. The people who owned those courts were the same people who had given our land to Pexton. The judges who would rule in our lawsuit might be the same ones who had condemned the Four to death. We had no chance at justice there.

^^^^^^^

THROUGHOUT THE VILLAGE THAT DAY and the next, it was as if an eternal night had settled and the sun would never come up. We went to our farms, and to the forest, and to the market, but our thoughts were seldom on what our hands were doing, or where our feet were going. Our minds swirled with questions: How could this be? What do we do now?

With every subsequent visit to Kosawa, Thula seemed to be sinking deeper into the same darkness that had consumed her when her father vanished. She spoke little and she wouldn't eat, though we offered to make her favorite meals. When the children ran to her, she looked at them blankly. She and the Five sat in the square late into the night, whispering. It was from one of the wives of the Five that we learned that there was even worse news than Thula had told us: Pexton had filed a lawsuit against Kosawa, demanding that Kosawa pay its lawyers, since it was our fault that they'd needed to hire lawyers. If we lost that lawsuit, whatever we owned of worth would go to Pexton.

Thula told us at a meeting that we had no reason to worry about the lawsuit: no judge would ever place such a punishment on us. Pexton was only doing it to warn those who would dare follow in our footsteps—they didn't want villagers thinking they could rise against corporations with impunity. "Do you really believe an American judge will side with us and not allow Pexton to take everything we own?" someone shouted. Hadn't a judge just doomed us to perpetual terror? Thula did not seem to know what she believed; she spoke without conviction. We heard little hope in her voice when she said that she'd had many conversations with her friends in America, friends who still believed in her dream, and she had also spoken to Carlos. They had all reminded her that there were other courts we could take Pexton to, courts in Europe whose jobs were to protect people from their governments. But who among us still trusted courts?

If we were walking around with broken hearts, our friends the Five were sitting in one spot, sharpening machetes in their heads. In the week after Thula told us the news, whenever we happened upon any of them, they had no patience for inconsequential conversations—they were in a hurry to get on to the next phase of Kosawa's war. Though their zeal for Kosawa always awed us, we never wondered why they were the ones to dedicate their lives to Thula's ideals. Even as children, they were the most aggrieved of us, the ones who kept count of the number of spills in a given month, the ones who helped their fathers and uncles carry picks and shovels whenever the time came to dig a new grave. Yet they were the ones who rarely cried at the news of a death. We could tell, even then, that their pain was bound to find a violent form of release. As we got older, they bonded closer to each other by virtue of this shared determination to save Kosawa.

Like us, they'd dreamed of dying in Kosawa after living lives unfettered by toxic matter and the fists of men with no regard for our worth. Unlike us, however, they couldn't accept that such a destiny might never come to be. We admired their wives, who stayed with them, though we knew, because we were friends with them, that their marriages were full of silence and uncommunicated agony, circumscribed by the worst kind of loneliness.

If we had known how close they were to an explosion, we would have said something—anything—to prevent it, but how could we have known? In the months after learning of the verdict from America, our hearts were still heavy, but Thula's visits to the village put little smiles on our faces, even if she was nearly devoid of hope. Most of us had decided to take each day as it came and leave everything to the Spirit. Who knew, Pexton might decide the next day that it had taken all the oil it needed and that the time for it to leave had come. But the Five—they entertained no such fantasies. While we were beginning our long, slow march toward resignation, the Five were making plans.

∧∧∧∧∧∧∧/
ﮩﮩﮩﮩ

THULA WAS IN THE VILLAGE the day the Five exploded.
Nothing about that morning was extraordinary.
We sent our children to school. We went to work.
Some of us entertained relatives visiting from other
villages. A wedding was coming up in a few days—
one of our young men was marrying a girl in one
of the sibling-villages—and the women of Kosawa
busied themselves talking about the newest girl who
would be moving to Kosawa. Maybe it wouldn't be
long before all the huts filled up again, they said; may
the Spirit be thanked for love that causes blindness.

Thula was excited about the wedding too. It
was the first time she looked happy in the months
since the verdict—seeing her eyes aglow again was
like stepping out of a smoky kitchen. She and Sonni
and two of the Five attended a meeting at the district office in Lokunja in the afternoon, the details of
which Sonni was going to tell us at the next village
meeting. Thula had dinner with the wife and children of the one of the Five in whose hut she always
stayed. After dinner she helped the children with their
homework. She laughed hard when one of them read
to her an essay about why every country ought to be
like America—it sounded like a place where everyone
had everything. Thula went to bed smiling. The truth
about what happened after that, we'll never know.

. . .

We believe the Five woke Thula up and told her that they had Mr. Fish and his wife.

We don't know when the Five left Kosawa to go to Gardens and kidnap Mr. Fish and his wife. The Five were in the village in the morning: we saw a couple of them leaving to go hunting. We saw them in the evening, sitting on their verandas or visiting relatives. They must have left for Gardens after most of the village was asleep.

How great was Thula's disappointment and shock when she found out?

What did she say? What could she have said?

Did she attempt to stay out of it, wanting nothing to do with a crime? Did the Five command her to join them, or else? They wouldn't have. They revered her. But Thula would never have wanted to leave Mr. Fish and his wife at the mercy of angry gunmen. Mr. Fish was an oilman, but we did not hate him; he had never been unkind to us. Thula respected and appreciated him for what he'd tried to do. It seemed to sadden him that he derived his livelihood from our suffering—and Thula, though her meetings with him were heated, believed he truly wanted Pexton and Kosawa to reconcile. We all wished he could do more than say that the decision about the cleanup of our land and waters rested with headquarters in New York, but Thula would never have wanted him dead.

. . .

Mr. Fish and his wife were in Thula's family's hut for three days, and we did not know it. Sahel had given the hut's key to Thula, and Thula kept it in the care of one of the Five, so she could open the hut whenever she wanted to be in it. She couldn't have imagined that the Five would open it one night and put Mr. Fish and his wife there. What did Thula say to the Americans when, likely still wearing her sleeping clothes, she entered her family's hut that night and saw them? Did she offer the couple her mother and father's room, in which she had installed a bed and table and chair? Did she take the Five aside and plead with them to take the Americans back to Gardens? Did she truly write those ransom letters, or did the Five write them and sign them with her name? Thula's handwriting was made up of tightly packed, slender letters; the handwriting in the letter the government released was chunky and spacious.

The morning after the Five kidnapped the Americans, the wife in whose hut Thula was staying woke up and prepared breakfast. When she went into Thula's room and found the bed empty, her husband told her not to be alarmed, Thula had been stirred to wake up before dawn and do some writing. Thula needed to be alone for some time in her family's hut, he added. The husband took all of Thula's belongings from their hut to the Nangis' hut, along with extra kerosene, supposedly for Thula's lamp. His wife understood—it wasn't surprising for Thula, during her visits to Kosawa, to open her family's hut and spend time alone in there, writing in her notebooks.

We imagine Thula and Mrs. Fish chatted about New York during those three days as they waited for the two ransom letters to be delivered to Lokunja and Gardens and for the government and Pexton to make their move. Thula would have felt the need to keep the mood in the hut cordial so the Americans would not be in a permanent state of fright. No matter what their state was, we're confident they were well fed, because the wives of the Five set aside meals for their husbands every day, which their husbands took to the Nangi family's hut, saying something had come up, they needed to eat with their friends while they discussed it. The wives had shrugged; they'd heard that too many times. In those three days, Thula did not come out of the hut. It must have been the decision of the Five. She would have wanted to come out at the end of the day if she could—she loved sitting with her women friends and their children on verandas in the evenings.

While Mr. Fish and his wife were in the hut, the Five must have taken turns guarding them, likely two at a time, guns in hand. The rest of them carried on around us so we would not suspect that anything was awry. And we never suspected; nothing seemed peculiar; their manners were ordinary. We did not notice when they went to Gardens and Lokunja to drop off the ransom letters the government claims Thula wrote.

. . .

Pexton wanted to heed the letters' warning that soldiers be kept out of the negotiations. It wanted its man and his wife free to return to their children in America, it wanted no more blood on its hands, Pexton had not come to our country to get involved in our lunacy and carnage. We heard that His Excellency's men in Bézam told the Pexton men that the decision was not Pexton's to make: His Excellency did not take take orders, particularly from women. They say Pexton's leader in New York called His Excellency and asked again that soldiers not be sent to Kosawa, Pexton would give the kidnappers whatever they wanted. Some say Pexton's leader warned His Excellency that, if he sent the soldiers and there was bloodshed, Pexton would have to cease doing business with our country—Pexton held the highest regard for all human life. His Excellency is said to have laughed and told Pexton's leader to stop wasting his time with stupid bluffs.

Pexton, having no choice, sent its men along with the soldiers.

They arrived in a truck and parked it at the entrance to our village. Seeing them, we began spilling out of our huts, confused, not daring to go too close. We held our children's hands, though we did not need to worry about their getting close—they'd been born with a fear of soldiers, they knew from birth what men with guns could do to them.

A Pexton man in a black suit spoke into a bullhorn. "We hear you have our people," he said. "Bring them out now and we'll give you whatever you want."

It was early evening. Panic arose. We did not understand what he meant.

Who was in the village? Laborers? Supervisors? Why would Pexton workers be in Kosawa? No one thought it could be Mr. Fish. Only later did we realize that none of the Five had come out of their huts when the truck entered the village.

A soldier took the bullhorn. "Everyone get out of your huts and put your hands up right now," he said. "Come out before we start shooting."

Thula must have heard them. Did she consider leaving the hut with her hands up? She knew what the government would do if she did. She knew the soldiers wouldn't simply free the Americans and tell the Five never to do it again. Versed in the ways of Bézam, she knew what their punishments would be: a short prison sentence for her, execution for her friends. She must have known the Five wouldn't go down easy.

Standing before the soldiers, we saw it coming. Another massacre. Except this time we were warned. Sonni, barely any eyesight left, cane in one hand, walked close to the truck and asked the men, "Can you tell us what's happening? Who are you looking for?"

The soldier with the bullhorn said, "I'll say it one more time: everyone, get whatever you need and clear this village immediately."

We ran into our huts and began packing up whatever we could.

We yelled at our wives to stop crying, screamed at our children to put on their shoes. The sick and the old forgot how to be slow. On their mother's backs, tired babies whimpered and yawned; their hunger would have to wait. We threw items into baskets and raffia bags. Some of us packed too much, others too little. We all thought of something that we might need but had no time to search for: the soldier had given us five minutes.

We half-ran to Gardens, our provisions on our heads.

Under the skies we laid our blankets, behind the laborers' houses. Some of the laborers offered us water as they asked us questions we had no answers for; others looked at us askance, not knowing what to make of us. We were nothing to them, much as they were nothing to us, merely beings with whom we shared space.

We slept like animals that night, at the mercy of nature. No moon revealed itself, as if we were undeserving of light. The children, afraid to play, stayed by our sides. We shared with each other what food we'd packed. We felt rocks beneath our heads when we lay down to sleep. We heard gunshots in the distance, those of us who had stayed awake. We'd figured by then that it had to do with Thula and the Five, but out in the open, we dared not speak of it. Even that night, we knew we would never sleep in our huts again.

ΛΛΛΛΛΛΛ

IN THE MORNING THE BUSES from Gardens took us to Lokunja, and from there we made our way to relatives across the other seven villages, searching for refuge, so weary we could scarcely see our paths. We heard the news before we arrived in our new villages. We heard it from those who had come out to watch us lumbering. They told us that the Five were dead. Four soldiers were dead. Mr. Fish and his wife were dead. Thula was dead.

The story the world would hear about the last days of Kosawa was of how Thula and the Five, with guns in their hands, went to Gardens, sneaked past multiple guards, stormed into Mr. Fish's house, went into his bedroom, and kidnapped him and his wife, who was visiting from America. The government would tell of how Thula and the Five blindfolded Mr. Fish and his wife as they pleaded for mercy, and how they brought them to Kosawa. They wouldn't say how come no one at Gardens raised an alarm. They wouldn't wonder, as we did, if Mr. Fish and his wife came to Kosawa of their own volition. They would show one of the letters Thula wrote to Pexton saying we'd waited for too long. They would underline the section where Thula wrote that if a delegation did not arrive on foot from Gardens to negotiate, Mr. Fish and his wife would be killed and their bodies thrown into the big river. They would underline, also, the line where Thula wrote that if soldiers showed up instead of negotiators, the captives would be stripped naked, gagged, and whipped, before being executed. In stories written in newspapers here and abroad, they said she was a radical, they called her the Fire Lady.

No one will ever convince us that these stories are true.

Our Thula was angry, but she'd long lost her capacity for hatred. When some of our younger brothers started stealing from Pexton, breaking pipelines and filling buckets with crude so they could sell it in distant markets, Thula decried it all at a meeting, telling us we must be what we wanted our enemies to be. But the Five—we could be convinced they did what the government claimed. The American judge gave them permission to.

Only after their deaths did we learn that they were behind the phantom killings.

We had thought it could be the case—we'd discussed it in low voices, lest the trees be agents of the government—but we had no evidence that they owned guns, and how could we imagine that our friends had become murderers as insidious as our enemies? The wives of the Five, they suffered the worst in their wondering. But what right did they have to ask their husbands if they were killers? What marriage could ever survive such doubt of the other's decency? Like us, the wives decided to believe rumors of vengeful spirits. Whenever soldiers came to our villages to harass confessions out of us—something they continued doing years after the phantom killings stopped—the wives made up whatever lies they needed to make up for their husbands' sakes. They spent many evenings when their husbands were not at home visiting each other to commiserate; they told their children that their absent fathers would one day start spending more time at home, they would give them the attention they so craved, all would soon be well.

We were often overcome with doubt that Thula's movement would someday defeat His Excellency and Pexton, but that did not stop us from marching in Lokunja, or occupying Gardens, or attending planning meetings that she called for. Thula believed, the Five were resolute, and though our spirits were far more willing than our flesh to rise on some days and raise fists and chant, year after year, we did it because Thula believed.

THE SOLDIERS BROUGHT THE BODIES of the Five to Lokunja. They laid them at the entrance to the big market so that passersby could take pictures in their minds, spread the story far and wide. Our friends' eyes were still open, their bodies covered in dust and blood. We wrapped them in sheets to carry them away on our shoulders.

We asked for Thula's body.

They did not have Thula's body.

We mourned for our Thula without a body.

Some say she jumped into the big river, and, with her body bullet-ridden, sank to the bottom. Others say she ran into the forest, wanting to die alone. We went into the forest to search for her. From morning till night we called out, Thula, Thula. We never found a body. Thula, Thula. Thula never answered. Thula was gone.

The twins, Bamako and Cotonou, they went to their father, in the hut of the uncle to which their family had fled. They told their father about the child they'd put in Thula's womb. They were a medicine man and a medium, but they were also children who'd lost homes—could they have wondered, as children are wont to do, if they were responsible for what had happened to us? Their father, he was one of us, he told us what his children and the Five had done. We did not blame them; they had done what the Spirit had commanded them to do. We cried for Thula, for her baby. Would he have grown up to be our savior? A man conceived of the Spirit—who would have dared to stand against him? Sometimes we imagine that Thula ran deep into the forest and there the Spirit caused her belly to swell, and birds and leopards tended to her, wiped her brow, and watered her lips as she pushed forth the child, and in unison, all the living things sang: **For unto us a child is born.** Could this child someday return to us, reclaim for us what was stolen?

Sahel, Juba, Nubia, and Thula's new papa came from Bézam. We had no body for them. We buried the Five, but for Thula we only cried. We held Sahel, begged her to be strong. She fainted, again and again. She asked for a cup of poison; we refused to give it to her. Nubia told us she'd hidden all knives from Sahel when they got the news. The Spirit will restore, we told Sahel. We didn't believe it that day, but we told it to her, in desperation. Three times in one life. Three vanishes for one woman. Juba tried to be strong for his mother, but his own heartbreak wouldn't allow him. Nubia kept one arm around her husband, their son, Malabo Bongo, in her other arm.

Our fathers told us that Malabo Bongo was a replica of his father's big papa—the same small, sad eyes. We cried for the child too, as we did for our own children, the burden he would have to bear for the things done and undone to those before him. His life, like the lives of our descendants, in good ways and bad ways, would be only a continuation of our story—nothing could save him from that.

We were refused one last chance to enter Kosawa and empty our huts. The government decided the land had become too contaminated for human presence. His Excellency ordered Kosawa burned. What once were our huts became ashes. Our mothers' kitchens, ashes. Our barns and outhouses, ashes. Our ancestors' pride, ashes. Nothing remained of Kosawa, except for what we kept in our hearts. Hour after hour, day after day, year after year, winds of every kind came and blew away the ashes of what used to be our home.

Pexton took the bodies of the overseer and his wife back to America, to their sons. It was only months later that we learned their full names: Augustine and Evelyn Fish. In stories printed in our country, there were pictures of them, smiling, with their sons. A couple that loved life: executed. Their sons: orphaned. A tragedy in every sense. No one called Thula's death tragic. There were no pictures of her in most newspapers. Or of the Five. She was the Fire Lady. The Five, her disciples. Fire Lady, Fire Lady: how many readers of those stories cared for her real name, her full story?

The story told about her was mostly about her time in America, how she'd spent days in jail there for one misdeed or another. Some wrote of how His Excellency's freedom-loving government had allowed her and her followers to speak out and march. She was given privileges accorded to every citizen of the republic—why did she have to turn to violence? In America the newspapers wrote that New York was where she had learned violence; she wasn't the first and wouldn't be the last to travel to New York and leave as a radical. They wrote of how she had attended meetings in a place called the Village, a gathering of people who hadn't learned how to channel their anger positively. Others argued that violence had been in her blood long before she traveled to America: our government confirmed for those who inquired that, indeed, Thula's uncle Bongo had been one of the men responsible for the kidnapping of Pexton workers decades before. Thula had taken it further by acquiring guns and orchestrating killings. A violent family—how sad.

∧∧∧∧∧∧∧

HER FORMER STUDENTS AND BUSLOADS of devotees came from across the country for her one-year death celebration, which we held in her big papa's village. We'd stopped crying by then, but Sahel hadn't, though she now cried for her new husband too—he'd died months after Thula, leaving Sahel alone in a big house. She yearned to return to her birth village now that she was entering her final years, she wanted to sit on verandas and laugh old-woman laughs with Lulu and Cocody. But Juba and Nubia wanted her in Bézam so they could do everything to make her happy, visit her often, and spend nights at her house, so Sahel could feed and bathe and sing to Malabo Bongo and his little sister, Victoria.

Juba said Austin had written him a condolence letter in which he said Thula often talked about wishing everyone would wear yellow at her death celebration. So we all wore yellow. Flowing yellow dresses for the women, newly sewn for the occasion, along with yellow head-scarves and yellow earrings. Yellow trousers and yellow linen shirts for the men.

In the square where her big papa once sat in a corner, we beat the drums around a framed photo of Thula, taken by Austin, in which she's wearing a white dress, walking the streets of New York. Her hair is at the top of her head in a bun; she's smiling.

We felt her spirit around us as we sang and danced till the sun left us for a while. Before we dispersed, Juba thanked us for loving his sister. He told us that he would like to close the celebration by reading a poem Austin had written in honor of his princess.

We had learned from Thula that Austin had become a monk and was living in a neighboring country.
He left America the year after Thula returned home,
months after he buried his father. Thula told us he
had described his new life as the most joyous form
of existence he had ever known—having no possessions, living in stillness, daily tending to a garden
to help feed children at a nearby orphanage. Even
with no chance of a life together, the two of them
shared love letters in which they professed that their
spirits will be forever united, and that living
their callings had freed them to love each other without conditions.

Holding a pregnant Nubia's hand, his voice trembling, Juba read Austin's poem:

farewell to the revolution, weep not, silence lasts
for a night
rise children, get in formation, madness ignited,
fists clench up
burn, burn, burn; lift every voice; alive and
proud—or give us death
ten thousand systems, sipping on our souls,
onward yet we fight, until when
long may we live to see that glorious morning,
when the light shall emerge
when we'll gather, at the river, in the village
pure and clean
there'll be no more crying, no more bleeding,
no more sickness, only bliss

**oh boundless love, we are weary, won't you
come forth, guide us home?**

Pexton created a scholarship in honor of the overseer
and his wife, the Augustine and Evelyn Fish Memorial
Peace and Prosperity Scholarship. The scholarship was
for our children only. It would allow them to go to the
best schools and someday become learned, like Thula.
There was no land left to fight for, so Pexton had no
fear that our children might grow up to wage a war
against them. They'd already begun digging a new
well in what used to be our village square when they
announced the scholarship. They'd already uprooted
what was left of the mango tree under which we'd
played—whatever hadn't turned to ashes.

Most of our children got the scholarships.

We paid nothing for their education; Pexton made
sure of that. After finishing at the school in Lokunja,
they moved to bigger towns or to Bézam, where they
went to schools of higher learning, living and eating where they studied. Some of them got into the
government leadership school, others into lesser places
of advanced learning. Many traveled to Europe and
America, to study on other scholarships, or to start
new lives.

Today, in the year 2020, forty years since the night
Konga told us to rise, our children have good jobs
with our government, with corporations in Europe

and America. They live in lovely houses. They drive new cars. They've given us grandchildren. Several of us have been to America. Our children buy us nice things to show their gratitude.

Sometimes we ask our children about the cars they drive. The cars seem to be bigger than they've ever been, needing more oil. Do they think about it, about the children who will suffer as we once did just so they can have all the oil they want? Do they worry whether a day will come when there'll be no more oil left under the earth? They chuckle at our questions. They tell us that oil is still a thousand years away from depletion, by then no one would need it. We nod; we agree that a thousand years is too far away for anyone to worry.

WE HAVE NOW BEGUN OUR entrance into the last decades of our lives.

It marvels us how much suffering we bore, our parents bore, our ancestors bore, so our children could own cars and forget Kosawa. They do not speak our language to their children. They speak to them only in English. They do not recognize our Spirit, a

rejection that surely makes our ancestors weep. They
go to churches, if they have any awareness of a Spirit
at all. They believe in a Spirit in the sky when ours
lives within them. Some of us had taken our families'
umbilical-cord bundles before we fled Kosawa, hoping to pass them on to our children, but they have no
use for them. For births and deaths and marriages,
they celebrate in the ways of our former masters. They
dance to their music, as if ours was merely a relic to be
admired. They have village meetings, occasionally, but
it isn't to talk about how to keep alive their ancestors'
spirits, or how to revive Kosawa in any form. No, their
meetings are to plan dinner parties where they laugh
about things we don't understand. One day, we know,
our world and our ways will vanish in totality.

All the seven villages now have electricity. Most of
us live in brick houses. Many of us have cellphones
and flat-screen televisions. In Lokunja you can use the
thing called the Internet to read about our story, or
see huts like the ones in which we were born.

It may be long dead, Kosawa, but we never forget it,
the splendid piece of the earth it was. We can never
forget it, for there our spirits were whole. Amid oil
spills and gas flares, we looked behind us and saw
green hills where twin mambas hissed in gaiety, where
robust moles and porcupines zigzagged before falling
prey to the hunter's precision. We lived in a place

where caterpillars took twice as long to renovate into heavy butterflies. Ours was a village where the sky sang thunderous songs in the dry season, songs that made us wrap our legs around our siblings in fright and in delight. There were dire rainy days, when the rivers threatened to take our possessions to their resting place, and parched days, when the ground in the hills cracked from thirst and the palm trees rejoiced. Through it all, Kosawa remained a singular place—if not for the beauty of our surroundings, then for the people who called it home. How could we not want to return to those full-moon nights when we danced in the square? Even as we began leaving childhood and started realizing how determined death was to never let us see our old age, we still laughed on verandas, and skipped over pipelines. We sat under the mango tree, lazed and gossiped as if tomorrow would always be ours, a luminous tomorrow. We hoped, we believed, that we would die where we were born.

Often, while visiting our children in Bézam, or America, or Europe, we sit on the couch, looking at the television but not seeing it. We're there, but we're not there. We're somewhere else, thinking of Kosawa, thinking of Thula. We're wondering if Thula would still be fighting if she were alive. It's at such moments that the children of our children come to us and say, please, Yaya, please, Big Papa, tell us a story.

Acknowledgments

My editor, the incomparable Andy Ward, and my late publisher, Susan Kamil (I miss you so much), both believed I could tell this story; they nurtured me and nudged me, never once allowing me to indulge in self-doubt. I also thank Andy's assistants, Chayenne Skeete and Marie Pantojan, and the brilliant team of Rachel Rokicki, Melissa Sanford, Katie Tull, Taylor Noel, Avideh Bashirrad, and Barbara Fillon for their hard work and dedication. Profound gratitude to my literary agent, Susan Golomb, and my speaking agent, Christie Hinrichs, both of whom represent me with utmost passion and vigor. My former editor, David Ebershoff, is the greatest mentor any writer could ask for, and I thank him for his kindness. Much gratitude to my production editor, Steve Messina, and my copyeditor, Terry Zaroff-Evans, who both did an outstanding job. Jaya Miceli designed another superb book cover and I thank her.

My friends Howard Shaw, Lloyd Cheu and Douglas Mintz, Mark Salzman, Warren Goldstein, Zadie Smith, and Christina Baker Kline all read full or partial drafts of my manuscript—this story wouldn't be what it is without their dazzling critiques and I am indebted to them. The same goes for my countryman and fellow Anglophone Cameroonian writer Dibussi Tande, who, along with Joyce Ashuntantang, has been an incredible champion of my work. Many thanks also to Fiammetta Rocco for giving me advice when I needed it. For two summers, Mary Haft gave my family and me a lovely cottage in Nantucket where I could work near the ocean and I thank her for her generosity. I also thank Greyson Bryan and Bob Kohn for helping me understand elements of American corporate law. And huge thanks to my German team (Mona Lang, Eva Betzwieser, Maria Hummitzsch) et mon équipe française (Caroline Ast, Diane Du Perier, tout le monde à Belfond).

Finishing this novel was grueling and I am eternally grateful to my spiritual counselor and confidant, Rick Weaver, for his wisdom and wit, and for reminding me of the truth about who I am. My thanks also to Donna Schaper of Judson Memorial Church, Justin Epstein of the Unity Center of New York City, and Father Frank Desiderio of the Church of St. Paul the Apostle for the safe spaces they gave me to worship in.

Year after year, my wonderful friends have never asked me to be anything but what I am—what greater gift can one human give another? I thank them for making me laugh, for traveling to be with me because I needed them, for distracting me from my writing with endless text messages.

When I was a child, my mother sent me to live

with my aunt, a decision I was not thrilled about, but one that set me on this path, for it was in my aunt's house that I discovered literature. I thank my mother for her love and bravery, and I thank my aunt for welcoming me, and for making me go to Bethel Baptist Church, Kumba—it was the teachings I received there that pushed me to start questioning the world, and it was those same teachings that led me to become the person of faith I am today. I am deeply grateful, also, to all my relatives, by blood and by marriage, who have played roles big and small in my life and who have shown me many kindnesses. I am especially thankful to my cousins who, on my last visit to my hometown, reminded me with their affection that no matter how far I travel, my umbilical cord will remain buried in Limbe, in Cameroon, in Africa.

And my marvel of a husband. And my breathtaking children. To you, I say: thank you, thank you, thank you. For your love and a home that overflows with joy. For dance parties and countless other reasons to take a break from writing. For coming with me on this journey and cheering me on to stay the course, so that at the end of each day, when I lie down to sleep, I may do so to the words: Well done, good and faithful servant.

About the Author

Imbolo Mbue is the author of the **New York Times** bestseller **Behold the Dreamers,** which won the PEN/Faulkner Award for Fiction and was an Oprah's Book Club selection. The novel has been translated into eleven languages, adapted into an opera and a stage play, and optioned for a miniseries. A native of Limbe, Cameroon, Mbue lives in New York.

imbolombue.com

Facebook.com/imbolombue